As Time Goes By

Dear Doug and Lakshmi

A pleasure to eat, drink, and dance with you, as well as to learn a little bit more about our World!

Hope you enjoy the look —

Ben Baglio

First Edition Design Publishing

Patty says "Hi!"

As Time Goes By
Copyright 2012 Benedict Baglio
ISBN 978-1622870-43-1 EBOOK
ISBN 978-1622874-026 PRINT

LCCN 201394567

Published and Distributed by
First Edition Design Publishing, Inc.
September 2013
www.firsteditiondesignpublishing.com

Cover Art by Deborah E Gordon

ALL RIGHTS RESERVED. No part of this book publication may be reproduced, stored in a retrieval system, or transmitted in any form or by any means — electronic, mechanical, photo-copy, recording, or any other — except brief quotation in reviews, without the prior permission of the author or publisher.

Chapter 1

The little boy sat fascinated by the images the television presented to him. They were not in the colors he was used to, but that only intrigued him to look more closely at them. Airplanes flashed across the screen, seemingly chased by white dots and black cotton balls. Some of the airplanes suddenly would come apart in white flashes, while others streamed white cones to the collision with the water below. Yes, that was water, even though it wasn't the color he was used to seeing it, because he recognized the ships that plowed through it as the airplanes chased them. He even recognized some of the ships. Sometimes, daddy and mommy would take him to the beach and he would see the ships come and go. Some of the ships he saw from the beach were like the big white ship that mommy and daddy had taken him on when they went to the place with the warm beach, the big waves and the water that was so clear you could see the fish right through it. Most of the ships that passed by the beach near where he lived were gray. He saw two gray ships today. One was very large and flat, except for the building with the big white numbers painted on it. The other was smaller, and had a white number painted on its front.

Some of the airplanes hit the ships, and when they did, he saw the flashes of white again, followed by the black clouds. He saw people running around the ships, squirting water and using other tools. The flashes must be fire! He had to force himself to look because the fire frightened him. He remembered the time when the fire came to the house across the street, and big red trucks with colored flashing lights and scary sounds came with men dressed in black coats. The men used big hoses to squirt the fire, and axes to try to cut the fire out from the rest of the house. He remembered the fire left the people across the street very sad, and their house was all dirty and smelly.

What excitement! Now airplanes with white stars were landing on one of the ships. Some stopped very nicely. Others would come apart, and some would have the fire come when this happened. People on the ships would try to put the fire out, as other people got the man out of the broken airplane. Then other men would push the broken airplane off the ship into the water. Some of the men looked sad as they tried to help the men who looked very sick. Those ships with the airplanes seemed to be very busy places. The big ship he had seen today must carry airplanes, because it looked a lot like the ship on the television.

AS TIME GOES BY

It would be exciting to go on one of these ships with airplanes on it! He liked being on airplanes and ships, and he certainly liked looking at the ships as they came and went by the beach near his house. Being on one of the ships with the airplanes would be great fun!

He turned to his father, who sat behind him turning the pages in a big flat book. "Daddy?" he said, waiting for his father to look up.

"Yes, Steven," his father said, with the smile that always came when he looked at his son.

"Want to go on a ships with airpanes!" he said, pointing at the television and smiling to this father.

His father looked at the television, raised his eyebrows and looked back at his son, who was still pointing and smiling. He gathered his thoughts in a manner he hoped his son would understand, and after a few seconds, he said, "I don't think you would like it, Steven. Those ships aren't very pretty or nice places for little boys to be."

The little boy was incredulous! Not nice places to be? Didn't his father see what was happening? Maybe he didn't understand him. When that happened, he would have to repeat himself, and then daddy would get him what he wanted. Well, most of the time anyway. So, a bit more loudly, and with his hands on his hips, just like mommy did when she wanted him to do something right away, he said, "Want to go on a ships with airpanes now!"

His father laughed at the precocious little boy. Steven was so very bright, and would spend hours reading books and the sports pages of the newspaper, and he wasn't quite three years old. He reached for the little boy, brought him to his lap and hugged him and kissed him. "Maybe someday, Steven."

The little boy could not know that his father was hoping the last place the little boy would be someday was on one of those "ships with airpanes on it." He had been on one of those ships off the frigid coast of a mountainous hellhole called Korea in 1953. He saw many "airpanes" leave the ship, and far too many failed to come back, and he thanked his stars that his unkeen eyesight prevented him from fulfilling the dream he himself had as a youth. He was very happy as the officer in charge of the ship's electronics equipment. In fact, he had made a nice living for his family as a result. Norfolk was a great place to work, and the fantastic ships he was designing electronics for were true marvels of science and technology. But he didn't want his son on one, especially one with "airpanes" on it. He had done enough of that for both of them.

Chapter 2

Steven Amato was twelve years of age in 1972. Over the years he proved to be an amazingly bright boy who managed to confound and surprise his teachers with his absolute brilliance, as he endeared himself to them with his sensitivity, sense of humor and impish smile.

His interests ranged from all sports to chess, from *Bonanza* to Flip Wilson, from the legitimate theater to science fiction thrillers. He glued himself to the television set as Gemini and then Apollo blasted their way into the heavens. But more than the machines which fascinated him to no end, he was awed by the men who flew them. He read and reread their biographies until he felt he knew each man personally. While he admired their courage in breaking through the new frontier, their exploits in their past lives as fighter pilots was the issue that earned them his respect and adoration. He was more interested in John Glenn's experiences as fighter pilot than his three loops around the earth as an astronaut, like the time he landed a severely battle-damaged Panther Jet on a carrier off the coast of Korea. There he stood by the mutilated tail of the aircraft, smiling as if nothing happened at all. To his mind John Glenn certainly was a man of courage, more for his grit in battle than his exploits at the pinnacle of an Atlas rocket. After all, what more did he have to do in the Mercury capsule than just sit there? If it blew up, it wasn't because of his dereliction. If that Panther spun in though, it was probably because there was another pilot better than he was, or because he made himself a good target for some anti-aircraft gunner. In the fighter, John Glenn was in total control, and if things went badly, luck had less to do with his fate than at the top of that rocket. Even the astronauts referred to themselves as "spam in a can."

Others of his heroes had flown aircraft whose official designation began with the letter "X," setting new altitude and speed records with each flight. Still others took the newest military aircraft to heretofore unknown limits. What could be more exciting, he thought? To him, these men dared to defy death, more for the cause of country than for the cause of science. Those who had their country's pride and strength on the line in the heat of battle fascinated him the most.

As with many intellectuals, the present state of affairs only served to make Steven curious about the past, for he reasoned that to fully understand what is referred to as "now," a thorough understanding of "then" was deductively necessary. Thus driven by what he felt as necessity, he opened himself to what could be termed "unintended consequence." Steven discovered that his love of planes and pilots, of aviation and aviators, could only be fully satisfied by knowing as much about the past, inclusive of the societal values and technology of the times that formed the men and the machines that were consuming more and more of his thoughts and efforts. And, as he progressed from building static plastic models of "airpanes" (his father still teased him by referring to them as such) to radio-controlled balsawood flying machines that buzzed loudly as they soared over the fields near his home, Steven became a student of history. More correctly, he became a student of the history of aerial warfare.

The late sixties and early seventies were confusing to adults, let alone a young boy who lived in a society with a set of values that seemed completely antithetical to the one that existed a scant twenty-five years ago. He would read the heroic exploits of the great pilots of World War II, and how the country profited by their courage, while it totally dedicated itself to the cause that might consume them. Then, he would turn on his television set, and saw the men who flew those fantastic Phantoms, Crusaders, Super Sabres, and Delta Darts seemingly vilified by their countrymen, whom they were only trying to serve as their predecessors had. It seemed just saying the word "Vietnam" got the same response as blaspheming the name of God. There was scant information on the Korean War, and it was readily apparent that everyone, including his own father, was trying very hard to forget it ever happened. Yet, when he saw the movies and read the books of World War II, the men who flew those propellered machines were idolized. Everyone seemed to support and respect them, as individuals and aviators. There was more...sanity; yes, that was it-sanity, he thought. Everyone knew where they stood and what the rules were. To the observer, a wholesomeness that was hard to define pervaded life then. And everyone seemed so much happier "then" than "now," even though the country was in so much more danger then, than now, and even though people had so much more "now," than "then." A whole way of life, a whole world, was at stake then. Now, a little country of questionable strategic merit, of no great military strength, with few resources, was giving his country, the same country that defeated the embodiment of Evil not thirty years ago, an extremely bad time of things.

It seemed the men and war machines of "then" were the right instruments at the right time, as opposed to the current state of affairs where war machines didn't work, and men were reluctant to work them. Perhaps this was the reasoning that drove him to study the past so intently. "Then" seemed so much more pleasant than "now." He transcended time when he played *Moonlight Serenade* on the piano. *The Glenn Miller Story* was a favorite movie because of the gentleness, yet firmness in which the times were portrayed. Would any modern band continue to play as buzz bombs sent the audience for cover?

Those movies- to Steven, most of the movies today were drivel compared to those movies. He was enchanted by the movies of "then." *Casablanca*; was there ever a woman born as beautiful as Ingrid Bergman was in *Casablanca*? The tears on her perfectly shadowed face only enhanced her beauty, and caused those strange but pleasant feelings to stir within him that were becoming more and more common the older he grew. His fondness for this movie was so intense that he used the dialogue in regular conversation every chance he could. For example, Steven's mother rocked with laughter when she inquired as to who had broken a favorite decorative plate, and Steven responded by saying, "Round up the usual suspects." Was there ever a tougher guy than Humphrey Bogart? His name was weird, but none of the movie stars today compared to this guy. And what about Katherine Hepburn in that beautiful white dress, dancing with a dashingly uniformed Spencer Tracy in "*A Guy Named Joe?*" Has a woman ever looked more appealing in a white dress than Katherine Hepburn did? Had there ever been anybody funnier than Abbott and Costello *In the Navy*? He loved that movie for its comedy, and the fact that it showed a number of the battleships that would be broken at Pearl Harbor a few months after the movie's release. They were still alive and well on that film.

One movie more than the others captured his imagination, and personified and solidified all he had come to know and assume about "then." *On a Wing and a Prayer* told a story of a Navy torpedo squadron that came of age during the pivotal Battle of Midway. It truly gripped his soul. As he read the historical accounts of the battle, he realized the movie was a glamorized version of fact, but it served as another impetus to decide that he really wanted to fly "airpanes onna ships."

A friend of his fathers who knew of Steven's interest in naval aviation and history gave him a book to read entitled "*The Big E*". It was written by Commander Edward Stafford, and told the story of the World War II aircraft carrier U.S.S. *Enterprise*. The *Big E* was the most decorated ship in the history of the United States Navy, and served in practically every campaign in the Pacific War. More than a story about a ship, it was truly the story of the men who flew the Wildcats, Dauntlesses, Avengers, Hellcats, Corsairs, and Helldivers from her wooden flight deck against the Empire of Japan. The *Big E*'s most substantial claim to historical fame was that its air group was responsible for sinking three of the four Japanese aircraft carriers that had taken part in the engagement off Midway Island. As Midway was seen as a turning point of the Pacific War, the ship's fame became eternal.

If there was any doubt, reading "*The Big E*" only served to whet his appetite to fly "airpanes onna ships." When his father took him aboard the *Enterprise*'s nuclear-powered namesake after a recent refit at the Newport News Shipyards, a carrier so gigantic it was nearly twice the size of its predecessor, he felt he was somehow more connected to history. He talked with several of the carrier's officers who were so amazed by his knowledge of their ship that he was given a VIP tour. The ship's executive officer made it a special point of showing him a porthole taken from the World War II carrier before it was broken up for scrap in a dreary Bayonne, New Jersey shipyard. The officer said he thought it was incongruent that the richest country in the world could not preserve its most famous warship, if only as a shrine to the men who left her deck never to return, or those that died from Japanese bombs or the kamikaze pilot that blew her out of the war just before it ended.

"It's almost unfair that the *Enterprise* was denied honor of seeing the Japanese surrender in Tokyo Bay to honor her crew and her air groups." He himself touched the porthole as he continued, "Her two sister ships had died during the war, the *Yorktown* at Midway, and the *Hornet* at Santa Cruz. She was the only survivor of her class of carriers, a war hero of no equal and the last shred of the United States her men had known before they died terrible deaths in some far flung corner of the Pacific Ocean, " he said, as his eyes seemed to glisten as he talked. He felt chills course through his body as he gently rubbed the tarnished brass of the relic.

"If you could talk, what would you say?" he uttered.

"It would probably say it was glad to see its sacrifices weren't in vain, because there are young men like you around who profited from them," the officer offered.

As Steven's ear-to-ear grin grew, the officer's mood changed quickly, and he said, "Hey Steve! How'd you like to sit in a Phantom? Everybody's almost gone, so we can make a few adjustments to the program, so to speak. What do you say?" The officer's eyes were now wide with pride and excitement.

"Would I? Oh, boy!"

Paul Amato broke in, "It's not necessary, commander. Steve is just happy to be here, right son?" he said with a nervous smile.

At first, Paul couldn't understand why he had said what he had, but then he immediately put together the puzzle that had defied all previous efforts this day as to why he was becoming more anxious to get his kid off the ship. Sitting in the seat of that damned "airpane" would no doubt put aside any logical second thoughts his son may have had about military flying. But how could he deny him this extra special treat? Steven's eyes were almost out of his head. The kid was as perfect as a kid could get. Why say no? It wasn't his damned business; he was his father, not his warden, and he couldn't take looking at the kid's eyes as they dimmed from disappointment.

"Okay, Steve, but only for a few minutes. The commander has lots to do."

"Allllrightttt!"

They went up to the hangar deck to be greeted by an F4J Phantom that sat menacingly with its wings fully extended to give the onlooker an appreciation of its size. Its nose was painted with a shark's face, like it needed to look any fiercer than its design demanded. Its pylons were loaded with evil-looking missiles. The damned thing looked ready to kill, skin, and eat any misfortunate that was foolish enough to get too close, Paul Amato thought - and his kid was about to get inside it!

Eagerly, Steven climbed in to the cockpit while a few pilots put a flight helmet on his head, and strapped him in. Great, just fucking great! thought Paul Amato. The only way he was going to get the kid home was to take that fucking plane with him, if it didn't snap off his leg when he got close enough. It may have liked his kid and those grown up kids standing on its wings, but he would not trust it. Never! He reluctantly took several pictures of Steven, the commander and the two fighter jocks, all smiling, all giving the aviator's thumbs-up for the camera.

Leaving was easier than he thought. The ship's loudspeaker informed everyone who was a visitor that the day's program was over. Like any good officer, gentleman and fighter pilot, Steven obeyed the orders and left the cockpit without being told twice. As he did, he noticed that one of the pilots wore a patch on his leather jacket that was different from all the others. One particular patch showed an old-type propellered plane loosing what appeared to be a torpedo. The insignia said *VT-6*.

"Where did you get that?" Steven asked incredulously.

Taken aback by the young boy's excitement, the pilot answered, "My dad gave it to me."

"You mean your dad was at Midway? In VT-6?" the young boy asked. "Did he... you know, is he...?"

"No, Steven. My dad made it back You really know your stuff, don't you? You're real good, kid," the pilot said, scruffing the boy's hair.

"And you are too! Thanks a ton, sir. This was great fun!"

"My pleasure. See you in the funny papers!" the pilot said with a salute.

"It's a wonderful life, Lieutenant," Steven said returning the salute with a smile.

AS TIME GOES BY

The pilot walked away in laughter, shaking his head. Steven's father was dumbfounded. What was this VT-6 thing all about? He decided he would ask on the ride home.

The tragedy of VT-6 was a thorn in the claw of his love of flying. For all his love of military aviation, its story constantly caused him to re-evaluate himself and his dreams not because of trepidation, but the self-doubts it created. He read and read again the history of that battle around Midway Island, hoping somehow that VT-6 would suffer a kinder fate, but it never did. Midway produced many heroes, but those that gripped his heart were the pilots of VT-3, VT-6 and VT-8, the torpedo squadrons that flew from the *Yorktown*, *Enterprise* and *Hornet* that beautiful spring day. He couldn't quite understand why the Fates chose to turn their backs under the bright Pacific sun. When he expanded his reading to try to gain an acceptable understanding, he came to realize that to this very day he wasn't alone in his difficulty to come to terms with the tragedy of VT-3, VT-6 and VT-8, as forthright as the "official" facts were. It all seemed too cruel and out of context with what was assumed to be the accepted underlying tactical doctrine of how the United States fought all its battles. But that day, when the outcome of the Pacific War was held in the balance, the rules did not apply as VT-3, VT-6, and VT-8 determinedly flung themselves at the Japanese fleet-and were crushed by withering anti-aircraft fire and deadly Zero fighters.

And after the ill-fated attack, while the torpedo squadron ready rooms aboard *Enterprise* and were consumed by grief for the many dead squadron mates, no one grieved in the *Hornet*'s VT-8 ready room. The reason wasn't bravado that warriors developed to hide fear and pain. It was simply because not one torpedo-carrying Devastator aircraft from VT-8 that was launched from the *Hornet*'s flight deck that morning made it back from its encounter with *Kido Butai*, the Japanese Imperial Fleet. The tragedy, of course, wasn't that just the machines were wasted. Every man in the squadron save one, died in a fusillade of steel, blinding fire, or upon impact with the Pacific Ocean at 150 knots, as they bravely, vengefully, but vainly, tried to put torpedoes into the Japanese aircraft carriers called *Kaga*, *Akagi*, *Hiryu* and *Soryu*, the same ships only six months past that had massacred the battleships at Pearl Harbor.

When young boys discover heroes, as much as they want to emulate them, they do not want to recognize their mortality. Steven's thoughts wandered again to what it must have been like to fly an obsolete and underpowered airplane into the jaws of certain death. What thoughts coursed through the pilots' minds as tracer bullets crossed their paths as they flew through puffs of heavy caliber antiaircraft fire, and while Zero fighters spat explosive projectiles from their guns? What drove men to do this, as burning aircraft carried men they had known for years to the bottom of the Pacific Ocean? What madness would possess men to do this madness? Was the hope of sinking an aircraft carrier so possessing? Were they driven by the need to avenge the Sunday murders? Did they think they had a miracle in their pockets to guarantee their survival, even though the odds, by plan or chance, were heavily against success, or survival? Why didn't they just...turn away?

Then, the question arose that always troubled him; what would he do if he was called upon to do what the pilots and gunners of VT-3, VT-6 and VT-8 were called upon to do? Did he really want to fly "airpanes onna ships" that much? He wanted to ask those fighter pilots he just met about that, but he forgot in the excitement. Maybe it was a stupid question to ask. But they were Navy pilots, weren't they? And didn't that one guy's father fly with VT-6 that day? He must have known all about the events of June 4, 1942, and he still chose to fly "airpanes onna ships," just like his dad. Vietnam wasn't World War II, but the SAM missiles and MiGs these guys flew against could make you just as dead as a Zero could. But did these guys of "now" feel as strongly as the guys of "then" in those torpedo squadrons? Would they try to crash their burning planes into a target as some those torpedo guys tried in vain to do with a Japanese aircraft carrier?

"Why do they do it, dad?" Steven said, as they drove home.

"Why do who do what?"

"The men who fly the airplanes from ships?" he chuckled.

"I guess because it's what they feel they have to do. They think they have a calling to do it. It's a love." Some love, his father thought.

"Yeah, but you say you love what you do, right dad?"

"Of course. But it's different in their cases. My job doesn't call for me to risk my life. Those pilots you spoke to today have done that countless times, but they're ready to go tomorrow or tonight, if need be. I'm sure that they know that there is a chance that their next launch from the *Big E*'s deck might be their last, but they still have the calling to do it." Great! He's having second thoughts, Paul Amato thought.

"I wonder if that's how Waldron felt about the odds that day?" Steven said, looking off to the ocean.

"Waldron? Was he one of the pilots you talked with today?"

"No-but in a way, yes. He's the guy who commanded VT-8 the day they took off from the *Hornet* to attack the Japanese fleet at Midway. The whole squadron died, except a guy named Ensign George Gay from Texas. I mean, the pilots flying from the new *Enterprise* are just like him, don't you think?"

AS TIME GOES BY

"I would guess so," Paul Amato said uncomfortably. He remembered reading newspaper accounts about the great losses at Midway when he was a teenager. "While the news of victory came quickly, the news of casualties came in dribs and drabs, but I don't remember reading of a whole squadron being destroyed. Even if they did know, people tried to hide that kind of pain, because they believed tomorrow would be better than today, and were willing to accept the cruel sacrifices of the war. The times were different. People were different. As bad as the times your grandma and grandpa lived through, they were always optimistic."

"Hmm," Steven replied, still looking out onto the Chesapeake Bay. "After all, the American air groups sunk four Japanese aircraft carriers that had attacked Pearl Harbor, and because of that great victory the losses might have been overlooked, or ignored. And I can see the aviators coming to terms with that kind of thinking, too. I'm just wondering if old John Waldron knew how very high the probability was that he was going to be killed that day, and that the probability increased as he winged his way to the Japanese fleet because the battle plan came apart. I wonder if he really thought his torpedo would work that day, because they were notoriously faulty. Did he feel that this was the wrong battle at the wrong time for him, considering the odds? His old Devastator torpedo-bomber was due to be replaced in a few weeks by the brand new Grumman TBF Avenger with a better torpedo. Did he take this as an omen that his time was up? Did he think about turning back or conveniently missing the Japanese fleet? Or did he just get up, wash his face, eat breakfast, and do the job he was trained to do?"

"Whoa! This is some pretty heavy metaphysical stuff you're thinking about! Are you sure you're only twelve?"

"Do you think he thought he'd secure a place in history?"

"Do you think the Orioles will beat the Yankees tonight?" his father said with a laugh.

"Huh?" His father did it again. He caught him by surprise and lightened the load. As his father laughed, he laughed. His dad always put things in perspective. He didn't want to be depressed, and he was looking forward to watching the game and munching on hot dogs in the backyard under the Virginia summer sky with his family. He couldn't change the circumstances of Waldron's demise, no matter how much he studied it. And his father was right-he was only twelve years old. Perhaps he was too young to understand it all, but he still felt he should care.

Jim Palmer ended the baseball game by throwing a fastball on the outside corner to Thurman Munson for a called strike three, with a man on first. Immediately after, the news came on to show Muhammed Ali preparing for heavyweight bout. .It occurred to Steven that John C.

Waldron had boxed at Annapolis way back in 1920. Now how did he know that, he wondered? Had he read it somewhere?

"Dad, could you cook me another hotdog?" he asked, as his eyes looked upward and focused on the flashing lights of a jetliner in its final approach to Dulles International Airport. He followed the lights until they became indistinguishable among the star-studded Virginia summer sky.

Chapter 3

Paul Amato looked anxiously up at the azure sky, his hand spread across the middle of his forehead to shade his eyes from the bright August sun. His son's seventeenth birthday was a benchmark event for a few reasons. Steve had received his driver's license just this morning, and this afternoon, he was in the midst of demonstrating his level of competence in another machine. The Cessna he had gently lifted into the warm, humid Virginia air had vanished fifteen minutes ago into the eastern horizon, and this solo flight was only supposed to be ten minutes long. Paul Amato, being the precise engineer he was, had allowed himself only ten minutes before he would blatantly panic. Now he nervously swiveled his head to cover as much of the heavens as his eyes could blanket to catch a glimpse of the machine that kidnapped his son, just as an evil eagle might snatch up an unwary fawn.

Paul Amato did not torment himself by going over the old ground that led to this particular moment of eternal time, to stand as a nervous wreck on this patch of concrete, and his son to soar in the gases above. Suffice to say that Steven was very difficult to deny anything to that came as a result of his carefully contrived deductive processes. His well-prepared arguments were backed by statistics that proved his point irrefutably, so much so that he would have led his father to believe that blasting into outer space was safer than crossing the street.

A few hangars down the flight line from where Paul Amato stood, several distinguished-looking, middle-aged gentleman also eagerly searched the skies for a sign of the Cessna. Their bodies were lean, their temples gray, but their piercing eyes were younger looking than would be expected. They had watched and cheered as the Cessna's wheels left the ground for the ether above, and they kept their sharp eyes on the tiny plane as it lost its familiar shape to become a slowly disappearing dot in the sky. The men had taken a special interest in this teenaged fledgling who was so smart, yet so gullible, so introspective, yet so gregarious, so theoretical, yet so practical, and so full of questions that there never was enough detail to fill him. His interest in them was at once flattering, yet abusive, because few young people today were as interested in their past and their passionate past-time as Steven, but his questions often stirred memories that were painful even today, twenty-five years after the fact. They knew the kid would do anything to sit in the cockpits of their relics, but when he did, they drew a deep breath, for the questions came fast and furious. Some of their answers required emotional preparation as well, so they smiled when he approached, yet were on guard. But they loved him, so much so that when he didn't come around for a few weeks, they called his home to see if he was all right. Usually, his absences were due to his academic or athletic pursuits, which were the only things he attacked with more tenacity and aggressiveness than aviation.

Steven was about to begin his senior year in high school. In fact, this was his last day of relative freedom before the dreaded varsity football "two-a-days" began. He had spent part of the summer at the University of Virginia in a special program for prospective engineers, and part of it playing summer league baseball, the other sport he lettered in last year. He would serve as the Class of 78's president in September, and played tenor sax in the high school concert band and jazz ensemble. Every dollar he made working for the middle-aged gentlemen or from the part-time job he had at the local drugstore went to pay the for gas for his beloved 1963 Chevrolet Impala Super Sport convertible he and his dad restored, or for his "airpane" lessons, as Paul Amato still said teasingly. For this investment of time, energy, and money, Steven Amato now sought to own piece of the sky.

Paul Amato tapped his pipe empty, as the smoke was hot and bitter-tasting. He reminded himself that a pipe was meant to be smoked gently, its tobacco savored to mellow the spirit. In his anxiety ridden state, he puffed on it like a dragon, and the pipe became so heated its bowl was painful to the touch.

Suddenly, thunder roared across the sky, so loud that he dropped the pipe in fright, using both hands to shelter his head. Even the middle-aged gentlemen were taken to duck their heads and cover their ears as the thunder rolled across the airfield. When they dared a glance upward, two Navy Phantom fighters blasted through the air, not two hundred feet above the ground. Then their noses pointed upwards, and flame jutted from their tail pipes. They vanished. The little airstrip was so close to Oceana Naval Air Station that the Navy fighter jocks sometimes asked for cleared air space to practice low-level penetration and evasion tactics. The small airport was remarkably similar in size and configuration to the early-warning MiG strips in the Soviet Union. The Navy had set up radar stations that used Eastern Bloc frequencies along the approach routes to help the pilots perfect their tactics. Paul Amato reasoned that the cameo appearance by the Navy fighters was the reason as to why his son was overdue. The air controllers wanted to keep the skies clear while those two monsters devoured the clouds on their rampage across the little airfield. Those modern-day mechanical pterodactyls would chew up that little Cessna and spit out its bones, Paul Amato surmised, his mouth twisting out of shape at the thought of it.

A slight purr from the west reached the ears of the onlookers. A little dot in the direction of the purr grew wings and wheels and a spinning propeller. The plane's wing flaps were down as it descended in a gentle dive headed for the runway's end. As it crossed the concrete ribbon, the nose gently came up and the engine's noise faded a little. The main wheels beneath the high wing touched the concrete, spewing little puffs of white smoke. The tail wheel gently touched, and the little aircraft rolled out to a halt on the taxiway. A jubilant instructor rushed to meet it as the propeller's rotation ceased. He was followed by the gray-templed gentlemen and Paul Amato, whose progress was impeded by eyes blurred by the tears that welled in them, and legs that were somewhat reluctant to move as commanded.

As the veteran aviators customarily cut the fledgling's shirt tails, Steven Amato, while happily taken with the ceremony, never took his eyes from his father. He knew his dad must have been having palpitations, and was anxious for him to join the melee. Steven escaped from their grasps and rushed to meet his father's opened arms.

"I did it, dad! I did it! Did you see? Did you?" he said in short, excited gasps.

"I sure did, son. I sure did! I've never seen a prettier landing. For a moment though, I thought those two Navy jets had eaten you for lunch." He hugged his son tightly, partly out of pride, relief, and to hide his tears.

"The tower sent me out farther than planned because of them. I saw them as they approached the field," Steven replied matter-of-factly, but hugging back just as hard.

Paul Amato came to some crushing realizations just then. He noted that there was not a trace of baby fat left on the body he embraced. He also realized that his son was at least three inches taller than he, at almost six feet. The face had a shadow, and was more angular than he remembered it to be not a half hour ago. He was holding his child for sure, but the child was, for all intents and purposes, a man.

Steven turned to one of the distinguished gentlemen and said, "Mr. Whitney? You think it would be all right if I sat in the TBD for a few minutes?"

"Sit in it?" Whitney replied, with pride an excitement. "I wish I could let you fly it! Let's go for a visit!"

The group of aviators, and Paul Amato, headed for the hangar, and entered. They were greeted by three venerable and noble aircraft, all in pristine condition, but only two were air-worthy. The Douglas TBD Devastator couldn't make it out of the hangar on its own power, because its 900 horsepower Pratt and Whitney Twin Wasp engine wouldn't turn over, despite a complete rebuild. It stubbornly cranked and cranked but would not catch fire, and the reason as to why remained an exasperating mystery. The Grumman TBF-1 Avenger was factory-fresh in every sense. The Douglas SBD-3 Dauntless dive bomber seemed as ready to put a 1,000 pound bomb into a Japanese aircraft carrier as it was in 1941, when it left the California factory that created it. For some strange reason, an unexplained force drew Steven to the Devastator, which was presently little more than a beautiful static display piece. As impotent as it was, it drew his attention each and every time he was around it, as if by some strange power it was communicating with him, perhaps to tell him firsthand about that awful day in the spring of 1942 when it was to carry a crew of two young Americans from the USS *Enterprise* to the Japanese Imperial Fleet. It seemed to want to scream its anguish at watching its brothers tumble like falling leaves flaming in a maelstrom, all in vain. It seemed to crave validation of its mission, as futile as it was, perhaps not for itself, but for its brothers and their dead crews. Its hangar mates seemed to comfort it, but more as a pitied cripple than as a fellow warrior.

Steve climbed into the Devastator's immaculate cockpit, painstakingly refurbished by the veteran Navy airmen. He pushed the rudder pedals and played with the control stick, watching the control surfaces on the tail and wings respond to his commands. He peered into the torpedo sight while the men below congratulated his father on his success at raising such a wonderful young man. Their voices fell away as he pressed his eye to the torpedo sight that conjured a vision of long ago. The confines of the hangar gave way to bright blue sky and shimmering cobalt sea. An aircraft carrier's shape loomed before him. He immediately identified it by its low bow and small port-side island structure. It was *Akagi*! She was perfectly framed by the torpedo sight, only the blur of the Devastator's spinning propeller in the way. The carrier's bow wave indicated she was steaming at full battle speed. *Akagi*'s destroyer escorts closed to her, to protect her from this rapidly closing gnat that sought her death.

His right hand gripped the control stick tightly, his thumb moving over the red button at its top that would release the white-tipped torpedo, to streak to the hated veteran of Pearl Harbor and blow its side out.

Easy now, he told himself. Watch the throttle. You don't want the torpedo to break apart or go off course because you were going too fast when you "pickled" it. You want this fish to do its job! His left hand gingerly reached for the throttle on the left side of the cockpit, and eased it back.

The anti-aircraft fire was becoming more intense. The port side of *Akagi* seemed to catch fire as it slashed at the Devastator with guns of all calibres. Her escorts joined in the ominous display. Angry black puffs of heavy caliber guns joined the streaking red and orange tracers of lighter weapons as he drew closer. Where are the dive-bombers? He asked himself. Every gun seems to be on me! This was supposed to be a coordinated attack! A Zero fighter slashed across his path. It must have made a run on him. The Devastator felt fine, though. No smoke. He missed me. He heard the chatter of his rear-seat gunner's thirty caliber machine gun. Another Zero must be making a run. Holes appeared in his right wing. Steady, he told himself. This is no time to panic. You've trained too hard. Lindsey and Waldron would chew his ass out good if he missed, or worse, turned off the mark. He wouldn't let his squadron down. He wouldn't let Waldron or Lindsey down. No way in hell.

The *Akagi* loomed larger. Its captain was trying very hard to make him miss, as the carrier heeled hard to port in a severe, high speed starboard turn, the stern coming around to present the smallest target possible to the torpedo plane bearing down on his precious ship. Steven kicked his left rudder to adjust. You won't get away, Captain Aoki. Not you, nor Admiral Nagumo on your flag bridge. I saw what your planes did to *Arizona*. It's payback time! His thumb pressed the torpedo release button, and...

"Steve! Steven! Wake up!" A gentle nudging on his shoulder startled him, forcing his eye away from the sight. He turned in surprise to see his father and Mr. Whitney standing on the wing.

"Little man, you've had a busy day" Mr. Whitney said with a smile.

"Huh? I don't remem...You should have seen...!" He stopped himself. Was he really asleep, in a dream? Or, did he...Don't be ridiculous, he angrily told himself.

He climbed out of the cockpit with a big smile on his face. He knew John Waldron would be proud of him, all right. He earned his wings today. The Devastator looked proud too. It seemed to know something he didn't know. What was it? Why was this airplane so...beguiling? Yes, that was the word. It was a good SAT word. Beguiling. He would have to remember that word.

He drove home as his dad proudly sat in the passenger seat of the fire-engine red Chevy, his thick black hair almost immoveable as the wind rushed in to the convertible's interior. Steven was driving a little faster than usual, as he was anxious to tell his mom personally about this special day. He knew his father had already called her and told her to breathe again, but he wanted her to have all the details. His sister Susan was no doubt anxious as well. Unlike typical brothers and sisters, they got along famously. Only a year apart in age, they shared many interests and friends as well as the love of things mechanical. As a matter of fact, Susan had rebuilt the Chevy's carburetor and installed a new distributor during the restoration process. To repay her for her interest and help, Steven was working diligently on the restoration of a 1964 Mustang GT their father had bought for her.

Rena Amato waited nervously on the porch for her husband and son to arrive home. Her slim frame was covered by a light cardigan. Despite the heat and the embrace of her daughter, her nerves made her shiver. Her blonde hair was cut short, and her blue eyes were the same color as her children's. Her slight northern Italian features contrasted sharply with her husband's chiseled Sicilian features, but their children were absolutely beautiful, Steven having his father's rugged looks and dark complexion, softened by his mother's delicate pronouncements, and Susan, having the most dazzling eyes, set off by thick jet black hair and a milk-white complexion that was broken only by the natural blush of health. Both children were lean, and tall. Rena Amato never failed to smile when she saw them standing together.

The Chevy rounded the corner, its horn honking loudly. Susan and her mother rushed to the car.

"Mom!" Steven exclaimed, "I flew an "airpane" all by myself! And I landed it, too!"

She hugged him tightly, his sister joining them.

Steven offered himself a compliment. He was only starting to realize how special he really was. Now if only he could convince the admissions office at the United States Naval Academy at Annapolis of this by April 15, 1978 he would really have done something special. This was going to be a benchmark year, he thought.

Then the thought of the first two-a-day football practice tomorrow entered his mind. He winced.

Chapter 4

Steven Amato swung at the fastball, but the bat came around a hair too late. He heard the ball thud into the catcher's mitt behind him, and he cursed himself for being too cautious. A split second afterwards, he heard the umpire bark out "STRIKE TWO!" Dammit! I saw it was a fastball the instant it left his hand! What the hell am I doing? He grit his teeth in disgust.

The pitcher turned around to face second with a smirk on his face after receiving the ball from the catcher, who also took time to wryly smile at Steven while getting back into his crouch behind the plate. This pitcher had already struck him out twice today, and had struck him out or grounded him out, or popped him out every time their two teams met for the last three years. The kid managed to defy the laws of physics with a baseball. Steven could not hate him, because he knew Danny Morello to be a true sportsman and athlete. When Steven ran in the game winning touchdown last November with zero time remaining on the clock to have his high school win the Virginia State championship, Danny Morello was the first kid on the field from the opposing team to shake his hand and wish him well. But now, the kid throwing fire from the mound of dirt sixty feet, six inches away was on the verge of shutting him out-again.

Steven got closer to the plate to shrink the strike zone and force the pitcher to come outside and low. The pitcher wound up, and threw what was obviously another fastball-right at his head. Steven threw himself backwards just in time, immediately concluding that the bullshit tactic of shrinking the strike zone was a risky thing to do with Daniel L. Morello on the mound. Steven got up, dusted the dirt off his uniform, knocked the caked clay from his cleats with his bat, ignored the chuckles of the catcher, and got into his stance. He asked the umpire for the count.

"Three and two. Two out." Steven thanked him.

Danny Morello wound up again. His motion indicated a fastball, but...his fingers...were showing...curveball! The ball hurtled to the plate, as Steven Amato's brain calculated its flight dynamics, he concluded that it would arrive a bit higher and slower than the previous two pitches, right about...here and... now! Swing!

The particular sound of the crack of the bat coupled with observation of the baseball's first second of flight, were all those who knew the sport needed to know to decide where the ball was going. It cleared the left field fence, 330 feet away. Steven "broke into the trot," never looking at Danny Morello, who hung his head in dismay and anger for hanging that curve. Steven stepped on home plate, taking only a millisecond to smile wryly at the catcher. Danny Morello's team went oh-for-three for their bottom half of the inning. The score was tied. That game was going to extra innings.

The game remained a stalemate for three cycles. Danny Morello came to the plate with a man on third, and two outs. He took his time in getting his long body set in his batting stance. He was as perfect a model of batting mechanics that ever played high school baseball. Danny's whole body went into a perfectly synchronized motion to hit the pitch. His swing was perfect. It was powerful. It generated tremendous bat speed. It knocked the first pitch over the center field fence 400 feet away with room to spare. It won the Virginia State High School Baseball Semi-Final Championship, and knocked Steven's team out of the playoffs. Now it was Steve Amato's turn to be a sportsman, despite the agony gripping his throat.

He sought Danny out from the mob of bodies that had swallowed him in their victorious hysteria. Danny saw him as well, and shook his outstretched hand. "Nice shot, Danny. Great game. Congratulations." Somehow, he felt better by saying it.

"Nice hit, too. I didn't think you'd be looking for the curve."

"I was looking for the smoke but I noticed your fingers gripped the ball differently."

Danny was incredulous. "You saw my fingers, from way back there? You got the eyes of a hawk. Without my contacts, I can't even see my catcher's signs. I hope it doesn't knock me out of the Naval Academy. I got a waiver, but I think you have to be perfect to get in."

Steven smiled surprise. "I applied to Annapolis too! We're supposed to hear any day now, I guess. How about you give me a call when you hear, or I'll give you a call when I hear. Deal?"

"Deal! It'd be great finally playing on the same team," Danny said. They wrote their phone numbers on each other's tee shirts.

"You bet! Good luck. See you in the funny papers."

"Funny papers? What are you talking about?"

"Just a saying. I gotta go," Steve said, rushing off to his team's bus, the only smiling face among twenty-five others.

When he got to the front door, he yelled the cry of the American teenager. "Mom! I'm home!"

"We're in here, Steven," she replied in a tentative voice.

His internal alarm went off. Something was out of joint. He went inside to find his whole family sitting at the kitchen table that had an envelope solely resting upon it.

"It's from the Naval Academy son," his father said.

"What's it say?" he asked, with anxiety's fever rising, his mouth suddenly dry, his stomach gripping tightly.

"We were waiting for you to open it," Susan replied.

"Oh," he said, trying to maintain his calm while staring wide-eyed at the envelope that held his future within.

"Well open it, Steven!" his sister shouted, her nerves frayed.

He fumbled the envelope and dropped it. His sister shouted at him, almost delirious with anticipation. His father covered his eyes nervously. Steven tried to brace himself for disappointment. He did everything he could to get in, he told himself. He couldn't have done anymore. He'd go to the University of Virginia. That's all. They had accepted him already. To hell with the Navy. To hell with airpanes onna ships.

"Read it out loud, dear," his mother said, as he removed the sheet of paper. "We're in this together." She wound her thin arm around his thick wrist, and pulled him closer.

He smiled at her as he unfolded the sheet of paper, taking time to notice the Academy's pennant on the letterhead. "Dear Steven, It is my pleasure to offer you admission to the United States Naval Academy as a member of the Class of 1982," he read. Suddenly, his eyes blurred, and his sister knocked him to the ground, smothering him with kisses. His mother and father joined the fray. Even Halsey, the family bulldog, joined in.

The phone was ringing in the background. His father answered it, and called to him. "Son, it's someone named Danny Morello for you." His father was puzzled, as this was a strange name among the many that rang the phone frequently.

"Danny. I got in," he said softly. "What's the scoop with you? Did you get..." He was hesitant. He knew how painful the disappointment could have been.

"You wouldn't think they'd let two Italians from Virginia into the same class. It looks like you and I will finally be on the same side, Amato!"

"Fantastic!" Steven screamed into the phone.

"You bet! Are people at your house going nuts too? My mother and father haven't stopped crying since I opened the envelope. My grandmother almost sucked my face off she kissed me so much."

"Ditto here. I played football for eight years and never got an injury, and I think my sister broke my shoulder with the tackle she threw at me! But I guess it's better than facing you again."

"Hey, pal, you're the one who touched me for the round trip today."

"Yeah, pal, and you're the one playing in the state finals next week."

"I guess we're both blessed," Danny Morello said. "I tell you what. I'll call you when we get back from Richmond next week. Maybe we can hang out for a while together. Okay?"

"That'd be great! Good luck up there!"

"Thanks Steve. I'll be calling you."

"Yeah. And Danny?"

"Yeah?"

"Beat ARMY!"

"Yeah!"

Steven told the story to his parents, and they marveled at the whim of the Fates.

"You must invite Danny and his parents to dinner," his mother said.

"That's a great idea, Mom."

"Holy cow. Annapolis," his father said. "The same place that Halsey, Nimitz, President Carter and Alan Shepard went to school. What a tradition!"

"Don't forget John C. Waldron, dad. It seems that everybody forgets that guy."

His father raised a glass of lemonade. "To John C. Waldron, then. And the Midshipmen of Annapolis!"

"Here, here!" the family replied.

Steven Amato reached for the phone again. He quickly punched in the seven digits and waited impatiently for the ring. "Hello?" he finally heard.

"Mr. Whitney? Yes, it's me, Steven. I got in! Thank you. And now you owe me a ride. Tomorrow will be fine. I'll see you bright and early. Right. That would be great, too! Thank you. Good bye."

"Ride? What ride was that all about," his father said, feeling his throat tighten. It was "airpane" time again.

"Mr. Whitney promised I could fly the Avenger if I got into Annapolis. Tomorrow is the day he makes good on the promise."

"Are you qualified? That's a pretty powerful machine. You've been loping around in Cessnas. Are you ready for that?" his father asked tentatively. Those damn planes!

"I'm ready. I've been reading the pilot's manual and practicing for months. Hey, what do you say I take you guys out for dinner?" Steven said, nervously changing the subject.

"That would be fine, but I'll treat. It's not every day your kid gets into Annapolis!" his father beamed, realizing that arguing about "airpanes" was an exercise in futility.

The family jumped into the red Impala. The April sun was still bright in the sky, shedding the warmth of spring and lengthening the late afternoon shadows. He left the convertible top down, and as he pulled out of the driveway, he began singing *Anchors Aweigh*. His whole family joined in the chorus.

Chapter 5

Steven's first year at Annapolis had passed without incident. He earned a 3.80 grade point average and was confident in his ability to make the varsity football and baseball teams in his sophomore, or "youngster," year. Danny Morello made varsity baseball his first year, already throwing his patented fireball at opposing batters with almost as much success as he had at the high school level, and batting a very respectable .301. There was also very little doubt that he would give Navy's senior quarterback a run for the starting position. Danny could throw a football for miles and already had established himself as a fiery leader.

Steven added an inch of height and fifteen pounds of solidity to his broad shouldered frame, in no small part due to the regimen of lifting weights, running, and swimming that was the norm for midshipmen, but more intense for jayvee and varsity athletes. He drove Susan's friends absolutely nuts when he wore his dress whites that spring for his Mother's Day visit. He had spent so much time outdoors his dark skin already took an even deeper luster that highlighted his blue eyes and jet black hair. He heard the word "hunk" mentioned for the first time, and it took him awhile before he realized he should be flattered by it, but Rena and Paul Amato knew the definition all the while. They were moved to tears as he ran up the walk to greet them.

Steven and Danny spent their four-week Academy summer commitment at the Naval Air Station at Pensacola, where each of them was taken up in a Buckeye jet trainer as well as a propeller-driven Texan. Although his eyesight was not perfect for pilot training, Danny's urge to "be up there" was strong, and he hoped to be trained as a Radar Intercept Officer (RIO). Steven, on the other hand, was in his element "up front" in the cockpit. His instructor and he rented a Cessna for the day and soared across Florida to Disney's new park near Orlando, with Danny Morello as a passenger. The instructor, Commander Thomas "Bengal" Lancer, was a Vietnam veteran with over three-hundred combat missions. He was impressed with Steven's flying skill "behind the stick," that validated his notions that he would soon fly "airpanes onna ships."

At the beginning of his sophomore year, he began to seriously think about his senior thesis. The Academy faculty encouraged foresight in this endeavor. The project's theme, research, and conclusion were developed to the point where the author could in fact be deemed expert. He had an idea as to what he wanted to write about. In fact, it came to him just a few weeks before when he soloed in Mr. Whitney's TBF Avenger, then sat yet again in the cockpit of TBD Devastator 6-T-7, the designation indicating it was the number seven plane of the *Enterprise*'s Torpedo Squadron 6. It was still little more than a giant paper weight, but it possessed the mysterious powers to attract and entrap him in its past. Again, Whitney had to shake him awake, just as he and the plane were attacking Japanese shipping off Marcus Island. He quickly extricated himself from what had to be a haunted cockpit.

He decided that the first piece of research for the thesis should be done in the Academy alumni archives, for if he was to fully understand the decisive Battle of Midway as it pertained to his thesis, he would really need to understand the men, beginning with:

John C. Waldron, Lieutenant Commander, United States Navy
United States Naval Academy Class of 1924.
Born 21August 1900 in Fort Pierre, South Dakota.
Died in the Line of Duty 4 June 1942-body never recovered.
Survived by Adelaide Waldron (wife), and two daughters.

Steven became engrossed in Waldron's official Annapolis file that contained everything from his declaration sheet, to his health file, to his yearbook picture. The declaration sheet that bore Waldron's signature indicated that he had "completed the theory of quadratics in algebra," and had gone "through five books of plane geometry." Waldron had been through the Naval Academy prep school, which was then located in Annapolis for "two months and a half." His signature, obviously done carefully with a broad pointed fountain pen in blue-black ink, appeared on the neatly typed USNA oath that he signed on 16 June 1920 upon his appointment as a midshipman. His physical examination for the academy was conducted on 15, June 1920, where he was found to be "physically sound, well formed, of robust constitution". A receipt for his "outfit and textbooks" of $350 also appeared, dated 21 August 1920. A voucher indicated he received $79.85 for the 1597 miles he traveled from Fort Pierre to Washington D.C. to take his entrance exams, which, by the way, old John C. did very well on, scoring a 3.6 of 4.0, Steven mused. Another form (Steven realized the Navy had a history of forms) indicated that Waldron was a Roman Catholic, and that his mother's occupation was "farming and stock raising". A farmer and rancher, Steven thought. That explained the personality traits that were reflected by his leadership as related by the Midway narratives: Waldron worked hard, and, as a result, so did everyone he commanded. He was as honest as the day was long, had high moral standards, was probably a physical bull, and had tremendous faith in his abilities and his fellows. He had one serious offense though, and it cost him 25 demerits. It involved him "sitting in park in rear of B.H with..." Steven couldn't make out the final handwritten word.

Waldron's Academy health record indicated he was afflicted by a few boils, impetigo, the flu, sprained ankles, knees, and shoulders, and a reaction to an inoculation that required medical attention.

Sometime before he graduated, as early as 1923, the address on several documents indicated Waldron's mother moved to Lashburn, Saskatchewan, Canada. There was no mention of a father on any of the forms. Was it because his father passed away? Waldron boasted that he had Sioux bloodlines, but none of this was in his official record.

He viewed his official academic transcript. It seemed that Waldron's best grades (3.0 and above) came in leadership, languages and seamanship. Other grades in engineering and mathematics were surprisingly low. What really threw Steven into outright laughter was Waldron's 2.69 in navigation, with 2.50 being identified on the transcript as "tolerable." He thought this strangely ironic, as it was Waldron's excellent navigation and well-known "Sioux Sense" that led VT-8 to the Japanese fleet on that beautiful June day, while the rest of his air group got lost.

Steven was most taken by what his classmates had to say about John C. Waldron in their senior yearbook. The camaraderie he cherished at the Academy, the one thing that made Annapolis so special, was alive and well at least as far back as the Class of '24.

"Stranger, pause! Look at this strange specimen. Reading from the outboard halliard, we make out the ambitious student, the inspiring athoolete, the snake par excellence and, last but not least, the sea-going cow-puncher. Here is a man who is lord of fluttering hearts, scattered from hither to yon, wherever he has travelled. And yet, he wouldn't let Helen herself in his room after study call has busted. The "Busy Day" sign is always in evidence on "Jawn's" door during boning hours. Lady Luck has given him a cold shoulder as far as athletics are concerned. "Jawn" comes across with the desire and ability, but the aforementioned damsel steps in with the sand and rocks. Having taken a shot at everything, he has at last decided to choose the sport which will keep him in the hospital for the shortest time, sort of a cross between boxing and wrestling. His ambition is laudable, since the doctors need a rest." Class Wrestling (2): Class Boxing (3)

"Jawn?" His fellow classmates must have mimicked his western accent in the pronouncement of his name, and the word "athoolete." Even in the Navy of "then", nicknames and call signs were alive and well. The text also confirmed his suspicions that young guys throughout the ages were assholes first, then students. The medical record of sprains evidently was due to the nature of Waldron's chosen athletic pursuits, Steven surmised. You could get pretty well banged up in those two sports. Who was Helen, he wondered- Helen of Troy? And, yes, they knew of his farmer/rancher pedigree, as evidenced by the teasing "cowpuncher" reference.

His classmates went out of their way to mention he spent a good deal of time in study, "in the boning hours." Coupled with the mostly "tolerable" grades he received, his time at the academy prep school, and his penchant for hard work and driving spirit that became his trademark, Steven concluded that Waldron was the classic overachiever. He busted his hump to get what he wanted, and wouldn't ever, under any circumstances, be deterred from it. Indefatigable, persevering, intrepid - these words would define Waldron to polite society. The Navy had another idiom: one tough son-of-a-bitch. Yes, Steven thought, that was the most appropriate summation of his personality. This guy was the pattern, the real life model for World War II Navy officers, the characters John Wayne, Dana Andrews, Don Ameche, and all the other actors portrayed

Steven looked long and hard at Waldron's face - his nose was large, and his jaw square. A bit of the Sioux was certainly evident. His face seemed stern and yet kind, with the eyes showing humility, sort of an inner peace that indicated he was pleased and proud about who he was. A driving sense of purpose shined through. There was even a trace of a smile on the corners of his lips, but Waldron, it appeared, wouldn't let it out, as he rightly assumed the picture was for posterity. Could it be he didn't want to look to flippant? That had to be it, Steven surmised with a grin.

He returned WALDRON, JOHN C to the archivist, put his cap on and turned to leave. Waldron was a fine officer, and a ...patriot? Yes! That was it; a patriot, who did his duty as ordered....no, duty was too easy an explanation. WALDRON, JOHN C was above and beyond that. His was a higher purpose than sheer duty; it was unqualified love of America, the American Navy, and the American men who served him, and Waldron, like any great officer, felt privileged and honored to serve and lead them. He felt the tears welling in his eyes, and initially, he couldn't explain why. No doubt, it was Waldron's and Torpedo 8's tragedy that had something to do with it, and the more he knew of him, the more he felt Waldron was an acquaintance, not a just player in his thesis. After all, the story of Torpedo 8 brought tears to the eyes of Winston Churchill.

But something else was playing in his head, and he finally came to identify it, with WALDRON, JOHN C's help. Could it be that the history of USNA Annapolis, the tradition of honor, the call for sacrifice that led to it being called the best of its kind in the world, had finally caught up to him?

Yes, that was it. In his heart at that moment he understood what the demeanor of the upperclassmen was all about, and what the old admirals who hung around were trying to get across in words that just didn't come all that easily. That...creed was evident when their eyes became misty as they looked over the Midshipmen passing in review. He really loved this place and was proud to be a part of its tradition, and the seafaring tradition of his country and its Navy. What other occupation could be more honorable than this?

"Hey, Amats! What's up?" Danny Morello yelled.

"Nothing at all. Why do you ask?"

"You have a face on that looks like the same one Moses had on when he saw the Burning Bush."

"Oh," he chuckled. "I was just doing some research for my thesis. I think I've got a topic."

"Well jolly for you. What might that be, may I most humbly ask?"

"I'm calling it "Torpedo Squadron 8 at Midway - Tragedy by Tactics or Planned Sacrifice?"

"You're playing with some deep shit here. This better be good. The old men are still ready to come to blows over that issue."

"I know. But I have this need to write it. I can't explain why. Whenever I hear the name Waldron, I go off someplace. Every time I go home and visit Mr. Whitney and look at that damned Devastator, it seems to cry to me. I guess I have to put it all together, for my sake."

"Well, a man's gotta do what a man's gotta do." Morello hesitated a moment as a demon seized him. "What do you say we go knock on some plebes?"

This was never his cup of tea. Steven heretofore didn't think it did a thing to inspire aggressiveness or loyalty, and while he made it through his own plebe year with few problems, he despised some of the crap that went on endlessly. But now he knew "Jawn" better and what he stood for, and the traditions that made this place "the Yard." He smiled at Danny and said, "Let's!"

They approached one plebe that did his best to try to turn a corner before they closed. It didn't work.

"You can run, but you can't hide, Mister....Lynch!" he screamed, viewing the name tag. "Where are you off to?" he screamed not five inches from the horrified face in front of him.

"Nowhere, sir!"

"Oh, just great! Another dumb smack who is going nowhere! Mr. Morello, can you believe this?"

"No, Mister Amato, I cannot!"

"Tell me, Mister Lynch. Have you any idea of who John C. Waldron was?"

"No sir! I don't sir!"

"You don't know? Did I hear you say you don't know? Mr. Morello, did Mr. Lynch say he didn't know?"

"I'm sorry, tragic as it is, but I must confirm that, Mr. Amato!"

"Mr. Lynch! You are to meet me here this evening right after, and you are to know exactly who John C. Waldron was. Do not keep me waiting long. If you don't know by then, I will expect that I will have heard that you left the Yard stripped naked and in total disgrace. Am I clear?"

"Sir! Yes sir!"

"Get out of my sight. On the double!" Amato said, through gritted teeth.

"On the double, Mr. Lynch!" Morello screamed for effect.

The two looked at each other and smiled. "Mister Lynch will make a new friend, don't you think?"

"Yeah. Boy, can that kid run!" Morello offered. "Look at him go!"

"I hear he's a halfback, if that's the same Lynch. Perhaps we will scrimmage the plebes and see what he's made of."

Steven was at the designated sight at the designated time waiting for Lynch, Danny Morello at his side. Lynch came pounding up the pavement, a grin on his broad face. He had a likeable face, Steven thought, and it almost - almost - made him smile. But he looked at Danny's stern face and held it in.

"Sir! I've found out some information about WALDRON, JOHN C, and would like to report out to you, sir!" Lynch screamed.

"Report, Mr. Lynch, and make it quick. We've got better things to do than stand here with the likes of you!" Morello retorted. The grin left Lynch's face.

"Sir! WALDRON, JOHN C graduated from the Yard in June of 1924. He achieved the rank of Lieutenant Commander, before being killed in action during the Battle of Midway, June 4, 1942 as commanding officer of Torpedo Squadron 8."

"On what carrier was Torpedo 8 assigned, Mr. Lynch?" Steven interrupted.

"Sir! That would be the USS *Hornet*, later sunk during the Battle of Santa Cruz by Japanese carrier-based aircraft, probably from the carriers *Shokaku* and *Zuikaku*, sir!"

"How many men survived from Torpedo 8, Mr. Lynch?"

"Sir! Only one, sir. Ensign George Gay. And one officer and a crewman who flew one of six TBFs from Midway Island itself. They were attached to Torpedo 8, but never flew from the *Hornet*."

A TBF flown from Midway, attached to Torpedo 8? It was something Steven Amato never knew. This was going to be a great thesis, he thought. He almost forgot about Lynch, who was obviously in pain from standing at brace for so long.

"Are you made of the same stuff as Waldron, Lynch?"

"Sir! Yes sir! I look forward to the day when I can fly for our country, sir!"

"Very well done, Mr. Lynch! Thank you. Where did you find your information?"

"Sir! My grandfather flew with Torpedo 3 from the USS *Yorktown* during Midway. He never returned, sir! I called my grandmother, sir. I assumed Mr. Waldron was an Academy graduate, as most of the questions I've been getting have been about the history of the Yard, sir! She knew right away. My grandfather graduated from here back in 1926, sir!"

"Well done, Mr. Lynch. I admire your resourcefulness, and I'm jealous of your family's history. I hope you get what you want," Steven said.

"Sir! And I hope you do too, sir!"

Steven saluted Lynch, who returned a sharp, perfectly executed response. It was obvious this kid had saltwater in his veins as well. And he had given Steven another lead. TBFs at Midway? He thought their introduction was too late for the battle. Maybe not.

He laughed to himself. If that damned Devastator could talk to him all the time, why didn't that damned Avenger make the attempt?

Chapter 6

"So it is your contention that all the American torpedo squadrons, including *Hornet's* VT-8, were purposely sacrificed to keep the Japanese fighter squadrons and AAA down on the deck, so as to insure the dive bombers had no problem in cutting open the Japanese carriers? Is that a correct on my side, Midshipman?" Captain D'Couer asked, his eyes peering above the reading glasses perched at the end of his nose.

"Sir! Yes sir!" Steven answered smartly.

"May I ask why that policy was not adopted heretofore, such as at Coral Sea, or any of the raids that preceded Midway?"

"Sir, my thesis explains the fact that the various sorties before Coral Sea and Midway conducted by the task forces built around the carriers *Enterprise*, *Yorktown*, *Lexington* and *Saratoga* were forays, not major engagements, sir. Their successes were predicated on the element of surprise, and the old, obsolete TBD Devastator was at its limited best attacking merchant shipping and stationary men-of-war in the calm waters of the lagoon anchorages of the South Pacific. The torpedo squadrons were provided yet another advantage by attacking at dawn when the South Pacific horizon was at its colorful peak with limited visibility. Spotting, identifying, and targeting low-flying aircraft was a difficult task for half-asleep and surprised anti-aircraft gunners. In each instance, the Zero fighters were caught on the deck or were up in such few numbers that escorting F4F Wildcat fighters had no trouble in engaging them and keeping them off the torpedo planes, and for that matter, the dive bombers."

"Okay, I'll buy part of that, Midshipman Amato. But what about Coral Sea? No sacrifice needed there?" Captain D'Couer raised his bushy eyebrows in an apparent mocking of Steven Amato's precept.

"Sir, at Coral Sea the newest of the Japanese carriers, *Shokaku* and *Zuikaku*, along with the tiny *Shoho*, had untried crews manning their AAA batteries, and the youngest, most inexperienced and scorned air groups in their fleet. In addition, the force was really under strength for the mission that they were called upon to complete, that being the invasion of Tulagi in the Solomons. *Akagi*, *Kaga*, *Hiryu* and *Soryu* had the veteran 1st and 2nd Air Squadrons and ships' crews that were sailing together since the Manchurian invasion. And even though *Shokaku*'s and *Zuikaku*'s 5th Air Squadron had been on the Pearl Harbor raid, it too was an attack on stationary targets, carried out in surprise, against a sheltered anchorage where even the most inexperienced airman could look like a hero. At

Midway, the varsity was playing in a big major league stadium, and all the cards were on the table. It was the Decisive Battle scenario that ruled Japanese naval doctrine. Be reminded, sir, that Doolittle's Tokyo raid was the motivating factor for the Japanese to seize Midway. They saw the invasion as not only a way to draw out and destroy the American carrier fleet, but to also secure their defensive perimeter and neutralize, then possibly invade, Hawaii. There is even an historical perspective that claims that the Midway island chain isn't a separate island grouping at all, but actually a part of Hawaii, sir. We can only imagine if this bit of trivia played any part at all in the cards Admiral Nimitz chose to play."

"I see. So you contend that the Battle of the Coral Sea was somewhat of a standoff between amateurs, and the torpedo squadrons were more successful and survivable because of this, correct?"

Captain Thaddeus D'Couer was an expert on Midway, and the whole of the United States Naval history of the Second World War. He had published several books on various battles, skirmishes and naval encounters of both World Wars, and his quest for absolute historical accuracy was legendary. He described the *Yorktown*'s sinking at Midway with such detail that her own captain learned about incidents of which he was totally unaware prior to the publication of D'Couer's manuscript. He was grilling Steven into trying to compromise his thesis, but the first classmen would have none of this.

"No, sir. You are only partially right. If you will recall during the Coral Sea engagement, neither force had any clue as to the other's strength. They had no idea as to how many carriers each of them possessed, or for that matter, what each other's missions were. At Midway, the Japanese mission was known weeks ahead of time because of Commanders Rochefort's Japanese naval code-breaking activities. As a result, Admiral Nimitz knew well in advance how many carriers the Japanese had, how many battleships, cruisers, troop transports, submarines, destroyers and oilers. He knew Yamamoto's tactical plans, and that only four of the six carriers that were the Pearl Harbor raiders would make the cruise, because at Coral Sea *Shokaku* had been laid open by *Yorktown*'s air group, and *Zuikaku* lost most of her air group in their attacks on *Yorktown* and *Lexington*. Nimitz also knew the Japanese thought *Yorktown* was sunk. As you know, she was severely damaged, but deployable for Midway through a superhuman effort over three days at the Pearl Harbor Navy Yard. Because of Rochefort's superhuman efforts, Nimitz also knew the Japanese were aware *Saratoga* was recuperating on the west coast from a torpedo hit, and the *Lexington* had been sunk at Coral Sea."

"That still doesn't explain why the torpedo squadrons should be singled out as the sacrificial lambs of Midway. If Nimitz knew so much, he must have known the limitations of the Devastator. Nimitz had full knowledge of what was coming at him, and the costs of losing this battle. Wouldn't that make sacrifice, any sacrifice, acceptable? Sometimes leaders have to do that, Midshipman Amato. It comes with the fancy uniform".

Captain D'Couer sat back and raised his bushy eyebrows again. He wants me to fold and say the torpedo squadrons' fate was either predetermined at the highest levels, or just the way things happened to have worked out, chalked up to the fortunes of war. Bullshit! Don't worry, John. I won't let that stand. The good Captain doesn't know who he's fucking with.

"Begging your pardon sir, but you're way off base." He saw D'Couer's eyebrows rise again, but this time. Coupled with the slowly clenching fists and taut lips, they betrayed a seething anger. Good! "Nimitz set the strategy. Tactics were developed by CAGS, air officers, captains, Admiral Fletcher aboard *Yorktown* and Admiral Spruance aboard *Enterprise*. To this day, the fact that Gene Lindsey, the CO of *Enterprise*'s Torpedo 6, had his prearranged single with Jim Flatley, CO of Fighting Six, ignored points to the lack of confidence among naval airmen in their own torpedo comrades. Lindsey was to holler "Come on down, Jim!" if his Devastators were swarmed over by Zeros. When he frantically screamed that phrase as his planes were cartwheeling into the sea, Flatley elected to stay with the dive bombers, even though the Zeros were swarming downward and cutting all three torpedo squadrons, VT-3, VT-6 and VT-8 to ribbons. The few that survived the Zeros were left to draw the concentrated fire of the Japanese fleet's AAA gunners. There are some who suggest Flatley never heard it. I suggest he ignored it."

"There are some to this day who would say you are accusing the fighter commanders of cowardice. That started world-class brawls even up to a few years ago, Mr. Amato. Are you saying Flatley was a coward?" D'Couer leaned forward in his chair menacingly.

Midshipmen Amato didn't flinch. Waldron wouldn't have let him. There would be no wavering here. "No sir, not at all. The torpedomen knew what was expected of them that June 4th, sir. If Flatley could be accused of being a coward, what would you say about Commander Stanhope Ring of *Hornet*'s Air Group 8? Ring took all his fighters along with the bombers to refuel at Midway when they failed to follow Waldron's bearings. They missed the entire battle! Not a bomb or even a single bullet from the rest of *Hornet*'s air group, hit a Japanese ship. If sacrifice was expected, it seems that the brunt of it was expected from the torpedo squadrons, sir. There seems to have been a plan, unwritten, maybe even unspoken, to use the tactics of torpedoing a ship at sea as a ruse to keep the guns and Zeros down on the deck while the dive bombers did their work."

D'Couer's face changed from anger to reasonable doubt. He thought a few seconds, than uttered, "Going solely on the sense of urgency demanded by the battle situation of June 4, why weren't the divebombers also expendable, then?" D'Couer asked.

"The SBD was a more modern airplane, sir. Its effectiveness was already proven in previous engagements. Therefore they weren't as expendable as an old TBD Devastator, whose attack and evasion tactics were best described as sitting ducksmanship, and whose torpedo armament was not at all reliable. The torpedo squadrons were sure they'd have the new TBF for Midway, with its bigger torpedo that had greater range and speed that would increase their survivability. Even when the Devastators attacked the tiny *Shoho* at Coral Sea with fighter cover to keep the Zeros at bay, only two torpedoes of the four that made contact detonated. As a matter of fact, the Navy did not develop a reliable aerial torpedo until the following year. Again sir, don't forget the surprising fact that Commander Stanhope Ring of Air Group 8, *Hornet*'s CAG, was given permission to land his SBD dive bombers and F4F fighters at Midway to refuel, after failing to find the Japanese Fleet. This happened even after Commander John Waldron and his VT-8 had been denied this same permission after finding the Japanese fleet. They were the first naval airmen to do it since the crews of the patrol aircraft made their initial contacts. Waldron was still thinking in terms of a coordinated divebomber and torpedo attack. Even considering that the element of surprise was tantamount to Nimitz's strategy, and continuous attack was primary to tactics, it's difficult to understand why Waldron was denied permission to refuel, unless you factor in the obsolescence and unreliability of Waldron's weapon, and the fact that he alone now had the Japanese fleet in his sights. Waldron knew full well that his critical fuel situation would not permit him to return to the *Hornet*, even if his torpedo attack was successful. But it was critical for Admiral Spruance to catch the Japanese carriers between the strike they had already carried out on Midway and the strike they were preparing for the American fleet. He had to have had reasoned that if the Japanese were forced to maneuver to avoid unrelenting aerial attacks, their defensive formations would be compromised, and they couldn't turn their carriers into the wind to launch heavily loaded aircraft. If the torpedo planes did nothing more than keep the Japanese off balance and on the defensive, Spruance would have accomplished his mission of striking at the more powerful enemy while preventing the enemy from striking at him. It was better to lose obsolete planes rather than the dive bombers with the real and reliable punch. Carrying this a step further, it was far better to lose torpedo planes than three carriers. Nimitz's only guideline to Fletcher and Spruance was that they risk their precious carriers only if they could be absolutely sure that the damage inflicted on the enemy was worth the risk. If Midway were to be lost, it was better than losing the only three carriers left to the Pacific Fleet, even if their air groups were decimated. Air groups could have always been replaced. That's why Spruance's response to John Waldron's request was "ATTACK! REPEAT: ATTACK!" Still, I just cannot understand why Commander Ring was allowed to land at Midway, rather than ordered to fly to Waldron's radioed position."

"Midshipman Amato, you are making light of the fact that this attack was to be coordinated with dive bombers. Didn't everyone get lost and separated? It wasn't just Ring. Wade McCluskey of *Enterprise*'s Bombing Six squadron found the Japanese fleet by luck. He followed the wake of a destroyer left behind to depth charge a submarine, the *Nautilus*, that stalked the Japanese Fleet all day, and finally finished off *Kaga* after she was laid open by the dive bombers. It was meant to be coordinated." D'Couer leaned forward, only to see Steven Amato's jaw tighten.

"Then, quite simply sir, why wasn't it? There were hundreds of American planes in the air. Why didn't someone, anyone, take over, or be placed in command? There wasn't one overall air officer assigned for the American attack, not for the attacks coming from Midway, and not for the attacks coming from Spruance's and Fletcher's three carriers. That led me to conclude that the element of surprise was tantamount to offset the huge Japanese advantage, even more so than coordination. Nimitz, by his calculated risk axiom, had set the stage for Spruance and Fletcher to develop their attritional tactics. They wanted purposely to keep the Japanese off balance, unable to launch a strike at the Americans, whose strength and numbers were largely unknown to the Japanese until it was too late. This tactic of constant uncoordinated attack was risky, but it would prohibit the Japanese from efficiently recovering and rearming their Midway attack planes, all with the hope of catching *Akagi*, *Kaga*, *Hiryu* and *Soryu* with deck loads of armed and gassed aircraft waiting to take off, and their armories laid wide open. It wouldn't have taken a whole lot of bomb hits to at least severely damage a carrier in that condition. A strafing fighter plane would have done it. You will note, too sir, that the Japanese carriers burned viciously after they were hit, consuming themselves in the fuel and bombs their aircraft were to use to sink the American fleet. The strategy and the tactics worked. It was a masterful, if uncoordinated ambush. I'm not condemning anyone for it, sir. I just propose that the torpedo squadrons did what they were ordered to do, willingly and aggressively, even when they knew they were being tossed away. In short, the Devastator was condemned to demonstrate with great success how outclassed and under armed it was. It was at its best as a sacrificial lamb. The torpedo squadrons were ordered to attack alone, forfeiting the advantage of fighter cover and dive-bomber attacks to disperse the enemy's defenses. I can only conclude that the thinking was to take advantage of their one true and unarguable asset - their expendability, based upon their vulnerability and unreliability, all in the urgency to sink the Japanese carriers by keeping them off balance, sir. I think events were too complicated and too intense to give the Fates and Luck credit for this happening. Nonetheless, it made this sacrifice much easier to explain to an American public that was badly in need of heroes in 1942."

"What do you say if I argued that Fate and Luck had finally deserted the Japanese? That's why they roll dice in war games to decide each move. It allows the element of chance to come into play, Midshipman Amato." D'Couer was smiling now. It put Steven more at ease. D'Couer was now discussing his thesis, not attacking it.

"Considering the number of B-17 and B-26 missions the Army flew from Midway, and the number of missions the Marines and Navy flew from Midway, all dispersed intermittently to apply constant pressure to keep the Japanese fleet defensive, the tactic left Admiral Nagumo no time to think about what devils were about. He didn't know the number or positions of the American carriers until well into the battle. He didn't even know how many carriers he was facing until his own carriers were on the bottom. It took advantage of the cockiness of the Japanese Navy bred from it string of successes since Pearl Harbor. The breaking of their fleet code was the joker in the deck. It made planning that much more effective, essentially giving Nimitz what amounted to another task force. Look at what there was to gain. After Midway, the Japanese fleet never again took the offensive. They lost the heart of their striking power and their best airmen. And it fulfilled Yamamoto's prophecy that he would run wild for six months, but after that he wouldn't guarantee anything. He knew on the midnight stroke ending June 4, 1942 that Japan's days were numbered. He lost the decisive battle he needed to win. Luck didn't desert Yamamoto and Nagumo, sir. They gave it away by making a critical rookie mistake; they underestimated their enemy, and overestimated their own power."

Captain D'Couer continued to smile and allowed himself to settle back in his chair. He crossed his legs and tossed his eyeglasses on the table. The kid was good. Now it was time to test his depth. He already knew the kid had brains and spirit. And, he was onto something that no one had yet articulated, despite the years and books written on the Battle of Midway.

"How so? What about the Japanese? Even if Luck deserted the Japanese, or if they gave it away as you contend, why did they fail so badly? They still out-gunned and out-shipped and out-planed us. If it wasn't all bad luck, then what was it, Midshipman Amato?"

"Sir! To the Japanese, the protection of their sacred Homeland against further bomber raids was tantamount. They knew how important it was to win this decisive battle for which they had planned, war-gamed, and trained for years. It was the heart of their war strategy. Even though their last war-games exercise prior to Midway resulted in the sinking of *Kaga* and *Akagi*, they pressed on with a plan that was too intricate and complicated. It doomed them to failure because Nimitz ambushed them way before they had actually planned on the intervention of the American Navy. They they had no respect for their enemy. They actually believed the Americans would do what they wanted them to do precisely when and where they wanted them to do it. They assumed, for example, that the American fleet would sortie from Hawaii only after Midway had been bombed, invaded, and secured as an unsinkable carrier to use against the puny American fleet. Their timetable left no room for something going awry. It was all part of Nimitz's strategy to take advantage of this because his codebreakers had given him the heart of Yamamoto's battle plan. Why their intelligence failed them is a mystery to this day, considering how thorough it was for the Pearl Harbor raid. But considering their astonishing string of victories across the Pacific, Pearl Harbor, The Philippines, and Wake Island, Singapore and in the Indian Ocean against the British Navy, they had every right to be cocky. Nonetheless, it was still go-for-broke time, and everyone on every carrier knew it. As Commander Stafford said in his book, *"The Big E"*, the war narrative of the USS *Enterprise*, there were no cowards flying from any carriers on June 4, 1942. It's interesting to note, sir, that the Japanese were stunned by the selflessness of all the American Army and Navy airmen as they pressed home their attacks to can't-miss range, or rammed their planes into their ships. They made the fatal mistake of doing what all of us are taught never to do, in football or in war-they underestimated their enemy. Admiral Kusaka, Admiral Nagumo's Chief of Staff, was so taken back by the ferocity and perseverance of the Americans that he found himself praying for the torpedo plane crews as they died. Admiral Yamaguchi, captain of *Hiryu*, was moved to tears at their bravery and sacrifice. Those Americans- they were some kinda guys. Sir."

"Yes. They were some kinda guys, Midshipmen. The best kinda guys" D'Couer said, allowing himself to use Amato's vernacular. He smiled broadly, and even chanced a wink at the young, handsome face sitting across from him. You have heart and you're some kinda guy yourself,

Amato, he thought. And it's nice someone your age remembers the boys of VT-3, VT-6, and especially VT-8. He cleared the apple that was choking him from his throat. "Midshipman Amato, in your opinion, if VT-3, VT-6 and VT-8 had been equipped with the new TBF Avenger, do you think tactics or outcome would have been different?"

He thought of Lynch, whom he had harassed three years ago, and smiled. "No sir. I don't, unless the strategy of attrition and constant attack was cast aside. The detachment of Torpedo 8 that flew the six Avengers from Midway had no better luck than their brothers on the *Hornet*. Only five of the six planes returned, and the one that did come back was so shot up it would never fly again. Neither would its dead turret gunner. The problem was that the torpedo squadrons would still have an unreliable torpedo that had to be launched very close to its target to have a chance of destroying it. And if the strategy was to constantly attack without fighter cover in piecemeal fashion to keep the Japanese from launching their air groups, they would still have been picked off by the Zeros. Remember too, that the TBF was so new that its pilots barely had twenty hours of flying time in it. You can't develop proficiency in flying and fighting it in that time frame. It's a great airplane to fly, sir, but it wasn't a superweapon."

D'Couer looked up in surprise. You sound like you know the aircraft intimately, Midshipman."

"I do, sir. I've got twenty hours myself in an Avenger that belongs to a group of World War II veterans, all Navy flyers, all who flew at Midway. Comparing the Avenger to the Devastator is comparing an F-14 Tomcat to an F9F Cougar, but still, enough Cougars under the right conditions could splash a Tomcat, sir."

"That's astonishing, Amato. I'd like to meet these men someday."

"Sir! It would be my pleasure to introduce you to Mr. Whitney and his comrades.

"You're on. Midshipmen Amato, what led you to choose this topic for your senior thesis?"

"I think it's been with me all of my life, sir. I've always wanted to fly Navy Air. I can't remember a time in my life when I have ever thought of doing anything else. Lieutenant Commander Waldron's story seems to have literally possessed me. Even the Devastator that Mr. Whitney owns has a magic to it."

"This Whitney fellow owns a TBD too?" D'Couer almost jumped out of his seat in amazement.

"Yes sir, and it flew with VT-6 from the *Enterprise*, and was designated the squadron's number 7 aircraft. Did you know, sir, that the Devastators that survived Midway were the number 7 or 11 ship, no matter what squadron they were attached to? From what we can determine, it has never flown since. Mr. Whitney was able to finally get the old Pratt and Whitney Twin Wasp engine rebuilt five years ago, after spending decades locating spare parts, or having them painstakingly replicated. But even though it's perfect mechanically, it won't start. The aircraft seems bewitched, sir. It has the power to captivate and confound you."

"Are you trying to spook me, Amato?" D'Couer let out with a laugh.

"No sir. Just come and look for yourself."

"I intend to, Midshipman. A wonderful job was completed here, Amato. You are to be congratulated. May I call the Naval Institute and try to get your paper published?"

Steven was dumbfounded. "Sir? Did you say published?"

"Yes. The Naval Institute might want to publish it in *"Proceedings."* You certainly have an interesting premise here, and no doubt some old admirals will surely get into a fistfight after reading it, but I like your approach. What do you say, Mr. Amato?"

"I say, aye aye, sir! Thank you! Thank you very much!"

"Dismissed. And don't forget you owe me a visit with those airplanes."

"Sir, I'll set it up right away. Thank you!"

Steven ran down the campus looking for Danny Morello, who he found sitting with Ernie the Chevrolet dealer, looking over the contract for a new Corvette. It was two weeks until graduation, and every car dealer in the world descended on Annapolis to sell eager graduation candidates the objects of their automotive lust.

"Amats! What's up? You got that look again, just like the one you had on when you scored the TD against Army. Do you like red or white?" he asked, holding up a picture of a new Corvette. The dealer looked on and smiled.

"D'Couer is going to get my thesis published in Proceedings! Isn't that something?"

"Holy Hannah! That is something! Congratulations!" Danny said, pumping his hand.

"Yes, that is great," chimed Ernie the Chevrolet dealer. "You should celebrate and buy yourself a new Corvette! What do you say, Mr. Amato?" A greedy smile crossed is face.

"Ernie, you don't know my pal Amats. Unless you got an old Corvette, a very old Corvette, Amats here won't even look at it, right, paisano?" Danny said, chucking his arm.

"I'm afraid he's right, Ernie. See that red '63 SS convertible over there? It's mine, and as far as I'm concerned, even that's too new."

"Ah, you're an antique freak. Nice hobby. That car's gorgeous!"

"Thanks. There's just seems to be something about the objects of the past that help you determine where you came from, and maybe where you're going. I dunno. I guess it's an obsession. I've always been that way."

"Well, I'll keep my eye peeled for something you might like. I never lose a customer, Mr. Amato."

"You know where to find me, Ernie, at least for another two weeks. After that, you'll have to look me up at Pensacola Naval Air Station."

"You're going to be a fighter pilot, huh?"

"I hope so, but the Navy might find better use for me flying a Hawkeye, or an Intruder; or an Orion, God forbid. Who knows?"

"What about you, Mr. Morello? Where are you off to?" Ernie asked.

"I'm off to Oceana Naval Air Station to learn to fly the back seat as a radar intercept officer. Amats and I are going to be bosom buddies forever, right Amats? Just like I quarterbacked and handed off to him, like I pitched and he caught, we are inseparable, and I just know the Navy is going to be smart enough to realize that."

"They had better. You get to know a guy very well over four years. I've never had a brother, but I tell you, soon-to-be-Ensign Morello is as good as my flesh and blood."

Steven couldn't believe what he had just said. Why was he... gushing like this? Was it that graduation a few days away was marking the end of what had been a superlative educational and social experience? He saw Danny's eyes swell as his were. This place was really something, wasn't it? He came to realize that tossing up his cap at graduation wouldn't solely be a demonstration of relief for having survived this place. His cap would be one of a thousand that showed a unity of spirit among the Navy's newest officers, a kinship that Lord Nelson had referred to as his "Band of Brothers." It was a relationship thicker than blood, and he realized fully why those alumni acted as crazy as they did during their reunions, and why men with gobs of gold braid on their uniforms were moved to near insensibility when the weekends were over, and why they all took one long last look at Annapolis before they drove away. He found himself hugging Danny Morello, and saw Ernie unabashedly wiping a tear from his eye at the sight of it. Maybe Ernie's smile wasn't gratuitous after all, Steven thought.

Chapter 7

Steven Amato sat watching the Orioles losing to the Minnesota Twins at the bottom of the seventh inning. Susan had brought yet another of her girlfriends home from the University of Virginia, hoping that Steven would show some interest. The young blonde-haired beauty from Georgia in the heels and short, tight-fitting dress sitting next to him was trying her damndest to attract him without being an outright slut about it. He was trying to be above it all, totally platonic, always steering the conversation to the game on TV, and the hopes he had for being assigned to a fighter squadron after his year of pilot training. He didn't even care to know her name. He just called her Miss Georgia.

Susan couldn't figure out her brother. Every woman who knew him wanted to love him, and he could have cared less. Sure, he had a "bevy of beauties on his six," as Danny Morello would say (Susan adored Danny Morello, but like her brother, he also seemed seemed...preoccupied), but whenever a women got too close, he'd abruptly cut off the relationship. His last close girlfriend had broken off their relationship in their first year away from each other at college. Steven wasn't so heartbroken, but the girl called Susan every night for a month and cried for hours.

The phone rang, and with noticeable frustration, Susan jumped up to get it. She listened intently for a minute, and said, "Ensign Amato. It's for you."

"Who is it, Susan?" he asked coming to the phone with Miss Georgia in tow.

"A fellow named Ernie."

He looked at Miss Georgia and smiled at Susan as she sneered at him, perplexed as to why she might be angry with him. Paul Amato, reading the newspaper at the kitchen table, looked up as his son took the phone.

"Ernie?"

"Yes, it's Ernie the Chevy salesman. Have you reconsidered the Corvette?"

"No, Ernie. I'm sorry, but it doesn't do a whole lot for me. Danny loves his, though."

"I kind of figured that. Anyway, when do you leave for Pensacola?"

"I'm leaving Sunday."

"So you have a few days. Good. I do have something I'd like you to look at. I remember you told me that the older the car, the more you liked it. I just attended an auto auction down your way, near Richmond. That's how the dealership stocks our used cars. In any event, I met an elderly gentleman who said he had a car for sale, but couldn't bring it down to the auction lot because it wasn't drivable. All the other dealers there scoffed, but I didn't have the heart to turn my back on him. Are you still with me, Ensign?"

"I'm here. Please continue, Ernie." An antique, perhaps? He sat down at the table, and got his father's attention by pointing at the phone's receiver. Paul Amato lowered his newspaper to listen to the conversation.

"I walk with the gent to the parking lot, and we head toward a Cadillac limousine attended by a chauffeur, who's all done up in a beautiful gray pinstripe and black cap. The chauffeur simply says, "My name is Derek, sir. Please follow me. We have a twenty-minute drive to Mr. Moore's residence."

"A limousine, huh? It sounds like the gentleman has found the secret to the good life, Ernie."

"That isn't the half of it, Ensign."

"Moore. That name rings a bell with the city of Richmond. I..."

"Hold on, Ensign. You'll get the connection, believe me. Twenty minutes later we're in a wealthy suburb of Richmond. We go through a wrought iron gate up a driveway that's at least an eighth of a mile to this fellow's house, or more rightly, his estate's manor house. You cannot believe the beauty of the place. I park behind the Caddy, and the chauffeur directs me to follow him and the old gent inside. A maid serves us iced tea in his walnut-paneled library. He asks if I'm hungry and I say no thanks, but the maid returns with some finger sandwiches anyway. I'm polite and I have a few."

"Of course," Steven said with a chuckle.

"Yeah," Ernie replied, chuckling back. "Then I see a picture of a young man in a white Navy uniform and officer's cap on the mantle. I ask the gent who he is. He says he'll explain in a moment, but when he says this, his whole face becomes pained. I think that maybe he's taken ill and I move to help him, but the old fellow waves me back. Derek the chauffeur returns, and I follow him and the gentleman back to the limousine. I get in and the gentleman introduces himself as Richard Moore, and offers his hand."

"Richard Moore? There's something about that name. I don't know what it is, but I..."

"You'll get it all in a second, Ensign Amato."

"OK, Ernie. What happens next?"

"He takes us to a carriage house. Parked outside is a Rolls Royce and a Jaguar XKE. I ask him if these are the cars he was talking about. He smiles at me and says no, they are not. The Jaguar belongs to his daughter, the Rolls was his wife's car. When he said "was," I realize his wife must have passed on. He asks me to follow him into the carriage house as the chauffeur opens the door. I see a tarp covering a car. I immediately know it's an old car, probably from the thirties or forties, just by the height. All those old machines were built tall, you know?"

"Holy Hanna! What are you getting at here?" Steven asked. The connection between Moore and Richmond was still computing in his head. He was aggravated that he hadn't come up with a solution as yet, but its impending arrival made his heart beat faster. He knew he was on to something.

"Don't push it. You'll ruin it for yourself. Derek pulls off the tarp, and there sits a burgundy-colored 1939 Ford convertible. The paint is faded and the interior is musty and worn, not from use, but from time. The canvas top is a mess. The odometer reads only 18,421 miles. The chauffeur hands me the owner's manual."

"A '39 Ford convertible! Ernie, you are a super salesman. I'll take it!" He would have paid whatever Ernie wanted for the car. Even Paul Amato was excited about his son's discovery. The Moore-Richmond solution, though, was just about there, and the delay was torturing him, despite the fact that the Ford was the car of his dreams.

"Hold on, Ensign. There's more here."

"Sorry. Please go on."

"I ask how long the car has been in storage. The gent tells me since just after Pearl Harbor. It was his son's car, and he..."

" Ernie, I got the connection. Sweet Jesus!"

"I figured you would, Ensign. I saw your article in *Proceedings* last week, and me being the naval buff that I am..."

"The car belonged to Lieutenant Raymond A. Moore, and Ray Moore belonged to Torpedo 8."

"Bull's eye. Mr. Moore told me Raymond himself parked the car in that exact spot a few days before he left with Torpedo 8 on the *Hornet*'s shakedown cruise, just before Christmas, 1941. The old man cried. You know the rest, Ensign."

"Yeah, Ernie, I do." An overwhelming sadness gripped him, followed by a sense of luck and eerie timing. Nonetheless, he had to ask the next question. "Where's the car now?"

"I'm calling from Mr. Moore's home. He insisted I stay with him, and became more insistent when I told him I had probably had a buyer. When I told him who and what you were, he smiled and fell into a chair. He was so happy and sad at the same time. He told me his son loved the Navy, loved the *Hornet,* and thought the world of John Waldron. He said his son died doing what he loved, and he was so happy that someone who was following in his footsteps was getting the car."

"How much does he want for it?"

"He won't give me a price. He says he'll give you a real bargain if you want it."

"Tell Mr. Moore I'll meet him tomorrow morning at his home at 9:00 a.m., if that's all right with him."

"I'll call you right back."

Steve relayed the details to his father, whose open-mouthed expression reflected the circumstances of the find.

"It's like finding Amelia Earhart," he said.

The phone rang again a few seconds later. "Hello?" Steven answered.

"It's Ernie. Tomorrow at nine will be fine."

Steven took down directions, thanked Ernie again, and hung up the phone. He looked at his dad, who was sitting back in his chair, his eyeglasses held across his chest. Paul Amato, smiled and said, "I guess we're going up to Richmond tomorrow."

"I would certainly appreciate the company, dad."

"Fine. I'd better get up to bed then."

Steve then looked at Miss Georgia, who looked on with interest throughout the entire conversation. She was really beautiful, and the romance of owning the Ford, with all its historical connections to what Steven thought was the most romantic time in history, further stirred his emotions. He smiled at her, and she returned it with a smile that indicated she was willing to give her undivided attention to his story of Ernie, the Ford, and Raymond Moore.

"How about we take a bottle of wine, some cheese and grapes and look at the June moon rise over the Chesapeake, Miss Georgia?"

"On one condition," she said, folding her arms and crossing her legs as she leaned against the door jam, trying to look incredibly sexy. From the look in his eyes, she was succeeding, she thought.

"And what might that be?" he asked, gently putting his arm around her waist.

"That you call me by my real name," she said, draping an arm around his shoulder.

"And what might that be?" he asked. He would have been really embarrassed had he known his sister was hiding at the top of the steps, watching and listening to his every move.

She laughed, and put her forehead to his chin, and her other arm around his neck. "Julie. Julie Ann Tate. Got it?" She couldn't believe how hard she had to work to get this far.

"I've got it, Julie Ann."

I certainly do, don't I? He allowed himself wryly, as he escorted her out the door to the waiting Chevy.

His sister almost gave herself away as she giggled with excitement. Rena Amato put her hand over her daughter's mouth just in the nick of time.

Chapter 8

Steven Amato extended his hand to the frail, silver-haired gentleman sitting in the large brown leather chair before him.

"I'm Steven Amato, Mr. Moore. It's my pleasure to meet you, sir."

The old man looked up through tired blue eyes and smiled faintly at the tall sailor in the summer white uniform. The corners of his mouth turned down slightly and his eyes reflected a remembrance of days long gone as he took the young man's strong hand. He had known a grip like this, and for a moment it was only yesterday that his Raymond shook his hand and hugged him tightly when he said good-bye to avenge the Sunday murders with his comrades, flying his Devastator from the deck of a brand new ship built not eighty miles from here.

"Hello, Ensign Amato," he uttered with a smile. "It's so good to know you. Ernie here was most kind to me, and spoke so highly of you. I read your article last night. It was good to see you remembered the boys as the heroes they truly were. Is this gentleman here your dad?"

"Oh, how rude of me. Yes, sir. May I introduce Paul Amato." As his father shook Moore's hand, Steven continued, "It was an honor to do the research on Torpedo 8, Mr. Moore. I hope that every naval aviator reads that thesis. It helped clarify a number of items, including the concepts of leadership and sacrifice."

"Surely. I hope Raymond appreciates it, too. Ah, well. I've been conjecturing for forty years about what Raymond thinks now. It's time I stopped. Let me take you to the car, Steven. Let's go, Derek," he said, motioning to the chauffeur to lead them out.

"I think you'll be pleased, Ensign. It's a beauty!" Ernie gushed, as they all walked to the waiting Cadillac limousine.

At the carriage house, Steven noted a car-carrier was parked off to the side. They went in, and Ernie helped Derek take off the tarpaulin. Mr. Moore was not at all disappointed by the smile that crossed the young officer's face.

"You seem to like it, Steven," Mr. Moore said softly.

"Like it? Mr. Moore, I love it! It's...it's superb! What price are you asking for it?"

Ernie looked at Mr. Moore intently, as he had not discussed price with him at all. Moore just smiled, knowing what Ernie was thinking. He was the middle man who had been cut out of this unusual transaction, but somehow Ernie didn't seem to mind as much as he could have. He realized this wasn't simply a car, but a family heirloom, a relic of historical significance.

"The look on your face is the price, Steven. Take her, but on one condition. You must restore her to the same pristine condition she was in the day my son parked it here. No one has moved it since. I've ignored it all these years, thinking that by some miracle Raymond would return, and I could chide him about how terribly he took care of things. I should have known better. I just couldn't bring myself to sell it, or take care of it." Mr. Moore's face was contorted with agony.

Ernie was incredulous. Moore saw that as well. He put his anguish aside yet again and said, "Ernie, I know you're a businessman. I'll tell you what I'll do to make your kindness and the time you spent with me worthwhile. Derek tells me a new Mustang convertible, which I think would be the modern-day equivalent to the old Ford here, would run about $17,000. I guess your commission would be about six percent. So here's a check for $1500. It will cover your time and your efforts on Steven's behalf. Are we square?"

"More than square, sir," Ernie beamed.

"Good. Now then, Steven. Can you restore this old horse?" Mr. Moore asked as he kicked at a wire wheel that held a very flat Firestone white-wall tire.

"I drive a '63 Impala Super Sport that my dad and I restored, sir. This will be more of a challenge in finding parts, but I guarantee you I'll spend every spare moment I have to get it on the road."

"I understand you're headed for Pensacola. That's where Raymond learned to fly for the Navy, too. If things are the same, you'll find yourself pretty busy over the next year, so don't be disappointed that things take longer than you wish them to. It's been a relic for forty years. Another few won't hurt it," Moore said, forcing a smile.

"I'll bring it up as soon as it's done, Mr. Moore. If you give me your number, I'll call before..."

Moore cut Steven off abruptly. "That won't be necessary, Steven. That uniform indicates you're a man of your word." He quickly turned to the chauffeur and said, "Derek, please get the truck we hired, load up the Ford, and drive it back for the Amato's. I won't be needing you anymore today, so you might as well spend the evening at Virginia Beach. Here's some money that should cover your expenses," he said, handing Derek a brown clasped envelope, tightly sealed with tape. "Enjoy the evening on me."

"Yes sir." Derek replied. "Thank you."

"Derek, we would be pleased if you stayed with us this evening," Paul Amato offered. It was the least he could do, he reasoned.

Derek was a tall, quiet, and seemingly an emotionless young man of no more than twenty-five years. He had a muscular build, and a fair complexion. The only time he smiled broadly throughout this day was at Paul Amato's invitation.

"Why, thank you sir!" Derek turned to Mr. Moore and offered back the envelope.

Moore pushed Derek's hand back, and promptly said, "You're taking a trip, Derek. Keep it for...well, for whatever."

"Yes, sir".

"Well, gentleman, I'll take my leave of you. Thank you so much for your help in seeing me clear of this problem. Oh, and Ernie. I have another favor to ask of you. Would you consider driving the Rolls to your dealership and selling it for me? I have no need for it, and it's time I got rid of it. I'd send Derek, but he's already busy with the Amato's. I'll have Derek take your car back to Annapolis and take the train home. Get the best price you can for it. I'll trust your judgment." He gave Ernie a devilish wink.

"I'd be pleased, Mr. Moore. But don't be troubled. I'll ask someone from the dealership to pick up the Rolls today. Then I'll follow it..."

"Nonsense!" Moore interrupted. "I absolutely insist you drive the Rolls Royce back to Annapolis. I'll see that Derek drives your car back to you in a few days. In the meantime, use the Rolls as your own."

"Yes, sir." Ernie surmised that arguing with this old codger was useless. He must have been one hell of a businessman. That much was obvious just from this conversation. He planned everything down to the most minute detail, Ernie thought.

"Fine, then. Off with you all!" he said with a flare. "Derek, I'll walk back to the house. Thank you all again." And with a wave of his frail hand, Mr. Moore turned a corner as was out of sight.

The trip back to Virginia Beach was filled with questions about Mr. Moore. Was he eccentric, or had his heart finally caved in to the emotions that resulted from Raymond's death? Derek was close-mouthed, except to say that Mr. Moore's daughter rarely drove her Jaguar, as she spent most of her time in Europe. When Steven asked what it was she did, Derek gave a weak smile and said, "Nothing at all." She was obviously out of favor with her father. Derek also confirmed that Mrs. Moore had passed on after battling Alzheimer's disease for years. Mr. Moore swore it was Raymond's loss that brought it on, because she hadn't been right since.

Later that evening, Derek was invited out on the town by Steven Amato and Danny Morello. He opened the envelope Mr. Moore had given him for expenses, and was shocked to see it contained one hundred hundred-dollar bills and a cashier's check for $500,000 made out to him.

AS TIME GOES BY

There was also a scribbled note that reminded him to get Ernie's car back to him. He tried to call Mr. Moore, but the line was continuously busy.

At about the same time, just outside Annapolis, Ernie Martinos, in the company of his wife and two children, had been pulled over by a state trooper for exceeding the speed limit in the Rolls. He luckily found the registration and insurance card in the glove box, and quickly gave it to the trooper while he fumbled for his wallet to produce his license. The trooper, while inspecting the registration slip, said something that caused Ernie's mouth to drop.

"Do you know how fast you were going, Mr. Martinos?"

At about the same time, Mr. Richard Moore gazed at the picture of his son in his gleaming white uniform and felt the tears come to his eyes for what had to be the millionth time. He then cradled his wedding portrait to his chest, but pulled it away and forced himself to look at his beloved wife. She was so vibrant in her youth, so beautiful, the expression on her face portraying a lust for life. He looked at his daughter's picture, and forgave her for all her sins against him, and wrote her a quick note to that effect. He also begged her forgiveness of him. It was all his fault-all of it. He knew it, he wrote, but he couldn't help it. It was difficult living in this house after Ray died, and his daughter bore the brunt of his and his wife's unhappiness. He signed the note, "Affectionately, Dad." He slipped a sheath of papers in the large brown clasped envelope, addressed it to his daughter's apartment in London, and over stamped it, just in case. He then called the maid, and asked her to walk the envelope to a mailbox and drop it in.

He looked again to Raymond's picture and said, "I did what you wished, son. It's done, all of it. Please, may I come to see you now? I've missed you and your mother so!"

He heard the answer he prayed would come. Then the mantle clock began striking off its twelve bells. This was the penultimate sound Raymond Moore heard. Then the Smith and Wesson snub-nosed .38 went off at his temple.

The date on the mantle clock changed to June 4, 1982.

*****

Steven and Danny Morello were looking over the '39 Ford with wonder. Paul Amato was buried under the hood, quietly poking around the V-8 engine. The garage was warm, but nobody seemed to notice.

"I wonder what kind of action this car has seen?" Danny said.

"I dunno. Mr. Moore was very close mouthed about it. His son was good-looking and rich, so I guess it has seen its share. And, he was Navy. How could he miss?" They both laughed as Steven continued, "Can you imagine the radio blaring out *In the Mood,* or *Moonlight Serenade* while

Raymond Moore put the moves on some sweet thing? There's a certain sadness to this car, though, just like that Devastator Mr. Whitney has."

"You gotta get a grip on yourself and this history thing!" Morello exclaimed, raising his long arms above his head. "It's starting to overtake you, man. And, you're giving me the creeps as well. You should be putting the moves on some sweet young thing in a Corvette or Porsche yourself. The fact that you would wind up with a car that belonged to a Midway casualty is eerie enough, you know? Why don't you sell the thing and..."

"Shut you blasphemous mouth!" he yelled, spitting a mouthful of beer all over himself, unable to contain his laughter.

"Oh, pardon me, I was just thinking that maybe..."

"Hush a minute. You hear that?" Steven's face changed suddenly.

"Hear what? The bells? So what?"

"So it's June 4, that's what. This is the fortieth anniversary of Midway. This car became ownerless forty years ago today."

Danny listened intently for a moment, as he stared at the far-away countenance on his best friend's face. He felt he was being overtaken, but just before giving in, he yelled, "Ah, you're nuts! I'm going to find your sister. She's the only child in this house who's sane. Susan! Where are you?" Danny yelled. As he walked out, he was stopped by the ringing of the phone on the garage wall.

"Hi, Mr. Whitney," Danny said.

"Hi, Danny. Is Steve about?"

"Yes. He's lusting over his newly acquired antiquity. Hold on." Danny motioned to his friend to come and get the phone, as he said, "Here, Amats. It's Mr. Whitney. He said he found the condoms Raymond Moore used on his last date."

"You're a jackass! Give me the phone. Condoms, for chrissake," Steven said with exaggerated annoyance. The sound of some sort of powerful machinery filled the background.

"Hi, Mr. Whitney. What's going on over there? It's so noisy."

"I've got some news."

"You'll have to speak up. I can barely hear you over that racket."

"I got the Devastator to start tonight, Steven. That's what you hear."

"Danny! The Devastator's running!"

"That's it! I'm getting the hell outta here right now. You're whacked out. Susan! Dammit! Where the hell are you? I'm shipping out in a few days, Susan. Come and love me while you can!" Danny yelled, as he rampaged through the house, trying to avoid Mrs. Amato's playful slaps for his blatant intent to dishonor her daughter.

Paul Amato stared at the Ford's V-8, wondering if it would suddenly jump to life as well after its forty-year slumber. There was something more to this coincidence that eerily defied recognition, and it made him feel very uncomfortable. The fact that his son was reveling in it made it all the more disturbing.

Chapter 9

The little Buckeye soared gracefully and responded quickly to the commands of control stick, rudder pedals and throttle that Steven gave as he closed to one-quarter mile of the end of the *Lexington*'s flight deck. The sky was crystal azure, and the sea a warm and inviting midnight blue glistening under the morning sun. The *Lexington*'s white wake made the scene just perfect. It was hard to imagine that any peril was lying in wait here. One errant move of hand or foot, or one wire that didn't send its prescribed electronic signal, or a malfunctioning switch could add a fiery red smear to the beautiful scene below, and "would just ruin my day," Steven's flight instructor said, just before he took off from Jacksonville NAS. This would be the first of what he hoped would be many carrier landings. For luck, he carried John C. Waldron's Annapolis yearbook picture in his wallet.

"Fledgling one, you are a quarter of a mile out. Call the ball." The Landing Signal Officer (LSO) of the *Lexington* was monitoring Steven's approach. The "ball" was a system of colored lights and mirrors that an approaching pilot had to keep perfectly aligned for a "trap" on the *Lexington*. His plane's arresting hook was to snag one of five cables stretched across the aft end of the angled flight deck, the number three cable being the most preferred. For their first landing, however, the young pilots circling overhead would have given their first child for a guarantee that they'd snag any wire, Ensign Steven Amato included. He couldn't believe how he was sweating. How do they do this at night in the rain, he wondered, but quickly dismissed the thought; one thing at a time, Amato.

He caught the amber light in the mirror that signified his fast-approaching Buckeye, and announced, "Roger, ball" to the radio microphone that lay buried in the facemask that covered his nose and mouth.

The black deck quickly grew as he approached it a 120 knots, its white and yellow lines clearly distinguishable, and her flight deck crew materializing from scurrying dots to the figures of men. The instrument panel lights indicated his hook and his landing gear were down. Easy, he told himself. Stay calm. Keep the ball centered, that's it.

"Steady," he heard in his earphones, as the LSO watched his approach intently, making sure this fledgling didn't become a statistic. "Good approach. Very good. Nice flair! Excellent!"

He felt his wheels touch the deck and applied full power, just in case his hook failed to snag a wire. Then he felt the plane decelerate quickly as his shoulders strained against the seat harness. He trapped! He throttled back the engines, then quickly looked for the deck officer who told him by hand signal to raise his hook to disengage the wire and taxi to the catapult. There would be no layover on the *Lexington*. He would leave this ship by steam-powered catapult as soon as the Buckeye could get connected to the catapult's sled on the carrier's forward end. The deck officer held up three fingers - he trapped the third wire! A "thumbs-up" and a smile followed. He returned the signal gleefully.

Now, for the second part of the ordeal- the roller coaster acceleration to 150 knots in three hundred feet, then off the bow and into the sky. Steven maneuvered the Buckeye to the port catapult in accordance with the signals he received from the Air Boss on *Lexington*'s bridge and from the catapult crew. The catapult's sled was attached to the nose gear, and the restraining bar connected. He was ordered to go to full power. The catapult officer signaled him with a thumbs-up and a salute; Steven returned it, then put the back of his helmet firmly into the headrest, and checked the trim of the Buckeye one last time. In an instant, he heard the roller coaster rumble beneath him and saw the deck's end approach very quickly. Then...nothing but the hum of the twin jet engines as the Buckeye left the *Lexington*'s deck. He rolled left as he retracted the landing gear.

He was elated. At long last, he fulfilled a lifelong quest: he flew "an airpane onna ships." He laughed out loud as he headed back with his wingman to Jacksonville, most eager to phone his father and mother and Susan.

Back at the base, their instructor waited with a camera to record his fledglings' successes. Steven's elation commenced as soon as his feet hit the tarmac. He leapt up and down, and the pumped his arm into the air around him. Every new carrier pilot felt that way, including Louis Thatcher, a black man from Michigan who had used the ROTC route to get to where he was. He had become Steven's closest friend at Pensacola, and he posed with him for the instructor's photo.

Just before the camera lens was to be exposed, Steven said, "Sir? Please wait...just one second. I want someone else in the picture."

"Who? C'mon, hurry it up! It's party time Amats!" Thatcher said.

"He's right here," Steven replied, as he reached into his wallet and pulled out John C. Waldron's photograph.

"Oh, right. We shouldn't forget John C. Good choice Ensign Amato," Lieutenant Commander Robinson said, as he readjusted his shot, and pushed the shutter button.

Chapter 10

Lieutenant (jg) Steven Amato opened the envelope containing his orders carefully. The last time he remembered being this nervous was when his family sat around the table as he fumbled with the envelope that contained the admission decision from Annapolis. He told himself he was older and wiser now, and that any kind of U.S. Navy aircraft was fine by him, even if it was an Orion, or C-2, or a Hawkeye. Like Commander Robinson had told him, everyone couldn't fly an F-14. Still, he was first in his class, he reasoned, and that would mean he would be preferenced, but the class that graduated just before his had their number one assigned to A-6s. Not that in itself was so bad, but an A-6 Intruder was no F-14 Tomcat. He also reminded himself that Waldron had wanted fighters, too. The Navy was his boss, just like it was Waldron's, and Waldron bought his own immortality by flying torpedo planes.

His eyes scanned the orders, and stopped at the training squadron call sign "VF". He got fighters! He read a little further, and saw the designation he was looking for... F-14! He yelled so loud and carried on so that those around him thought he had been stricken or possessed by a demonic entity. His next move was to run full force into a door that did not open as quickly as he had planned, causing him to lose his balance and flop down three steps, landing in a heap on the barracks sidewalk. He staggered to a pay phone, hurriedly plunked in ten quarters, and dialed his parent's phone number.

"Hello?" It was his father.

"Dad! I got it! F-14s! I'm assigned to a VF training squadron to learn to fly the Tomcat! Isn't that great, dad?"

"I'm really happy for you son! That's wonderful! Rena, Steve got F-14s! He's going crazy!"

"Steven, it's Mom! That's wonderful news! Susan will be thrilled when she hears about it. So will Julie!"

She said "so will Julie." Again. He had no interest in Julie Ann Tate, though her interest in him continued unabated. He answered her emotion-filled letters just to be courteous, but she was reading things between the lines that simply were not there. He wrote, for example, that "you shouldn't be wasting your time on someone who isn't ready for a commitment," and she would write back "waiting for you isn't a waste of time, Steven." He shouldn't have led her on and taken of her that night last June almost a year ago, not that they had gone all the way, but came pretty damned close. No, he told himself; she was a more-than-willing participant. Had he unwittingly led her on? Had his sister been too good a friend by bolstering her spirits, trying not to let her be hurt by what was obvious? He didn't think so.

"Mom, I've got a few weeks of leave before I have to report to my new squadron. I'm looking forward to coming home for some of your world-class cooking."

"That's wonderful, Steven. When can we expect you? I'll have Susan tell Julie..."

She wanted him to be with her. His mother wanted him married and taken care of. She liked Julie. Obviously Julie had been the perfect daughter-in-law-in-waiting while he was away.

After some hesitancy, he said, "Mom, that's not a good idea."

There was a long pause. Rena Amato realized what Susan said was true. He had no interest in this young, blonde, beautiful, bright, well-educated, well-heeled woman who would no doubt make him as happy as could be.

"Very well, Steven," she said, doing little to hide the annoyance in her voice.

"Mom, can I, uh, talk to dad again, please?"

"Certainly. And Steven?"

"Yes mom?"

"Although you're making a terrible mistake, want you to know I love you and I'm very happy things are working out for you."

"You're still my best girl, mom."

"I know. Here's your dad."

"Son, the Ford is really coming along nicely. The engine is purring like a kitten. I hardly had to do anything to it. The body still needs work, and you know you'll have to tear out the interior. Nothing is going to get that musty stink out. I'm trying to get Mr. Staminsky to do the upholstery work after you strip it down. You won't have too much time to dither with it."

"Yeah, I know. I want to be sure I keep that promise to Mr. Moore. Shit, I still get the willies when I think about how he set that whole thing up. It's eerie."

"Yeah, the whole experience was eerie. By the way, Derek wrote to us and said he's living near Annapolis now, and started his own limousine business. Ernie loves the Rolls, too. He stopped by last week to see how the Ford was coming along, and how you were doing."

"I'll have to call him when I get home, which by the way, will be in two days. My training cycle doesn't begin until the beginning of July, so I've got four weeks to work on the Ford. Have you heard from Danny?"

"Your sister has. Suzan says he's due home in a few days as well, so it looks like you two will get the opportunity to hook up again. I know your sister is on pins and needles waiting for him to come home.

"Yeah. Is he still interested in Susan?"

"Yes, he is."

The bluntness of the statement indicated that he thought his wife was right about Miss Georgia and her son. He could only manage to say, "Oh."

"Well, I'd better get going. I'll see you in a few days. Kiss mom for me, will you dad?"

"It would be my pleasure."

"And Susan, too. Bye, dad."

"Bye, son. And watch yourself with those damned airpanes!"

He wanted to ask about Mr. Whitney and the Devastator and the Avenger, but the line waiting for the phone was too long. There were smiling young men everywhere he looked, and it was obvious a lot of good news had to be spread around. Those brightly polished gold wings he and his fellow newly-crowned naval aviators had been awarded just this morning were something to behold. He couldn't get his eyes to drift from the insignia for too long. All these men felt a strong kinship that, to him, was only marginally secondary to the USNA Class of 1982. If the "red balloon went up", it would be with these men that he would carry the fight to his country's enemies-and destroy them. Even though it would be months before he would be assigned to an operational squadron, the feeling of camaraderie among the newest members of the "Navy Air" fraternity was already intense. He reflected on this for a moment, and thanked John Waldron yet again. This 'esprit de corps', this intangible yet so evident quality that linked men beyond the flesh and blood, the sense of significance, his...love, could only be experienced by men-at-arms, but especially those that lifted fantastic machinery into the air from unbelievable ships to perform superhuman feats. It was Waldron's legacy.

What in the world could compare to flying "airpanes onna ships?" He smiled at himself when he realized he was right all along, from age three to this day in June of 1983.

*****

The '39 Ford convertible greeted him in the driveway, with his mother, father and sister standing next to it. He quickly pulled the Chevy off to the side, and received the embrace of his family. His father proudly displayed the fact that he had registered the car, the shiny new vanity license plates spelling out "39 FORD." The license plate frame, however, caused him to laugh and with pride. On the bottom part of the frame, neatly printed in shiny red lettering next to a slyly grinning tomcat with two tails and a holstered six-gun, were the words, "*MY OTHER CAR IS A F-14 TOMCAT.*" The tomcat wore a badge that was the F-14's motto, applied by the Grumman Corporation that read, "*ANYTIME, BABY.*"

He jumped into the seat that Paul Amato had covered with a plastic drop cloth to avoid possible smudges of the omnipresent mildew on clothing. He turned the ignition key, and pushed the starter button. The V-8 jumped to life, and purred like...well, a kitten. The gauges registered the oil pressure and water temperature, and the power output of the six-volt battery and its generator.

He looked to his father and said, "Dad, I see you bought a signal light conversion kit."

"I had to. It wouldn't have passed inspection if I hadn't. I bought seat belts for it, but I didn't put 'em in because the interior has to be redone. Boy, that motor is sweet, and so easy to work on. Come and give it a look."

The motor was sparkling clean. Paul Amato's perfectionist touch was evident here; new ignition wires, a new distributor, new ignition points and spark plugs, and a pristinely painted block and heads. The little valve-in-head V-8 barely shook as it ran smoothly. "I see you replaced the motor mounts. Were they rusted out?"

"One of them had a crack in it. I guess it must have hit a pot hole or a bump at too high a speed. The suspension on this thing is all leaf springs, so you don't get that `boulevard ride.' I had the radiator redone, and I put in a new water pump, and belts. Some of the seals, gaskets and freeze-out plugs needed replacement, too. But, I had no problem getting parts. They were expensive, but I got them. I tell you, son, it's decent. Hell, why are we talking about it? Let's go for a ride!"

His family got it. Steven depressed the clutch, and put the floor mounted gear shift into its reverse slot. He backed out of the driveway, and then found first gear. He was amazed at the get-up-and-go the car had. It really was fun to drive, and the beautiful Virginian June day begged for a convertible.

"Where are we headed?" his father asked after a few minutes.

"I want to see Mr. Whitney. I need to look at something on the TBF for a professor I had at Annapolis. And, more importantly, I want to see the Devastator. Mr. Whitney got it going a year ago, but he hasn't flown it yet, at least not up until a few months ago when I called him."

"Why doesn't this surprise me?" his father said sarcastically.

Steven went directly to the hangar and parked the car to the side of the big folding doors. He went inside to see that the Avenger and Dauntless were still there, but the Devastator was not. He looked in the shop area but there was not a soul around. Just then, he heard the unmistakable drone of a high-powered aircraft piston engine, and headed for the door. He got outside just in time to see it. There, two hundred feet above, running at one hundred fifty knots, the Devastator dipped its right wing, then its left, in salute. The pilot waved as he passed his audience, a white scarf flapping behind him. He was recognizable even though he wore a leather helmet and goggles. Mr. Whitney's elation was evident.

The old plane swung around in a broad circle as it lined up with the runway, its nose coming up slightly as Mr. Whitney gently flared for a landing. As he taxied the Devastator to the hangar, both fists were pumping the air with elation.

"She flies! At long last she flies! The others will be furious with me because I didn't tell them that I was going to take her up, but who cares! I flew her and I landed her just as I did twenty-one years ago. If Gene Lindsey could see me now, he'd be elated!"

"Who's Gene Lindsay?" Paul Amato asked.

"He commanded Torpedo 6 off the *Enterprise* at Midway, dad." He turned to Whitney, who seemed to have lost twenty years of age. "I'm very happy for you, Mr. Whitney."

Paul Amato saw something beyond the old gentleman's obvious elation that transcended the moment, and his son's quick answer fortified his sense that there was more to this flight than met the eye. Hell, this Whitney guy had flown throughout World War II. He commanded an air group at its end. Why the faraway look in his eyes? However, Steven's facial expressions told him not to pursue it.

Whitney changed the subject quickly. "So this is Ray Moore's car! It's a beauty."

"Did you know Ray Moore, Mr. Whitney?" Paul Amato asked.

"Yes. Our torpedo squadrons were great rivals. We were in constant competition that was rooted in genuine mutual admiration. Torpedo 8 was brand new, and we taunted them constantly about their "greenness" and their swagger. John Waldron had instilled a great deal of pride in them. They wore shoulder holsters and carried huge non-regulation knives in their belts. We called them the "Flying Circus," or the "Mexican Panchos", but they worked their asses off. Waldron wouldn't let them rest a second, physically or mentally. He ran them and classroomed and flew them until they were ready to drop. Ray Moore once questioned Waldron if they would have enough gas to complete a rigorous training mission, and Waldron said that when Moore's gas ran out, he expected him to climb out on the wing and piss in the tank. He was hell on wheels, that Waldron. Our squadrons never socialized much. You know, the pride thing, the rivalry. But we had a great deal of professional respect for each other."

Whitney circled the car, and skimmed his fingers along the trunk lid. "This car was well-known around Norfolk, I tell you. This one, and Gus Widhelm's Lincoln Zephyr convertible." Whitney's eyes stared at something far away, as he touched the curve of the Ford's fender.

"Begging your pardon, Mr. Whitney, but who was Gus Widhelm," Paul Amato asked.

"Oh, I'm sorry. That was a SBD pilot with Bombing 8 on the *Hornet*. He was quite a character, that Gus."

"Mr. Whitney, do you think I could get a few hours in the Avenger? I also need to check some details on the turret for a professor of mine at Annapolis."

"Of course, especially now that you have those beautiful gold wings. You've entered a really select group of snobs, I tell you," Whitney chuckled.

"So I see," Steven said, gently poking the gold wings the old flyer wore on his flight suit. "I'll stop by later this week."

"I'll look forward to it. Thanks for coming by."

Whitney climbed back into the Devastator's cockpit, and busied himself with a few adjustments as the Amato's pulled away.

"What was that all about?" Paul Amato asked.

"That plane, 7-T-6, was not launched from the *Enterprise* on June 4, 1942 for the Midway battle. It was on the bow, ready to go, when its engine inexplicably conked out and wouldn't restart, no matter what was tried. The plane was almost shoved overboard to clear a very busy deck, but the pilot begged and pleaded for it to be pushed off to the side of the island. It snarled the deck for a few precious seconds, but he frantically reasoned with the deck officer that this was not the time to push a perfectly flyable, fully armed and gassed plane over the side. He tried and tried again to restart it, but the damned engine wouldn't catch. After *Enterprise*'s strike group became airborne, the plane was pushed on an elevator and struck below to the hangar deck and worked on, but no one could find a thing wrong with it. When the remnants of Torpedo Six returned to the *Enterprise* after engaging the Japanese fleet, and the surviving pilots told the story of the massacre that transpired, all work on the plane ceased. *Enterprise*'s CAG ordered it in complete disgust and remorse for the eighteen dead pilots and crew. Considering the losses of all the air groups, it was a ballsy kind of decision, as the Americans needed every plane they had, just in case. And remember, even though three Japanese carriers had been ripped open, the fourth, *Hiryu*, hadn't been touched as yet, but it made no difference to CAG. That plane was going nowhere."

"Was the plane's pilot Mr. Whitney?"

"Yes," Steven said, straight-faced, "and he hasn't forgiven himself or that plane to this day. He had flown it on earlier raids, and it worked perfectly fine, but on June 4, it wouldn't budge."

"How did he get to own it?"

"He found the plane in an old hangar at Miramar Naval Air Station in California right after V-J Day. It had been shipped back from Hawaii right after Midway. The new TBF Avengers were re-equipped the torpedo squadrons, so there was no need for it. There were barely enough of them to use as trainers, and after Midway no one wanted to even look at them, let alone use them as auxiliaries. He made an offer to rid the Navy of it, and they were more than glad to oblige him. He had it shipped here right after that. You know the rest."

Paul Amato stared straight ahead. What was it with his son and this old stuff? Here he was, capable of buying any car he wanted to, about to be trained to fly the arguably best fighter in the world, and yet, he was happy driving a `39 Ford and he hung on to that Devastator and that Avenger. What really tipped him over was the "new" album Steven pulled out of his suitcase when they had gotten home and he unpacked.

"Hey Dad, look at this. It's an original 78 rpm Glenn Miller recording of *Pennsylvania Six Five Thousand*. I got it at garage sale on my way up here."

"You listen to it. I'm going to put on my new *CHICAGO* cassette." Glenn Miller, for chrissake!

Chapter 11

Danny Morello thoroughly enjoyed the flights in the TBF. For almost a year, he and Steven had flown the old bird almost monthly, greatly appreciating these occasional weekend interludes loping about in the air, or helping their World War II predecessors with aircraft maintenance and insuring FAA aircraft certification requirements were met. Mr. Whitney's tutelage had them doing "dry" torpedo runs against the Chesapeake Bay's merchant marine traffic, he flying the Devastator, while they brought up the rear in the Avenger. It was great fun and a welcome respite to the high intensity flying they were doing almost eight hours a day at Virginia's Oceana Naval Air Station, where they were learning to fly and fight the F-14 Tomcat. Danny was finding it quite comfortable to sit behind his best friend and future brother-in-law, either in the F-14 during the week, or now, as they soared above the Chesapeake in a plane that was built forty years before they were born. The steady, deep drone of the big Pratt and Whitney 2,000 horsepower radial engine was vastly different from the high pitched whine of the dual Pratt and Whitney turbojets the F-14 carried, and it stimulated nostalgia for an era long gone by. The instruments on the panel before them were quaint compared to the high-tech buzzers, bells, switches, digital and infrared imaging displays, radars and electronic countermeasure indicators they had assimilated in the Tomcat. In 1942 the TBF was as advanced as a military aircraft could have been then, but now in 1984, the differences that forty-two years of technology had made were the truly amazing. They often flew with the Avenger's cockpit wide open. Danny mused what that would be like in an F-14 traveling at its "cruising speed" of over six hundred knots! However, one thing remained constant in terms of comparing the two planes, and that was brutish and robust construction of both aircraft, given the differences in aeronautical design advancements over the last four decades. It was no wonder that the Grumman Aircraft Corporation was affectionately known throughout the Navy as the "Ironworks," Danny thought.

They both loved flying the Tomcat. It was absolutely a phenomenal experience. The plane could do it all, be it down on the deck or at its maximum classified altitude. It could out-dogfight practically anything in the air, and could run away from something it couldn't. Its weapons assortment could kill an enemy a hundred miles away, or a few yards away. There was no such thing as going down to the deck to launch a torpedo and holding a precise course while being shot at by the wildly maneuvering target or its defending fighters. They had developed a true appreciation for the awesome capability of the Tomcat, now that their first fleet deployment was only weeks away. It had been a long fourteen months, but it was almost over.

To celebrate their accomplishments, Mr. Whitney had given each of them a classic leather bomber jacket, festooned with the squadron insignia patches of VT-3, VT-6, and VT-8, in addition to F-14 patches he had procured from an engineer friend at the Grumman Corporation on Long Island. They wore their jackets everywhere.

After they had post-flighted the Avenger and bid farewell to Mr. Whitney, Danny and Steven motored (Danny always used the word "motored"-you didn't "drive" a Corvette-you "motored.") to the upholsterer who had promised to complete the interior of the '39 Ford by this afternoon. It had been almost two years since Steven had been given it, and he was anxious to meet his obligation to Mr. Moore. He and his father had completed all the work on its body and mechanicals. The car had been repainted in its original deep burgundy enamel, and buffed and waxed to a brilliant luster. The only deviation from original standard equipment Steven and Paul Amato had made was to have camel-colored leather seating and rugs installed to compliment the new camel colored canvas top.

The upholsterer was a friend of Paul Amato and had done work on the Chevy and Susan's Mustang. Mr. Arthur Staminski, a retired shipfitter, was a perfectionist who was genuinely delighted when he saw the Ford for the first time. When he heard the story of how the car had come to be Steven's, he told him that he would rip it out himself. "You need some time for yourself," he said. "I'll handle it." A robust and jovial man who chewed on cigars more than he smoked them, he was happiest covered with grime and talking like a sailor as he worked on old automobiles. He himself drove around a 1956 Cadillac Sedan De Ville that looked as if it had been just delivered to his home straight from the factory. It was one of six classic machines that shared an immaculate garage and restoration shop behind his home.

When they arrived, Mr. Staminski was standing outside his shop next to the Ford, proud as could be. Inspection of the beautifully fitting convertible top and the detailed leather interior told why. The car literally looked better than new.

"How do you like it?" he asked, an ear-to-ear grin on his face, as he removed the ever-present cigar from his mouth, waiting for the compliment that was sure to come.

"God, it's beautiful Mr. Staminski! Just beautiful!" Steven's eyes opened wide as Staminski opened the door for him to sit in his masterpiece. The unmistakably rich aroma and texture of new leather filled his senses. The dashboard had been painstakingly restored, and each gauge refurbished and reinstalled. The steering wheel had been detailed beautifully. Even the clock ran perfectly.

"I'm glad you liked it. It was time consuming. It was expensive, but it was worth it. This car is concourse ready, Steve. You and your dad did a great job on the body and mechanicals."

Staminski stopped his platitudes, and turned suddenly serious. "By the way, I found this tucked up under the front seat, like it was purposely hidden there," he said, as he fumbled in the pockets of his overalls. "I tried to get it ticking, but...damn! Where the hell is it?" Finally, out came his hand, grasping what appeared to be a wristwatch. "Here," he said with some relief. "Did you lose this?"

"No, I didn't," Steven said examining the watch, "but I guess Ray Moore did." It was a Hamilton chronograph from the 1940's. Its leather band was dried and peeling, and the crystal covering its face was cracked. The back had an inscription that read:

To Raymond, love Mother and Father - Christmas, 1941

Winding it seemed to do no good as the second hand didn't budge. The hour and minute hand refused to move, and the little buttons that worked the stopwatch were frozen as well. "Hmm. The guts must be screwed up. I'll see if I can get someone to fix it. Thanks, Mr. Staminski. I appreciate your honesty."

"Ah, hell. I know your dad practically all my life. A broken down old watch isn't worth your family's friendship. Besides, I've got a drawer-full of broken down, old watches," he said with a chuckle.

"Well, thanks again. Here's a check to cover your bill. You've outdone yourself."

"Enjoy it. Your dad says you're about to head out to the fleet in a few days. I hope you have a great time."

"It's what I've wanted all my life."

"And when you visit some of those fancy ports-of-call, don't forget to screw one for me," he said, twisting his right arm as his left hand held its elbow.

"I'll keep you in mind," Steven said with a smile.

Back at his house, before Danny Morello had even shut down his Corvette, Steven said, "Danny, take a ride with me. I want to drop this thing off at a jewelry store to see if it's worth fixing." He noted Danny's lustful stare at his sister's bedroom window. "No, she's not home from work yet. I wouldn't draw you away if she were."

"I want your sister, Amato. I want her bad. You know that."

"Yeah, I know that, and so does everybody in the house. Even Halsey knows that. That's why he growls every time you walk in the door. Perhaps in six months, after we're back from the Med, and you make it official, well, then you might, and I say might get your chance."

"Let's go," he said, after giving him a long stare. "If you were a real pal, you'd talk her into it for me."

"I am a real pal. I'm also her big brother. Now, get in the Ford."

Danny directed him to the same Norfolk jeweler that sold him Susan's engagement ring. They parked outside a storefront sign that advertised *Sam's Jewelers,* and under the gold-lettered sign on the window was the wording, *SERVING VIRGINIANS AND THE FLEET FOR FIVE DECADES.*

Norfolk was a Navy town, and every merchant took every opportunity to make sure that the connection to "the fleet" was included in every advertisement. They walked into the richly decorated shop with its gray rug, brilliant lighting and mahogany and glass display cases. An elderly gentleman sat at a cluttered work counter behind the showcases full of sparkling gems and precious metals.

"Sam? How're you doing?" Danny said, as the gentleman turned to face his customers. The gentleman squinted above his thick microscopic lenses to see his visitors. "This is Steven Amato, my future brother-in-law and best friend. He's got something he'd like to show you."

"Hi, Sam. Pleased to meet you," he said as he extended his hand.

"And nice to meet you," Sam said, as he stood to shake Steven's hand. "What do you have?" Sam Levine said, smiling at his prospective client. Sam was portly and mostly bald, about sixty years old with a kind face highlighted by pleasant green eyes. He wore a brilliant white starched shirt and a conservative striped tie. A picture stood on the cluttered counter of what had to be his son and daughter standing next to an attractively slender older woman with deep set eyes and jet black hair. Three little children clustered around the older woman.

"This," Steven replied, taking out the watch, carefully putting it into the thick but unusually clean and soft hands of the jeweler. "Can you get it running?"

"Where did you get this?" Sam asked. The jeweler smiled as he gently fingered the Hamilton. All jewelers seemed to caress their wares in a way no one else could.

"I found it in an old car I've just finished restoring. Is it possible to..."

"That answers it," Sam interrupted. "Steven, this is a true treasure you have here. It was one of only five hundred chronographs that Hamilton made of this model in 1940 and 1941. It was very expensive to produce and market. The profit margin was too slim for Hamilton to continue production. It was practically all hand-made, and has twenty-three jewels, or gears, to keep very accurate time. Feel the weight of it. It was all stainless steel and gold. Only the rich could afford it. I would guess the car is from the thirties or forties, right?"

"1939, to be exact. As a matter of fact, it's right outside there. See?" Steven said, proudly pointing to his Ford.

"It's beautiful. I knew a young man who had one just like it many years ago. He lived up in Richmond, and his father and mother came in here on the Sunday that Pearl Harbor was bombed to..." Sam stopped short, as he read the inscription on the watch's back. His eyes and mouth opened wide as he looked hastily at the Ford, then back at the watch. He felt his knees suddenly buckling, and he sat down in a heap as he fought the tears that came to his eyes and drained his complexion. "This is Raymond Moore's watch, isn't it?"

Steve and Danny looked at each other wide-eyed, each of them having difficulty swallowing. "Yes. Cripes, this is really something," Steven managed to say, almost in a whisper. "How...how did you know? I mean..." He barely managed to utter the words as he placed his hand on the jeweler's shoulder to steady him, as Sam looked on verge of passing out.

"The car, the watch...It had to be Raymond's watch. How many watches and cars go together like this? My memory really kicked me in the pants just then. The inscription confirmed it. I did the engraving. Me. Dear God, the pain comes back, even after forty years!" he said, as the tears came.

"Sam, could you please explain this a little?" Steven said, almost pleading. "I know it's hard on you, but the circumstances surrounding me and that car is almost beyond belief."

"Sure. It's a story that deserves telling," Sam said, drying his eyes with a precisely folded handkerchief he produced from his pants pocket. "My father was the jeweler to the Moore's. Raymond was kind of a hero to me. A flyer, a college graduate... hell, he even looked like Clark Gable. You should have seen him wearing that white uniform, so very handsome and dashing. Women loved him. He was everything I wanted to be. I was only fifteen or so when he died. The Moore's were wonderful people. My father had a store in Richmond as well as here in Norfolk before the war. That's how he came to know the family. My brother still runs the Richmond store. Anyway, Raymond's parents had called my father with a sense of urgency on that Sunday, and Mr. Moore asked if he would please extend the courtesy of opening this store up for him. Asking somebody to work on a Sunday back then was asking for the ultimate favor, but he wanted to buy Raymond this watch. Raymond had been in here and hinted to his father that he admired it. They were going to take Ray out for Sunday dinner and present him with the watch as an early Christmas present, because Raymond's ship, the *Hornet*, was about to leave on its first cruise. There's a special name the Navy uses for it. What is it? Something like shook up..."

"It's called a shakedown cruise, Sam," Danny said.

"That's it, its shakedown cruise. The *Hornet* was a brand new aircraft carrier that had been built right here in Norfolk, and Raymond had been assigned to one of her squadrons. He was a torpedo plane pilot, you know."

"Yes, I know, Sam," Steven said with a faint smile, still trying to digest the surreal course of events that led him here and another encounter with Raymond Moore.

"It's interesting you're pilots, too. Well, anyway, they realized that he would probably not be home for Christmas, so they thought they would surprise him with an early gift. It seems almost ironic that the Sunday they were here was December 7, and the Moore's heard of the Pearl Harbor raid while having dinner. And now, this watch has come full circle. Here it is, back where it started forty-three years ago. I guess Raymond left it in the car for one reason or another. For all these years I thought it rested on the bottom of the Pacific Ocean." He looked at the watch for a moment, then asked, "How did you come by the car?"

Steven told the story of the Ford, and noted the anguished expression that painted Sam's face when Steven told him of Mr. Richard Moore's demise.

"What a tragedy. They were fine people, the Moore's, really wonderful. They were never the same after Raymond died at Midway. Ah, well." He looked again at the watch, and then gave Steven a look that, while absolutely kind, still held an air of mystery.

"I will fix it for you, Steven. I'll have it brand new. I'll need some time, though. This isn't a cheap quartz movement in here," he said, forcing a smile.

"Take as long as you want. We'll be gone six months anyway for our first fleet deployment. I'll pick it up when we get back with the *Nimitz*. Does around Christmas seem reasonable?"

"That's fine. And, just for the record, I'm so glad it was a naval officer who came upon this-you know, for Raymond's sake. He loved the Navy, absolutely loved it. He would bring his squadron mates to the store to buy engagement rings for their girlfriends. Even his squadron commander came in with him one day. This Waldron fellow wanted to buy his wife a broach for her birthday." He noted that Steven and Danny were staring at each other again. Each had a stilted look on their faces. He continued anyway, still fondling the Hamilton. "You know it took over five hundred

1941 dollars to buy this? A Hamilton back then was equivalent to today's Rolex."

Steven just nodded his head, taking in what Sam had said, his mind trying to comprehend all this "coincidence." Finally, he said, "Okay then. We'll see you around Christmas. Take care, Sam."

"You too. Oh, and Steven, Danny. Take these," Sam added, his face blushing with a heart-felt smile, as he fumbled with two wrapped packages he produced from a drawer beneath his cluttered counter. He tossed them the packages, and they opened them as Sam beamed. They contained brand new Breitling watches. "It's their aerial chronometer version. Every pilot should have one."

"It's beautiful, Sam", Steven said in surprise, "but I'm a bit low on cash now, and I really can't afford..."

"What's to afford?" Sam interrupted. "It's a gift to you, for your first fleet deployment. I feel someone should carry on the tradition the Moore's started here with Raymond."

"We couldn't possibly take them, Sam," Danny said humbly. "It's much too..."

"Take it. You brought back my youth today. Anyway you'll buy your engagement and wedding rings here someday, right? I'll get even then," Sam said with a laugh.

"Okay, it's a deal! Thank you so much," Steven said, putting the watch on his thick wrist. "I'll wear it and think of you, Sam."

"Mazeltoff!" Sam replied, raising his hands above his head. "By the way, Danny, did you give her the ring?"

"Tonight, Sam. Tonight. Tonight won't be just any night. Tonight there will be no morning sun. Tonight...."

"Let's go, Tony, before the Sharks catch up to us," Steven said, dragging out the singing and gesturing Morello. Sam's smile never waned as they left his establishment.

"At least I made Sam laugh. You made him cry," Danny chuckled.

"He'd drop dead if he knew the significance of the time at which the watch's hands froze."

"What time would that be? I didn't notice."

"The hands indicated 3:25 p.m. Eastern Daylight Time".

"And?" Danny said, his hands motioning his desire for a conclusion to the melodrama.

"It's all dumb coincidence, I guess, but at Midway, that would be 9:25 a.m. That's the exact time Torpedo 8 began its attack run on the *Akagi*."

Danny stared at him for a long moment as he opened the door to the Ford. He finally said, "Do me a big favor."

"I'm not going to talk my sister into sleeping with you."

"It's more important than that," he said straight-faced. "Tell Sam to keep that fucking watch." Then he got in the car.

Steven didn't know if Danny Morello was kidding him or not. Neither did Danny Morello.

Sam Levine took the old watch into his little work room and removed the old leather band. He retrieved a clean jar from a cabinet and put a cupful of jeweler's cleaning fluid into it. He removed the Hamilton's cracked crystal, all the hands, then the watch's face. He then unscrewed the two halves and gently placed them into the solution. Capping the jar, he placed it in a safe, along with a small plastic case that contained the watch's hands and face, and locked it. This was no ordinary antique. It was an heirloom that belonged to one of his best customers, and he would take every pain to be sure his best work was evident upon delivery when the *Hornet...Nimitz*, yes, the *Nimitz* returned from her cruise.

Chapter 12

The vector they had been given from the *Nimitz*'s combat information center was exactly the same as the vector the E-2C Hawkeye AWACS aircraft had given them. Steven Amato pushed his throttles forward and felt the Tomcat surge into the left turn, its swing wings coming back to a full delta configuration as it went supersonic.

"Danny, you got `em?"

"Roger that," Danny said, examining the radar scope. "The vector's perfect. Eight bandits climbing to angels 45, at Mach 1.2."

"OK, arm the missiles."

Danny flipped a few switches and seconds later reported, "Phoenix missiles in target acquisition mode, armed and standing by. Sparrows armed and ready."

"Roger that. Thatch! We're supersonic. We'll be there in five minutes. Repeat five minutes. *Nimitz* launched the alert five. He's on the way, too. Hold On! Do you read?"

"You better hurry your asses! These pricks mean business!"

Louis Thatcher, Steven's best pal from his days at Pensacola and Jacksonville, was in deep trouble. He had taken his F/A-18 on a photo reconnaissance mission with an escort just off the Libyan coast, but well within international waters in the Gulf of Sidra. Several Libyan warships were operating together in that area about three hundred miles from the *Nimitz*'s battle group. No one expected any real trouble, but keeping an eye on forces that could turn hostile at any moment was an established procedure. These forces were under the control of Colonel Qaddaffy, and that made it all the more necessary to have as much up-to-date information as possible. Sending two planes rather than six would appear less aggressive to the Russians standing by. Qaddaffy's generals were at the same time given the message that the American fleet was within striking distance. Things began to turn sour when Thatcher's wingman had to return to the *Nimitz* with a balky engine. Thatch's job wasn't totally completed, and he decided to linger there a few more minutes to be sure his photos were perfect. That's when the MiG-27 Floggers left their patrols above the Libyan airfields and headed right for him at almost Mach 2. He was trapped in a giant pincers from aircraft approaching on both sides of him in the cup of the Gulf. Amato and Morello, *The Flying Ronzoni's* as they had come to be known in VF-41, were assigned combat air patrol for the *Nimitz* and her battle group when Thatcher's call for help came. Apparently, the MiGs wouldn't let him leave and had their radars in attack mode, their missiles locked on his aircraft. In addition, they took turns flying right at him, causing him to constantly turn off his heading back to the *Nimitz*. It was apparent to everyone that the game had gone beyond harassment, but nobody fired a shot. Not yet, anyway.

"The bogies are closing on our guy. Radar signature indicates Floggers. That confirms Thatch's report. Phoenixes are locked on targets," Danny reported, very matter-of-factly. Actually, he felt like he did at the beginning of a football game. Here he was, in an aerial matchup against Warsaw Pact weapons and tactics, and personally, although outnumbered eight to one, he thought the odds were fairly even. Judging by the way Steve was driving the Tomcat, he concluded the feeling was mutual. The six Phoenix missiles under the Tomcat told Danny they had selected their separate targets. "Steve, the birds are ready to go."

"Haul ass, Amats! They're all over me like stink on shit!"

"I gotcha, Thatch. We're locked on."

"Shoot, goddammit! Shoot! They're locking me up! They're gonna launch any second, for chrissake! All my ECM is in the red!"

"Dog one to Kennel. We have primary weapons radar lock. Request permission to engage, over," Steven said.

"Acknowledge your readiness. Do not, I repeat, do not engage targets."

Steven was incredulous. "Repeat, Kennel!"

"Do not fire!" came the terse reply.

"This is Taffy 1. I got tone on one of the bastards! I got tone! Request permission to fire, over!"

Thatcher had managed to maneuver his brand new lightweight Hornet fighter behind one of the MiGs. One of the two Sidewinder missiles he carried told him it had locked onto the heat generated by the "enemy" plane. His Hornet was a dogfighter, a lightweight fighter and attack plane that could more than match any enemy aircraft one-on-one, or even outnumbered two or three, and in certain situations, four to one. However, it was now overwhelmed. The Tomcat, on the other hand, was designed to engage at least eight targets. Bigger, heavier, and capable of carrying the more sophisticated and longer-range Phoenix missiles, the Tomcat was in its element engaging multiple targets. The little Hornet wasn't.

"Do not fire," came the terse reply.

"Kennel from Dog 1! He's gonna get smoked! Goddammit, at least let him defend himself!"

"Kennel to Dog 1. Stay off the frequency unless you have updated information."

The voice was as terse as could be. Obviously, there were reasons, probably political, for this totally defensive action. But Thatch was being engaged very aggressively, and the farther out he got from the Libyan territorial limit, the more aggressive the Libyan fighters were becoming.

"Kennel, they're baiting me! They're waiting for me to get closer to you to smoke me. Christ, Kennel, they're setting me up for..."

"Stay defensive."

"Bingo fuel! I'm almost outta gas! This high speed chase shit is costing me! I gotta slow down! Request a KA-6 to fuel me, over!"

"Reduce speed. The tactical situation prevents tanker link up," came the reply from Kennel.

"Let me at least close, Kennel. Maybe they'll let Thatch go if they can fuck with me a little bit. Over."

"Dog 1. Permission denied. Keep your distance. Keep missile lock. Do NOT fire. Repeat. Do NOT fire."

"Jesus H. Christ!" he screamed. Steven was looking for something in the canopy to punch that wouldn't break or upset the aircraft's systems.

"They're locking me up again! I can't slow down."

It was obvious the Libyans knew the game, if in fact it was actually Libyans in those MiG-27s. Steven reasoned they were too smart and too sophisticated. They had to be Russian-led, at the least. They knew that they were baiting the American to fire, or run out of gas in fleeing. They wanted an incident, but on their terms. If the American plane spun in for lack of fuel, it was an accident that could not be directly blamed on the Libyan government, and therefore the Americans could not legitimately retaliate. If the Americans downed some or all the Libyan planes over the open ocean, the Americans would be the aggressors. If the Libyans downed the American plane by firing on it, it would be easy to apologize for it because they were so close to Libyan airspace that the international community would call it a toss-up. The Libyans and their allies had very little to lose by this blatant act of aerial terrorism.

A few more minutes passed, with Steven and Danny's F-14 circling off in the distance, and Louis Thatcher turning himself inside out in desperate maneuvers trying to get away from his eight pursuers. Finally, the inevitable message they had been waiting for came.

"I'm outta gas. I'm ejecting. Send rescue. Repeat send rescue." Thatcher matter-of-factly gave his position. The message came in a calm, quiet and evidently disgusted voice. Then, in a most muted tone, "I hope you fuckers are happy."

The F/A-18 disappeared off the radarscopes of Amato's Tomcat, then the Hawkeye's. The radars also showed that seven of the MiG-27s were seen heading for home. One of the Libyan planes, however, was losing altitude in a wide turn, ending up barely above the surface of the sea, hopefully in an attempt to see if the American had in fact escaped his aircraft successfully. The Hawkeye, monitoring the Libyan radio frequency reported no transmission was heard to that effect, nor did the Hawkeye or the *Nimitz*. The rescue helicopter reported it had picked up Thatcher's rescue transmitter signal.

"Kennel, this is Dog One. Request permission to check on the status of the downed pilot, over."

There was an unusually long period of waiting for the reply. Steven was almost ready to send his request again, when Kennel replied. "Roger that, Dog one. Alert Five, you are assigned rescue CAP". The alert five pilot retorted with a "roger that."

"Yeah, five, now you can jerk me off if the Libs return," Steven said in a voice just above a whisper, but forgetting how sensitive the microphone in his face mask was.

"Repeat, Dog one?"

"As you were, Kennel," Amato said.

Danny Morello, on the other hand, was not muted in his expression of opinions regarding this whole affair. He had shut his mike off, and was screaming at the top of his lungs. "Fuckin' A! What the fuck are we doing out here? Fucking Thatcher is swimming, we lose a twenty-million dollar bird, and we don't even fart at those towel-headed pricks! What the fuck is up?"

"Calm down, Danny. I don't need an excuse right now," he said, switching the mike to the plane's intercom.

"Mother fucker!"

A low sweep over the sea's surface at the coordinates that Louis Thatcher gave just before he ejected showed nothing. Steven adjusted his course a bit to account for the wind drift of the parachute's descent, and came upon what looked like a rubber raft. Upon closer inspection, the raft was practically deflated. Thatcher's parachute was visible under water, and what appeared to be a reddened mass of green floated next to it. Steven and Danny's blood turned to ice water.

"I've got our guy! Hurry your ass up!" he yelled to the rescue chopper's pilot. "He's banged up bad!"

A carrier's air group becomes a fraternity. It happens because of the tactical organization, the way it trains, and how it is expected to fight. Each squadron, be it an attack squadron, a fighter squadron, an electronic countermeasure contingent, or the choppers that work rescue, begins to respect, rely and enjoy each other's company. After a few months at sea in the confining space of the carrier, friendships blossom from the interdependency and mutual respect for each other's missions. The rescue guys knew Louis Thatcher. They also knew Steven Amato and Danny Morello, and the alert five guy, whomever he was, knew each of them as well. There was concern, if evidenced only in the tone of voice and the nuance of expression.

Five minutes later, the chopper appeared. A man in a wetsuit dropped into the water and swam to Thatcher through the chop churned up by the helicopter's thumping blades. He signaled for another man to jump into the sea. Both of them put Lieutenant (jg) Louis Thatcher in the sling and sent him up. From the look of Thatch's bloodied body as it hung limply in the sling, the situation was not going to end happily.

"Rescue. What's the status of the pilot you just fished out?"

"Who's this?" came the very unofficial reply.

"It's Dog One, your escort. What's the story with Thatch?"

The hesitation said it all. It was confirmed by a low speaking voice. "This is Hobbs here. Thatcher's dead. From the looks of things, I'd say he was murdered."

"Rescue one. Repeat report status of downed pilot, over". It was *Nimitz* again.

"I said he's been murdered. One of those fuckers must have strafed his chute. He's been blown apart. I don't know...what's holding him...together. Oh, shit, Thatch. Dear God." Several sobs were heard.

"Rescue one. You are ordered to maintain radio silence. Acknowledge."

"Yeah. Loud and clear, Kennel. Loud and fucking clear."

Steven could not remember a time when he had been so angry, so consumed that the Tomcat's course and altitude varied wildly. He found it impossible to contain his anger, pain and frustration. They let Thach die! They fucked him like they fucked Waldron. They used the poor bastard by not helping him. He had a good mind to plant the Tomcat right in the middle of the *Nimitz*'s deck. What would another plane matter, or the whole fucking ship? They let the Libyans fuck them over good, and no one fired so much as a fucking cannon shell in return. It sounded like the song of VT-8 all over again, but this time it wasn't for a tactical advantage. This time it was for some shithole diplomatic reason. If he could have at that moment, he would have quit the Navy, and told it to shove their "airpanes on a ships" up its collective ass.

He brought the Tomcat aboard *Nimitz*, and as angry as he was, he still trapped the third arresting wire. His rage was so pent up that it grew geometrically. Even Danny Morello, who knew something was amiss from Steve's silence all the way home, couldn't contain him. He was absolutely bonkers. He jumped the distance to the deck, pushing aside the crewman who was there to assist him in his egress from the cockpit. He threw his helmet against the carrier's island structure with such force that the visor cracked and the helmet dented. His squadron mates had listened in on

Thatcher's ordeal in the ready room, and although their anger was apparent, they weren't "up there" when it played out. Amato was, and the fury had possessed his being so much so that it took ten of them to restrain him as he headed for the *Nimitz*'s bridge. They weren't about to let him ruin his career. Even the CAG (Commander Air Group) Commander James Ebbet, and VF-41's commanding officer, Lieutenant Commander Bruce Riley, had thrown themselves on the pile that quaked every time Steven Amato flexed his muscular fullback legs in a rage to free himself and continue his rampage. If it weren't for the tragic circumstance, the scene on the flight deck was almost comical, as an ever growing pile of men was stationary for a second, then hopped a few feet, and again came to rest.

Ebbet and Riley thought Amato to be the absolute best "first-timer" they had ever seen. They weren't about to let him throw his career or his life away by trying to punch out an admiral or captain.

"Amato! You listen to me! This is your CO, and the CAG is right here with me. If you don't stop this shit right this fucking second, I'm going to bring you up for a court-martial! I fucking mean it, Amats. I swear on my daughter I'll do it!" Riley screamed, right into Steven's ear.

"Where'd it get Thatcher?" Steven screamed back. "He died doing what you told him! He was fucking slaughtered, and we let it happen! I let it happen!" The pile quaked again.

"Thatcher followed orders! He did what we told him to do. That's what we do, Amato, we follow orders, or were you absent the day they covered that at Annapolis? The ROTC guys must have covered it with Thatch, though!" Ebbet screamed.

"Steve! Enough! Stop it, man. Please!"

He recognized Morello's voice, and he relaxed a moment. Then reason came. What was he going to do, beat up everybody on the bridge? On the carrier? The Marine guard would have shot him before he punched anybody in "flag country" anyway. This wasn't him at all. But they let Thatcher die! But could he bring him back by this...this...display? He relaxed. He took a deep breath. Then he cried, and Riley and Ebbet held him close. Thatcher was one of their boys as well.

"Let's go get you showered up." Riley said after a moment.

"Yeah. Sir, I'm sorry. It's just that I felt so frustrated about not..."

"Save it. We train you to fight aggressively, and then we tell you not to throw a punch as you watch your buddy spin in. We'll talk later. Go shower up. Take a nap," Ebbet said.

"I'm sorry this happened, sir," he said to Ebbet.

"Sorry what happened?" Ebbet said with a smile and wink. "Excuse me now, Lieutenant. I've got an air group to look after."

That evening, there was a knock on Steven's cabin door. He opened it to see the *Nimitz*'s captain, Peter Clark, the battle group commander, Admiral Justin T. Travis, accompanying Riley and Ebbet. Before he could jump to attention, Travis put his arm on his shoulder, and instructed him to sit down.

"How are you doing, Amats?" Travis asked.

"Okay, sir," he replied.

"Ebbet and Riley here told me you wanted to beat up the ship's crew today, is that right?"

"Yes sir, but they talked me out of it."

"They also told me you wanted to beat me up too," he said with a slight smile and a cocked eyebrow.

"I'm sure I would have been shot before I got up to you, sir."

"Nah! I would have ordered them to let you through. Then I would have knocked you on your ass in a minute." Even the admiral laughed at that. "Well, are you feeling better?"

"I'm still aggravated about Thatcher, sir".

"It's a hazard we put up with in our business, Lieutenant," Clark said, looking at the pictures Steven had on his dresser.

"I would have better accepted it if he had died fighting, sir."

"In my last war, Amato, we were forced to fly with one hand tied behind our backs and one eye patched. We had to fly the same egress and ingress routes every day. We couldn't run AAA suppression mission because they were afraid we'd kill some Ruskies on the ground who handled the North Vietnamese air defenses. We couldn't deviate from our primary targets. We were warded away from China. We couldn't even use the advantage our long range air-to-air missiles had because we had to eyeball and identify the enemy plane before we could fire. They thought we wind up hitting a Russian airliner. I spent three years as a POW but I never accepted the idea that my country gave up on me, Lieutenant. Not for one moment, even though the fuckers that held me prisoner told me so every day."

Steven looked directly into Travis's blue eyes. They showed absolute sincerity. His grandfather said that the eyes were the window to the soul, and Italians had a gift for looking through that window better than anybody. Steven saw pride and resolve. And pain. And...suppressed grief. "You're more pissed than I am, aren't you?"

When he said that, Ebbet and Riley turned away. Clark stared off at the pictures on the desk. Travis gritted his teeth, as evidenced by his pulsating jaw muscles.

"There's a phone up on the flag bridge that's missing a receiver. They'll never find it because it's at the bottom of the Mediterranean right now. I don't know who did it, but I'd say the person who did felt the same way about Thatch as you do. Oh, maybe he was a little more removed, but Thatch was one of his boys, one of many boys he knew who left the deck of a ship but didn't come back."

Steven smiled at Travis, who smiled back reassuringly. "Well, then. I'd better go. I have a battle group to get back to Norfolk in time for Christmas, and I'm not going to get it there by wet nursing some JG. Let's go, gentleman." With that, Clark, Riley, and Ebbet left the room. Travis stopped for a moment, closing the door behind him, and moved to Steven's desk. "Why do you have Waldron facing the wall?" he asked.

"I couldn't bear to look at him, or worse, have him look at me after today," Steven responded.

"I'd venture he'd be prouder of you today than ever before. Shit, son, I think you'd better reread your own senior thesis." A smile crossed Travis's face. "Yeah, I read it, Amato. It was a great piece of work. You're a special kinda guy with your brains and your flying ability. You've been chosen. That's why I took the time to be here. Goodnight."

Steven stared at Waldron's picture, the one of him in full flying regalia, hands on hips, pistol in his shoulder harness, survival knife jutting from his belt. The photographer lay on the ground to take it, and it gave Waldron a heroic and indestructible image. Waldron, he thought, another great guy joined your squadron today. Take good care of him. He paid the price like you did, except we had the chance to fire back, but we didn't. We obeyed our orders. The Fates and we set him up, just like you-and like you, he, and we, did what we had to do, too.

He shut off the light over his bunk, and soon fell fast asleep.

A few minutes later, Danny Morello came into their room and saw he was asleep. That's good, he thought. As he undressed, he recounted how it was really something the way the brass had taken the time to talk to each of them about what happened today. Somehow, though, he knew neither of them would be the same again. He saw John C's picture staring at him in the dim light. Waldron would no doubt have been proud of *The Flying Ronzonis* for their actions today. It took more guts to sit tight than to fight. These were hellish times, and besides being without benefit, dying was also without glory. No one would remember Louis Thatcher. He died on a routine peacetime mission because his aircraft had a major malfunction. End of story.

Chapter 13

Steven Amato and Danny Morello flew into Oceana Naval Air Station with the rest of VF-41, about a half day ahead of the *Nimitz's* arrival at Norfolk. Admiral Travis had made good on his desire to get the ship and its accompanying battle group in port prior to Christmas; the calendar read December 20, 1984. They turned the F-14's log over to the base's aircraft maintenance facility, and then Danny phoned his fiancé to tell her they were back. Susan Amato was naturally overjoyed by the call. Each of them was burdened with so many gifts from such exotic places as Naples, Rome, Sicily, Bahrain and Athens, that he advised her to bring Paul Amato's station wagon.

No sooner had Susan parked the wagon than she saw Danny Morello waving to her not twenty yards away. She rushed from the car, removing her high heels to run as quickly as she could. Susan leapt into Danny's outstretched arms, her long raven black hair all askew, and her makeup washing down her face in the tracks of her tears. He picked her trim body off the ground and whirled her around several times.

They smothered each other with more kisses than Steven could count. He ventured that people couldn't get any closer, physically or emotionally, than this. He wondered if his sister had even noticed him. For the first time in his life, Steven Amato felt like he was missing something, and a lonely, vacuous feeling was developing in his innards that made him feel uncomfortable. Everywhere, women were running to the outstretched arms of men, and vice versa. Everyone but him seemed to have somebody to caress. He thought of Miss Georgia, but quickly dismissed her. It wasn't right, and he would be doing her a terrible disservice by stringing her along, taking his advantage, wasting her time, just to have the privilege of someone to meet him when he got back from wherever the Navy would happen to send him. There were trade-offs on the credit side of the ledger regarding his relationship status, to be sure. For example, while Danny was obliged to play it safe in Naples, he had the absolute time of his life with an Italian model in her apartment overlooking the bay for three days. Then he thought of Louis Thatcher and felt his lone wolf status was even more justified. Thatch's wife was nowhere to be found, for sure. Merry Christmas, Mrs. Thatcher, where ever you are, he thought, shaking his bowed head.

He turned again to find his sister leaping to him and hugging him closely.

"Hi there, sailor!" she said, kissing him on his cheek and hugging him closely. It wasn't the same hug Danny got, but it felt good. "Why the long puss? Lonely, are we?" she said coyly, a smirk emerging on her pretty face.

"I know what you're getting at Susan, and Miss Georgia had better not be sitting on the couch next to mom when we get home," he said with a smile.

"Ah, you're a stick in the mud, big brother. But at least you got my Danny boy home, safe and sound." She hugged and kissed Danny again. "I guess you're pretty good at this flyin' airpanes onna ships stuff, huh?" he laughed. Every Amato laughed when they said or heard the now idiomatic term.

"I'm not all that good, Susan," he said, bowing his head, "just very lucky."

"Don't let him kid you Susan. He's the best. Even CAG and Admiral Travis told him so."

Nevertheless, she sensed that something was wrong with her big brother. She had known that face since they were children, and it hadn't changed a bit when something disappointing happened to him.

"Hey, let's get going. I've got a lot of stuff to wrap when we get home. And I want to stop by Mr. Levine's shop and pick up that watch I found in the Ford," Steven said, checking the time on his Breitling.

Danny Morello got a chill that could not be attributed to the December wind blowing off the Atlantic. "Amats. Forget about the damned thing," he blurted. "Let old Sam keep it. You've got too much old shit already. What do you say we buy you a brand new Porsche? You've earned it, pal."

He turned to look incredulously at his friend. His sister's expression changed to alarm almost immediately when she saw the glare in his eyes. "I can't do that! It's my watch. I got it when Moore gave me the Ford. What is it with you, anyway? Every time I mention that watch or my car, you seem to act like you saw a ghost, or you're about to be possessed."

"I dunno. It seems you're giving up your future and forsaking the present. And the circumstances surrounding all this stuff you get seem too contrived. When Levine said that he recognized the watch as Raymond Moore's, I almost peed my pants. It's too eerie."

"Ah, you're being a baby. Besides, it's all good fortune that I'm able to piece together the last few days of the life of a real hero, especially one that has been ignored all these years. And, I'm a student of history. Add to that what happened on this cruise, and Ray Moore and John Waldron are closer to me than I ever thought."

Danny hesitated a moment, looking into Steven's eyes to detect the degree of resolve he had on this topic. They showed intimidating firmness. "I don't know, Amats. I'm starting to think all those tales my grandmother told me about turn-of-the-century Sicily, with witches, ghosts, devils and saints all running around together and playing with people's lives may be true. If I were you, I'd forget that damned thing. Let Levine have it and call it an even trade for the watch he gave you."

"Bullshit. I want my watch and I want it now. C'mon Susan. Let's get going before he puts a wooden stake through my heart."

He looked at Susan and noted something wasn't quite right with her either. She never saw Danny as upset with her brother as he was now. What the hell went on "out there," she wondered, that would have such a pronounced effect on both of them?

"Why don't we go home first, Steve. Mom and dad are waiting for you. Then we can find out if..."

"Susan, for Christ's sake, what's the deal? You two have to..." He realized he was losing his temper with the sister he adored and the best friend he loved. He took a deep breath and began again slowly. "Listen, take all this stuff home for me. I'll be there in a little while. You two need the time alone anyway, and I get the feeling I'll only be getting in the way."

"Steven, I didn't mean..." Susan said, raising her arms to hold him, concern all over her smudged face.

"Then you didn't. It's okay, Susan. Maybe I need some time to walk this cruise off anyway. I'll take a cab or the bus, or I'll bum a ride. Tell mom I'll be home by seven, okay? I had better get going. Take care of my sister, Danny." With that, he walked quickly across the parking lot and disappeared.

Susan looked over at Danny. "What's with him? He's got me worried."

"Don't be. It's just that he had some misconceptions about what we are supposed to be doing, and he learned about them the hard way."

"What happened out there?" Susan asked him.

"I can't say right now. When priests in the Catholic Church start doubting themselves, their mission, and their God, the term they use for it is crisis of faith. That's what Steven has, pure and simple. He'll get over it. He'll be okay." He turned to her, and by the look in her eyes, he knew he had not convinced her. Nevertheless, he thought it would be best to get her moving. "Come on. Let's get going. I'm freezing here!"

Sam Levine looked as if he was expecting him. He stood there behind a gleaming showcase, all smiles.

"Welcome back, Lieutenant Amato. I see you've been promoted," he said, gently lifting the collar of his shirt that contained two silver bars of a Navy Lieutenant. Congratulations."

"Thanks, Sam," he replied, taking the jeweler's soft outstretched hands into his.

"How was your first cruise?" Sam inquired.

"Invigorating, disappointing, happy, tragic, the best of times, the worst of times. But, it's my job and I love it. How's the watch coming?"

"I somehow knew you would be in today to pick it up. I thought of making you an offer for the piece, but somehow, something told me not to."

Steven thought for a moment of his conversation with Danny. Maybe he was right. Maybe he should give it up, let Sam have it. "Sam, perhaps I should let you keep it in exchange for the watch you gave me. It works wonderfully well, and the Hamilton seems to have more sentimental value to you than to me."

"No. I cannot accept it. It's not in the scheme of things for me...no. It's not right. It is your property. Let me get it for you, Lieutenant."

Steven was taken aback by this abrupt response. Sam disappeared in his back room momentarily, plagued by indecision, and torn by desire. Not in the scheme of things? Now what the hell does that mean, Steven thought. It's only a fucking watch. Sam emerged from the recesses of his establishment holding the watch in both hands, as if it were an offering. The watch gleamed and sparkled like a precious gem.

"Sam, it's beautiful. It looks brand new," he said, gently taking it from the jeweler's hands.

"I'm proud of it myself. Even I didn't think it would come out as nicely as this. I even replaced the strap with the kind of leather they used back in the forties. The Hamilton Watch Company sent it to me at no charge when I told them the story of the watch. The gentleman I talked to was the official company historian. He knew this model watch well. Many pilots and other officers coveted it during the World War. Put it to your ear. It is a sound you don't hear much anymore."

The red second hand ticked off precise intervals of time. The stop watch worked accurately, the little knobs that started and stopped it moving freely. The new crystal gleamed, reflecting the intense lighting that highlighted every facet of every jewel in Sam's showcases. The leather band felt smooth and rich in his hands as he strapped it on his right wrist. He felt a sudden gush of warmth course through his body. He felt he had left this place for an instant. He closed his eyes and felt suddenly light. He forced himself back.

"How much do I owe you, Sam?" he asked, still feeling a little out of sorts, but not at all unpleasant.

Sam Levine saw the watch had the same effect on him as it did when he put it on his own wrist just after he completed the repair process. He saw the young naval officer close his eyes a moment, just like he had done.

"One hundred and twenty dollars, Lieutenant. Much of that was for the special crystal this watch calls for. The Hamilton people made me pay for it. They're generous, but not fools!"

Steven laughed. "Thank you, Sam. It's really a beautiful job." He peeled off six twenty dollar bills from a money clip he held in his wallet. "Happy Holidays."

"And to you, Lieutenant Moore...er,...Amato. Happy holidays!" he said nervously.

Steven raised his eyebrows in slight surprise, still feeling a bit of phase. He nevertheless raised his hand in a wave to Sam Levine, pulled up the zipper on his leather flight jacket, and left the store. He walked to the corner, hailed a taxi, and gave the driver his address. The ride would be expensive, but it was worth not having to wait for the bus. A feeling of accomplishment came over him. He suddenly felt very warm and taken with himself. He looked at the Breitling on his left wrist and compared it to the time on the Hamilton on his right. Both were dead accurate. He found himself whistling *White Christmas.*

Chapter 14

The phone rang in the den, and even though he was only an arm's-length away, he ignored it, continuing to lay on the couch unabatedly watching the *Today* show. When he answered it last night, Julie-Miss Georgia was the caller, and he felt awkward in having to be polite when it was really an effort to just talk with her. He despised himself for having to be so obviously arrogant to a young woman any other man would die to have, but he really did want her to leave him alone. She would be much happier with someone who really wanted her.

"Honestly, Steven!" his sister said in a huff, as she turned the corner of the den and saw him still prone and ignoring the phone's incessant ringing. Someone picked it up in the kitchen.

"Hello?" It was his mother's voice. "Yes, Commander Riley, he's here. Sure. Please hold on. Steven, it's your CO."

Thank God, he thought. He picked up the phone and spoke smartly into the receiver. "Yes sir", he said, fending off his sister's playful slaps.

"Did you get laid yet, Amats?"

"No sir, I didn't. But I've only been home two days. I should be able to do something to that end soon."

"You got a date tonight? Any plans at all?"

"No sir, I don't."

"I'd like to offer you a proposition. I'm asking all the single and unattached guys first, because it's almost Christmas and I don't want to screw with the married guys with families, or the single guys with fiancés."

"Then whatever it is, sir, I'm in."

"I knew you'd say that, Amats, and I'm glad I can offer you something that will pay you off. We were authorized four new Tomcats, and they need to be picked up tomorrow. I'm sending eight guys up to the factory on Long Island this morning by C-2. You should arrive at 1000 hours at Grumman's Bethpage facility. After you sign in with the Naval Procurement office, you'll have the whole evening to yourself. Bethpage is about a half hour from New York City, if you get my drift. You'll go out to the Calverton plant in eastern Long Island tomorrow afternoon at 1600 to fly the birds home. You should be back by dinner time. You still interested?"

Christmas in New York should be something, he thought. He hadn't been to the city since his third year at the Academy, where a bunch of midshipmen ventured north to visit the Big Apple. They saw *A Chorus Line* and had dinner in Little Italy at a place called Puglia's that was great fun.

"Like I said, Commander, count me in. It sounds like a good deal to me."

"Thanks, Amats. You're doing the guys a real favor."

"Sounds like I'm doing myself a real favor too!"

"Great. See you in an hour, okay?"

"Roger that, sir. Oh, what about my RIO, Morello the big mouth?"

"Wha...? Oh, I get it. Did he tell someone about the Italian Incident?"

"Try everyone, sir. I ran into a guy I knew from Pensacola last night, and he went on and on about it. He told me Morello was his source."

"Son of a bitch," Riley said, almost in a whisper. "Ah, anyway, he's got the flu. He called the O.D. just an hour ago. He's coming in to the base hospital to get checked out. Don't worry about it, though. I'll get you a back-seater."

"See you in an hour Commander Riley."

Even before he hung up the phone he felt The Presence. That's what he called Rena Amato when she eavesdropped.

"And where are you off to, may I ask?"

"I'm gonna fly an airpanes, but not onnaships."

"Very funny. Where are you going?"

Steven told her the story as he hurriedly packed his toilet gear his dress blues.

"Brand new planes? Has anybody made sure the wings won't fall off?"

"Sure, mom. The Grumman test guys do that. Besides, we can go to New York tonight and have a few laughs."

"Is that all, just a few laughs? And you're going to fly tomorrow? Promise me you'll get some sleep and don't drink too much tonight, okay?"

"I promise mom." He couldn't believe how she still lectured him and worried about him. If she only knew the real nature of his job, like landing a jet at night on a carrier-in a storm, or screwing with the Russkies and their Libyan buddies. Ah, that's what mothers are for. Besides, his mom had a double deficit; she was a mother and Italian.

"Make sure you're home by supper time like you said you would be tomorrow night. We're having company," she added, almost as a casual afterthought.

"Whom might that be, Mama Amato?" he said.

"Never you mind. Just be here."

"Mom, if it's Miss Georgia, I don't think..."

"I don't care what you think!" she snapped. "And stop calling Julie Ann Miss Georgia! It's demeaning! You could do a whole lot worse, mister hot-shot jet pilot! You can't cavort with models in Naples all your life, you know. We didn't bring you up that way!"

Red alert! She was pissed. This was totally uncharacteristic for the normally reserved Rena Amato. And now, he was going to have to kill Danny Morello, who, probably in a childish, jealous prissy-fit, told Susan about what everybody in the squadron, and practically the Navy, and now the world, called "the Italian Incident." Susan, being Susan, wasted no time in telling their mother-all this "agita," because he was still upset about Thatcher when he arrived at Norfolk, and he wanted to get his watch from the jeweler rather than come right home. Now, everybody worried he was going crazy. The Italian folk-cure to being a crazed single man was marriage. And, here we are, folks. "Mom, you're jumping to conclusions. I don't want to string Julie Ann along. She's an absolute knockout in every way, but she just doesn't do it for me."

"Oh? And what doesn't she "do" for you that Miss Naples did for you?" She stared at him, and tried not to laugh as he started to laugh, she realizing she left herself wide open for one of the world's greatest punch lines. Rena Amato still had her sense of humor.

"I don't think you want the details, Mom. And, I didn't marry Miss Naples. And don't call her that! It's demeaning! Her name is Ariana. And she likes to cavort, and I could do a lot worse than that, Missus hot-shot Italian lady!" mimicking her voice and her mannerisms.

She had to laugh. She couldn't help it. She couldn't get angry at him, no matter how hard she tried. He was too sweet, too smart and too witty. Even as a little boy, he had that way about him that forced everybody to love him even more when he got into mischief. She hugged him. What else could she do?

"All right. Invite Julie Ann to dinner. But, mom, don't push it. Maybe seeing her again is a good thing to do. It was a tough six months out there. The last few weeks were terrible. Maybe I need someone to slobber over me."

"Who better than her? Get going," she said as she kissed him while he put on his leather jacket.

"Right. See you tomorrow night."

"Oh, Steven. You forgot your watch," his mother said, pointing to the Hamilton on his dresser.

"Oh yeah. Perhaps the guys would like to see it. Thanks, mom. Say goodbye to dad for me."

"I will. And be careful flying those damned airpanes onna ships!"

"You betcha. And Mom. Make linguini and clams tomorrow, okay?"

"It's on the menu." She kissed him again.

He thrust the Hamilton in his pocket, not taking the time to put it on his wrist. He wanted to make the fastest getaway possible. He jumped into the Ford, pushed the starter button, and was gone.

AS TIME GOES BY

Steven decided to drop the top at the next stoplight. It was unusually mild for a Virginia December, and the fresh air felt good. He looked up at the sky and noted it was clear blue. The weather report on the *Today* show indicated that it was clear on the east coast, and would remain that way through tomorrow, though light snow was expected tomorrow night. It was great weather to fly, especially if you were doing it in a brand-new-right-out-of-the-box F-14 Tomcat.

He parked the Ford next to Riley's station wagon in a covered garage facility on the base, and quickly secured the canvas top. He jumped out with his uniform bag and saw Commander Riley urging him to hurry. The C-2 transport was just starting its engines in the background. He hurried into the squadron's ready room to change from his civilian clothes to his flying suit and to secure his helmet. He was greeted by Tom "Silver" Ware and Todd "Roto" Reuter.

"Where's the other part of the Flying Ronzoni's?" Ware asked.

"He's got the flu. I'll need RIO," Steven responded.

"No, you won't, Steve." He turned to see Commander Riley behind him. "Grumman is sending one of their flight test guys back with you to do some research on a new piece of equipment they installed in the plane you'll bring back. He'll RIO you. He's no Morello, but I don't think you'll run into any MiGs between here and New York," Riley mused.

"I'd just like to run into the one that did Thatcher".

The group of seven men got a copy of their orders from Riley, and then hurried off to the waiting C-2 transport. As soon as they were aboard, Riley gave the thumbs-up to the C-2 pilot, who revved the plane's two turbo-prop engines, and slipped up the taxi-way and onto the runway. As he waited for his take-off clearance, a red-haired enlisted man with a bright smile and a freshly scrubbed freckled face by the name of O'Toole ran down the aisle to make sure his passengers were all buckled up and ready to go. The pilot's voice came on the intercom.

"Good morning, gentlemen. This is Navy flight 110 nonstop to Bethpage, New York. I'm your pilot, Commander Manny L Fiske. You're copilot, like you give a shit, is Lieutenant Eduardo Almos. He'd rather be flying F-14's, but he got fucked like me, and we're stuck flying this piece of shit around. Okay, first some rules. It's almost Christmas, and I don't need any shit. O'Toole, the ugly fucker with the three hash marks on his sleeve, will be your lovely stewardess on this flight. If you want anything, get your lazy ass up and get it yourself. O'Toole's pissed because he can't get home for the holidays. And don't let his boyish looks fool you, because I know he killed a guy over a hooker in a New Orleans cat house, and he joined the Navy to avoid prosecution. I think he has a gun, so watch your fucking step. In case of an emergency, O'Toole will be the first one out the fucking door if he isn't killed outright in the crash, so he ain't gonna help your ugly ass. Therefore, if I were you, I'd read the manual in your front seat pocket, cause I'm out the door right after O'Toole. You guys will have to fight Almos to be the next guy out. Watch out for him though, because all those spics carry knives. Contrary to public opinion, your seat cushion will sink faster than you do if we go down in the drink, so don't think of using it as a flotation device. There are some egg sandwiches and fruit and coffee in the boxes in front of you, if O'Toole hasn't sold them to a soup kitchen by now. I've just received take-off clearance, so adjust your balls. This ain't a carrier cat shot, so I know you Tomcat jocks will be a bit disappointed, but this is the most fun I have all day. O'Toole, sit your dead ass down and buckle it up. Here we go."

O'Toole just shook his head. "I've been flying with him for a year now, and every day is still an adventure," he said as his passengers reeled with laughter.

The one hour and fifteen minute flight to Bethpage was quite uneventful. The pilots and RIOs busied themselves playing poker, or reading, or just looking out the window at the wintry landscapes below. Steven reached in his pocket for a Lifesaver, and the feel of the Hamilton watch reminded him he had brought it along.

"Hey, Roto, take a look at this," he said taking the watch out and pulling down the TIME magazine Todd Reuter was scanning. Reuter's eyes widened with curiosity.

"Where'd you get it?" he said, taking the watch from Amato's outstretched hand and carefully examining it. "This isn't a copy or anything, is it?"

"No sir. This is the real McCoy. The guy who did my Ford's upholstery found it tucked under the front seat."

"Who the hell is Raymond?" Reuter asked, reading the inscription.

"He's one of us. Or, actually, he was. He died at Midway flying a torpedo plane from the *Hornet*."

"I guess he forgot to take his watch, huh?" Reuter said, as he let it rest on his wrist. His eyes got sleepy suddenly.

"Wow, I just got a case of the yawns you wouldn't believe."

"It must be the damned watch," Amato said with a smile. "I put it on in the jeweler's shop where I had it restored, and I got a bit light-headed myself. I haven't worn it yet. I'm afraid I'm going to break it or something, so I'm saving it as a kind of dress watch. As a matter of fact, I don't know why I brought it along with me. It must have been because I was hurrying to get away from my mother. She wants me to get married, and she handed it to me as I rushed out of the house, figuring it would be easier to take than to explain why I wasn't wearing it."

"You're mother too? God, I can't believe it. I'm supposed to be going home Christmas day, and I know she's going to ask me if I'm seeing anyone."

"You think that's bad? Rena the Matchmaker found me a bride already. All I have to do is screw her and it'll be official," Steven said, carefully burying the watch in his jacket pocket.

"Then if that's all she wants, you should tell her you're already married to the beautiful Ariana."

"Oh, Christ, don't bring her up! Morello told my sister, which is almost like telling my mother directly. My mother brought it up to me this morning when she lectured me on the lewd and lascivious life I'm leading, and how she was disappointed in me because she brought me up better than that."

"Okay, cherubs, make sure your seat belts are buckled. We're on final approach and I anticipate that we'll be on the ground in ten minutes. O'Toole, please make sure are passengers are buckled in. Shoot anyone who isn't."

Fiske's skills as a pilot were apparent by the smooth touchdown he made on Grumman's runway. The C-2 Greyhound rolled out smoothly and came to halt in front of a rather nondescript building, outside of which a Navy officer and two civilians stood. Steven surmised the temperature was frigid, as the vapor from their breathing was thick. When the C-2's hatch was opened, his deduction was substantiated. The wind was gusting, adding to the chilliness of the air. As he left the aircraft, the C-2's still-rotating propellers further exacerbated the chill, so they quickly filed into the building with the Navy officer in the lead. Fiske wasted no time on the ground. He quickly turned the aircraft on to the taxiway and was gone. After all, Steven mused, it was almost Christmas.

After walking down several hallways, they were led into a small amphitheatre. After they settled in, the Navy man, who Steven noted held the rank of Captain, greeted them.

"Good morning, men. My name is Captain John Munson, and I work here at the Naval Procurement office. I understand you represent VF-41, and you're to take delivery of four F-14 Tomcats that have just come off the assembly line out at the Calverton Plant, which is about an hour due east of here. I also understand that Commander Riley has promised you an evening in New York. Well, I'm here to see it gets done, so let me tell you about the itinerary. I've take the liberty to make hotel reservations for you at the Hyatt Grand Regency. It's one of New York's newest hotels. We'll drive you there in about an hour, and your stay is on the Navy. The hotel concierge will help you with dinner reservations and theater tickets, or whatever else you would like to do that is in the limit of the law. There's a locker room at the end of the hall where you can dress. You can leave your flight gear here, as we'll assemble here tomorrow at 1300 hours for lunch before going out to pick up your new aircraft at Calverton. Therefore, be ready to leave New York by 1130 hours. Transport will be waiting outside the hotel at that time.

"We'll give you a brief plant tour at Calverton and let you meet some of the men and women who made your airplanes. You should be in the air by 1530 hours and back to Oceana by...well, I'll let you decide the flight plan tomorrow," he said with a broad smile. The pilots chuckled as this. Munson knew damn well the fighter jocks would head due east over the Atlantic out to fifty miles, then head due south at Mach 2, then head west to Oceana, bleeding off airspeed, and landing about thirty minutes after they took off. After the guffaws subsided, Moore called out, "Lieutenant Amato?"

"Sir!"

"I'd like you to stay a few minutes and talk to Vincent Capo here," he said, introducing the young, slenderly built civilian who had accompanied them into the room. "Vince will tell you about the special black box your Tomcat is fitted with. He'll RIO for you on the way back to test it out. The rest of you can get changed, but no one leaves without Amato. Dismissed."

"Hello Lieutenant Amato. Glad to meet you," the dark haired, olive complexioned man said to him as he extended his hand. Capo was in his early thirties. His clothing was conservative and neatly tailored. Steven noted he wore a wedding ring, and a school ring that contained a "P" in the stone. A Princeton man, Steven thought-smart guy, probably an engineer.

"It's Steve, Vince. So what kind of stuff you testing?"

"Well, we are always trying to keep the aircraft upgraded and prepared to assume new missions. The Tomcat is wired for bombs, but it never carries any."

"We were told that we would never carry them. We're even forbidden to do air to ground training."

"Yeah, I know, but the F-14 could be a super air-to-ground aircraft, even superior to the Air Force's F-15C model. It can carry a tremendous load of all kinds of dumb and smart bombs and air to surface missiles. The only thing we need is a laser targeting system and an upgraded air-to-ground radar package and software. And we're there." Capo smiled.

"And that's what my aircraft will have, right?"

"I didn't say that, but on the way back I'm going to test some equipment that may have an awful lot to do with that."

"I take it you're working on this stuff?"

"Well, Steve, I'm working. And no one else can fly this, because I've got to make some calibrations on the hardware and software to continue what I'm doing, and that's why I'm going."

"I see. Do you need me to follow a specific flight plan?"

"Not really. We'll pass over lots of ground targets that have been entered in the software. We'll also pass some shipping that I can target as well. I don't have that much to do, because this is the first time the system's been airborne, at least in an F-14. It works well in....well, let's say it works well. When I get to Oceana, I'll be training some RIOs in your squadron on it. Support aircraft and equipment will meet me down there after the holidays."

"You'll miss Christmas with your family, won't you Vince?" Steven asked.

"No. My family's from Southern Maryland. I'll drive up to see them tomorrow, Christmas Eve. My wife is already down there. I couldn't leave with her because of my work."

"Okay, I'll see you tomorrow," Steven said, extending his hand. "I promise you a smooth ride home."

"Great! This is my first time up in at Tomcat, and I'm a little nervous. Funny thing, but I've worked on the plane for six years, and now when I get the chance to fly it I get butterflies."

"Nonsense. You'll love it. I promise you that."

"I'm gonna hold you to that. See you tomorrow."

"So Amats. What's the story with the black box. What are you carrying, a new death ray or something?" Reuter asked.

"No big thing, believe me. Just calibrating some standard gear for the Tomcat and Vince Capo is the engineer in charge of the effort. That's all."

"Hurry up and get dressed. New York beckons. And there is a lovely city maid awaiting me!" Ware said.

"The only New York city women waiting for you aren't particular. Trust me."

The Hyatt was as busy as New York itself. That Captain Munson was able to get room reservations in such a hotel at Christmas was in itself a small miracle. Someone must have pulled a government string. The city literally throbbed, as if it itself was a living, breathing entity. Steven thought of what it must have been like during its heyday in the forties, when New York was unrivaled as the Queen of American Cities. It was not quite two o'clock in the afternoon when they arrived, and everyone wanted to see something different. So they decided to spend a few hours on their own, then gather back at the hotel at seven, and check with the concierge to see if she could gather up any theatre tickets. Then they would have a late dinner, sleep late the next morning, have a late breakfast and be off by 1130 hours. It was a dress blues night, and they quickly showered and changed after they were shown to their rooms. Steven had a solo, as all the other pilots shared a room with their RIOs. He put on his Hamilton watch, admiring it as it glistened in the dress mirror's reflection. Damn, he thought. There's that dreamy feeling again. It passed quickly.

As he waited in the lobby for his comrades, Steven noted that the New York Times advertised a *Sentimental Journey Week* at the Radio City Music Hall. Beginning at four today, a showing of the *Maltese Falcon* was to be followed by a concert of the Glenn Miller Orchestra. What better a way to spend three or so hours, he thought. "Hey, Reuter, you want to do something a little different?" he asked.

"Like what?"

"Like this," he said, showing the ad in the Times to his friend.

"Why not, Amats? Hell, I'll only get into trouble if I'm left to my own devices." "Maybe you can teach me something as well. I'm such a dumbass about history, and you're so into it with your car and your other antiques that you might make it interesting. And, I like that Bogart guy. He was a real bad ass," he said, nodding to the ad with Humphrey Bogart's picture on it. "We'd better get going if we're going to make the show. Hey, Amats. You still with me?"

"Huh?" He felt dreamy again. And then he realized he had the Hamilton on his wrist, but the feeling again quickly faded. "Yeah, I am. I guess I got too engrossed in where we are. Let's get going."

Amato and Reuter walked into the darkened theater after the movie had already started. Their taxi had gotten caught up in a traffic jam that delayed them twenty minutes. Bogart was already pointing a big .45 automatic at Peter Lorre, protecting Mary Astor from his demonic ways. He felt a bit lightheaded throughout most of the movie, jabbing Reuter with his elbow when Bogie beat the bad guys yet again. However, when the movie was over and the theatre lights came back up, and they made their way to the lobby for a drink, something was definitely amiss. It wasn't at first obvious, but when he finally digested his surroundings, he was in shock.

The first cue that things were amiss was the clothing everybody wore. They weren't the fashions of the eighties. Women wore hats and short jackets. Their hair was...waved. Their shoes were opened toe with ankle straps. Their nylons had...seams? Men wore double breasted suits and loud ties. And everyone who smoked was smoking an unfiltered cigarette; Lucky Strikes, Camels, Chesterfields, he even saw a pack of Sweet Caporals. Children were wearing knee length socks and knickers, and argyle sweaters.

A man carrying a fedora approached him and Reuter and said, "I see your Navy guys huh? Pilots too?" he said, poking the gold wings on his breast.

"Yes we are," Steven answered wide-eyed, his head still turning to make sense of what was around him.

"Well, when you get your chance, give them sneaky Jap bastards and krauts hell. We're behind you all the way!" he said, defiantly thrusting his fist in the air.

"We...we certainly will," he replied. He looked at Reuter, who was totally aghast. Women and children were waving at them, and men smiled proudly making the "V for Victory" sign with their fingers. One even bought them popcorn and soda.

"What's going on here, Amats? Why are these people so weird?"

"The show is called *Sentimental Journey*, isn't it? They're probably actors, and we're part of the show. That's gotta be it!" He wasn't totally convinced himself, but he had read of audience involvement segments in the newest Broadway shows. This must be one of them, he reasoned.

Reuter looked relieved, and convinced. But to Steven, everything was much too real to be contrived. Even the glasses they were drinking from were from the forties. The soda fountain itself was from the forties-the soda jerk made their cokes from syrup and seltzer. So was the packaging of their popcorn.

The lights flashed and they made their way back to their seats, their brains still trying to come to terms with what their senses perceived as reality. An announcer walked to a microphone on stage whose design was straight from the era.

"And now, for your listening pleasure, the Radio City Music Hall is proud to present Glenn Miller and the Glenn Miller Orchestra!" The crowd roared to the opening strains of *Moonlight Serenade*" as the huge curtains opened. On the stage, a tall bespectacled man in a white jacket and bow tie stood in front of the orchestra, playing a trombone. The man was a doppleganger for Glenn Miller himself.

"This is getting interesting!" Reuter said to a bemused Amato.

Amato could only reply, "Yes. Very!" He was too busy studying the faces of the musicians in the band, and becoming more disconcerted with each face he scanned. There could be two or three look-a-likes, but judging from the photographs he had seen and the album covers he had, the whole band looked exactly like Glenn Miller's band did back in 1941, man for man. What finally brought everything to doubtless reality was the gentleman who put aside his saxophone to come up to the microphone at Glenn Miller's invitation to sing *I've Got a Gal in Kalamazoo*. That's when the ice water replaced the blood in Steven Amato's veins.

There was no doubt about it. It was confirmed by the present sights and sounds, and cross-referenced by his memory of the sights and sounds of the numerous newsreels and records that he owned and had watched and listened to hundreds of times since his early childhood, with what appeared before him now. That was the real Tex Beneke, backed up by the quartet of singers known as the Modernaires. The Modernaires traveled with Glenn Miller's band, and he knew the special sound of their harmonies very well. The Modernaires on the stage sounded too real to be duplicates.

And all this deduction also led to another inescapable truth: the man on the stage with the trombone and easy-going conducting style was, in fact, Glenn Miller.

He watched Reuter singing and tapping along to the song, in total ignorance of exactly what was happening to them. Steven was just too dumbfounded to do a damned thing but stare with his eyes wide and his mouth agape.

Benecke finished his number to rousing applause. Glenn Miller came to the microphone and said, "Thanks, Tex! And now we have a little something to put you in the mood, so to speak." The band began to play the first well-known musical bars of what was no doubt the most famous tune of the big band era. Everyone knew *In the Mood,* whether they were seventeen or seventy. The crowd cheered wildly.

Steven smiled and shook his head gently. He knew the day to be Wednesday and the date to be December 23. He glanced at the Hamilton watch, and its face told him it was almost 6:30 p.m. He mused that the watch had told him the time; now, if only could get it to tell him the year.

Roto Reuter never knew that anything extraordinary had happened. When they exited the building to the street, nothing was amiss. Modern cars and modernly dressed people were going about their business. Back at the hotel, Tom "Silver" Ware held four tickets to *Sugar Babies,* a Vaudeville revival starring Mickey Rooney and Ann Miller. How appropriate, Steven mused.

"But hurry!" Ware urged, his facial expression reinforcing his excited speech pattern. "It starts at eight and that's only twenty minutes from now."

Steven took the elevator to his room on the tenth floor to wash his face, taking the New York Times with him. Before he immersed his hands in the running water, he rolled up his sleeves and removed the Hamilton to set it on the vanity. After drying himself, he picked up the Times again to check the theater that hosted *Sugar Babies.* Oddly, he couldn't find a thing about the *Sentimental Journey* show, even though he scanned the entertainment section again and again.

He was dumbfounded. Roto was knocking on his door, telling him to hurry his ass up. He quickly rolled down his sleeves and reached for the Hamilton. He stared at it for a second, and then stuffed it in his uniform jacket.

Chapter 15

"All set back there, Vince?" Steven asked.

"I guess so," he replied nervously. "I can't believe I'm actually sitting back here."

"Like I said before, you're going to love it." He had been reassuring Vincent Capo for an hour now, doting over him as he put on his flight gear, making sure he was securely strapped in to the Tomcat's rear seat, and fully briefed on what he was supposed to do and when he was supposed to do it.

The brand new Tomcat felt absolutely wonderful beneath him, solid and indestructible like all the Tomcats he had flown, but it had that special feeling that might be associated with a new, expensive automobile. It even had that new-car smell. Meeting the plane's builders and engineers had proven to be a valuable experience. It demonstrated the commitment the Grumman "Ironworks" community had to building the world's best fighter plane, and he gained a new appreciation for the Navy's expression that the name Grumman on an airplane was like Sterling on silver.

As he checked his instruments again, the Grumman tower gave him and the other three planes permission to take off.

"Okay, they say we can go flying. Blast-off time, Vince. Sit back and enjoy."

"Roger," came the feeble reply. Vince didn't know it, but the sheepish reply brought a smile to Steven's face. He really wished he hadn't used the term "blast-off."

Steven pushed the throttles forward and released the brakes. The jet responded by setting back on its main gear and lifting its nose slightly. Vince watched the airspeed indicator rise to 150 knots. Suddenly the ride became quiet, and he felt his head bob slightly to his chest. He took his eyes off the instruments and looked out the canopy. They were flying! He felt the nose of the aircraft come up higher as the wings folded back slightly. Steve rolled the F-14 as it climbed.

"How are we doing back there, Vince?"

"This is fucking awesome!" What else could he say? It was. He heard Steven communicating with the other three planes that joined up on their wings. They made a coordinated turn due east staying at....500knots! He couldn't believe the gauge. He checked to see his test equipment was functioning properly. It was. The system was identifying and tracking targets as the software and hardware was designed to do. A few minutes later, he noted that they were passing over the Montauk Point lighthouse at 7500 feet. He punched in orders to the radar to track surface vessels, which it did. Fifteen seconds later several small fishing boats, a Russian trawler and a tanker were identified. The boats were just beneath them. The trawler and tanker were thirty miles away. The system asked for weapons choices. He input the necessary data by punching a few buttons. The system instantly told him they were ready to fire. It was working much better than even he had anticipated.

"Are your gizmos working out all right?" Steven asked. He turned south-south west.

"Better than I expected. This stuff is dangerous."

"Okay, we're out over fifty miles. Let's go to Mach 1.2."

The engines changed their pitch and the Tomcat's wings came back fully to a delta configuration.

"We're going faster than sound now, Vince. We're supersonic."

"This is really great!" He could not remember the last time he had been so elated. And these guys did this for a living! Lucky pilots. His black boxes continued to function even at this speed, routinely locating and tracking potential targets, and engaging them in mock attacks.

Time passed quickly. The jet was slowing, and he noted that the wings of the Tomcats began to come forward as the planes headed due west. He also saw his altimeter indicate a loss of altitude, as his headphones came alive with the voice of Steven Amato asking for landing instructions.

"Did you enjoy the ride, Vince?"

"I'll say. What a time!"

"Great. I think you had better shut your stuff down. We don't want to complicate the electronics for Oceana. We're on the glide path and should be on the ground in about five minutes."

The pilots turned in their log books, and affectionately patted the new planes on their snouts. Steve asked the squadron maintenance officer to paint the word *JAWN* on the nose of the Tomcat he had flown home. The officer was a bit perplexed by this request, but after Steven explained the significance he heartily agreed to see it was done. Further, to Steve's elation, he said he would paint *The Flying Ronzonis* under the cockpit as well.

Steven briefly spoke to Vince Capo about setting up a training and testing schedule next week to further refine the air to ground system with the squadron RIOs. He drove him to a Hertz rental car agency in Norfolk, insured the car Vince had reserved was in fact there, and then departed for home. It was Christmas Eve and his mother had planned the usual traditional Italian seafood Feast of the Seven Fishes.

He then remembered that Miss Georgia (oops!-JULIE ANN), would be there. And so would Big Mouth Morello, slobbering over his sister. Nevertheless, the houses with their decorative holiday lights, the brightly lit trees and the radio station's Christmas carols stirred in him the warmth of the Season and feelings of gratitude to the Man whose birthday was being celebrated. The radio station played *Silent Night*. It was his favorite carol, and he quietly sang along.

He parked the car in the garage and walked to the front door, carrying his garment bag over his shoulder. It was snowing ever so lightly. The warm glow of a fire beckoned through the windows of the living room, and he felt like a child again, full of anticipation of what might be under the tree tomorrow. The robust aroma of Italian food caused his stomach to growl.

He tried the door but it was locked, and he had forgotten his key. He rang the doorbell, and his father answered it.

"Merry Christmas, son!" he said, giving him a bear hug.

His sister ran to him and hugged him warmly. Danny Morello sniffled as he hugged him as well. Ah, 'tis the season. Forgive him, he thought, and he did. His mother hugged him best.

"Hi, Steven. It's so good to see you. How are you?"

He turned to see Julie Ann Tate, dressed in a scooped-top, form-fitting green velvet dress cut just above her knee. It perfectly accentuated her slim body and full bosom. Her thick, long blonde hair was done up in a loose bun from which a few curly strands hung in a most seductive manner. Her fair skin was ever so slightly flushed, highlighting her beautiful blue eyes and high cheekbones. She was ...gorgeous! Why did he try to resist her so? She was too good for him, that was for sure.

"Hi, Julie. I'm fine. You're certainly looking well. It's nice to see you too. How's work?" He tried very hard to insure his eyes were not hanging too far out of their sockets.

"I'm doing okay. It's fun working for the Washington Post. I'm certainly learning a lot. I understand you were in New York. How was that?"

He thought a moment before he answered. "Interesting," he finally said.

Rena Amato saw the look on her son's face before she went into the kitchen to check on her pasta. She smiled broadly to herself. She knew her son wouldn't let her down. Paul Amato came up behind her as she stirred the pot bubbling with linguine, putting his hands just under her breasts and nibbling her ear.

"You were right, Rena."

"Mr. Hot Shot Jet Pilot or not, he's still my son, and I know best. Now get your hands away from my boobs and help me serve. The pasta's done." She smiled broadly as she stirred the pot with a big wooden spoon one last time.

Paul Amato laughed heartily, but he didn't take his hands away from her breasts. At least not right away.

Over dinner, Steven asked, "Julie, have you seen your parents yet?"

"No. I'm leaving early tomorrow morning for Georgia. It's a six hour drive and..."

"Where do your parents live?" he interrupted.

"Just outside Atlanta. Why?"

"Well, I figure we could have an early breakfast tomorrow morning with my folks and go to Mass. I could fly you home, and then fly you back here late tomorrow night. This way we could spend a little time together. I'm off until January 9, unless the world goes south. What do you think?"

He noted everyone had stopped eating, mouths in mid-chew, forks-full in mid-flight, and they were staring at him. Danny Morello was caught with his tongue sticking slightly out of his wide-open mouth, strands of linguine just touching it.

"What are you all staring at?" he said defiantly.

"Are you going to steal a Tomcat from the Navy, Steve?" his sister giggled.

"Nnnooh!" he said sarcastically, shaking his head slightly to add effect. "I'll rent a Cessna Twin at the airport," he said turning to Julie. "I'll have you home in less than two hours. What do you say, Julie?"

"Sure! I'll phone my dad tomorrow and have him pick us up at the airport. You'll love my dad, Steven. He's an engineer. You'll have plenty to talk about."

"Great! Dad, please pass the calamari?"

He hated to admit it, but his mother was right. He must have been out of his head to ignore the girl whose eyes sparkled every time she looked at him. He stopped to listen to the Christmas music coming from the stereo, and wistfully looked at Julie Ann.

"This is *White Christmas*! Did you know that this song was composed by Irving Berlin for the 1942 musical *Holiday Inn*?"

"Is that right?" she said, looking at him just as wistfully.

"Uh-huh. Bing Crosby got it right on the first take. The director of the film was furious because he found Irving Berlin lurking on the set to be sure the song was performed beautifully. Even Bing's promise that he'd do the song justice didn't make Berlin feel better. Berlin had done a number of..."

His sister couldn't believe the crap he got away with! And here he was, stuffing his self-confident face, like this was the way he had planned it all along, that one of the most beautiful and sweetest and smartest girls in the world would cave in exactly when he wanted her to, at his leisure. What nerve! What conceit! She was steaming. She looked at her mother, who smiled so broadly it looked like her face would crack. Why didn't she see this negative obnoxious trait of his? Rena's apparent indifference only made her angrier.

    Then she caught herself. Her brother had a high risk, high pressure job. Even Danny held him in the highest professional regard and was slightly in awe of him, and he flew with him every day. Danny also mentioned other things about the cruise besides the Italian Incident. He wouldn't elaborate, but the six months her big brother was away from home wasn't exactly a cruise on the Love Boat. Being sure-footed and cocky was a defense mechanism, Danny assured her. He explained to her that even though the country was at peace, they were always at war at sea. Being a bit conceited and aloof helped them to stay alive-and, if need be, to accept death. She surmised there was a lot more to "flyin an airpanes onna ships" than she realized.

Chapter 16

Julie Ann Tate was a player. The more Steven got to know her throughout Christmas Day, the more enamored he became. She was so witty, especially after she felt more comfortable with him. He gave her a quick rudimentary lesson in flying the Cessna, and marveled at how quickly she picked up the nuances of flight. She was also right about her father. He was a very interesting man indeed, doing working in cryogenics and superconductivity. Her mother made no bones about how wonderful she thought her Julie's new "friend" was. Her older sister seemed fond of him as well.

On the flight home, she asked, "So, what's on your agenda for tomorrow?"

"I have to drop in on an old friend, a guy who was one of my heroes while I was growing up. He was the fellow who let me hang around and fly his historical group's airplanes. He's not feeling all that well, and I promised I'd take one of his planes up so it maintains its FAA certification."

"That would be Mr. Whitney."

"How'd you know that?" he asked in astonishment.

"You called him when I was at your house once, in one of my many visits to see your, ahem, sister. You were much too involved with your life to speak with me, except that time we walked on the beach and..."

He laughed. This was her way of telling him what a jerk he had been. "Okay, okay! Mea Culpa! I'm sorry! I'm more mature now. I've...grown!"

"Hey, Julie! Why don't you come up with me in the TBF? It'll be a brief flight. You'll get to ride in a genuine antique. You'll love it. Then we can do something with my sister and Danny for dinner. What do you say?"

"Sold." She kissed him on his cheek.

They arrived at eight the next morning at Whitney's hangar. Julie Ann loved the old Ford. He even let her drive it the last few miles. Even early in the morning, Julie Ann Tate glowed, and he found himself constantly staring at her. Her makeup was always perfect and her hair was always suited to the occasion. Today, it hung lightly on her shoulders and down her back, and waves of blonde accentuated her movements. As he was consumed in ogling her and not hearing a word she said, Whitney was hobbling out with a cane to greet them.

"Hi there, sailor!" he said, waving the cane above his head. "Who's your friend?"

"Hello, Mr. Whitney. This is Julie Ann Tate."

"Wow! You certainly are a looker. Are you sure you're not wasting your time with this guy? How about a nice, mature older man?" he said with a wink.

"Don't you go teasing me, Mr. Whitney" she responded, laying on her Georgia accent.

"Why the cane, Mr. Whitney?" Steven asked.

"They tell me I need a new hip. I'm scheduled to go to John Hopkins and get it done next month. They also advised me not to fly until this whole thing is done. You're doing me a great favor in getting this FAA thing done for me with the TBF, Steven. I know your time is precious, but the FAA just notified us of their new certification procedures and timelines last week, and they caught us by surprise. That's just like the government. None of the other guys are around. They're all in Florida playing golf or visiting their grandchildren for the holidays, were I should be!" he laughed.

"Thanks for thinking of me. You know what a kick I get out of this old bird. It's like an old friend. Julie Ann is going up with me, if that's okay with you."

Whitney laughed. "I can remember back in World War II that we would have given anything to take a beauty like you flying, Julie. Watch Amato, though. He's not all that good at this pilot stuff."

"I beg to differ with you, sir. I've been flying with him and I think he does it exquisitely." She pecked him on the cheek for emphasis.

"Oh, well. Shot down again. Okay, you win. Take care of her, Amato."

"You don't have to worry about the Avenger, Mr. Whitney. She's in good hands."'

"I'm not talking about the Avenger! But take care of that too!"

As he laughed, a thought came to him. "Oh. Mr. Whitney. I thought you'd like to see this" he said, pushing up his jacket sleeve and then removing the watch on his wrist. "Here, take a look."

"So this is the watch you told me about. Oh, yes. I remember it well. We World War II aviators coveted this watch. What a beauty it is. Expensive as hell, as I can remember." He turned it over to read the inscription. "Ah, Ray Moore. What a guy. Handsome, rich, educated. He could really fly, too. A shame, a real shame," Whitney said as he passed the watch back to Steven. "But I guess you're getting to know about real shames personally, aren't you?"

"You heard?"

"Ah! I know everything that happens out there."

Julie Ann looked on confused about this last banter, but Danny already pleaded with her not to ask Steven about what happened "out there." Not yet anyway. However, this Raymond Moore fellow was fair game, and being a newspaperwoman meant to be curious.

"Is that the same Ray Moore who owned the Ford?" she asked.

"Yes. I'm surprised my sister didn't tell you about the watch. It got me in all kinds of hell as soon as I got home."

"No, she didn't," she said, expecting the explanation.

"Let's go flying." He put the watch on his wrist and the lightheadedness came for an instant.

When he brought her into the hangar, Julie walked around the TBF several times as Steven pre-flighted it, her eyes widening with each orbit.

"Are you sure this plane is forty years old? It looks brand new!" she exclaimed.

"Actually, it's better than new. When Whitney and his guys did its ground up restoration, they upgraded it with state-of-the-art communications gear. The engine has been rebuilt to better-than-new specifications, because they used optic measuring devices and lasers to come to tolerances that were unheard of in the forties. Yeah, it's a beauty, all right."

Steven changed into one of group's World War II issue khaki colored flying suits. This particular one had the squadron insignia for VT-6 on its sleeve, and the insignia of a lieutenant's rank on its collar. Julie Ann wore his leather jacket over a flight suit Steven gave her to wear. She climbed into the Avenger's portside hatch and he guided her to the ball turret seat behind his. He instructed her how to secure her seat and shoulder belts. Once he was sure she was safe, he climbed into the cockpit and secured it. He started the big Pratt and Whitney radial, and slowly taxied to the end of the runway. He reviewed the flight plan once more Whitney gave them to follow, received clearance from the tower, and then began his takeoff roll.

"How are we doing, Julie?" he asked.

"Boy, this thing is noisy!" she responded.

"Yes it is. It'll get a little better when we get airborne."

He rolled the plane's nose upward and banked slightly to the west, heading out over the Chesapeake. It was a bright, crisp morning, perfect for flying. The surface traffic on the bay below was light, as the holiday season would dictate. He continued to climb gently to two thousand feet.

"I'll fly over my parent's house, Julie. We'll see if my sister and Danny are up. If not, maybe we can rouse them."

"Sounds like fun!" she replied. He strained to see her face behind him. She blew him a kiss.

They soared and gently dove on the Amato residence, bringing the neighbors as well as his parents and Danny and Susan out of their houses.

He waggled his wings and flew a course that would take them out over the Atlantic along the Virginia coast, taking care to remain outside of Oceana's airspace.

Fifteen minutes later, his eye caught the oil pressure gauge beginning to fluctuate. The engine began to trail a very thin cloud of blue smoke. He eased back on the throttle and cut the engine rpm. He looked for fire, but none, to his great relief. This leak wasn't bad, but he still had to get the Avenger on the ground. The nearest strip was Oceana's. Julie must have seen the smoke, because she asked what was happening.

Calmly, he replied, "We're losing oil pressure, and from the smoke, I would say we've sprung a small oil leak. Don't worry, though. We're only a few miles from Oceana Naval Air Station. I'll radio a mayday and request permission to land. Why don't you sit in the bombardier's seat below, Julie, just in case we have to make a quick exit?"

"Okay," she replied calmly.

Boy she was tough, he thought. She must totally trust me, or be the bravest person I know. He hated to admit it, but his mother was right about her all the while. He turned to a heading that would put him on the glide path for Oceana's longest runway. In fact, it was the same one he had brought the new Tomcat down on just a few days ago.

"Mayday, Mayday! Oceana NAS, this is TBF 62-1190 requesting permission for an emergency landing. I have your runway 14 Left in sight, over."

"TBF 62-1190, this is Oceana control. We roger your mayday. Permission granted for landing. Continue your approach to runway 14 Left. Wind from the west at 10 knots."

"Roger, Oceana. Please give me radar confirmation of my altitude, over." He was concerned that the altimeter might be giving him a false reading, as it wasn't responding to the slight dive he had the plane in to keep up his airspeed.

"Repeat, TBF?" came the reply, after a long pause."

"Roger that. Request radar fix for altitude, Oceana."

Again, a pause. "We do not understand your request, TBF. Come again, please.

What the hell was there to understand, he asked himself angrily. Just look at the number on your...radarscope. He got that ice water feeling again, further heightened by his first full view of Oceana's runway as he came out of thin, low-level bank of clouds. The runway looked about a mile shorter than he knew it should be. The whole base looked smaller. Could he have possibly used the wrong heading? Was this Oceana, or the smaller emergency strip to the north? Or was it the small general aviation airport where he first learned to fly? He probably used the wrong heading. How could have he made such a dumb error? But how many airports have a runway 14 Left? He cleared his mind quickly and put first things first, namely, the slightly wounded bird that he was trying to successfully bring to earth.

He came over the runway a little faster than was prescribed, but he wanted to maintain airspeed in case of the unlikely event that the engine seized from the lack of oil. He flared perfectly, and his wheels hit the concrete in unison. He rolled out the landing, the plane still emitting a trail of blue smoke. The base's fire trucks surrounded the TBF, and men began dragging CO_2 fire extinguishers to the aircraft, putting their nozzles in and around the cowling. The plane was engulfed in a cloud of carbon dioxide fog.

Something was definitely amiss. He looked at the fire trucks. They did not look at all like the trucks he had seen hundreds of times at Oceana. They were smaller, their fenders and bodies were smaller and rounder, and they were painted red, not the new high-visibility yellow. They looked nothing like the squared-off high-tech firefighting vehicles he knew. Their headlights sat on top of their fenders, not integrated into the bumpers on front face of the vehicles he saw daily. The ambulance that approached them was a ... 1941 Ford wagon!

"Julie, you okay?" he asked over the intercom.

"I'm fine. I'm coming up to..."

"Julie. Please stay there. I think its better that I come over to get you. The plane is okay, but we had better get out. It's standard procedure."

"Okay, but where did all those old cars and trucks come from?"

"I'll explain later." Oh, good Christ!

An enlisted man helped him out of the cockpit. He saw others poking in the cowling, and confirming to each other there wasn't a fire.

"You okay, sir?" the man asked.

"Fine, thank you. I have a passenger inside that I'd better evacuate," Steven said as he looked anxiously over the TBF's long nose, backing off the wing, wondering what happened to the mile of runway that was definitely missing.

"No fire, sir. I think you just popped an oil line is all. Is this one of them new TBF's we've been hearin' about?"

It was happening again. He began to doubt his sanity. Nevertheless, they had to get away from the plane as quickly as possible. That was procedure, just like he told Julie.

"Yes, it is", he answered nervously, opening the hatch for Julie to step out.

Every man gawked when she exited from the hatch. A crusty old chief petty officer barked for them to get back to work.

"Who's that?" an enlisted man asked, mouth agape.

"Her? She's..."

"Julie Ann Tate. Washington Post. Pleased to meetcha!" she said, extending her hand to the enlisted man, a smile wide across her pretty face. The young man blushed. She glanced at Steven and winked, as if she was going to play along.

But how did she know to play along?

"What are you doing in a Navy plane, miss?" the crusty old chief asked, his eyes showing his consternation at this flagrant breech of Navy protocol.

"She's doing a story on this new airplane and the Navy squadrons in general, chief. We were on our way to Pensacola when the oil line came undone. She was going to interview our newest fledglings, right Miss Tate?" He winked at her, as she had just done, hoping she would continue to...play along?

She giggled. "That's right, sugar."

The old chief shook his head as an enlisted man came up to Steven and said, "It's definitely an oil line, sir. I'll have it fixed in a jiffy. We gotta get it to the maintenance area. You should be on your way in no time, sir," he said looking at Steven.

"Very well, Dobbs. Lieutenant, let's get going, shall we? We don't want to keep those Pensacola boys waiting, now do we?" the old chief sneered, as an aircraft tractor hooked on to the tail wheel of the Avenger and took it under tow.

"Better get used to different procedures and developments, chief. It's a whole new ballgame out there." He cuffed the chief's shoulder as he said it, trying to buy his confidence. He looked to his wrist to check the time. The Hamilton was gone.

"I guess the Japs saw to that," he replied, his face showing obvious pain. Steven Amato saw his assumptions coming together, if for nothing else to give a degree of reality to an enigma.

They rode back in the ambulance, Julie smiling brightly at everything going on around her, snapping pictures with a little Nikon camera she had brought with her. When they got back to the maintenance facility, the next sight almost pushed Steven over the edge.

Fifteen TBD Devastators were being lovingly worked over by their ground crews. Out from a building that Steven knew to be an office complex in 1985, but had one time been a torpedo squadron staging area before and during the World War, came fifteen naval aviators. Each one had an unusual pistol or knife, or a combination of pistols, cartridge belts, and knives across their chests, or slung around their hips. They walked with a swagger, each holding a clipboard, their leather helmets and goggles pushed up on their heads, or held in their free hands. Some chewed gum confidently, others puffed on unfiltered cigarettes, as in the fashion of Clark Gable or Humphrey Bogart. He looked at their faces as the ambulance came to a halt. The pilots started to run when they saw the tractor pulling in an unusual looking aircraft.

One yelled, "Hey! It's that new Grumman TBF!" Another yelled, "That one's mine!" Another yelled, "Not if I get to it first!"

The pilots raced by the ambulance as Steven got out. He looked at their faces as they raced past. God! That was Woodson. This other guy is Campbell. This one's Creamer. Shit, that's Johnny Gray! And Bob Miles. And, Christ- Billy Evans! And Tex Gay!

And Raymond Moore...

Steven plodded after them like a man in shock, his mouth and eyes wide in disbelief. He started walking back to the TBF being swarmed over by the other pilots. She decided to stay by the ambulance. The sight of all those howling men momentarily caused her caution.

As he walked, he felt a tap on the shoulder.

"Julie. Wait just a minute. I got..."

"Who the hell you calling Julie?" a voice boomed behind him.

He turned immediately around, and the sight before him almost caused his heart to seize. He would have recognized Lieutenant Commander John C. Waldron from a block away, let alone the six inches away from his nose where he stood.

"Sorry, sir. I thought it was that reporter I'm flying shepherding." He came to attention and saluted, his eyes still wide in disbelief, and his brow forming a sweat despite the frigid December air.

"The broad with the leather jacket on? What's she reporting on?"

"Naval Aviation, sir. For the war effort. She's from the Washington Post. I'm escorting her in the new TBF as a public relations initiative for the Navy Department."

"Oh, that's just great! We need that fucking plane, and the Navy decides to go Hollywood with it." Waldron looked to the ground, shaking his head. He quickly recovered. "Well, I shouldn't be surprised. Anyway, so that's the new TBF. How's it fly?" Waldron looked back at Steven and noticed his pale face. "Are you all right, son?"

Steven was scanning Waldron's face in total disbelief, wanting so very bad to reach out and touch him, just to see if he was real. Based on Waldron's confused face, he must have looked like a dumb ass, for sure.

"I'm fine, sir. Yes sir, that's the TBF Avenger."

"Avenger? Is that its name? What, like avenging Pearl Harbor?"

Steven almost blew it. The TBF wasn't named the Avenger because of Pearl Harbor, but as a vengeful memoriam to the slaughter of the torpedo squadrons at Midway. But how was he going to tell Waldron that?

"Yes. That's right, sir", he managed.

"What squadron you from?" Waldron asked.

"VT-6, sir," he said, displaying his patch.

"It figures that Gene Lindsey's boys would get the Hollywood assignments. You tell Gene that I still think he's a pussy. Got it?" Waldron laughed heartily.

"Yes sir."

"I'm gonna sneak a look at that plane of yours, Lieutenant... Lieutenant...?

"Amato, sir. Steven L."

"An I-Talian, huh? That's unusual. We don't get many I-Talians in the Navy Air Corps. Come and tell me about it." He grabbed Steven by the shoulder as a father would to a son, and walked with him to the TBF. The grip was real enough...

They passed Raymond Moore going the opposite way, his eye set on Julie.

"Hey, Moore. Don't you disappear on me, you little sneak. We got to get going real soon."

"I'll be right here, Commander Waldron," he answered with a wink, his thumb pointing to Julie.

"That son of a bitch would screw a snake if you held its head. He thinks it's because he's a Clark Gable look-alike. Must be the case, because he gets more pussy than anybody I know. He's a rich bastard too!"

"Yeah, I've heard that, sir." Moore put his arm around Julie, and directed her toward the Ford Convertible that was ... who's?

"Where are you off to?" Waldron asked.

Keep the story going, Steven, he told himself. "I'm flying Miss Tate down to Pensacola, sir. She's doing a story on Navy Aviation Training, and I guess the thinking is that the story will help the war effort. I'm assigned to test the TBF through carrier qualification." It worked on the chief. Would it work on Waldron?

"The *Big E* and your squadron have been quite busy from what I hear. They're trying to make sure those fucking slant eyes don't make another try for Pearl."

"So I understand. I wish I was with them. From what I've been allowed to hear, I think we took it on the chin pretty badly, sir." This was the most difficult conversation Steven ever had. He knew the outcome, whereas his partner had only speculation and scuttlebutt.

"The official Navy is not saying shit. So I agree with you. I think we got clobbered. We're the only guys not surprised. Those battleship admirals learned the lesson Billy Mitchell was trying to teach them the hard way. Shit, the Italian battleships got clobbered at Taranto last year by the British the same way we got it at Pearl, but nobody listened. And we've been underestimating those Jap bastards for years. Not me, though. I knew those guys were good, just from reading the news and talking to guys coming back from China with Chennault's Flying Tigers. Hey, this bird is beautiful!" Waldron said as he climbed up onto the TBF's wing. "And it's a big bastard too! And solid! How big is the engine?"

Then the others began questioning him.

"Is it designed to carry the new Mark 13 22 inch torpedo? From what we heard, that's the same size of the ones the Japs carried at Pearl Harbor. They need to be that big to blow the bottom out of those Jap battlewagons. I heard their *Yamato* was in on the Pearl raid. Have you heard that?"

"A ball turret! That should add to its lifespan."

"Is that a thirty caliber or fifty caliber in the nose?"

"Wow! Look at this armor. Hey Amato! How thick is it?"

"You can fit two thousand pounders in the bomb bay easy!"

"This radio gear is so small. Where are the tubes?"

Steven answered all their questions, but stood awed at men he knew to be long dead. Waldron was every bit the leader he had researched him to be. His men at once loved him and respected him. They did not fear him. It was evident from the wise-ass that was going on. They knew what the limit was in joking with their CO, and never crossed it.

"This radio is really different," Johnny Gray said. "And it's so small."

"Don't say it too loud, you know what I mean. Shit, if they knew I even let you guys near the cockpit I'd get horsewhipped," Steven laughed.

"We won't tell. We promise. Hell, who would we tell anyway? We're gone for a least a month," Bob Miles said.

Steven thought a moment. If the date of the twenty-sixth was right, it must have to be December 1941. Waldron was talking about Pearl Harbor as a recent event. It couldn't have been December of 1942, because by then, all these men were...dead. They were flying out to meet the *Hornet* on its shakedown cruise today! That's where they were heading before his forced landing interrupted their plans.

As he looked upon them, laughing, joking, talking about flying and fighting, he realized that they could be his own squadron mates. That 'esprit de corps' was there, even way back.. here. Suddenly, his chin quivered and his eyes moistened over.

"You okay, Amato?" Waldron asked.

"Yes sir. Just allergy, sir."

"Well get this airplane out to us pronto. Those Devastators we're flying are crap, even though seven or eight years ago they were the best in the world. It took long enough for our esteemed representatives in Washington to realize we needed a replacement. I hope we don't have to bleed for their mistakes. Here," he said, taking a calling card from his breast pocket, and signing it with a Parker Duofold fountain pen. "You give this to LeRoy Grumman, and tell him John Waldron gets the first production Avenger. Got it?"

Steven swallowed hard. "I got it, Commander Waldron. Where are you off to anyway? Do you have a training flight scheduled?" Maybe he could get Waldron to confirm their intentions.

"I can't tell you that, son. But if you take a heading due south of the tower there, you'll see our destination before too long."

He was correct. Waldron and VT-8 were going out to meet the brand new *Hornet*.

"Okay, guys, let's get the lead out. It's time to go flying," Waldron yelled looking at his watch. "We don't want to start off on CAG's shit list. Amato! I hope to see you soon, pal. And make sure you bring fifteen of those TBF's with you! And even though you're one of Gene Lindsey's boys, let me give you a word of fatherly advice. Broads and airplanes don't mix. Look what happened to Amelia Earhart a few years back!" Waldron said, as he slapped Steven on the shoulder, returned his salute, smiled and winked at him, and then went off after his men.

Torpedo 8 jogged to their Devastators. Each man had an ear to ear grin on his face. As they passed Waldron, he made it a point of slapping each one on the shoulder or on the ass. Those initially out of his reach changed their course to insure their commander touched each of them. It was like a coach psyching up his team just before a big game. Steven postulated that there had never been a bigger game in the history of the world, before or since. Other men were coming out of other squadron ready areas. Fifteen SBD Dauntless dive bombers were parked just beyond Torpedo 8's ready area. A man jumped out of a Lincoln Zephyr as it came to a screeching halt. A beautiful redhead in a flowing pink dress waved good bye to him as he back-peddled and blew a kiss to her. It was Lieutenant Commander Gus Wildhelm, the CO of Scouting 8, living up to his reputation as a swashbuckler with a lust for life. Fighting 8 was already taxiing its F4F-3's to the runway, with its CO Sam Mitchell in the lead plane. Lieutenant Commander Al Tucker had Bombing 8 airborne already.

Amidst the roar of aircraft taxiing and taking off, a rather dour looking man appeared quite upset, seemingly about the method and timetable of deployment, as he alternately pointed to aircraft and his watch. Waldron and Widhelm were pointing to their clipboards and watches, in obvious disagreement with the gentleman. Judging by Waldron's and Widhelm's reaction to his gesticulations, the commander said what had to be a few terse words to them, then quickly climbed aboard an SBD with a "00" designation, and taxied to the runway. Just as it was in Steven's day, the "double nuts" plane belonged to the Commander-Air Group, or CAG, in this case Commander Stanhope Cotton Ring. As he stormed off, it was obvious from the looks on their faces that Widhelm and Waldron were disgruntled. Again, they pointed to their watches and the clipboards that carried the day's operational orders, then shook their hands and waved in disgust at Ring's fast disappearing Dauntless. No doubt, they were right on the schedule Ring himself had prescribed, and had no tolerance for Ring's needless tantrums. Ring was known in the Navy historical circles to have a penchant for exerting his authority without cause or provocation, as this instance had demonstrated. Steven had noted this in his senior thesis at Annapolis as a probable cause leading to a miscalculation that resulted in all of Air Group 8 missing the engagement of the Japanese aircraft carriers during Battle of Midway on the critical day of June 4, except for Torpedo 8. What surprised him then was that Captain D'Couer didn't question or berate him on this charge, which led him to believe his assertion was more than not true.

Waldron looked as each of his pilots and gunners climb aboard their aircraft, and noted that one was missing. He saw Waldron have what would be currently called a "shitfit." He screamed at Raymond Moore, who was obliviously still talking with Julie Ann Tate, his eyes all dreamy.

"Moore! Get your ass into your aircraft pronto!"

"I thought we were to go at 0930, sir. My watch tells me it's only 0845!" He pointed to a Hamilton chronometer.

"That's before CAG changed the rules. Now move your ass!"

Steven felt his own pulse quicken with....jealousy? He began to walk to Moore, but Moore was quick to heed Waldron, his body stiffening at the sound of Waldron's roar. Moore began to run, only to trip and fall on expansion stripping. He got up quickly looking at his wrist, and Steven ran to see if he was okay. Moore put his index finger up to Waldron in a "just a minute please, chief" sign, then ran back to his car. Waldron slapped his own forehead so hard, Steven thought he would pass out with a concussion.

Moore quickly opened the Ford convertible's door as he talked with Julie. He reached down into its interior, got up and closed the door with a slam, and began to run again to his plane. He passed Steven, who said, "Nice car, Moore."

AS TIME GOES BY

"Thanks! Moore said in a huff, slowing his pace briefly. "Maybe I'll sell it to you one day!"

Steven looked at his wrist. As he suspected, the Hamilton chronometer had reappeared. That worried him, because he now concluded he was making sense of insanity. Julie came to him as he watched Torpedo 8 take off and head south on to meet the *Hornet*.

"Wow! This is quite a show, Steven. Thanks for sharing it! It made me feel like I was really back in 1941. That guy who played Ray Moore was awfully cute."

He let the comment go. "What'd he say to you, Julie? Just now, I mean, when he went back to the car."

"You know what he said, Steven Amato. Who do you think you're kidding?" she said, holding his arm.

"I just want to be sure, Julie. What did he say?" He tried to keep his cool, but it was getting really hard.

"He said his father would be really aggravated at him if he found out that he had broken the watch he had just given him a few weeks ago, and that he had better hide it under the front seat until he got back to have it fixed. You know that." She pulled at his arm and put her head on his shoulder.

The crusty chief reappeared and said, "Lieutenant, you're all patched up. We replaced the oil you lost. You should be fine."

"Thanks, Chief. Let's go, Julie Ann."

He just had to be sure. He headed due south after taking off, keeping his altitude at 1500 feet. Sure enough, fifteen minutes later, he had his answer.

Below him, a bright number 8 painted on each end of its deck, the brand new carrier USS *Hornet*, CV-8, plowed through the Atlantic at thirty knots, already with a bone in her teeth. The morning sun sparkled off her new deck, and highlighted her fresh gray paint. With her were two brand new battleships Steven knew to be the *South Dakota* and *North Carolina*, and several destroyers. Steven grinned in his disbelief, and good fortune, or whatever it was that he was feeling now.

"Look, Steven! An aircraft carrier! Which one is it?"

Shit! What does he say now?

"It's the USS *Guam*, Julie Ann. It's really an assault ship, not a carrier." In fact, the new class of assault ship had almost the same dimensions as the YORKTOWN class carriers, and even bore a striking resemblance to them from altitude.

"But all those old planes we saw are on the deck."

"We'd better get back. Mr. Whitney is probably worried waiting for us," he said quickly.

She snapped a few photos of the ship as Steven turned back North, now escorted by two of Sam Mitchell's Wildcat fighters that had intercepted them, vectored out by the carrier's crude top secret radar from their combat air patrol. It was just 19 days after Pearl Harbor, and even though the only real threat to the *Hornet* might be a lurking German submarine, nobody was making any more assumptions about the capabilities of the Japanese or the Germans. They waved to the Wildcat pilots, who, after five minutes of escort, waggled their wings and headed back to their ship.

They were on the ground a half hour later. There sat the Ford convertible, just outside the hangar. Mr. Whitney sat on a stool next to the Ford. Julie Ann ran from the airplane and hugged him and began babbling the adventure of the morning. Whitney just smiled and raised his eyebrows at her as she excitedly told her story. She then ran to the car to fetch her purse and redo her face.

"How did the *Guam* look, Steve?" Whitney asked.

"Just fine," he said, taking off his flying gloves and trying not to look Whitney directly in the eye. "The Avenger's all checked out. I've signed the log and the certification. There is an oil line that needs to be checked though."

"Why should I check it? From what I've been told, it's been fixed by experts," Whitney replied matter-of-factly.

Steven smiled at the old gent, and nodded his head. What did he know? Was he playing off Julie Ann's story?

Or, did he know better?

What Julie would tell his parents, his sister Susan and her fiancé Danny Morello was his chief concern, though he didn't seem to care what the outcome would be. Whether it was reality, some mental condition, or sorcery, he knew, somehow or other, he met the hero of his youth today.

Julie catnapped on the way home, and he gently nudged her awake when they rolled up his parent's driveway.

"Wake up, sleepy head," he said, kissing her forehead gently.

"That was a lot of excitement today. When you take a girl out, you take a girl out, don't you?" She hugged him tightly.

Susan ran from the house in excitement, with Danny Morello trailing behind him. "Did you enjoy the flight, Julie?" she asked.

Steven just cringed. He didn't want to hear the answer.

"Oh, yes Susan! We had some excitement! The plane sprouted an oil leak and Steven had to make an emergency landing at Oceana. We met a lot of Steve's fellow pilots, while the mechanics fixed the leak. Then Steven took us out over the Atlantic again, and we saw the USS *Guam*, right Steve?"

"Right, Julie," he said warily, unable to look Danny Morello in the eye.

"Then two fighter planes flew with us awhile and then took off. It was the best date I've ever had! Your big brother is one kind of flyboy, Susan!"

"Who'd you meet, Julie?" Danny asked, his eyes still on Steven.

"Oh, this guy named Moore and Waldron, this Lieutenant Moore was real interested in me, I tell ya, Suzie Q," she said, winking to her to see if Steven's jealousy would be aroused.

He turned quickly, as he felt his face coming off. He couldn't believe it. He was knotted up by confusion, and its accompanying rage. His sister picked up on the expression, but misinterpreted it.

"Jealous are we, Mister Naples?" Susan said.

"Yeah! You're my girl, Miss Georgia, and don't you forget it!" he said forcefully, pointing his finger at the smiling Julie Ann Tate. It helped release the rage, because this is one thing that happened today that he was in control over and was determined to get straight.

"You mean that Steve. I know I'm no Italian jet-setter, but..."

"Hell yes, I mean it!"

Despite all the voodoo, he really wanted to spend at least the rest of his life with Miss Georgia. "You're a player, Julie Ann Tate," he said as he held her close.

With that done, there was one more thing to take care of.

"Julie, give me the film. I'll go get it developed at that one hour photo center while I pick up some lobsters and scallops and clams for a mid-winter clambake. How's that sound?"

"That sounds like a great idea!" Susan said. The weather was beautifully crisp, and it would be fun to bundle up and eat on the beach from a big can full of the fruits of the Chesapeake.

"And you," he said, targeting his finger at Danny, "be useful and come with me."

Julie gave him the camera. He and Danny got in the car and were off.

"Okay, out with it. The *Guam* is with the Pacific Fleet, last I heard. What happened today?" Danny asked.

Straight-faced, Steven looked directly at him. After a moment's hesitation, he told him the whole story, both of today's incident and the incident on Christmas Eve. Danny didn't flinch.

They dropped off the film and then went about their errands picking up the seafood, with Danny pressing him for details. Steven willingly supplying them, as they both tried to come to terms with this warp of reality. They went back to the photo center an hour later and nervously opened the package.

Some of the photos were blurry, others were double exposed, but the picture of Steven talking with Commander John C. Waldron was clear as a bell, as was the picture Julie had snapped of Raymond Moore posed against his car. And there was no doubt about it-that was the USS *Hornet* steaming southward, and the two F4F fighters providing escort had the markings of VF-8.

"Did she know who she was talking to?" Danny asked.

"How would she know? Everybody sees the truth as they think it to be, even if the details that come from specific knowledge are absent. It's like trying to come to terms with UFOs and aliens. What I do know is that each experience for the wearer and the person who accompanies the wearer becomes reality. If Reuter knew that he was seeing the real Glenn Miller Orchestra with Glenn Miller leading it, he would have died. But he didn't know better. To his mind, he was watching a modern day imposter with the modern day Glenn Miller Orchestra. He doesn't know what the real Glenn Miller looked like-but I did. He saw all those people in forties clothes and assimilated it into the theme his mind's knowledge created."

"He didn't know enough to ask the right questions."

"But I did, and here are a few more. Why did the ad for the show in the New York Times disappear when I took off this fucking watch? That episode was much more contained than what happened with Julie Ann today. She talked to the same people I did today. Like the Glenn Miller situation, she didn't know who they were, including that flirting son-of-a-bitch Raymond Moore. However, Susan's got pictures. She recorded the past. She also said that Moore told her that his old man would be pissed if he knew that he smashed the watch he had just given him, as he hid it under the front seat. The watch disappeared from my wrist when I landed the TBF at Oceana. It reappeared when Ray Moore stuck it under the front seat of the Ford. "

He sighed deeply and ran his fingers through his thick black hair. "Who the fuck knows? And I could wear this damned watch all day today, and nothing would happen, unless I go someplace that was around..."

"When the watch was new, like Radio City Music Hall, or Oceana Naval Air Station," Danny cut in.

"Right. And I wonder where Levine went with it. He had that gleam in his eye, and wouldn't hear of me giving him the watch in trade for the Breitling," Steven said, taking the Hamilton off his wrist. "And what the hell did Whitney mean about getting the oil line in the Avenger fixed by experts? What does he know beyond what we told him about getting the line fixed at Oceana? He seemed to know more than he led on. He even smirked when he asked me how the *Guam* looked, like he knew I had seen the old *Hornet*. Ah, shit! I'm so shitless I'm witless. I just don't know."

Danny took the Hamilton from Steven's hand, and stared at it for a long second, then he looked at his best friend, and said, "I told you a week ago to get rid of this fucking thing. Please, please, please do it."

"You think I'm crazy, don't you?"

"No. And that's what worries me. I believe you because I believe in you. These pictures here tell me you're not bullshitting me, and you're not crazy enough to doctor them, nor did you have the time, unless Tate is in on this with you. I know she's not that crazy. Just get rid of this," he said, flipping the watch in the air to Steven, who caught it in his right hand. "It's got what my grandmother called malocchio, the evil eye.

"And if I were you, I would give Julie the blurred pictures and tell her that her fucking Nikon is broken and needs to be fixed."

"Oh, great! I'm supposed to start off this relationship with a lie?"

"Amats, think about it," he said, hesitating from the task of putting the groceries in the Ford's trunk. "I still think that us former Midshipmen believe in the Honor Code. But telling a lie is an act based on knowing the truth."

"Okay. Then explain this bit of truth," Steven said, reaching into his shirt pocket and pulling out a business card. As he gave it over to Danny he said, "I was handed this today."

On its printed side he noted the bearer's name, rank, and unit embossed in black ink. He turned it over to see a brief note written with a fountain pen in green ink, a color that was fashionable in the late thirties and forties, to Leroy Grumman. It requested that the first fifteen Avengers to come off the assembly line be assigned directly to Torpedo 8. "Just call me directly when they're ready, and I'll have them picked up. I'll tell the Navy about our deal afterwards!" it read. It was signed LtCdr. J.C. WALDRON, CO, VT-8, USS *Hornet*.

Danny flicked the card with his free thumb and pursed his lips as he watched Steven Amato fill the trunk of the Ford convertible with several shopping bags full of lobsters, scallops, clams, corn, charcoal briquets, and charcoal lighter fluid.

"Reality is a bitch," he said.

"Tell me about it," Steven responded.

Now he was just as confused as Steven was, and he hoped that someone would steal that Hamilton watch, and soon. He knew Steve wouldn't discard it or sell it or trade it until he came to the bottom of the eerie thing. He would also drop by on Sam Levine, and soon. He had several questions that needed asking.

Back at his parent's house, Julie Ann Tate was taking a fitful nap. She wasn't a feature writer for the Post because of her magnificent appearance. She was a Magna Cum Laude graduate of the University of Virginia, and besides being exceptionally smart, she was curious and daring. Yet she was having a difficult time coming to grips with what she had seen today, and was glad that Steven hadn't pressed her to comment more fully on the day's events. She would research this out herself. She was curious to see the pictures, and now she regretted giving him the film to develop. If he wanted to keep this morning's escapade an enigmatic secret, he would no doubt doctor or destroy the film. From his relief at her story, she knew he couldn't explain what was happening himself, but she also concluded he had more facts that he wouldn't or couldn't share. She loved him deeply and she was convinced he was at beginning to love her. She trusted that what he was doing was to protect her from outcomes he could only postulate to explain. Anyone who graduated third in his class from Annapolis and flew thirty million dollar airplanes off ships at night in storms should at least be given every benefit of the doubt. She saw his face contort when those airmen swarmed passed them to the embrace the TBF, and the look in his eyes when he spoke to that big fellow Waldron.

And Raymond Moore. She knew the story of the car well enough to know Raymond Moore when she saw him. Not only had she recognized the Ford, she also recognized the watch Ray Moore was stuffing under the front seat as the same one Steven had shown to Whitney this morning.

She rushed to the door when Steve and Danny came home. "Hi, sweets. You have my pictures?" she said kissing his cheek.

"Yes, but half of the damned things didn't come out, and the ones that did were blurry. Must be something wrong with the camera."

He said it nervously, and his eyes pleaded for her to accept the lie. A reporter knows when she's being lied to. But his eyes...they were sincere. Was he afraid of the truth, or was he trying to keep it away from her? She hugged him closely, and felt his body relax. Yes. There was something there, all right.

She was due back to work in Washington on January 2. She didn't have the photos, but she still had her photographic mind, the Library of Congress, and the archives of the Washington Post. Her job was half research and investigation and half presentation. And nobody did research better than Julie Ann Tate.

She wasn't driven by this project to know the truth, or to prove her sanity, or for that matter, the sanity of Steven Amato; it was driven to help the man she wanted to spend the rest of her life with, and this made her all the more resolved to do a thorough a job of this.

Chapter 17

Danny Morello woke up bright and early on New Year's Eve and "motored" into Norfolk. He parked the Corvette just up the street from Sam Levine's jewelry store. The streets were near deserted, and there were few cars in the parking lots. Most of the stores were still closed, not opening until nine. His first view of Sam's establishment indicated a darkened interior. Nonetheless, he pushed on the door's large brass handle. Surprisingly, the door creaked open, and he went inside. He called out "Sam, Sam?" repeatedly, but nobody answered.

As he approached the counter, he noted all the showcases were empty and a light collection of dust accumulated on the once highly polished glass surfaces. He reasoned that the store could not have been vacant very long. After all, Steven had been there less than two weeks ago to pick up Raymond Moore's watch.

An uneasiness overtook him. A business that had been thriving here since before the Second World War seemed defunct. As he thought those last few words, his trepidation increased twofold. He felt there had to be a connection between that damned Hamilton watch and the situation he was trying to come to terms with now. He remembered Steven had told him that Levine had behaved strangely the night he came to pick it....

"May I help you?"

Even though the voice was low key and not threatening at all in tone, Danny almost jumped out of his shorts.

"I'm sorry. I didn't mean to startle you. Are you okay?"

Danny's eyes focused on a man about his age, accompanied by a woman. The man looked like a young Sam Levine. He didn't recognize the woman.

"Yes. I'm fine, thank you," he said with some relief. "I'm sorry, but I didn't mean to intrude. The door was unlocked, and I thought I might find Sam Levine in here."

"I'm Sam Levine Junior, he said extending his hand. "This is Rachel. May we be of some assistance?"

"Danny Morello," he said, taking first Sam junior's hand, then Rachel's. "It's a pleasure to meet both of you. As I was saying, he did some work for me and a friend, and I..."

"Was there something wrong with the articles you bought? If so, I can..."

"No. Actually, the articles are examples of superb craftsmanship. I just..."

"Ah! Then father would have been happy. He liked to hear those compliments, right Rachel?"

Rachel smiled slightly as she nodded her agreement. She did not say a word, though she just looked on slightly amused.

"You're talking in the past tense, Sam. Has something happened to your father?"

"I guess you haven't heard. My father passed away on Christmas Day. His heart gave out. My mother passed on a week before that. She died after a long bout with liver disease."

"My God! I'm so sorry" said. "You lost both parents in the less than the span of a month. How do you cope?"

"We cope. Please do not grieve. My father would have loved to have heard your complimentary words on his work. He was a master craftsman in every sense. We are here to remove the last of his personal effects. It's time for us to move on. Is there something you may have left here for repairs? Or perhaps a piece my father was completing for you?"

"No, I just needed to talk with Sam about a watch he had restored for a friend of mine."

"Oh? Is the watch broken? If so, I can honor..."

"It works perfectly fine. It's just that strange..."

He stopped himself. From the look on their faces, they were anxious to make him happy, and more so, to have him on his way. And what might he tell them about the mysteries of the watch that normal people would believe?

"Never mind. It's not important. I'm sorry even mentioned this triviality in your time of bereavement. Know well that your father was a decent and honest man. His creations still bring joy to his clients. He's alive in spirit and in our minds."

"He certainly is. Thank you for your thoughts and kind words, Mr. Morello. Goodbye."

As he walked out of the shop, he noted with sadness the family pictures that Sam kept on his little work counter behind the showcases. He didn't have his contact lenses in, and he left his glasses in the Vette. What a tragedy his children and grandchildren had to live with. Just before he entered the car, he decided to go across the street and around the corner to the little diner for a cup of coffee, a glass of orange juice, and an egg and bacon sandwich. He moved from the house with such alacrity this morning that he neglected to sit for his favorite meal, and he was headachy from hunger. Even on the rare occasion when the huge *Nimitz* rolled and yawed in an Atlantic storm and many felt queasy, Danny Morello never missed a meal.

He sat on a stool. Almost immediately, a pretty red-haired waitress came by and put a place setting in front of him. She smiled at him as she held her pencil to her pad. He returned the smile, and placed his order. Another patron had just finished his last sip of coffee and left his stool and the local newspaper he was reading. Danny picked it up and began to lazily leaf through it, thinking the day that started with such purpose fizzled in a most unusual way. Then the story and accompanying photo on the fifth page jolted him to his bones. He reacted so strongly that even the man cooking his eggs became alarmed.

"Jesus!" he exploded.

"What's the matter?" the wide-eyed waitress asked.

"This story on Sam Levine, the jeweler across the street-is this today's paper?" he said, fumbling to look for the front page date.

"Yeah, of course it is. We don't know what on earth happened to him. He just vanished, about two or three days before Christmas."

"His children...what about his children?"

"Sam had children? The poor dears must be crazy with concern," the waitress said.

He regained his composure and thought of his special circumstance. "Oh, I guess I mistook him for somebody else. I've been at sea too long," he said with a laugh, trying to conceal the fact that his heart was almost pounding out of his chest. He tried to look casual as he read the paper for another moment, then said as matter-of-factly as he could, "Make those eggs and coffee to go, please." He gulped down the orange juice. "And please hurry." He tried desperately to contain himself.

He paid for his breakfast and let the pretty waitress in the tightly fitting pink uniform keep the eight dollars in change to the ten dollar bill he thrust at her.

"Thanks, sugar! And a happy New Year to you too! By the way, I get off at six, if you need company to celebrate with tonight."

He ran out of the diner and rounded the corner, never taking his eyes from the jewelry store. He literally threw the sandwich and coffee into his car, and without losing a stride made for Sam Levine's shop. It was locked. He pounded noisily on the door for at least fifteen seconds, hoping "Sam and Rachel" would answer it, but somehow he knew better.

He judged the situation to be desperate, and desperate situations called for desperate actions. He quickly looked up and down the street, and when he saw no one, he kicked the door in, fully expecting to hear an alarm, and wryly thinking how wonderful it would be to start the New Year off with a court-martial.

But there was no ringing, whistling or any type of loud noise, only a "whoosh!" of air, then silence. He hurried behind the counter and into

Sam's little work room, and noted a shelf that held a large glass jar with a label that read "Raymond Moore-Hamilton" on it. The label was yellow with age and obviously lettered with a fountain pen. Contained in it was a small box and shipping envelope, both with the return address of the Hamilton Watch Company. The jar was bulky to conceal, but he took it anyway. A repair and parts order log sat on the desk, and Danny quickly put it into his jacket. He opened a drawer and noted a journal that he also procured, thinking all the while that the Adjutant General could now add petty larceny to the breaking and entering charge.

There was nothing else to be found, except a pack of cigarettes. He didn't know why, but he took them too. He made for the door, but stopped in midstride as he saw the photographs on Sam's little work counter. He took them as well.

He scanned the street in either direction and looked across it. No one stirred. He opened and closed the door casually, then tried to re-open it. Somehow, despite the damage he had caused it, it was locked again. He was tempted to kick it in again, just to see if it would open, but he decided to leave well enough alone.

He jumped into the Corvette, and set off to Steven Amato's house, breaking the speed limit by leaps and bounds, munching on his sandwich and gulping his coffee.

He was gratified to see it was Steven who answered the door.

Without giving Steve the opportunity to greet him, without asking about his fiancé, he said, "Get your coat, Amats. We're going to Richmond."

*****

They stopped at the first phone booth they came to within Richmond's city limits. They found what they were looking for in no time and headed directly to the location they sought, having to stop only once at a service station for directions and gas. Sol Levine's jewelry store was much like his brother's in size. It was located in a fashionable part of the city, not very far from Raymond Moore's home. They went in to see an old man with a pipe clenched in his teeth, hunched over a counter very similar to the one in Sam Levine's store in Norfolk. He was working on a diamond ring.

"Mr. Levine?" Steven asked.

The old man looked up in the same way his brother had the first time they entered his store, Steven noted with a sad smile.

"Yes?"

"Are you the brother of Sam Levine, of Norfolk?" Danny asked.

He abruptly turned around. "I've told the police all I know," he said defensively. "I don't know where my brother is. We haven't talked since

Thanksgiving." He began to turn back to his work, saying "I am terribly busy, so if you'll excuse me, I'd like to ..."

"It's nothing like that, Mr. Levine," Danny said, seeing the old man turn to face them again. "We were his customers and were saddened by his disappearance. We were wondering if we might make a few inquiries about him. That's all. If the time is inconvenient, or you feel uneasy, we'll leave."

Sol Levine studied their faces. They were young, well-scrubbed and clean cut, and they seemed sincere.

"You're military men, right?"

"Yes sir. United States Navy," Danny said.

"I knew it. My brother loves you Navy men, just like my father did." He sighed loudly and clapped his hands together. "Okay, sit." He pointed them to several stools by a showcase. "What can I do for you?" he said, forcing himself to smile.

"Was your brother's wife sick very long?" Steven asked.

"What sick?" he said, frowning and jerking his head back. "She was healthy as a horse when she died."

They looked at each other confused, and Sol Levine looked at them with consternation.

"Their children. We wanted to know if...."

"What children? Where did you get the idea they had children? Gentlemen, somehow I do not find your line of questioning the least bit comforting. Where did you hear that my brother had children?"

"From this picture. Isn't this his wife and his grandchildren?" Danny asked.

Sol Levine roughly took the picture from Danny's hands as he flashed him an angry look. He raised his eyebrows as he gazed upon it, and twisted his mouth. "This is my wife and my grandchildren. My brother cherished them."

"Oh, God," Steven muttered, to an utterly confused Danny Morello.

"How did Sam's wife die?" Danny asked.

"They made a pilgrimage to Israel in June of 1967. They were on a tour bus that was strafed by a rotten son-of-a-bitch Egyptian in a Russian MiG five hours after the Six-Day War started. She was killed. My brother was never the same. He treasured his Rachel. They wanted children so much that they were going to bring an Israeli orphan home. He never got over her death. Never."

Danny did not want to ask, but because he felt his sanity was on the line he had to, even if the response did in fact push him over the edge.

"Do you have a picture of your brother and his wife?"

"Sure I do," Sol replied, relighting his pipe.

"May I see it, please? I don't want to inconvenience you, Mr. Levine, but it's important to me..."

"I would say so, as it seems you don't know who's who, and somebody is pulling your chain! Wait here. I have to go in the back."

A minute later, he reappeared. "Here," he said. "It's an old picture, taken back in 1945 the day when they were married."

Danny swallowed hard, then calmly said, "Thank you. May I keep this, please?"

"Sure. I've got one just like it at home. Shove it in the face of anyone who's telling you lies about my brother. I don't know where he is now, but he has taken the worst life had to offer. I hope he's happy."

"This is a silly question, Mr. Levine, but I need to ask it. What was your father's name?"

"Sam. He named the stores after himself. He died a young man from a heart attack. My mother's death from hepatitis is what really killed him."

Steven rubbed his face so hard he hurt his nose. He looked directly at Sol Levine as he tried to muster his courage to ask the question he felt compelled to ask. He looked over at Danny, who kept his face buried in his hands muttering "dammit" incessantly.

"Mr. Levine. Did you know a young man by the name of Raymond Moore?"

"The spoiled rich kid? Of course I did. The Moore's were best customers to my father. His mother and father were devastated when he died during the war. Just before he left, he bought a watch from me and my father, right here in this store. He said his mother and father had given him another just like the one he was buying from me, but he wrecked it. He left it in the Norfolk shop to be fixed, but it wasn't ready when he was about to leave, because my brother couldn't get the parts from the Hamilton watch company in time. My brother called me to hold one for Raymond, as we got a shipment of them in just after the holidays, early in 1942. I had to engrave it and everything. He even made me swear to not tell my father, as he and Raymond's father were very close. That Sam," he continued, shaking his head and looking off to nowhere. "Just at Thanksgiving he said he knew Raymond Moore would be back to claim his watch. He wasn't feeling all that well lately, and I wonder if he was seeing things that weren't there."

Steven and Danny looked to each other yet again with what was becoming a normal countenance-wide eyes and opened mouths. Steven snapped himself out of it.

"This is important to me, Mr. Levine. Might you remember when Raymond Moore came in here?"

"Sure. Everything about those first few months of the war was branded in our memories. It was late February of 1942, early March the latest. His ship was leaving for its first war cruise. The *Hornet* it was, brand new aircraft carrier."

Sol Levine stared out his storefront window, smiling slightly as his mind painted a picture of yesteryear. "That spoiled rich kid. He smacked up on the curb so hard with the tire of that hot rod he drove around that I'm sure he did it damage. He was always in such a rush, and he pulled into that space right out front going at least forty miles an hour. Ah, when you're rich you can always get new toys. He told me he was going to get a Lincoln Zephyr when he got home, just like the one that followed him here to take him back to his ship. I guess the Japanese didn't realize they ended that dream."

"That explains the broken motor mount and the wheel alignment", Steven said.

They looked at each other and sighed. Sol Levine looked at them in confusion, showing his irritation by yelling "What? What? Now you're talking motor mounts?"

Danny finally said, "It's really nothing, sir. Thanks for your time."

"Poor Sam. I think he's found his peace. I don't know where he is, but I just know he's happy. He would disappear for a few days at a time on the weekends and holidays. But I know, deep in my heart that now he's gone forever," Sol Levine lamented, pointing to his chest and choking with tears.

"Thanks, Mr. Levine. We'll pray for him and his peace. Happy New Year." Steven rose to shake his hands.

"You too." Sol Levine shook their hands and showed them to the door. He relit his pipe and walked back to his counter.

"Mr. Levine, just one more thing. Did your brother Sam smoke?" Danny asked.

"Ah, only when we were teenagers, back during the war. He made believe he was Gary Cooper all the time. We all wanted to be tough guys, you know, but we were both 4-F. It didn't bother me so much, but Sam was devastated. He smoked those Sweet Caporal cigarettes. They don't even make them anymore. What a character. Gary Cooper, for God's sake." Sol managed a laugh.

They got back in the Corvette, and drove back to Norfolk.

"So now we have two watches, right?" Steven said.

"Yes, we do," Danny Morello replied. "And we also have an RIO about to go mad."

"How so?" Steven asked.

"That couple in the store today used the names Sam and Rachel..."

"They probably were casing the joint to rob it. They no doubt knew Sam's story. You startled them."

"It's more than that." Danny ran his fingers through his thick blonde hair, and just sighed.

"Well? What?" Steven said impatiently.

"I'm only telling you this because you confided in me about Glenn Miller and the guys of Torpedo 8. So if I'm crazy, you are also crazy, right?"

"For Christ's sake, what?"

"Those two people in that picture were the same two people in Sam's store this morning."

"Oh, shit. Here we go again."

"No, still. Look what else I dredged up from the haunted mansion."

Danny reached into his jacket pocket and pulled out the pack of cigarettes he found in Sam's store, and threw them in Steven's lap. They were Sweet Caporals.

"I wonder where Sam Levine went on those long weekends he disappeared with Ray Moore's other watch," he said.

"Probably the same place he's at right now, with his Rachel. He forgot his Sweet Caporals, though."

*****

They stopped back at the diner where the morning had started. After ordering coffee, they went through all the articles Danny "borrowed" from Sam's parts order log. No where did they find any order for spare parts from the Hamilton watch company, at least not in the last seven months.

Steven went to the pay phone and after a lengthy series of information operators and a fortune in quarters, he got in touch with the Hamilton watch company. The spokesman said that it would be impossible to repair the watch, as parts were not even made anymore for it, and only a precision watchmaker could remanufacture them. And, he added, it would take an enormous amount of time and a workshop full of precision instruments and machine tools.

"Wait! Didn't Sol say his brother Sam ordered parts for the Hamilton, but couldn't use them because Ray Moore had long gone? And if Ray Moore somehow broke two watches, wouldn't he order the spare parts for both? You saw him break one watch, right? Maybe you found the second watch old Ray broke. And maybe back at Norfolk, he gave the second watch to Sam Levine as well to fix, figuring he'd pick it up when he returned sometime."

"Danny, let me see that jar, the one with Raymond Moore's name on it." He opened the jar, and took out the envelope and box. He shuffled both of them, and studied the postmark. "Here are your parts. Note the dates. One says February 10, 1942, the other February 28, 1942. My guess is clumsy Raymond wrecked both watches. He brought the original one to be fixed right after the *Hornet* returned from her shakedown, and when the parts hadn't arrived on time, that's when Sam called his brother Sol to see if he had the another watch to sell. That's the one that Sol sold to Raymond in late February, just before the *Hornet* left..."

"For Tokyo," Danny Morello said.

"Correct-o-mundo. But look here," Steven said, fumbling the envelope. These parts arrived in December. Why didn't Levine fix the first one then?"

"Remember Sam said Raymond was his hero? Maybe Sam decided to hang on to a piece of his hero while he went off to battle the evil yellow thugs that did the Pearl Harbor job. Hell, maybe Ray gave the watch to Sam as payment to fix the second. Maybe he decided to not even pick it up, or forgot to pick it up. Who knows? In any event, figuring he'd catch hell from his papa, Ray thought he'd better pick up another one before he went home to park the Ford in his garage and say goodbye. He was probably followed by one of Gus Widhelm's boys in Gus's Lincoln Zephyr. Maybe he called Sam and told him to reorder the watch parts again. That's why he had them on hand when I brought my watch, or Raymond's second watch, to be fixed."

"You're probably more right than wrong. Look at this journal entry dated December 20, 1984. If you want to pass out, let me know and I'll catch you before you hit your head on the table."

Lieutenant Raymond Moore finally picked up his watch today. I had previously presented him with a brand new Breitling Chronometer in fair exchange for the Hamilton he gave to me so many years ago. Now I can go on with my Rachel. My work here is done at last.

After a long hesitation, Danny Morello cast his blank stare away from the window to his best friend. "Why us?" he asked.

"No offense, but I think you're the potatoes here, not the meat. You're involved because of me. Why did he think I'm Ray Moore? That's the question."

"I think it's obvious. You had the watch. All your life, you've been mystified by days gone by; your Academy thesis, your record collection, your association with Whitney and his band of merry men, all of it. Maybe you're Ray Moore's 1985 incarnation. Somebody is trying to tell you something, maybe trying to answer a question for you. And, amigo, if he is going to tell you, I'm going to make sure he'll have no choice but to tell me too, because, my friend, I'm going to be on you like stink on shit." He reached out and playfully smacked Steven's head. He reflected a moment, and blurted out, "I just wish my grandma was still around to give me one of her Sicilian good luck charms."

*****

Julie Ann Tate was at her desk at the Washington Post earlier than usual. She had a date to bring in the New Year with Steve and his squadron mates tonight and had to leave earlier than usual to make the trip to Susan and Steven's house in Norfolk, with enough time to spare to make herself absolutely breathtaking. She wanted to literally knock his socks off tonight, and as a boxer who had an opponent against the ropes, she wanted to put him away. She had shopped all day yesterday for the perfect black cocktail dress to help her provide the knockout punch. It cost a small fortune, but she knew it would work miracles, because even the department store saleswoman hustled her back into the dressing room after an ogler took a right, rather than a left, and fell ass over heels down the escalator. She sought out the military affairs editor as soon as she settled in her desk and logged on her computer.

Marcus White was a well-built man of forty years who stood a shade under six feet, with a full head of blond and gray hair that he wore a bit longer than would be considered fashionable for a man his age. He had piercing blue eyes and a fair, but roughhewn complexion. Marcus had written several widely read and highly regarded books on military history and weapons, and the relationship of geopolitics to military philosophy and doctrine. Coupled with a good sense of the stock market, he had made a substantial sum of money. His lifestyle demonstrated his wealth. He drove a Jaguar XK-6 from his exquisite Georgetown townhouse to work. He was always impeccably dressed, be it in a tuxedo or "on the job" in battle fatigues. He smoked an occasional pipe, cigarette or cigar, depending on the circumstance, the company or the mood he happened to be in.

Educated at the University of Chicago, Marcus had spent three years in the United States Army as a paratrooper and had done a tour of duty in Vietnam, where he was promoted to the rank of Captain and was awarded the Silver Star and the Purple Heart. He might be considered a "lady's man", but never married. He spent his nights and weekends with wealthy women, and as his job involved a good deal of travel to the far flung bases of American military might, Marcus knew women everywhere. His good looks and panache made him an attractive companion for dinner or the bedroom. Marcus loved Julie Tate, but only as an older brother loved a sister. He looked out for her, and even used his connections to get her interviews for her investigative pieces.

"Good morning Marcus. How's it hangin'?" she asked with a smile.

"Well, if it isn't the fabulous Julie Ann! It hangs well, dear girl. What brings you down to the land of olive drab?" he said, rising to kiss the cheek and shake the hand she offered.

"I need help with something, Marcus. I'm seeing a Navy flyer, and..."

"Dear God! Not a Navy man! And a pilot? Double dear God! Leave him now, Julie. He'll only break your heart. Those guys are totally nuts. Have you..."

"Save it. It's way beyond that. I'm gonna marry that sucker, Marcus. He knows it, too. I've put plenty of sweat into that man, and his sweet hard ass is mine."

"I love to hear a woman talk like that. It makes my nipples hard. That's why I took a liking to you, Tate."

"Very funny, White, very funny" she laughed.

"You said you needed my help. What can I do for you?"

"What United States Navy aircraft carrier has a number eight?" she asked.

"Number eight?" he said, a quizzical look on his face. "Considering they number way up into the seventies now, it must be a very old ship. Where did you see it?"

"In an old scrap book a friend of my boyfriend has. I'm going to a party tonight with his pals, and I don't want to stand out like a nerd. I figure if the book comes out again, I can provide some interesting footnotes."

He knew she was lying, but he figured she had good reason, and judging from the look on her face, she wasn't trying to hide the fact that she was being less than truthful. They were good enough friends and true news professionals to understand that sometimes it was better to lie than to tell the truth. It saved time in answering questions whose answers hadn't been fully documented, and dismissed immediate doubts to gain a higher purpose.

"Well, let's get out the Jane's Fighting Ships, and find out. A flattop with the number 8 had to be a World War II type. The *Coral Sea* is CV-43, and although she was completed just after the war ended, she's still in service." He fumbled with the index, and said, "Here we are! I've got a page and number reference." He picked up another volume and opened it up. He found the page he was looking for, and turned the book for Julie to see several photographs. "Is this your ship?" he asked with a smile.

"That's it, Marcus. You're a genius!"

"Nah. I just paid attention during English class in high school. I get a lot of broads by being able to look things up for them."

"Oh, you are something."

"You bet your baby blues I am. Let's read about your ship. It's called the USS *Hornet*. She's a *Yorktown* class carrier, meaning she was built with the same basic plan as the *Yorktown* and the *Enterprise*. They were sister ships. She was commissioned in late 1941, so we were right in assuming World War II vintage. It says here that she was delayed because her reduction gearing and boiler tubes needed to be replaced. Shit, even then they made boo-boos on major weapons systems. And cost overruns. The *Yorktown* cost only twenty one mil to build. The *Hornet*, last of the class, cost over thirty one mil three years later! Hah! And during a depression! Hah again! At least there's a precedent to the shit the Pentagon puts up with today!"

"Sounds like I just gave you a premise to put you on to another interesting piece," Julie Ann said.

"Where? Where?" he said, jumping to his feet, his head quickly moving from side to side.

"Read on Marcus," she said pushing him by the shoulder back into his seat.

"Sorry, Tate. You had my hopes up."

"Yeah, yeah. Go on," she said pointing to the book and shaking her head in exaggerated dismay.

"*Hornet* had a crew of 2,072. She was 809 feet long and 84 feet wide, and weighed in at 19,900 tons though she was probably heavier. Navies used to lie about tonnage to fool the enemy into thinking their ships were less capable than they actually were. It goes back to the Washington Naval Treaty, where all the big powers got together to limit the size of their navies in the hopes of preserving peace. It was sort of like the SALT talks today. I bet the *Hornet* was every bit of 30,000 tons. Considering the *Nimitz* weighs in at almost 100,000 tons, she was a peanut by today's standards. But in its day the *Hornet* was a potent ship. It says here she could carry over a hundred aircraft."

"She carried Doolittle's bombers on the Tokyo raid. She fought at Midway."

"Interesting. Where's the *Hornet* now?" she asked matter-of-factly.

"I think I know, but I should check the reference index." He punched in some numbers on his computer, and his screen gave him another reference text to check on.

"Are we off to the morgue or the library?" she asked.

"No need. It's right here."

Marcus White was the best in the business. He lived and felt great battles and events, and knew the blood and sweat of battle personally. To him, the machines of war were extensions of governmental philosophies and societal values, and to understand them was to understand the circumstances under which they were created and the men who wielded them in battle, be they the short swords of the Roman legionnaires or the cruise missile.

"World War II was the first instance where aircraft carriers were employed, so tactics and strategy were new and untried. Carriers operate in task forces. I know for a fact that the *Yorktown* was sunk during the Battle of Midway, where she operated with her two sisters. Now that was one of history's all time decisive battles. A lot hung on that one, I tell you. That one, and Guadalcanal. Ah, here we are." Marcus quickly read a few pages of texts, and frowned.

"Well, Marcus. Where is the *Hornet*?" she asked, playfully poking him in the ribs with an index finger. "It couldn't have gone to the breakers, because I..."

He didn't look up, but pursed his lips and shook his head. "I thought so, but I had to check to be sure about the date, not the event. You're right, Tate. It didn't go to the breakers, because it's on the bottom of the Pacific Ocean. The Japanese hit her with a rash of bombs and torpedoes dropped by aircraft from their carriers, the *Shokaku and Zuilkaku*. She was sunk during the Guadalcanal campaign on October 26, 1942 during an engagement known as the Battle of Santa Cruz."

"That can't be!" she gasped.

"It sure as hell can be. It's right here. Look for yourself," he said, turning the text for her to read. "The Santa Cruz Islands are just south and east of Guadalcanal. See?" He was perplexed as to the depth of her shock. He had never quite seen her this way before. "What gives with you and this ship?"

She tried to ignore him and maintain the line of questioning, but she knew she couldn't suppress her surprise. Not to Marcus. He knew her too well.

"Marcus. What does the designation VT-8 mean?"

"It complements with your *Hornet* inquiry," he began. "When the Navy had torpedo squadrons flying from aircraft carriers, the T in the designation meant torpedo squadron. The designations for all Navy squadrons start with the letter V. The V meant heavier than air.

I know it sounds silly today, but you have to remember the Navy had dirigibles back when naval aviation was new, and they thought the V would help to avoid confusion. An 'F' after the V indicated a fighter squadron. An 'S' after the V indicated a scout bomber squadron, while the B indicated a bombing squadron. Early on, before the war when carriers were relatively new weapons, it was thought that fighter, torpedo, and bomber squadrons assigned to a carrier would have the carrier's number. Therefore, VT-8 was *Hornet's* torpedo squadron." He saw her face continue its contortions, and that her body shifted nervously. "Why is this so tough on you?"

"Is there a VT-8 now? My boyfriend is with VF-41, so I know they use the fighter designation. He flies Tomcats. Does the Navy use torpedo planes now?"

He could see she wouldn't answer him. No problem. She's tough, and she knows where to find me if she needs me. "No. They were even obsolete way back during the war, but nobody wanted to admit it. Shit, they were sitting ducks when they attacked capital ships at sea. They had to go low and slow to aim their torpedoes, and were easy prey for ships' antiaircraft fire, and attacking fighters. Genda, the brilliant Japanese who planned the Pearl Harbor strike, decided that if the Japanese would launch a third wave, he would scratch torpedo planes, as the second wave reported that antiaircraft fire was already heavy, and Genda knew torpedo planes would be clay pigeons in the confines of the harbor. When they took part in the first wave of the raid under conditions of complete surprise, they really kicked ass."

Marcus's face lit up. "As a matter of fact, I remember reading an excellent article a few years back in the Naval Institute's journal *Proceedings* about VT-8 at Midway. It was written by a midshipman for his senior thesis. The kid's premise was that the torpedo squadrons at Midway were purposely sacrificed to clear the way for the dive bombers, the most effective weapons to do in the Japanese fleet. I've got it here somewhere," he said getting up to reaching high on his bookcase. "Here it is. It's brilliant work. Why don't you borrow it for a while? You'll wow that Navy faggot I still say you should dump before he breaks your heart."

"Not a chance, Marcus," she said as she took the magazine. "Thanks." She got up to leave.

He saw confusion on her face, but knew better than to press it. He still loved her and was concerned about her. "Hey, Tate. I know it's none of my business, and I know you're a tough bitch. But remember, I'm right down the hall if you need me."

She went behind the desk and hugged and kissed him. "I may take you up on that. Thanks, sweetie. Happy New Year. I hope you get laid tonight."

"Count on it," he said quite naturally, not hesitating as he took a yellow pad out of his desk, lowered his reading glasses, picked up a phone and punched in a number.

She now had some ideas as to why Steven had been so evasive. How could he ask her to share or confirm something as weird as this? One way or the other, she was determined to get to the bottom of this and stand by him.

Back at her own desk, Julie raised a cup of coffee to her lips as she opened the magazine to the story of VT-8. She choked and spit out a mouthful all over her desk when she saw the author's name.

Chapter 18

He awoke with his arm around her early on New Year's Day. She hadn't stirred as yet, and he was careful to let her peaceful, silent sleep continue as he moved from the bed and into a chair, just to look at her. She was absolutely the most beautiful and wonderful woman he could ever hope to have. When she walked down the stairs from Susan's bedroom last night with that black dress on, his knees wobbled and his head became feverish. She did it all for him, and the more he thought about it, and the closer to her he danced, the more he kissed and touched and made love with her, the more he couldn't believe what an absolute asshole he was for making her work so damned hard to get him, someone she should have cast in the gutter three years ago. Rena Amato, God bless you, he thought silently.

This wasn't lust. He knew lust. He had great lust with Miss Naples. It wasn't infatuation, either. He knew that, too. This girl did everything he asked, and was great fun to be with. She made great conversation, either talking about her job, or the jobs of the people with whom she mingled. She was gracious, always offering to help. She even argued football with Reuter last night. She was a pal, besides being a knockout to look at, and absolutely brilliant to talk to. Could she cook? He mused. Hell, we'll eat out.

He looked at her finger on her left hand that wore his Annapolis class ring, taped to fit tightly. Next week, he'd visit a jeweler and buy her a real engagement ring for sure, although just the word "jeweler" caused him trepidation.

She opened her eyes and smiled at him. "Hi there, sailor."

"Hi there Miss Georgia," he replied, moving to her outstretched arms.

"You did something strange last night, sailor."

"What was that, Miss Georgia?"

"You asked me to marry you, and you gave me this ring as a sign of your good intentions. 'On my honor as a midshipmen and an officer in the United States Navy,' you said, if I remember correctly. Do you still want me to keep this ring?"

"Only for a little while."

"Why? Just so you can have your way with me again?"

"No. I plan on having my way with you with or without the ring."

"Oh, is that so? Well, I don't sleep around with everybody that has a fancy blue suit with gold wings on it."

"I noticed. Are, uh... you okay, by the way?"

"I'm fine. I enjoyed it."

"Good, because I've been told that I'm pretty good at this stuff, so you don't have to shop around and compare."

"But how do I know I'm good at it?" she asked.

"You have my word."

"Well, I guess I will keep my word and marry you, then. It'll break a lot of hearts, but fuck 'em," she giggled.

"Yeah, fuck 'em," he laughed. "And because of that, I'm going to buy you a diamond ring that will knock people's eyes out from its brilliance."

"I think you had better ask my dad's permission first."

"I did, when we visited on Christmas Day."

She sat up in amazement, quickly grabbing the falling sheets to keep a modicum of privacy. "You knew then you would ask me?"

"Yup. You gave me no choice. I fell in love with you Christmas Eve. Or maybe it was back on the beach a few years ago. I dunno. What I do know is that you make me very happy, Miss Georgia."

"And you make me very happy, sailor".

She hugged him and he squeezed her tightly.

"And know that I'm right here besides you, no matter what. Just let me know when you want me to help."

He pushed her away slightly, and smiled, still holding her slim arms. "You know something's up, don't you?"

"Yes, I do. When we saw all those old planes, old cars, and old buildings, and the look on your face when you talked to all those pilots clustered around the Avenger-it was more than a show. I've read stories of people seeing things together, like that couple Betty and Barney in New Hampshire that swore they were captured by aliens from a UFO. Their story never wavered, even under hypnosis. Maybe there's something to that, or maybe we're both nuts. I don't know. Anyway, I've always wanted a mystery man."

"But there is so much more to this than that one episode." He had to explain the Glenn Miller band in New York to her, and the full story of his encounter with Richard Moore senior and the Ford convertible that started it all a few years ago. "It's all very weird," Steven said with a sigh.

"I know that. Just let me know when I can help. And no matter what, I'll trust you, and I'll always love you."

"And I'll always cherish you."

"And promise me you won't put me on, like telling me my camera's broken. You can't lie to me, even to protect me. I'm a newspaperwoman, and we like pain. We're funny that way. It makes us think the story is better if we bleed a little."

He realized he was getting more than a wife. He was getting a new best friend in the deal too.

"Then you know the ship we saw was the *Hornet*, not the *Guam*. You also know the *Hornet* was sunk during the war."

"At Santa Cruz. I told you I'm a newspaperwoman, you ditz! You can't lie to me!" she yelled, hitting him with a pillow.

He tackled her down, and made love to her again.

That ring will be a knockout, Julie Ann, he thought. He hoped his sister and Danny had this same thing going. It was great. He never, ever felt so...uplifted.

Chapter 19

Danny, Steven and Vincent Capo had become close friends, working tirelessly on getting the new Tomcat's air-to-ground electronics and configuration to work flawlessly. The hours of flying, modifying, flying again, and modifying again had brought the three of them from a collegial and professional relationship to one of true friendship. Steven had invited Vincent and his wife Donna to his and Julie's engagement party, and the three couples spent a good deal of social time together. Danny also added the Capo's to his and Susan's wedding list. Their wedding was planned for late July, while Steven and Julie planned a late August wedding, just to give Rena and Paul Amato a chance to breathe. Spring was vigorously making the warmth of its presence felt on this last day of March of 1985. Bulbs that lay in suspended animation for months had sprouted beautiful tulips and crocus. The cherry blossoms had erupted. Robins abounded, and everything was greener.

"I think the next step is to take this bird to China Lake and conduct some tests over the open desert. Then maybe we should put it up against the new F/A-18 and the Intruder, just to see how accurately it can put its ordnance on target," Steven said. "The second Tomcat that Reuter's flying gives us redundancy and the case for the systems reliability."

"I'd have to agree. I need data to complete the manual Danny and I are working on for the air-to-ground configuration. It will have to be pretty good stuff if we have any chance at all for the Navy to accept our work," Vince Capo added. "There's a powerful lobby out there who doesn't want the Tomcat carrying bombs. They know the best fighters in history were superb ground attack machines, and there isn't anything flying better than the Tomcat. If it works well in the air-to-ground role, not only will it save money for the taxpayer, it will also mean a lot more Tomcats and more modification work for Grumman. The other defense contractors will really hate that shit, I tell you."

"It's quite a world, isn't it?" Danny added.

"It certainly is. What do you say we get a few beers?"

"Here, here", Steven added.

As they downed Molson ale, Steven had come up with an idea that he thought might put to an end any disagreement regarding the merits of the proposed F-14 fighter-bomber.

"What do you say we ask the Navy to set up a mission profile, over land and water, in weather of their choosing to truly test your system's capability, Vince? You know, we'll use real ordnance, and attack a series of targets. Roto Reuter could fly one ship with his RIO, and I'll fly the other with Danny here. Roto is just as skilled as we are, and he believes in the mission. He's a top pilot, the best...except for me, of course."

"Of course," Vincent Capo added with a laugh.

The next day, the three of them accompanied by Roto Reuter and his RIO, Lieutenant (JG) John Donnelly, saw his squadron commander, Lieutenant Commander Paul Riley, whose intense interest in the project made the expedition of red tape all the easier. Riley had championed them from the start and had been pleased with its development. He listened intently to their pitch.

"I think you're on to something. Your right, the first thing you should do is test the stuff out at China Lake with the attack community watching and participating. You'll need to gain their support for this. Remember they love their Hornets and Intruders and Corsairs, so don't expect them to readily embrace this concept. In fact, look for them to try to tear it down. However, if you sell them, you've overcome a huge obstacle. Setting up the mission profile to get the Pentagon to buy this will be all the easier then. Is every detail in a row for this?"

"We're ready to go, skipper," Amato said.

"Okay! I'll call the fighter guys at Miramar and let them know what we're up to. Then I'll call out to China Lake and talk to a few friends in the attack community. Maybe I can call in a few chits and get this thing rolling. A few of those guys owe me big time from our Vietnam days. See me tomorrow, and be prepared to fly out there at a moment's notice."

As the men filed out to leave, Riley said. "Amats. How're you doing?"

"I'm fine, sir. Thank you," he said with a smile.

"You still interested in taking on the Admiral? He's bragging around the fleet that he could kick the living shit out of you, and you wussed out when he came to your quarters on the *Nimitz* ready to knock the snot out of you. Interested in a match?"

"No sir. I'm not," he laughed. "And thank you for your help."

"It wasn't help, Amats. Think of it as support. By the way, I hear you're engaged to a Playboy bunny. Is that true?" Riley said, leaning against his chair.

"Were you talking to Reuter?"

"He and your RIO say she's a real knockout, a heart-breaker for sure. They keep talking about this black dress she wore on New Year's Eve that stopped men's hearts and turned women's minds to evil thoughts."

"She's a reporter for the Washington Post. My mother and sister set me up with her. She was in my sister's sorority. Do you think they'd set me up with a Playboy bunny, especially after the Italian Incident?"

"You've made yourself a legend with that, Amats."

"I know that. So does my mom, and my sister. And Julie Ann isn't letting me forget it either. That's her name. Julie Ann Tate. I call her Miss Georgia sometimes. That's where she's from originally. And you were right about our engagement. We're going to be married at the end of the summer. You'll get the invitation in the mail, sir. And yes, that black dress was..., well, it just was," he said, shaking his head, and his eyes focusing on a picture his mind retrieved.

"Way to be, Amats. Good luck!"

"Thanks, sir."

Riley felt good about Amato's recovery from Thatcher's death. He saw him working and flying hard, putting the past in perspective, thinking about the future, and interested in making a contribution to the squadron and the fleet. And he was willing to take a chance against the establishment, something that Riley especially liked about him.

Riley was waiting for them the next morning in the squadron ready room. His eyes betrayed an eagerness to do battle.

"What's up, skipper?" Steven asked.

"You're on for China Lake. They'll be bringing the fighter guys from Miramar out to see you, so that is one less stop you have to make. The attack community is bonkers, by the way. And you can count on a surprise evaluation mission to perform as well. My guys at Miramar tell me that congressmen have been calling the Pentagon incessantly since I made my pitch yesterday. Obviously, we've ruffled a few feathers. I sure as hell hope your stuff is ready, Amats. If not, I'm going to look like a horse's ass."

"We're ready, skipper," Danny said assuredly. "When do we go?"

"How about 1400 today? The test is scheduled for 0800 on 3 April."

"That's the day after tomorrow!"

"Very good, Morello. You get an A in calendar."

"Let's get Vince Capo and go over..."

Riley cut him off. "Capo is on his way to the Lake as we speak. The Grumman guys picked him up an hour ago, and headed out there in a corporate jet."

"This is big, isn't it?" Danny offered.

"When you consider that billions of dollars in contracts may ride on this little innovation of yours, people have a tendency to get a little bit competitive and short-fused. Okay, enough bullshit," Riley said abruptly. "Go take care of your last minute details. Call your moms and girlfriends and tell them not to hold dinner. I'll leave word for Reuter to see me."

Danny dropped Steven off before proceeding to his own house to pack. Steven stuffed a few uniforms and some casual clothes in a garment bag, and his toilet articles and clean underwear in a satchel. He opened the top draw of his dresser for some socks, and saw the Hamilton Chronometer staring back at him. He hadn't wore it for a few months, purposely avoiding it, despite Julie's insistence that he do put it on, so something "really neat" might happen to them. He declined, courteously.

He didn't want to leave it here unattended for a long period of time, where some poor unsuspecting soul with a fervent imagination or checkered past might come upon it. What if an anachronism like himself somehow found it in his or her possession? What if it were stolen? What if Julie and Susan decided to play with it? The damn thing was akin to a drug like LSD that provided the user with fantasy...or reality, whichever label he or she decided upon to define the experience.

He started to go through the whole scenario of experiences again, looking for a solution, an answer, a closure, all which eluded him. Maybe it wasn't the watch at all, he thought. Perhaps he and Julie had some sort of psychotic or schizoid tendency, that grew geometrically when they were together. Maybe Danny became entangled in this bizarre web he weaved to cope and understand Thatcher's seemingly needless death, trying to give his sacrifice some meaning in using a past set of values. Was Danny initially right about that, that the watch was an excuse to go off to Serendipityville? Or perhaps they were all Barneys and Bettys, and rather than UFOs, they met their dreams, or answered long standing questions, or got involved in the dreams of others through the circumstances the Ford and the watch had brought about. Strangely , since the watch had stayed in the drawer, nothing had happened to anyone.

Maybe, maybe, maybe...if, if, if...perhaps, strange, eerie, odd, bizarre, creepy; he had literally had it with all these words.

Take the goddam watch, he concluded to himself, as he stuffed it in his garment bag. Mystical or not, shit happened to people when they were around it, and he didn't want to leave anything to chance. Anyway, he reasoned, there was no event he had a deep interest in that happened in March during the war years. Midway occurred in June, over two months from now, and though the temptation to take some leave and fly to Midway wearing the Hamilton on June 4, 1985 had sorely tempted him, he thought better of it. The temptation was getting stronger, though, with each successive day, but he was determined to fight it, even if it meant giving up the watch to the Chesapeake one morning while he fished for striped bass. He had Julie, and was having a grand time living in today. He didn't need yesterday any more. The question he asked of himself constantly, reiterated by Julie when he spoke about it, was if yesterday somehow needed him. Was there something back there for him to see to make him whole? Did someone need him to understand something?

He glanced at the top of his dresser to see the picture he had taken with Thatcher and "John C" the day they made their first landing and launch "onna ships." He kept the original in his wallet, but had the negative used to make the enlargement that stood on his dresser. Thatch was so very much alive. He wished he could have introduced him to Julie. He noted his eyes were misting over, and the heat of revenge to kill a few fucking Libyan murderers began to overtake him again. He fought it off.

He called Julie to tell her he would be leaving for a while, and that this weekend's plans were to be put on hold. A fellow reporter by the name of Marcus White, with whom Julie was working on a story, said she was out to lunch, but would leave her the message. He had met White last weekend, and came to really like him, and he felt comfortable in thinking the feeling was mutual on Marcus's part.

"I saw the ring you gave her, Amato. Pretty nice. It must have set you back plenty."

"My reenlistment bonus is going right to the jeweler," he said with a laugh. But she's worth every penny of it."

"I heartily agree. You'll like the piece we're working on together, Steve. It should be done by your wedding. Julie won't let me rest a moment. It's quite a project."

"So I've been told. She won't let out a single detail, though."

"A good reporter never reveals sources or progress on a story. As a matter of fact, there's some stuff in it she isn't even telling me. She's left me nothing but speculation. Damn, she's sickeningly good!"

"That's my girl!"

"That she is. Do you know she still wears that Annapolis class ring on her middle finger, like a high school kid?"

"Yeah. No matter how I beg, she won't give it back to me. And I love that ring!" he said, glancing at his Breitling. "Jeez! Look at the time. Listen, Marcus. I gotta go fly. Tell her I miss her, and I'll call her tonight."

"Be careful, Admiral."

"Roger that. Good bye."

He looked at the picture he took of her on New Year's Eve, posed so seductively in that black cocktail dress. And the picture Susan took of them embracing, her left hand displaying the ring, with her cheek against his chin. She felt so nice to hold, he thought, as he felt his legs go weak. He kissed the photos and smiled.

His thoughts were interrupted by Danny's beeping horn. As he ran out of the house, luggage in hand, Rena and Paul Amato were coming in with arms full of groceries.

"Ah, you're home and ... you're leaving. Where are you off to in such a rush?" Paul asked.

"I'm gonna fly an airpanes onna ships," he said kissing them both.

"Why?" his mother asked, realizing the obvious faux pas she made when he raised his eyebrows.

"It's what the Navy pays me for, ma. Remember?"

"When will you be home, mister wise guy?" she asked.

"Hopefully in time for my wedding, but more likely in a week to ten days. I'll call and let you know what's happening. See you." He kissed and hugged them both.

At precisely 1400 hours, Lieutenants Steven Amato and Todd Reuter pushed their throttles forward and released their brakes. The F-14 with the name *JAWN* on its nose and *Flying Ronzonis* under its cockpit, lifted gently into the warm spring air, immediately to the right of the F-14 with the name ROTO emblazoned under its cockpit. The planes headed west by northwest, flying a little under Mach 1 to avoid sonic booms on the earth below as they climbed to 50,000 feet to put them way above the airline traffic.

At altitude, Danny turned on the weapons system and called over to John Donnelly in Reuter's Tomcat.

"Hey, John. Have you powered up your system yet?"

"I'm doing it now. Are you tracking?"

"It's unbelievable. The damn thing is already asking me for weapons choices. It's engaged each target we programmed in so far. I just blew up the Sears Tower in Chicago with a SRAM."

"Hey! That was mine! No fair!"

"Okay, okay, you big baby. I'll let you blow up Wrigley Field. You locked on?"

"Firing!" Donnelly said. A minute later, he came on again. "It looks like the Cubbies will be playing all their games away for the rest of the year."

"Nice shooting."

"Little boys, little toys. Big boys, big toys", Steven said, just loud enough to be heard.

"And what do you call what you're doing up there, mister hot shot jet pilot."

"Leave my mother out of this," he said with a laugh.

About three hours later and an aerial refueling over Kansas, they received landing instructions from the tower at the China Lake Naval Weapons Test Facility. Situated just south of the Death Valley National Monument, China Lake was composed of two huge tracts of land in northeastern California. The Navy was constantly blowing the hell out of the desert as it perfected ordnance, ordnance delivery tactics, and hardware/software for its ships and aircraft. To the attack squadrons, China Lake was elevated to the same kind of Mecca status Miramar Naval

Air Station enjoyed with the fighter squadrons, so just seeing an F-14 put its wheels on the runway was considered a sacrilege of immense consequence. While the F/A-18 Hornet was considered a fighter, the A in its designation and its dual fighter/attack mission planned from the first blueprints, provided it a full pardon. However, there were A-6 Intruder drivers that thought even that was stretching the rules too far to qualify for clemency. The die-hards thought that if it carried a cannon, or if it carried any kind of air-to-air ordnance, it was a fighter. The A-7 Corsair guys were a little more lenient, in that the latest modification to their mounts provided the capability to fire a Sidewinder air-to-air missile, so they forgave the F/A-18. The fact that the F/A-18 was to replace their aging Corsairs probably had a lot to do with their emollient attitude.

Needless to say, no one rushed to the F-14s as they parked on the ramp. Even the ground crew, though militarily courteous, were minimally helpful. After they stored their gear, and were given billets by a chief petty officer who snarled at them, they decided to grab a meal at the base's officers' club. The ambiance was akin to the inside of a refrigerator. No one, except the enlisted men who served them, talked to them, even though the club was full.

"I sense an edge," Reuter remarked. "I think they know why we're here."

"Why do I feel like the world's a tuxedo and I'm a pair of brown shoes?" Donnelly said.

"Oh, I thought it was my basic ugly duckling insecurity," Danny said. "I feel so much better now." He turned to Steven and said, "Can we go home now?"

"What, and let these pricks take Riley and Capo out in the desert without any water and leave them there? No fucking way!" he said with a laugh. "And besides, I'm kind of enjoying this, as a matter of fact! I'll get us a round of beers."

"Uh-oh. Here we go," Danny said, putting napkin to his mouth.

"Here we go where?" Reuter asked, his senses telling him he should become somewhat alarmed, as Steven went up to the bar, and literally muscled his way to the rail.

"It's that look in his eye. I've seen it three times before. Once, we were still in high school and he hit a home run off of me after a brushback pitch I threw at him. The second time, we were playing Army in our senior year when a middle linebacker cheap shotted him long after the whistle blew. He came back to the huddle and demanded that I give him the ball on the next play, forcing me to call a time out. He glared at the coach until he got his way. He whacked that backer so hard, running right over his chest, that it took three minutes to get him to come back from Queersville. The third time was on the *Nimitz* last December. You remember that one, don't you? I believe you were on the living pile trying to hold him down, were you not?"

"Oh, shit," Reuter said, getting ready to rise.

"Eloquently put," Danny said. Donnelly sat back, as if he were watching a show.

"Don't get too comfortable, Donnelly. You may go from audience to cast in a flash. I believe the bartender is ignoring him, based upon the shit-eating grin on that lieutenant in the corner stool. Yes folks, get ready. It's almost showtime."

"Barkeep. We need a few beers here," they heard Steven say.

"I'm sorry sir. We seem to be out of beers," came the reply, accompanied by a smirk.

"Now how can that be, barkeep? I just saw you open the fridge and there had to be at least a case of Molson in there."

"You must be mistaken, sir. There isn't any more beer."

"I could have sworn that ...."

"You heard the man. There isn't any more beer," the Lieutenant said, rising and moving to Steven.

"Begging your pardon, but I believe you're mistaken as well."

"Trust me. I think you had better leave."

"I'm a guest here. And the least you could do is look in that fridge for me, officer and gentleman to officer and gentleman."

"I haven't got the time," the Lieutenant said, inching towards Steven's face.

"Oh, sure you do. It will only take a second."

With that, almost without his hand motion being seen, he lifted the man by his neck and jaw with his right hand, grabbed his crotch with his left hand, and threw him over the bar and into the bartender behind it. They both tumbled to the floor.

"Look again for me. Please?"

The lieutenant looked up at him, holding his back and grimacing with pain. His eyes opened slightly when he saw the glare in Steven's eyes. Pushing the bartender out of the way, he opened the refrigerator and pulled out a Molson.

"I need four Molsons, please," Steven said in a calm voice.

The lieutenant struggled to his feet, holding two beer bottles in each hand. He offered them to Steven, his jaw muscles pulsating to the grinding of his teeth.

"Thank you. I knew you could be helpful. By the way, what are you drinking? I'd like to buy you a round on me. I still think that we're on the same side."

"No thanks", the Lieutenant replied. "I gotta be going."
"Very well, then. Good night."

*****

"Amato, tell me it isn't so," Riley asked.
"Sir?"
"That you launched a guy in the O club last night. The word is that a former Annapolis football player and present day F-14 driver put a member of the attack community on the wrong side of the bar."
"It isn't so, sir," Amato replied.
"It isn't, huh?"
"No sir," Amato said with resolve. Then he tilted his head, closed his eyes slightly and brought up an index finger, as if trying very hard to put some explanation to the question Riley obviously wanted an answer to. "Unless, of course, you're referring to that unfortunate incident last evening when a fellow in the O club fell over the bar as he courteously looked to see if there was any beer left in the fridge. Poor guy took quite a spill. He even knocked the bartender down in the fall. I offered to buy him a round for all his trouble, but he declined."
"Oh," Riley replied, nodding his head. "It's amazing how these stories get taken all out of sorts when you get them second hand," Riley said.
"Isn't that the truth?"
"It better suffice to be. You're due at a briefing with the fighter and attack guys regarding your new toy."

As might be expected, the fighter guys were enthusiastic but the attack guys were not. They were, in fact, openly hostile. It was decided that the F-14s would be equipped with an array of weaponry to test the modified planes' ability to hit a variety of targets, inclusive of the Tomahawk cruise missile, the Short Range Attack Missile, the Maverick air to surface missile, and the Harpoon anti-ship missile, as well as an array of laser guided bombs, "smart" bombs and "dumb" bombs. The test was to be held the day after tomorrow, April 2. The pilots and RIOs spent the rest of the day with Vince Capo and a team of engineers from Grumman calibrating and testing their equipment. Only after an admiral pledged full cooperation did the ground crews and maintenance officers come around to service their planes.

As the evening rolled in, Steven managed to get hold of Julie on the phone.
"Where have you been? I've gotten nothing but your answering machine."
"Oh, Steve, I'm sorry. The research for this story has me zipping all over the place at all hours. I really miss you. Even hearing your voice on my answering machine makes me cry. How are you doing?"

"I'm getting by but I'm missing you too. Believe me, I'd rather be there with you than here. You would think we took a wrong turn and landed in the Soviet Union, what with all the hostility we're enduring. These jackasses don't want to realize we're all on the same side. Hell, I can understand some hostility between the services, but in the same service? I don't know. This isn't the way I planned it to be when I was at the Academy."

"Now, now. Don't get pouty. Just do the best you can. You can't make everybody happy," Julie said, trying to comfort him.

"Anyway, we're going to test the stuff tomorrow. Wish me luck."

"Good luck. How's Danny boy making out?"

"You can tell Susan he's fine and dandy. You can't believe how hot is here. But I also have to say that the sunsets and sunrises are breathtaking. And Julie, you should see the stars at night. The sky is absolutely painted with them."

"It must be beautiful."

"Yeah, it really is. Look, sweetheart, I've got to go. I've got to run a few more checks on the jet, and I want to turn in early. Tomorrow will be a busy day."

"Before you go, an old friend wanted me to say hello to you, and to wish you luck on your mission. He told me you'd run into a storm with this idea."

"Who is it?" he asked.

"Mr. Whitney. He's flying again. His hip is pretty well healed from the surgery. He's as spry as ever."

"That's great, Julie!" He was genuinely happy for him. The last time he had seen Whitney was right after he had been discharged from the Johns Hopkins Medical Center. He walked with difficulty, and relied on a cane.

"Not so fast, sailor. He's still a flirt. He told me to dump you and go dancing with him tonight. Can you believe it?"

"I think that whole generation is the horniest ever. Remember Miss Georgia, you belong to me." A thought suddenly occurred to him. "Why were you hanging around with Whitney anyway?" he asked.

"Jealous?" she said coyly, using her southern accent to really drive home the word.

"Yes, and curious."

"You'll see, sugar."

"I'd better get going. I miss you and love you."

"Same here, except I love you more."

"Don't start that, Julie. You know I love you more."

"Yes, but I loved you longer, so that means I love you more."

"Okay, you win," he laughed. "I'll see you soon."

"That's a roger," she giggled.
"Goodnight, Miss Georgia."
"Goodnight, sailor."

As he walked back to *Jawn* he suddenly realized what Julie had said about Whitney wishing him good luck in his mission, but that he'd run in to a storm with it. He hadn't mentioned this at all to him. How had he heard about it?

He dismissed it as coincidence.

*****

As he was taxiing his F-14 to its hangar, Todd Reuter was reminded of the poem "The Mighty Casey." There was no joy in Mudville to be sure, as evidenced by the long faces and steely glares. The attack community was shocked by the fantastic success the two Tomcats had. On each of the six scenarios flown this morning, not a single piece of ordnance landed outside its designated target area, or missed a free standing target. Every weapon had a hit. *The Flying Ronzonis* were just touching down on the runway, with Danny Morello pumping his fists in the air. In one, they fought through four "hostile" F-18's flying CAP over a target, shooting down all four.

Riley greeted them both and was smiling from ear to ear. "That was quite a display, boys. The phones in the offices of Congress will be ringing late in to the evening, that's for sure."

Vince Capo came over and congratulated them as well. "I can't believe you guys! Even when the software failed on the last mission, you compensated. How did you figure out what to do, Steve?"

"Shit, Capo, give me some credit." Steve said with a laugh. "I know I didn't go to Princeton, but I'm far from a dumb ass. And I have been flying this aircraft for a while, and so has Danny. We just analyzed and acted. We do it all the time. If we didn't these birds would never fly. It's far from perfect out there on deployment. It's why we train so hard. You gotta know your stuff."

"I guess that's why you get paid the big bucks," Vincent said.

"Not nearly big enough."

"Commander Riley. May I see you a moment in private?" a rear admiral said as he approached.

They noted obvious gestures of irritation, as Riley waved his arms and cocked his head, and put his hands on his hips and looked down at the ground. The admiral patted him on the shoulder, then slapped him on the back as Riley reluctantly nodded his head in the affirmative. He came back five minutes later fit to be tied.

"Those fuckers cried foul! You believe it? They said that the mission was too much of a set-up, and therefore invalid."

Vince Capo threw a clipboard to the ground and stomped on it. It was the first time any of them had seen him lose his temper. Riley looked at Steven Amato's glaring eyes and tight lips.

"Forget it, Amato. You can't beat anybody else up."

Donnelly screamed in a rage. There's never been an aircraft that did what we did today. Never! It was picture perfect!"

"That's the problem. It was too good to be true. However, Admiral Thomas came up with an idea. He said we should pursue a real mission profile. You know, get the real time intelligence and then attack, just like a war situation. He's detailing it out now. My guess is that you'll deploy on a carrier, and be assigned a mission flying from her deck with a mixed bag of ordnance."

"When do we know?" Roto asked.

"Very soon indeed."

Chapter 20

"Here's the profile," Lieutenant Commander Riley began.

They learned about the details of the test mission less than twenty-four hours before they would fly it. Admiral Thomas wanted to end speculation once and for all as to the system's merits by expediting a realistic combat conditions test. He argued it made good sense for the Navy to have the option to expand the role of the Tomcat, especially in view of the rapidly changing world situation. Just because it could carry air-to-ground ordnance didn't mean it had to. Pilots and RIOs could train with the equipment, just in case. Besides, throughout history, the world's best fighters had been superb ground attack machines, as evidenced by the spectacular success of the F-14's immediate predecessor, the F-4 Phantom. Why deny the F-14 that legacy?

"You'll fly out to Miramar immediately. There you will refuel and service the aircraft, and quarter for the night. Considering they are all fighter pilots out there, Amato, I don't expect any trouble, am I correct?"

"Absolutely, sir," he said above the chuckling.

"At 0400 on 6 April, you will fly out to the *Enterprise*. You will refuel enroute. She will be operating just north of Oahu. Her position will be radioed to you after the refueling. Once aboard, the aircraft will again be serviced and refueled as normal conditions dictate. Then you will be assigned a mission profile to be carried out within twenty four hours, no matter what the weather or sea conditions. The aircraft will be armed accordingly."

"Capo, you and your Grumman team will go aboard via C-2 Greyhound while she is underway. We'll get you to Ford Island on Oahu via jet transport. Your equipment is being loaded as we speak." Thomas saw the fear in his face and remembered he was talking to a civilian who probably barfed on roller coasters. Now he was asking him to land on a carrier, at night. "Sorry, Vince, but we can't use a helicopter because you Grumman guys need all that equipment. Bob Hope does it when he visits the guys on Christmas. You can do it."

"Yeah, but Bob Hope's old!"

"Don't tell that to Bob Hope!" Reilly responded.

As prescribed, Reuter, Amato and their RIOs took the short hop to Miramar and slept as best they could that night. Before the next day, as prescribed, they took off again across the Pacific to find the carrier USS *Enterprise*, lying just north of the island of Oahu, Hawaii. It was the first time Steven had ever flown this far west, and he thoroughly enjoyed it.

What he eagerly looked forward to was going aboard the *Enterprise* again, the first carrier he had ever touched as a precocious youngster.

They spotted the *Big E* and her battle group just before 0800 hours.

After reporting aboard, he led Danny down a few decks to view the porthole he had first seen back in 1972. He smiled to himself as he thought about that day, when it seemed it would be an eternity before he could "fly an airpanes onna ships." Yet here he was, again looking at a relic of the World War II namesake of the giant he was aboard now.

"It's amazing they tore that ship up for scrap. How could they?" Danny said, gently fingering the porthole.

"I don't know. Celebrities tried to stop it. Even Bill Halsey himself got involved, but to no avail. They got absolutely no help from the government, either. Christ, two Tomcats cost more to build than this ship did. How precious could money have been to have ..."

He was interrupted by the ship's PA system that requested he report to the hangar deck.

He climbed up the set of stairs through the battle hatch and saw *Jawn* and *Roto* being lovingly worked over by a team of Grumman personnel and Navy maintenance men. "Here, Steve!" he heard someone call out. It was Vince Capo.

"How'd you do with last night's trap, pal?" Steven asked.

"Like most things, the expectation is worse than the actual event. No wonder Bob Hope can do it."

"So how's my baby doing?" he said, slapping the nose of the Tomcat.

"She's doing just great. We've loaded the software package. I think this mission is going to be a beauty. Judging from what we've been instructed to program, you're going against a ship as well as land targets. My guess is a string of islands southwest of us. They're on the rim of the Hawaiian chain, and I know there's a target range out there. I also think that the fighter squadrons aboard this moving country will also get into the act too. You and Reuter are in for some real fun."

"That's what it's all about."

Commander Eric Lunt, *Enterprise's* CAG, approached the busy group, seeking out Amato and Reuter.

"You guys are really public enemy numbers one through four. I can't believe the ruckus you're causing."

"It's just a development for the Tomcat, sir. You know as well as I do that the potential for this aircraft has not even been remotely approached," Amato said.

"Just realize what's at stake here, Lieutenant. I'm an old A-6 driver myself. I can't believe that there is another aircraft designed as a fighter that could do the job as well as an Intruder could when it comes to putting ordnance on the ground. It's against my religion."

"Sir, that kind of loyalty is admirable, but dangerous. The Intruder was deployed in 1960. With upgrades in engines and avionics, it is still a most capable attack bomber, but it's still twenty years old. The Tomcat is also at a maturation point. We need new engines, and new avionics if it still is going to be the best fighter in the world ten years from now, just as it is today. However, maybe one of those upgrades should involve an air-to-ground capability, just in case the scenarios change. It would be an absolute tragedy if we ourselves took on the civilian point of view that a weapons system is still considered the best in the world ten years after it is introduced. We're asking for trouble then, sir," Steven concluded.

"Like the Devastator?" Lunt said with a smirk.

"Exactly like the Devastator. But the squadrons who flew it knew it was a disaster waiting to occur. Sure, when it was introduced in 1930, it was the best airplane in the world. In 1941, it was a turkey."

"I read your paper, Amato. When I heard you were part of this melee, I was not surprised at all. By the way, how'd you like China Lake?" Lunt laughed when he saw Steven's eyes open wide.

"Word travels fast, doesn't it?" Reuter said. "Here, almost four thousand miles away, in the middle of the Pacific, and everyone knows how much you like Molson, Amats."

"We got some replacement crews in from the Lake yesterday morning. That's how we heard. You guys should get some sleep. This mission profile you're going to fly is going to be a killer, believe me."

The look on Lunt's face made the suggestion an order, and Steven and Todd appreciated it. From Lunt's hint, it was going to be a night mission.

As they had guessed, they were awakened at 1900 hours, the Pacific sun having set only a few minutes ago at the ship's stern. It's showtime. The *Big E's* "red eye" combat air patrol was just getting off the deck when Steven, Danny, Todd, and John went to a ready room and were briefed by Lunt.

"You are designated Flight 442. You launch in an hour. Your targets are an old freighter here and destroyer here," he said, pointing to a map "and two armored vehicles and a blockhouse on this island called Layson, right here. You'll carry two Harpoons for the ships, two Mavericks for the armored vehicles, and two laser guided bombs for the blockhouse. You'll also carry some practice Sidewinders and Sparrows. You can count on getting jumped by our fighters on the way in and out to the target areas. Any questions?"

None came, prompting Lunt to remark, "Cocky little bastards, ain't ya?"

"Sir, what's the weather forecast?" Steven asked, with a chuckle.

"There's a line of violent squalls roaming the target area. Watch them, especially on low level runs. There's a lot of wind shear associated with them this time of the year in the Pacific. The seas are relatively calm though. Any other questions?"

He saw them jotting down notes and comparing their charts for headings, something pilots did as a matter of course for any mission.

"Shit!" Reuter exclaimed, frantically searching his pockets and both wrists.

"What's the matter?" Donnelly said.

"I lost my watch. Dammit!"

"So what do you need a watch for? There's a chronometer in the plane, and Donnelly's got a watch on," Danny offered.

"It's procedure. You know that. What if we go down?"

Donnelly was right. What if they did go down and he and Reuter were separated. Or if Donnelly's chute didn't...well it had to be considered, Steven thought, didn't it? How would he keep track of time and distance if he tried to navigate, or plan his rations if he were lost for more than a day? The Pacific was the biggest ocean in the world, and people could easily get lost on its surface. Even with today's lightning fast communications technology and satellite navigation positioning systems, people, planes, and ships regularly disappeared.

"Now here this! Flight 442 pilots, man your planes!" came the voice over the ready room's intercom.

"I thought you said an hour? It has only been five minutes," Steven said as he glared at Lunt, forgetting military courtesy for the moment.

"Somebody from the attack community is playing games, Amato. I'll kill the son-of-a-bitch. I don't..."

"Shit, shit, shit!" Reuter said, as he again went through the myriad of pockets in his flight suit.

A carrier's deck works like a precision instrument. If they didn't get catapulted off the deck precisely as ordered, their planes would be struck down to the hangar deck, the mission would be scrubbed and a lack of readiness would be cited as the reason. This in turn would be blamed on the equipment, not the fact that somebody on the *Big E's* air staff was a scumbag of immense proportions.

"Here, take my Breitling. I'll use my Hamilton. I guess the Fates were looking out for me when I had that urge to bring it along."

"Whoa! I got a bad feeling about this, Steve. Leave that fucking thing here," Danny said, looking down, hands on his hips.

"Danny, think about it. There's nothing I care to see anymore. It's just a watch now. I don't need the past. I've got Julie. Besides, nothing happened at this time that I'm interested in anyway. Is it worth scrubbing this mission?"

"What the hell are you talking about?" Lunt asked. If he hadn't, certainly Reuter and Donnelly would have, judging from the what-the-hell expressions on their faces.

"Nothing at all, sir. It would take a day to explain the happenings involving this watch I have," he said, pulling it out of his equipment bag and putting it on his wrist. Believe me, it's all in the past. Let's go," Steven said.

Danny followed them in morose silence. Too much was at stake to try to explain the uncanny events of the past several months, and if they had the time to explain them, Lunt would have them committed for sure, let alone order the mission scrubbed.

As they moved down the passageway that would lead them to the flight deck, they passed a familiar face that wore an I-ate-the-canary smirk. It explained the early launch. Steven scowled as they passed.

"Isn't that the fellow you helped over the bar at China Lake?" Reuter asked.

"Yes. And this is the way he says thank you. Some manners!"

Their two Tomcats launched off the *Big E's* bow catapults into the milky night sky. If one managed the fear, flying at night from a ship was a beguiling experience. Starlight glistened off the surface of the sea, and the Pacific sky was literally smeared with stars. Marine protozoans irradiated the bow wave with their bioluminescence. The ships' wakes were aglow with a brilliant blue-green. It was a lovely Pacific night capped off by an immensely bright full moon. Just momentarily, Steven thought of Julie Ann back in D.C. and wondered if she was working on the story she said he would love.

The image of a ship appeared on one of the Tomcat's CRTs. "Harpoon is locked on primary target. FLIR pod activated," Danny said. "I've got you, my friend," he whispered into his microphone.

"Donnelly, you got any bogies showing on the scope?"

"That's a negative, Roto. The scope is clear."

"Okay, Amats. You want to fire while I cover?"

"Firing!" Danny said.

Two minutes later, a red ball of flame shot through the sky. The infrared image on the screen disappeared in a white flash. The old freighter was hit and burning.

The same thing happened to Donnelly's target, the destroyer. This time however they were intercepted by defending air. Steven went after two other Tomcats that appeared on Danny's radar screen as Donnelly and Reuter launched their two Harpoons against the destroyer. One bogie got away. The other was "splashed" by a simulated direct hit from a Sparrow missile.

They encountered a rain squall over Layson Island, just as Lunt said they might during their briefing. However, this particular one was more like a major thunderstorm, and their planes were being tossed about mercilessly. Reuter tried a target run, but had to abort it. He couldn't get a laser lock for his laser guided bombs, as lasers were notoriously erratic in cloudy or rainy weather. The additional moisture and dust refracted and diffused the laser light, rendering it useless. Bogies were appearing on their radar scopes, as six additional fighters waited outside the squall line to ambush them as they made their way back to the *Big E*. The planes' electronic countermeasures gear began singing with its buzzers, bells, and flashing warning lights, indicating that they were being sought by powerful missile locking radars.

That's when things started to come apart, and quickly.

Jawn was rocked by an explosion coming from its starboard engine. The rudder and elevon on the starboard side was useless, if they even remained attached. Fire lights and buzzers filled the canopy.

"Roto! Are you with me? I've got major problems here!"
"Negative. Report your position."
"I'm losing it! I'm losing it!"
"Amats! Give me a fix!"
"Danny, what can you see? How does it look?"
"I can't see anything but fire! We're gonna have to get out of here!"
"I'm losing hydraulics. I'm losing it. Shit!"
"442, come in. Report your status, over?"

It was *Enterprise*. Her radars reported one of the planes was losing altitude, a little after an F/A-18 pilot flying interception on the exercise reported that one of his Sparrow air-to-air missiles had misfired when he was locking up one of the F-14's as it flew in support of his wingman attacking the target on Layson Island.

"*Enterprise*, this is 442 lead. We're going in. Position is fifty five miles due north of Layson Island," Steven reported.

"Roger that. We have you. Hang in there, guys. We're sending the choppers and a destroyer."

As he said, "Eject! Eject! Eject!" Steven couldn't help to think about Thatcher. An instant later, they were tumbling through the night, pelted by rain and buffeted by a 150-knot blast of wind.

The plane guard helicopter arrived fifteen minutes later and began to search the area, listening for the radio beacon all pilots carry to home in rescue aircraft. Traveling at flank speed, the destroyer arrived a few hours later. By the time they had reached Steven's and Danny's last reported position, the squall line had passed, and the seas were calm. The destroyer's powerful search lights and sensitive surface radar pierced the darkness, but in vain. Hope was placed in the hands of the dawn, about three hours away.

Be that as it may, the dawn could not persuade the Pacific to surrender the missing aviators. Parts of the Tomcat were found however, floating not three miles from their last reported position.

Aboard *Enterprise*, a young F/A-18 pilot on his first cruise could not be consoled, even after it was discovered the rack that had held the misfired missile was defective, causing a launch when the missile was only in its search mode. The young man, a JG named Lynch, said over and over again how sorry he was, and that Amato was sort of a hero to him from their Academy days. Amato had thanked him over and over again for the tip about the detachment of TBFs assigned to Torpedo 8 flying against the Japanese fleet from the airstrip at Midway during the climactic battle.

An enlisted man walking on the port catwalk barely caught Lynch as he tried to throw himself overboard later that day. The enlisted man had a hell of a time with it, and if it hadn't been for the six other men that came to his aid, Lynch would have had his way in a few more seconds. He learned later that Lynch had played football in the same backfield as Amato and Morello had, and that he possessed uncommon speed.

Chapter 21

Danny Morello reached for the still form of Steven Amato as they both drifted in their rubber life rafts under the bright Pacific sun. Even though a tether connected them, he felt more secure when the distance between them stayed at a few feet rather than a few yards.

The seas were heavy with wave heights exceeding ten feet, and they were tossed about brutally. Danny had discarded both their helmets, and had also discarded their "G" suits to lighten the load the rafts had to support. Danny managed to get one of their radio beacons going however, and apparently it still was broadcasting its signal. He anticipated they would be rescued in no time, and that would be none too soon.

Steven was slightly out of phase with a concussion. He had a large knot on his head that had bled quite a bit after they had landed, but had stopped when Danny applied a compress to it. Danny had a deep bruise on his thigh that was agonizingly throbbing with pain. He was sure his wrist was broken, as it was excruciatingly painful to manipulate. Both of them suffered a tremendous thirst, and Danny was petrified that a shark would find them to be a four-star breakfast.

Exhausted and suffering from exposure, Danny drifted in and out of sleep, but became awakened when he saw a destroyer not a mile away. He waved his hands and yelled at the top of his lungs. Steven was awakened as well, and joined the ruckus to attract the destroyer's attention. It obviously worked, as the destroyer made right for them. As the ship approached, Danny saw what appeared to be a carrier in the distance. Good, he thought. He managed to eject with *Jawn's* mission log and tape log tucked tight in a waterproof bag he kept inside his flight suit. He wanted Lunt, Reilly, and Thomas to have it, as it showed the mission's sequence had gone perfectly right. It also noted the time the F-14 had been hit by a missile, and Danny wanted to be sure that the guilty party was hung by his balls for this "accident".

Danny felt weak. Perhaps the anxiety and stress had finally taken its toll, he told himself. He looked to Steven whom he saw was out cold, before feeling his own eyelids uncontrollably shutting out the light. The destroyer was so close he could hear its engines.

By his own accounting, he awoke about four or five hours later in what appeared to be a shipboard sick bay, judging from the roll and the yaw. Seeing Steven sitting up to his right gazing out a porthole, and he reasoned they must have been rescued by the destroyer. His own wrist was in a cast, and he had nothing covering him but a sheet. Steven was wearing a khaki uniform, his head swathed in a bandage, and his own arm in sling.

"How are you, Amats,?"

"As well as can be expected," Steven said, wobbling his arm in the sling and pointing to his head. "They told me I dislocated my right shoulder. I also bruised my ribs," he said, rubbing his eyes. "Shit, I've got a headache to beat the band. Every time I turn my head and try to focus my eyes I get woozy. How are you feeling?"

"My wrist is throbbing. Judging from this cast, I guess I broke it. Otherwise I feel fine. I don't remember the doc who set it."

"Oh, he'll be back in a few minutes. You slept right through the whole procedure. He had those clothes brought in for you," Steven said, pointing to a khaki shirt and pants, brown shoes, and socks resting on a chair next to his bed. "Your log and tapes are there too. He asked some questions about them, as well as the flying suits. I made up a story of them being experimental stuff."

"What destroyer is this?" Danny asked. Made up a story?

"It's the *Gwin*."

"The *Gwin*? Is it a new *Arleigh Burke* class?" Danny said, heading for porthole. He noted the sun was a little to the port and astern of the destroyer's wake. They were heading in the wrong direction. "Is this part of the *Enterprise's* battle group?"

"So to speak," Steven said, "And no, I don't think Arleigh Burke made enough of a reputation yet to have a destroyer class named after him."

"You're talking in riddles, Amats. Are you really that woozy? When do we go back to the *Big E*? I want to shove the tape and the log in Lunt's face. I also want to fuck up that shitbird that shot us down."

"Oh, the doctor said we'd be back on the *Big E* by sunset. She's maneuvering to pick us up."

"Maneuvering? Why don't they just send in a chopper? It seems the battle group is heading in the wrong direction anyway," as he headed for Steven's porthole, to see what so interesting that he continued his gazing throughout their conversation.

It was precisely then that the view from Steven's porthole was partly obscured by the sides of what obviously was a carrier.

"Come take a look at this," Steven said.

A carrier with the number 8 stenciled on its island passed close by the *Gwin*, so close that she hissed. Her flight deck aft was covered with what appeared to be a good number of twin-tailed, propeller driven aircraft painted a dreary brown color. The aircraft were parked closely together, their dorsal gun turrets indistinguishable as to what aircraft they individually belonged to. Their national insignia showed clearly, a white star with a red ball in its center surrounded by a blue field.

Danny Morello couldn't believe his eyes. His face was painted with disbelief.

Matter-of-factly, Steven looked to Danny and said, "We're not heading in the wrong direction. I knew there was something about April that rang a bell. I just couldn't put my finger on it. Now I realize we're going to Tokyo with Jimmy Doolittle."

Danny noted that Steven was wearing the watch. He also noted an usual sereneness about him. Steven turned to him and smiled.

"It had to be, Danny," he said. "Somebody wants me to see something, or do something or be something or all of the above. It's been planned, perhaps since I was born. Who knows?"

"Oh, yeah? What about me? I just wanted a career in the Navy circa 1985! Why'd you drag me along? You, and the fucking time bomb on your wrist."

"I don't know, but I'm sure we'll find out."

"How long will it take? I've got a wedding waiting for me in the land of the future!" He looked again at the speeding *Hornet*, her deck full of B-25 Mitchell bombers. "Shit!" He ran his fingers through his thick blonde hair.

"I think we're here until June 4. About two months."

"You mean through Midway? Amats, I don't want to attack a Japanese carrier. Somebody already did that."

The doctor entered, taking a Camel cigarette from a pack he carried in his pocket. "Well, I see you're doing quite nicely. Good, good, good! The *Enterprise* is eager to have you back. That was quite a spectacular feat of survival, Lieutenant Amato. You and Morello are very lucky to have survived the night in the storm. I can't understand why it was so all damn important to qualify that new airplane for night landings now, especially with this mission we're on. Ah well, I'm just a country doctor, not some admiral. I'll leave these here for you," he said, placing the pack of cigarettes on Danny's pillow. "Feel free to smoke. I'm having some chow brought up for you. We'll have you back aboard the *The Big E* by the evening meal. Anything else?"

"No, sir. Thank you."

"Any pain in that wrist, Morello?"

"Just a throb."

"What about you, Amato?"

"I've got a headache, and it hurts when I breathe."

"Yes, that's normal," the doctor said, his southern accent becoming more pronounced as he continued to speak. "Those ribs will hurt for weeks. Well anyway, no more flying for you two for at least a month, and then only training missions. No combat."

"Thank you, sir."

"By the way, Amato, a guy named Waldron from one of the *Hornet's* squadrons sent us a message by signal light when he heard you were all right."

"Waldron? What'd he say, sir?"

"He said that the TBF you lost had better not be one of the bunch he asked you to have Leroy Grumman send to his squadron, and to get well soon."

"That would be Waldron", Steven said with a laugh.

Danny Morello stared at the *Hornet* plowing through the Pacific, sending up an immense bow wave, and looking as aggressive as a dog with a bone in its teeth as she began her first true combat engagement. He hoped it would disappear and he would awaken and laugh at the dream he had been having.

Somehow, he knew it was not to be.

Chapter 22

Julie decided it would be a good idea to visit Steven's parents while he was away. Paul and Rena Amato would be celebrating their twenty-eight wedding anniversary this month, and were holding off a family celebration until their son came home. The Amato's had a lifelong dream to go to Hawaii, and she was sure a certain son and daughter of hers had arranged an excursion, all expenses paid, and Julie made a contribution of a limousine to and from the airport. Of course, this was all top secret and Steven agreed to clear her, but only after she took an oath of secrecy, a violation of which would be a date with Mr. Whitney. She was such a good-natured blabber-mouth, he said, that she would let the cat out of the bag the minute she saw a palm tree in a commercial on TV. She smiled as she thought of that wacko she had fallen for.

Julie pulled in the driveway just in time to see a tall man dressed in Navy dress blues remove his hat as he entered the house, his station wagon parked at the curb. From a quick glance and the car, she thought it to be Steven's and Danny's commanding officer, Lieutenant Commander Riley. Now what would he be doing...

The horror gripped her so that she instantaneously grew goose bumps so large that for an instant her skin looked reptilian. The air was literally sucked from her lungs. She found it difficult to breathe and felt faint, as her stomach twisted and her forehead became feverish. She managed to control the car as it careened up the Amato's long driveway, jamming on its brakes, and skidding it to a screeching halt just short of the Ford convertible's rear bumper. She jammed the gearshift in park, and ran from her car without shutting off the ignition. As she ran to the front door, she lost one of her pumps and tripped, ripping her stockings and scraping her knees. The wails she heard from the inside of the house caused her to hesitate, and then, as she lay in a pathetic heap in a bed of beautiful red and yellow tulips, the tears gushed uncontrollably from her eyes.

She raised herself up and staggered weakly to the front door. As she opened it, her worst fears were realized. Rena Amato lay kneeling on the floor, her legs under her, her hand gripped by Riley and Lieutenant Ware. Paul Amato sat in a chair, his hands buried in his face. Susan was looking on, just stunned. Not only was her brother gone, but her fiancé as well. She managed to stumble to a chair, where she just sat catatonically, wide-eyed and pale. When Susan noticed Julie's presence, she held out her arms, began to tremble and cried and cried and cried.

Riley's own chin quivered. He had done this a few times before, most recently with Thatcher's wife. This was just as hard, if not harder. He reckoned that was a good sign-he never wanted it to become easier. When it did, he would burn his uniform, he resolved.

"How?" Rena managed to utter.

"We don't quite know what went wrong. Another plane involved in the exercise had a missile fire inadvertently. We were told it wasn't the pilot's fault, but a defective arming and release mechanism. The young man whose plane was involved knew Dan and Steve from the Academy. He played football on the same team with them. He tried to take his own life, we're told."

"Oh my God!" Julie said. "Have they recovered their..."

"No, Julie, but we did find some of the F-14's wreckage. We have them listed as missing. That's what gives us hope. It's a big ocean, and even though we had their exact location when they spun in, the storm might have carried them miles before daybreak. We heard their emergency radio beacon for a while, but not long enough get a fix on them. The signal just sort of faded away. We're still trying to figure out how and why that happened. It was eerie."

That's the word that sparked her out of the crushing rage and sorrow – eerie, the same word that had made a consistent reappearance in their vocabularies over the last few months. She looked at Steven's Annapolis class ring on her hand, and a grin began to work its way on her mascara-smeared face. They found pieces of the plane. The date...

"Susan, let's go up to Steven's room. Please."

"Oh, Julie. I can't go in there. He..."

"Susan, for me and for you. Please let's go. Mom, you too."

"Where are you all going?" Paul Amato said, a look of confusion joining the look of agony on his face.

"Up to Steven's room, dad. We'll be right back. Commander Riley, would you please see to my dad?" Julie said, hugging Paul and kissing him on his cheek. "Don't worry dad. I think our boys are all right. They won't be back for a while, but they're fine."

"Julie, please. Don't do this," Rena said, blowing her nose. "Steven is..."

"Mom, you have to go up there with me. Only his mom knows him well enough to find...I need to ask you a few questions. Come on."

As the three women entered Steven's impeccably kept room, Julie turned to Rena and asked, "Where does he keep his jewelry, mom?"

"In his top dresser drawer with his socks, in a little jewelry box."

"I just knew you'd know. A mother always does. I betcha Paul doesn't know, does he?"

Julie smiled broadly, and took a deep breath. Then she ripped open the drawer and found the little jewelry box that Rena Amato knew would be there. She took it out, and with her heart pounding and her eyes wide, she opened it. Sure enough, it was gone.

"Hah!" she yelled. It's gone. The watch! That fucking watch is gone!"

Rena Amato and Susan looked on in shock. What had possessed this woman?

Julie turned to them and said again. "It's gone. The watch Steven found in the Ford convertible is gone. He must have taken it with him. Don't you see? He took the watch and..."

It was then she realized that Rena Amato had no idea what Julie was talking about, but she saw signs of recognition in Susan's eyes.

"Danny said something about that watch having some kind of whammy attached to it. Julie, you don't think..."

"Let's get crazy, okay? How much did Dan the Man tell you, Suzie Q?" she said, glancing at Rena who was looking more confounded by the second.

"I didn't believe him. He's always joking and playing tricks on me, and scaring me half to death with his stories. I thought..."

"Well, sugar, I've got a few stories to tell you. And some stories to tell you to, mom. But first I got to make a phone call."

"Julie, please. I'm so confused. My son is ...."

"Going to turn up," she interrupted, dialing the phone. "I know where but I don't know when, but I will have a better edge on that right after...Marcus? This is Julie. Get your fat ass in that Jag of yours and get down here to Norfolk." She listened for a minute. "I don't care if you're about to boff Lady Chatterly. Get down here now. I need you. I really, really need you. Bring the research we've done, and some of those books you say you're doing research in when you're really screwing off. And your map tools." She listened again. "Hey, White, remember? You're talking to me, so hold the bullshit, okay? I know it's the weekend. It was on the news last night." She listened again, an eyebrow coming up. "That's exactly why I need you here, to make sure the admiral does marry me and gets me off your case."

She gave Marcus directions, and finished her conversation with, "See you in four hours. Again she listened. "Of course you can bring the bimbo. Haul ass. Goodbye."

Rena Amato sat on her son's bed, and sighed.

"I'm sorry about the language, mom. It's that Marcus has the clues we need to know about Steven, and he responds better to gutter language."

"I don't mind the language, Julie. I love you. I know why Steven loves you. And if you say he'll be back, I believe you."

Susan knelt beside her and took her hand and kissed it as she held it to her face. "Rena," she said, looking at her swollen blue eyes, "a pitcher from the '69 Mets said it best - Ya gotta believe."

"Julie, if you believe, then I believe. What choice do I have?"

When she put the jewelry box back in the drawer, the stereo sitting on a shelf next to the dresser caught her eye. She noted a cassette tape was in one of the two tape players. She pressed on the "play" button, and a scratchy recording of what had to be an old seventy- eight rpm record piped through the huge speakers on either side of the room. The woman forlornly sang one of the anthems of the Second War.

"I'll be seeing you, in all the old familiar places..."

"You bet your sweet ass you will, Amato. Thanks for the tip," she said, almost in a whisper. "And I'll be sure we're ready."

Julie went downstairs and sat next to Riley.

"I need your help, Commander Riley. Can you bring us a map of the exact location Steven's and Danny's plane wreckage was spotted?"

"Sure I can."

"Can you do it by two this afternoon?"

"That's a roger. What are you thinking of?" he said, noting the scheming look in her eye.

"If I told you, you wouldn't believe me. Be back here at two, and I'll let you in on a little secret. But if I do, you have to swear secrecy and total cooperation. Deal?"

"Those are my boys out there. I have no choice."

At two in the afternoon a British Racing Green Jaguar XJ6 pulled into the Amato's driveway. Out stepped a dapper gentleman, wearing dark brown flannel slacks and a brown tweed jacket around a bone colored turtleneck. A fashionably dressed woman of about thirty exited on the passenger's side. Upon further examination, the woman was deemed by the women spying from the house to be drop-dead gorgeous. She removed a hat that unleashed an avalanche of long eggplant colored hair that dropped to the middle of her back, offsetting dazzling green eyes, and white skin. The form fitting beige knit dress she wore betrayed a clock-stopping figure.

"The son-of-a-bitch hasn't lost his touch," Julie muttered.

"I guess he hasn't. I take it that's Marcus White?" Susan asked.

"In the flesh, and he brought the stuff we needed too. He may be a whoremaster, Suzie Q, but he's one great journalist-and friend."

Marcus White was greeted at the door by Julie, with Rena Amato and Susan behind her. After seeing her swollen eyes and the mascara streaked faces of the other women with her, it didn't take but a nanosecond for Marcus to realize a tragedy of immense proportion had struck. He grabbed Julie Tate and hugged her closely, and whispered, "I'm sorry, Tate, truly sorry. How did it happen?"

"His plane was accidentally shot down by an air-to-air missile."

"He was flying a Tomcat, wasn't he?"

"Yes. Why?"

"Because that airplane is one tough sucker. An air-to-air missile like a Sparrow or Sidewinder might force the plane down, but it's built for crew survivability. If your boys ejected, there's an excellent chance they survived."

"They went down in a severe squall with ten foot seas."

Marcus's eyebrows went up and his mouth formed a frown. "Then the added factor might reduce their chances. Where?"

"North and slightly west of Hawaii."

"That part of the ocean is treacherous this time of year."

"What if I told you I know, almost for a fact, that Steve and Dan are both alive?"

"Why are you choosing this time to play Karnak the Great?"

Just then, a loud "ahem" came from the woman Marcus had brought along.

"Oh, my goodness. Forgive my bad manners. This is Paula Nash. Paula, meet Julie Tate, and Mrs. Amato, I presume?" he said tilting his head slightly for a confirming sign as he looked at Rena, "and you must be Susan Amato."

"Pleased to meet you all," Paula said, extending her hand.

"What kind of work do you do, Paula?" Susan asked.

"I'm a surgical resident at Johns Hopkins Medical Center."

"I'm pleased to meet you too, Paula," Julie said. "Dr. Nash, I see Marcus's taste has improved by leaps and bounds.

"Yes, it has," she said with a laugh. "I'm terribly sorry for you, Julie. But from what you say, he may be..."

"He is alive. And so is Danny."

"Hi. I'm Paul Amato. Pleased to meet you. Rena, I'm going upstairs. Call me when Riley gets back."

Paul Amato had been expecting a day like this ever since he and Steven boarded the *Enterprise* that day when he was twelve. Goddam airplanes, goddam ships.

"Marcus, what events during the Second World War took place in the Pacific during April. Midway?"

"Not Midway. It was fought in early June."

Julie's heart sank. Her hypothesis was falling apart.

"But you know, Tate, a lot of historians think the Midway campaign was actually a Japanese defensive action, a counterthrust if you will, to secure their empire from another attack by marauding American bombers. The Japs were pissed to hell that Doolittle's planes actually got through to Tokyo."

"You mean the Tokyo Raid? The Thirty Seconds Over Tokyo Raid? When did that happen?"

"If we were in 1942, it would be as we speak. Here, look," Marcus said, opening up a text and his own draft of a story he was preparing. "The carrier *Enterprise* left Pearl Harbor on April 8 and was joined by the carrier *Hornet* on April 13. That's today."

"Did you say *Hornet*?" Julie said, grabbing Marcus's arm. "The same *Hornet* I asked you about in December?"

"The very same one," Marcus said, swiveling his head to take in the what-the-hell expressions of the women in the room. "She carried Doolittle's planes, sixteen B-25 Mitchell twin-engined bombers. They launched April 18."

A knock on the front door announced the return of Lt. Cmdr. Riley. He carried two cardboard tubes that contained official Navy Bureau of Navigation maps, one of intense detail of the area in question, and another that included the western Pacific through Japan.

"Okay, Marcus, let's earn your bucks. What was the route followed by the Doolittle task force?"

Marcus carefully took out several charting instruments and drew a series of lines as he carefully noted a series of numbers from one of the books he carried with him.

"Done. Now what?" Marcus said, looking up to see Paul Amato peering over his wife's shoulder.

"Commander Riley. Draw in the position where Danny and Steven supposedly were lost."

"Okay," Riley said. "May I borrow your instruments?" he asked Marcus.

"Of course, Commander." Marcus carefully placed the expensive and technical looking tools in Riley's hands.

"That's it, right...here." His eyes narrowed when he saw that Marcus's lines intersected the point that Riley drew on the map. "Isn't that a coincidence?"

"Marcus, what ships were on the Doolittle Raid besides the *Hornet*?" Julie asked.

"Well, there were two carriers, *Hornet* and..."

"*Enterprise*," Riley interjected; another coincidence. "Steve and Danny were operating off that ship's namesake, our very own nuclear powered supercarrier."

"It's more than coincidence, Commander. I knew it before you said the word *Enterprise*," Julie said.

"What's your point, Tate?" Marcus said.

She had to tell them, whether they believed her or not. If they thought it was a virulent psychosis that made fantasy reality, or some real "eerie stuff" wasn't the issue. She took a deep breath and began.

"Get ready for a real lollapalooza of a story, ladies and gentlemen. It all started with that car right outside. Well, actually, it all started way before that car came into the picture, with a little boy who was fascinated by airplanes, ships, antiques, a time long gone, and a pilot by the name of Lieutenant Commander John C. Waldron, the Commanding Officer of Torpedo Squadron 8."

Chapter 23

Because of anti-submarine precautions, Steven and Danny were transferred by bosun's chair to the *Hornet*, rather than to the *Enterprise*, their "assigned" ship. It was quite an experience hanging by a line between two huge ships in the middle of the ocean. Steve, then Danny, swung helplessly in the steel canyon and the river of ocean created by the two ships.

Because so much of her deck space was taken up by the Army bombers, *Hornet's* planes were struck below in her hangar deck. She relied on her sister *Enterprise* for aerial protection. Standing at the *Hornet's* rail to greet them was Lieutenant Commander John C. Waldron of Torpedo Squadron 8.

"Glad to see you boys made it. You had us worried," Waldron said as he welcomed them. "Gene Lindsey signaled us ten times until he was sure you were all right."

"Thanks, sir," Steven replied, taking every precaution to have Waldron do the talking. After all, Steven lost a Tomcat. Waldron thought he lost an Avenger. The ball was in Waldron's end of the court, so to speak.

"Was it structural failure?" Waldron asked.

"No sir," Danny intervened. "It was an engine fire, pure and simple. We couldn't put it out." What the hell, Danny thought. How much trouble could he get into talking to a...ghost? Yes, now I'm talking to a ghost, he thought. No, I'm lying to a ghost. He rubbed his temples as he was developing a terrible headache.

"I guess it was good fortune to have another pilot back there in an emergency, hey Steve?" he said, nodding to Danny.

Oh, even better, Danny thought. He thinks I'm a pilot. What if he asks me to fly something? Then what? Danny remembered that flying was an officer's occupation "here." Any other men aboard a plane were enlisted men, who served as gunners or radio operators. Maybe that wouldn't be a bad idea, though. He was tired of looking at the back of Amato's helmet, he told himself.

"It certainly was, Commander Waldron", Steven answered without flinching, and chucking Danny on his shoulder.

"You got off lucky. I was hoping you would have finished the fleet deployment tests with that bird before this mission is over. I would hate to get back to Pearl only to find out we have a squadron full of TBFs waiting for us on Ford Island, but we can't fly them because they weren't certified for fleet operations yet."

"I don't think that would be the case, sir," Steven said. "It's war. We carrier qualified that plane already. One crack up is not going to deter anyone from putting them out in the fleet. The problem is the plant at Bethpage is barely geared up to production. I think they won't be here anytime soon. But maybe Swede Larsen and Al Earnest and those other guys you left behind in Norfolk will get lucky."

"How did you know about them?" Waldron asked, tilting his head slightly, viewing them through narrowed eyes.

"Yes, Lieutenant Amato, how did you know about them?" Danny repeated, folding his arms and looking just as perplexed as Waldron.

"I met them just after you guys left in March. I was back down in Norfolk on another cross country hop checking out the new radio compass the TBF carries."

"Did you fellows play football at Annapolis with Swede?" Waldron asked.

"Yes sir. Swede graduated a year before we did."

"He was heartbroken to see the ship leave without him. Ah well. We'll catch up soon," Waldron said, lighting a cigarette.

"Judging from this deck load, I think the Japanese are in for a real treat, don't you think?" Steven said, nodding to the Mitchell bombers. "Admiral Halsey on *Enterprise* is excited about this, but he hasn't said a word."

"The Jap bastards deserve it, whatever the target." Waldron said as he exhaled a lung full of smoke. "I'm told those Army guys are more scared shitless of taking off those B-25s from the carrier that they are of the bombing run. It can be done, but it will certainly be something different for them. *Hornet* already launched a B-25 a few months back to prove the concept, but a Navy guy by the name of Miller did it. Doolittle's ship is the first one in line there. If he gets off, his boys will have all kinds of confidence. They're quite a bunch, for army guys."

"They are brave men for sure," Danny commented

"Since you're so banged up you can't fly, and we can't get you back to the *Big E* until we get back to Pearl, I'm going to put you to work helping those Army guys with navigation and flight deck procedures. I'm not going send you back to Lindsey overfed and underworked," Waldron said with a smile.

"Commander Waldron. Captain Mitscher needs you up on the bridge, sir. Oh, how are you doing, Amato?"

"Fine, Ray. Thanks. And you?"

"Great. Gee whiz, Dan. You gotta be more careful where you hang out," Ray Moore said noting his cast.

"What time you got?" Waldron asked Danny.

"It's 1730."

Doing a double-take, Waldron eyed the watch. His eyebrows were raised, and the only thing Danny could think of was "oh shit".

"What the hell kind of watch is that?" he asked.

"It's a chronometer, sir", Danny said, trying to hide his apprehension.

"I've never seen one like it. Hey, Moore, you're a watch freak, aren't you? Look at this one!"

Steven scratched his head, trying to look as nonchalant and detached as possible, while Danny's forehead broke out in perspiration.

"What the hell kind of watch is a Breitling? I've never seen one of these before," Moore responded.

Well, here goes nothing, Danny ventured. "It's German. My friend was a naval attaché in Berlin before the war. He sent it to me for my last birthday."

"German? How the hell can you wear a kraut watch?" Waldron fumed. "Let me see that damned thing."

Danny took it hurriedly off his wrist and handed it to Waldron.

"What kind of watch band is this, all these clasps?" Waldron said, bringing it to his ear. "And something else, Morello. The damned thing isn't even ticking, for heaven's sake. Look at how slow the second hand is moving." He tried to wind it. "And the goddam winder doesn't work either!"

Waldron slapped the watch into Danny's hand and said, "Son, your best friend got you a cheap piece of made-in-Germany crap. Give it up and get a Hamilton, like Amato's."

Ray Moore saw the watch on Steven's wrist, and smiled. "Hey! I got one just like it. Where did you get it?"

"At Sam's Jewelry Shop in Norfolk the last time I was there."

"Jeez! That's where I got mine... uh, my two, actually. My dad bought me one and I wrecked it the day you saw me take header at Norfolk. When we got back from the shakedown cruise, I took it to Sam junior to fix, but he didn't have the parts. He called his brother in Richmond, and fortunately he had one just like it in his jewelry shop. Sam ordered the parts to fix my first. I didn't want to run into Sam senior, because he and my dad are good friends, and this watch cost a bundle, but I guess you know that."

"I sure do," Steve said with a nod, while Danny looked on amazed.

"Anyway, I took the one I brought home so my dad could see me wearing it. One of Gus's guys was with me to drive me back to Norfolk, because I knew we were going to war, and I didn't want to leave my car on the base at Oceana. We had dinner with my parents. As we were leaving, I went to see my car one last time, and son-of-gun, I tripped again and smashed the watch I bought not four hours before. I just shoved it up under the seat of my Ford. I'll get it fixed when we get back."

Steven's heart skipped a beat just then.

"So, I got a thousand dollars' worth of watches, and I still have to ask people for the time!" Moore laughed.

"Well, you still got the Ford," Steven said in jest.

"I screwed that up pretty well too. I hit the curb in front of Levine's jewelry store in Richmond pretty hard. I know I did some heavy gauge damage to it, because it veered to the right something terrible. I want a Lincoln Zephyr like Widhelm's anyway. You want the Ford? I know you admired it. I'll pay to have it fixed before you take it away."

Steven's heart skipped a beat again. "I'll get it fixed. Just give me a good price."

"I'll give you the best price, Amats."

Ray Moore called him "Amats".

"How's the blond broad you were flying around? What happened between you two? Anything...uh, special?" Moore said with the wink of his eye.

"We got engaged."

Moore turned twelve shades of red. "Gee, Steve, I'm sorry, I didn't mean to... be so... disparaging. My dad is right about me. I'm really a..."

"Save it, Ray. I know you meant no harm. It's fine."

"Thanks. I...I...better see what Waldron needs me to do this evening. He made me squadron maintenance officer, and it keeps me pretty busy. Sorry again, Amats. See you later, Danny."

"You betcha." Danny turned to Steven and said, "Well, we certainly got a good deal of our questions answered. Waldron is going to have me dropped over Tokyo for wearing a German watch. Ray Moore wanted to screw your fiancé. And, I would like to find out when we graduated from Annapolis."

"And it appears Raymond and his pop are not the best of friends. Let's find the ready room. Perhaps there's a yearbook there."

VT-8's ready room was a far cry from one on a modern carrier. The ready room chairs had high backs and arms, and were fastened to the deck. They were covered in a rich leather to make them durable. A chair in one of the ready rooms of *Nimitz* or ENTERPRISE was made of durable fireproof nylon fabric, much less expensive than leather. There was no TV, and the flight data board was a simple blackboard, not a high tech acrylic plastic with a capability for projection. One thing was common though, and that was the ever-present coffee urn.

The ship's loudspeaker blared. "Now hear this! The captain will address the crew."

The crew looked at the ship's loudspeakers as Captain Mitscher spoke. "We have just received word that the island of Bataan in the Philippines has just fallen. General MacArthur has ordered his command to the island of Corregidor."

There was a hesitation in Mitscher's voice, and when Steven and Danny looked about, they noted that there were grim faces and hanging, shaking heads everywhere. Others looked angry enough to eat nails. Still others had quivering chins. Mitscher, a most popular commander, continued.

"Men, you may have wondered what our mission is as we press northwestward, again far away from the apparent battles in which the *Hornet* could no doubt participate and give a fine accounting for herself. You may have also wondered why we're carrying Army Mitchell bombers, and some of you have noted that we have a celebrity in our midst in the form of Colonel James Doolittle. Colonel Doolittle and his Army fliers have asked our help in carrying out a very special mission with those B-25s on deck, and if you think this is another ferry mission, you're wrong. Men, I will use the words of our task force commander, Admiral Halsey, to tell you our mission, just received as official by signal a moment ago from his flagship *Enterprise*. I quote."

THIS FORCE IS BOUND FOR TOKYO

The *Hornet* vibrated with a crescendo of shouts, war whoops, clapping hands and whistles throughout her entire length, and continued to do so for at least ten minutes. Danny and Steve looked at each other and smiled, as enlisted men and officers hugged each other, and men were driven to near tears. The shouts on *Enterprise* could be heard over the mile of water between the two sisters.

"Holy cow! I never heard anything like it except during the Army-Navy game," Danny said.

"Think about it. Bataan just fell. Since *Hornet* was commissioned, the ship hasn't done anything but qualify air groups and ferry planes. These guys just saw the wrecks at Pearl Harbor for the first time. They had friends on those ships. The Japanese have taken Wake Island. America has been getting the crap kicked out of it for four months now, and this ship hasn't fired a shot in anger, but now they're going after the bastards to whack them where they live!"

"They don't seem to think there's much the risk at all. Just listen to them!" Danny said.

"These guys are classic Americans, Danny. John Wayne just portrayed them, he didn't make the up. They don't like taking any shit, especially the guys of this generation. They just finished with a depression that really tested their mettle. They are so fucking pissed off over the Sunday murders and the general thrashing the Japanese have given us that they're ready to fight off Zeros with slingshots. What a time in history! God, it's America's darkest hour, and these guys are full of piss and vinegar. Unbelievable!"

"Don't you think we're the same way now?" Danny asked.

"I don't think we're as spontaneous, nor would we be as morally outraged. Maybe we're not as morally elevated, from the leadership on down. Ask a Vietnam vet. Look how we cowered with the Ayatollah. Hell, look how we cowered with Thatcher. Before we would do something like this, we'd probably have to get a lawyer's permission or something. These guys are taking it right to the bastards, full speed ahead."

"I just got a funny notion. Are we here to change anything?"

"Dan my man, we're going to find out, aren't we?"

As soon as he said Dan my Man, he thought of her. "Susan! What the hell is Susan thinking? What about your mom and dad, or my mom and dad? And Julie?"

"I haven't forgotten them. But if I know my Julie, she's getting her act together right now about us. I just know it. She's got to keep the faith about this, whatever this is."

They found several Annapolis yearbooks in VT-8's ready room. They opened the Class of 1936's and found out what they needed to know. In alphabetical order, there was a picture of Steven L. Amato and Daniel B. Morello, with their nicknames of "Amats" and "D-Man" under their pictures. It also listed them as having played baseball and football, and gave a brief description of their activities, just as they had been when they attended the Academy thirty-five years later.

To break their spell of disbelief, or perhaps amplify it, came Ray Moore.

"Hey, Amats. The CO wants you up on the bridge. You too, D-Man."

Chapter 24

Paul Amato sat and just shook his head from side to side, never taking his eyes from the rug in his den. Rena Amato was so confused she didn't know where to begin to formulate questions. Marcus White and Paula Nash stared at each other with pursed lips. Lieutenant Commander Riley didn't know quite what to do, or how to express his feelings in response to the story he just heard. He glanced at "Silver" Ware and "Roto" Reuter who had come to comfort Steve's family just after Julie began her story. Susan looked at everyone, and couldn't for the life of her figure out why they weren't at least pleased with Julie's hypothesis. After all, it was the only hope they had.

"Julie," Paula Nash said, as she came to her and put her arm around her trim waist, "perhaps it would be better for you to lie down. I have my little black bag in the car. I didn't carry it in because I didn't want it to clash with my outfit," she said, trying to evoke a smile from Julie, who was becoming increasingly distressed at the reaction she was receiving. "I have some medication that will help you relax. I'll be right back with it. Marcus, may I have the keys to the...?"

"Marcus, you move and I'll cut your nuts off and feed them to a wolf," she said with a glare. Everyone turned to face her, their attention now centered on her. Marcus just raised his eyebrows as the beginning of a grin took hold at the corners of his mouth.

"Easy, Tate", Marcus said.

"I'm not easy, Marcus. You of all people should know that. And I don't think you're drugs are going to work, Paula. It's not drugs I need. It's your help."

She saw Commander Riley shake his head as he retrieved his coat. "You don't believe me either, am I right Commander Riley?"

"Julie, this is slightly preposterous," he said softly. "I know you're hurting, but to blame this all on a watch?" he said, trying at once to be comforting as well as realistic.

"Commander, Julie's right about one thing. When I tried that watch on in the C-2 that took us to New York in December, I do remember becoming momentarily lightheaded, just like it happened to Steven. And sir? That was the most realistic costume party I had ever been to. And the music was great."

"Hey, Reuter. I have an idea. Call Radio City Music Hall and confirm the name of the show that played there, just for the hell of it," Julie said. She saw Reuter's face betray uneasiness. "Aw, go ahead, Reuter. Just humor this daughter of the South. And Rena; why don't you and Paul listen in on the extension?"

As Rena and Paul got up to go to the kitchen, Marcus's grin grew to a full-fledged smile. He didn't know what the hell happened to the Admiral, as he called Steven, but his instincts told him Julie Ann Tate was on to something. As Reuter pushed the buttons on the phone, he saw her patented "take the bull by the cogliones" style coming to full steam.

"Yes, you can help me, please," Reuter said into the receiver. "I was in New York this last Christmas. I was wondering if you might be able to tell me the name of the band in the Christmas show? It seems that I've forgotten...you know, the one that played after the *Maltese Falcon*? Huh?" Reuter's face was losing its color. "I distinctly saw that movie and then heard the band. It was Glenn something-or-other. No, I'm not kidding you! I distinctly saw that movie and heard a 'forties big band. Even the cast was dressed in 'forties garb in the audience. I do not drink! Listen, you! I'm going to....hey! Hello? Hello? Son of a bitch! She hung up on me!"

"Roto. What day were you in New York?" Julie asked, becoming more resolute by the second.

"December 23. We flew the new Tomcats home Christmas Eve."

"Marcus. Get the Post's morgue on the line. Check the New York Times of December 23, 1984 entertainment section for a show called "*Sentimental Journey*." That was the name of the show, right Roto?"

"Yes, it was. I remember Steve showing me the paper."

"Commander Riley, pay attention here. Try to relax, because in the next five minutes, you may need CPR. You might as well get your bag, Dr. Paula. He's gonna need it."

Marcus waited on the line as the clerk in the Washington Post's newspaper morgue ran her check.

"Nothing? Are you sure? Very well. Thank....."

"Hold it, White. I didn't dismiss you," she said with a smile. "Tell her to check the New York Times of December 23, 1941. Same entry."

"Julie, I don't know if..."

"Come here, Rena," she said reaching out as both Rena and Paul came back into the room. She hugged them both. "I told you he's okay. Unless he decides to go after a Jap aircraft carrier with..."

"It played at Radio City, December 23, 1941. Glenn Miller's band headlined the..." Marcus was in the initial stages of shock, uttering each word like it was his last. Riley sat in a heap, eyes goggled.

"Ha! I just fucking knew it!"

"Those people who wished us luck, the audience. They were really talking about the war! And the Japanese! Good Christ!" Reuter sat down, mumbling. "Shit. He didn't tell me," he managed. "He didn't tell me a thing."

"Would you have believed him, Roto?" Susan asked.

"I guess not."

"Commander Riley, let me show you a few pictures I found in my guy's sock drawer," Julie said, pulling several photos out of her bodice. "I keep them here for two reasons. One, because their precious, and two, because my precious hid them from me to protect my sanity too, Roto," she said, winking at Reuter's aghast face.

"Commander Riley, what kind of aircraft are these?" she asked.

"They're Grumman Wildcats- F4F-3s."

"Very good. Can you tell me when the Wildcat was deployed?"

Marcus White sat on the edge of his seat. All this research she had him doing on the story they were co-authoring began to make sense.

"In 1940 or 1941. Actually they were used throughout World War II. These two look brand new. Beautiful aerial shot, as well. Looks like they were just off Oceana, right there," Riley said, pointing to the little slip of land behind the planes.

"Very well, Commander. Now tell me. What ship is this?" Susan said with one eyebrow up, her red fingernail pointing to the vessel in the photo.

"It's a *Yorktown*-class carrier, also of World War II vintage. You can tell by the block-like island structure here," he said, as his eyes showed a tinge of alarm. "I see an "8" on her flight deck. That would be the...*Hornet*. Yes, the *Hornet*," he said, very proud of himself.

"Where's the *Hornet* now, Commander Riley?" Julie asked, seeing Rena's and Paul's faces light up, and Marcus moving to her side.

"It's at the bottom of the Pacific. It was sunk in the Battle of Santa Cruz during the Guadalcanal campaign. *Yorktown* was sunk earlier at Midway. *Enterprise* finished the war as the most decorated warship in our history, but shortsightedly was sold for scrap."

"So then, Commander, each of these ships are...gone?"

"Yes, Julie."

"Please look at the date of the photos, commander."

His face became flushed, then immediately pale. "This...this...cannot be...it's impossible!" He gaped at the two pictures over and over again.

"I took both these photos when Steven took me up in the TBF. It was quite a day, December 26, the day after Christmas. It was the day..."

"The *Hornet* left on its shakedown cruise, back in 1941. Why didn't you tell me about the photos, Julie?" Marcus asked, looking a little hurt.

"Because you would have started asking a lot of questions I couldn't answer when you saw the date. And Steven swore me to secrecy. And speaking of oaths of omerta, dear Suzie Q, what did the fabulous D-Man know?" Julie saw Susan's surprise at the question, and the beginnings of evasion in her eyes. "Out with it, sister. We're way beyond all that, as you already know."

"I think Danny was putting a lot of stuff together. He told Steven on a number of occasions to ditch the watch, but I know he and Steven went to see Mr. Levine, the jeweler who made up my engagement ring, to ask him about the watch, like if he experienced anything unusual while he was fixing it. It was a funny coincidence that Mr. Levine sold the watch to its original owner."

"That would be Lieutenant Raymond Moore, a torpedo plane pilot assigned to VT-8, deployed on the *Hornet*, Commander Riley. Right Marcus?" she said.

"Irrefutably," Marcus said.

"Danny was really shaken up to find out that Mr. Levine just vanished," Susan continued. "His store was completely empty of merchandise. He said he was so disturbed about Levine's disappearance that he had a dream that night where he was talking to Levine and his wife as newly-weds. It was really..."

"Eerie," Julie said.

"Yes! That's the exact word Danny used."

"Here is Levine's journal. I found it in Steven's room. Let's take a look. Do you see the entry here? Read it Rena. You'll understand how nuts this is."

Rena read the last journal entry, and gasped. "He thought my boy was this Raymond Moore fellow!"

"Why not? He was a young Navy pilot. He had Raymond Moore's car, and now he had Raymond's watch, or one of Raymond's watches. I got a hunch there was more than one, and Levine used the other to join his dead wife. Suzie Q, that was no dream your boy had. It was another brush with the...the..." Julie fumbled for words, trying to avoid another "eerie" type word.

"How about The Land of Then, Julie?" Paula said.

"For lack of a better term, okay."

"Commander Riley- back to you. What can you do to keep them looking for our guys?"

"Let's say I buy all this is so far. I'm not saying I am, but for argument's sake, let's say I do. Now...given that, what makes you think they'll be back? Levine never came back."

"Levine's best times were in the Land of Then. His wife died there. His hero Raymond Moore died in the Land of Then. My guy and Danny weren't around in the Land of Then. Their best times are in the Land of

Now. The basis of all this has got to be Steven's longing to know more about the Land of Then. Just look at his room and his collections and his car! But now, this longing for the Land of Then is fueled by the apparent unavenged murder of one Lieutenant Louis Thatcher at the hands of the Libyan Air Force. Perhaps it was the reason he insisted on getting the watch as soon as he got home. In the Land of Then, people didn't take any crap, apparently. All his heroes live in the Land of Then. Someone, or something, is allowing him to visit Then firsthand, for him to satisfy his curiosity or to make him whole, or to bring something back that will make him better understand the Now. When he was speaking to John Waldron, he looked like a kid who played little league baseball and got the chance to meet Reggie Jackson."

"John Waldron? The torpedo...?"

"One in the same, Commander Riley. But that's for another time."

"You know, when they came home after the cruise, Danny said that Steven was suffering a crisis of faith," Susan said. "What you just said reminded me of that."

"Perhaps it at least might help him come to better understand Thatcher death."

"I talked to him a few times about it. He didn't seem so overly burdened by Thatcher's death anymore. Right, Roto?" Riley said.

"I don't know about that, sir. When we visited New York he mentioned Thatch several times."

"And I've heard him mention his name in his sleep," Rena said. "Now I know who this fellow is."

Julie almost said the same thing, but discretion reared its head just in time.

"I guess he hasn't gotten over it, has he Commander?" Julie said, trying not to sound condescending. She really liked Riley, and felt his heart was in the right place. She couldn't legitimately judge him on this case of craziness.

"Neither have I," said Ware. He had been very quiet throughout this exercise, but now he looked up, his big brown eyes looking very sad. "And I'm embarrassed about it, and not because I feel so badly for Thatcher, which I do. I'm just wondering if my country will choose one day to use me, to string me out and then and cut me loose when I need her the most, just like they did to Thatcher. I mean, when is sacrifice necessary, justified, and appreciated? It wasn't with Thatcher."

"We're warriors, Ware. We're expected to take orders. We are expected to put it on the line," Riley said, very directly.

"Oh, I can do that, sir. But when can we fight back, like real warriors?"

"Gentlemen, we need to strategize," Marcus said, interrupting at the best time. "That is, about where they may happen to be. I would postulate they are aboard the *Hornet* or *Enterprise* on their way to Tokyo to launch Doolittle's bombers." Marcus couldn't believe his own statement. Dear God!

"I don't get the time frame," Paul Amato said. "My boy was interested in Midway, not the Doolittle raid."

"Mr. Amato, revisionist historians are looking at the Doolittle raid as the first salvo fired in the Midway engagement," Marcus said.

"I don't get you. Midway was two months away. That's a long battle," Riley said.

"Yes, but certain events precipitated by Doolittle's heroic foray must be taken into account. Remember, the Japanese were trying to draw out the American carriers to fight the Decisive Battle, around which their entire naval philosophy rotated. The concept of the Decisive Battle defined a major open water engagement where the Japanese would defeat the remnants of the American fleet, including the only striking power it had left after Pearl Harbor."

"The carriers," Roto said.

"Right, Lieutenant. Then too, they had to insure their promise that the holy ground of the Empire would never again be violated by bombs. To this end, they had to neutralize Hawaii and extend their defensive ring farther out across the Pacific. That was Midway."

"Wasn't there another major naval engagement, Marcus, just before Midway?" Julie asked.

"Coral Sea. That battle might actually be thought of as a sub-engagement of Midway as well. It was a defensive action on the American fleet's part to thwart the Japanese from taking Tulagi and New Guinea. The Japanese Army demanded air support against the marauding American carriers, whose air groups were harassing its efforts. Although we lost the *Lexington*, the Japanese were for the first time denied an objective. Their *Shokaku* was badly mauled, and, her sister *Zuikaku* practically lost her entire air group. Both would miss Midway. Admiral Yamamoto, the Japanese genius who planned Pearl Harbor, was resolved in his thinking that it was best to first destroy the American fleet, and then proceed with the scheduled conquests of the rich South Seas. Midway was a perfect choice because it was so close to Hawaii the Americans had to meet him with full force. From Midway, land based air and submarines could neutralize Hawaii to leave the Imperial Japanese Navy free to conquer all the Pacific, including Australia."

"Why the need to do it all so fast? Why not one step at a time? He was at the top of his game," Paula said. "When everyone turned to her in surprise, she said, "I minored in history at Georgetown. Hey, the School of Foreign Studies is there, you know?"

"Good question. Yamamoto knew time was also his enemy. Having lived here as a naval attaché, he had marveled at America's industrial might. He even studied at Harvard. He knew there were at least six carriers under construction with even more planned. They were the *Essex* class-bigger, faster, and more heavily armed than any afloat. His intelligence also told him that several of the battleships he sunk at Pearl Harbor were afloat again and being repaired."

"It still seemed he was on a roll," Paula offered.

"His battle plan overextended his forces. He had two less carriers than he planned on because of Coral Sea. Not only did he have to defeat the American fleet handily, he had to invade the island after neutralizing it with his carrier aircraft. With Midway secure, he could turn his full attention to destroying the American fleet when it sortied to battle his carrier and then retake the island. The United States would have to sue for peace. End of war, Japan wins the Pacific west of Hawaii."

"Yamamoto didn't think we'd ambush him while he was trying to take the island, right?"

"Right you are, Tate," Marcus said. "But the price was sacrificially incredible."

"Yes. I read the paper Steve did, Marcus. I know."

"It could very well be that Steve has been granted some subliminal wish, to be there in the times of his heroes to find what frame of mind was created by the battle on June 4, 1942. Even when he was just a boy he wanted to know what the justification was to ask men to die." Paul Amato had hit the nail directly on the head. He just hoped his son realized it as well, wherever he was.

Chapter 25

Steven and Danny climbed to the bridge to report to Waldron, who was quick to introduce them to the *Hornet's* skipper, Captain Pete Mitscher. His jutting jaw and craggy old salt face belied a brilliant mind and tireless force of will. He was beloved by his men for his no-nonsense attitude and his unqualified support. Mitscher had quite a history with the Navy, especially in the development of its air arm and aircraft carriers. He was destined to play a major part in the Pacific war, rising to the rank of Vice Admiral.

Mitscher sat in the elevated captain's chair on *Hornet's* bridge, Waldron at his side as they both watched the activity on the ship's aft flight deck. It was evident that the two had a special relationship that transcended differences of rank and age, as Mitscher laughed and joked with the commander of his torpedo squadron. He then focused his attention on the two none-the-less-for-wear naval aviators from another time, another space.

"You look pretty banged up," Mitscher said, surveying the two of them. "Just remember to tell Halsey it was all self-inflicted, and that the crew of *Hornet* isn't trying to outdo the *Big E* by beating up on her staff!" he said with a chuckle.

"We'll be sure of that, sir," Steven responded.

"Commander Waldron tells me that you fellows know the new TBF pretty well. Of course, I seriously doubt that since you cracked up and lost the only one in the fleet," he said, eyebrows up, choking a laugh that everyone else on the bridge let escape. "Anyway, are you physically able to spending some time in instruction with our torpedo pilots on the way back from Tokyo? If we have the TBFs waiting for us back at Ford Island, the ground instruction would have already been handled, and we can get right to flight training. Things are going to heat up after this little venture, I think." Mitscher grinned broadly.

Could he tell the captain that there wouldn't be any TBFs waiting for him when they got back, and that only six or seven TBFs would finally, but indirectly, make their way to him, not a whole squadron's worth someone had said might be there?

"Sure, sir. Anything we can do to help and not be in the way. As a matter of fact, the work might make us feel better about this bruising we took."

"That's the attitude!"

"Sir, is there anything we can do to help the Army guys?" Danny asked.

"Just be around to give them confidence in their take-offs from the ship and their mission. I think they're more afraid of the launch than the bombing run over Tokyo, but we've proved the B-25 can do it. We've got every department on this ship cooperating with them full-time. Even Frank Akers, my navigator, is helping them plot their course and update it with every possible alternative should something go amiss. Stephen Jurika, our intelligence officer, is providing target information, a little Japanese history, and the best way to get the hell out of there after they make their drops. The commander was attached to the embassy in Tokyo as naval attaché in 1939 specifically to make bombing maps. It appears we anticipated this little skirmish we're into at least two years ago."

"Don't tell the guys at Pearl, sir. They might be a bit annoyed at that," Waldron said.

"Indeed," Mitscher smirked, taking out a Camel cigarette and offering the pack to Waldron, who took one, and to Danny and Steven, who declined.

"Okay, gentlemen. Ground school will commence on the nineteenth, right after we get these Army bombers off the deck. Get some rest and heal up. And if you need anything, please don't be afraid to ask. You're family on my ship, not guests. We're in this together, all kidding aside."

As they descended a stairway from the bridge, Danny muttered, "We're in this together. That's what he said. I wish those apes at China Lake could have heard that."

"That's Mitscher. The Battle of the Philippine Sea marked the end of the Imperial Navy's offensive punch. He did something really ballsy during the simultaneous land campaign to capture the Mariana Islands. He was a rear admiral by then, and commanding a carrier task force. His flagship was the *Lexington*, the same one we all make our first carrier landings on now. His fleet was tethered to the Marianas to cover those landings. The islands would provide air bases for the B-29 bombers to really plaster the Japanese home islands, so the Imperial Fleet had to come out to fight. The Japanese launched an aerial armada against the U.S. fleet that was literally shredded in the most lopsided aerial battle in history.

"The Marianas Turkey Shoot; every Navy fighter pilot knows about that one."

"Right you are. Mitscher then launched a long range raid against the Japanese carriers that was very successful, but his strike was returning in the moonless black of night, very low on fuel. There were damaged planes and wounded crews searching for a deck to come home to. In the middle of submarine infested waters, he gave a simple order.

"Turn on the lights. That's what he said. I paid attention in Naval History."

"So you did. I am not surprised. Imagine; a blacked-out task force lighting up like the Fourth of July! No other admiral would have taken a chance like that."

"No one wants to take chances any more to do what's right. We're more concerned about our careers than our souls today. Then we brag about how wonderful we did the easy things, while we ignored the hard ones," Danny said.

Steven was surprised at those last comments. He was sounding more and more like him as the day wore on.

"Let's go find some Army guys. There's a few of them I'd really like to meet," Steven said, searching the flight deck.

"Like who?"

"Doolittle. Then Ted Lawson. Then three guys named Dean Hallmark of Texas, Harold Spatz of Kansas, and Bill Farrow from South Carolina."

"Everyone who ever flew a military airplane knows Doolittle, for sure. Lawson. Let me think. He...he wrote the book *Thirty Seconds Over Tokyo*! Hell, I saw that movie a hundred times when I was a kid! Van Johnson played him. And he's on this ship! Who were those other three guys though?"

"The bravest of them all. Let's get moving. I want to see those bombers."

The sixteen pristine B-25 Mitchell bombers were parked with their wings overhanging the ship's flight deck and packed as far aft as possible. The meticulous maintenance they each received was evidenced by their pristine condition. The planes' engines had just been run up to keep them in tune and free from the dampness and corrosive property of the sea's salt spray. Fueling personnel were topping off the tanks, just in case the airplanes had to be launched in a hurry. Interspersed were a few Dauntless dive bombers that couldn't be lowered into the hangar deck where the rest of the *Hornet's* hundred or so aircraft were placed. There wasn't any room, and the suggestion that the *Hornet* carry a few less of her own aircraft was met with disdain. What if the carriers had to fight their way back to Pearl Harbor? Would it be wise to do it with a few less planes? Standing next to an airplane named *The Ruptured Duck* whose nose bore a yellow duck in crutches, was Lieutenant Ted Lawson.

"Ted? They told me I would find you here. I'm Steve Amato. This is Danny Morello."

"More Navy guys? What do you need, another sap for poker? I'm tapped out. I got fourteen bucks left of the seventy I came aboard this scow with. That Gus Widhelm guy asked me to put my jacket in the pot when I couldn't see his ante. Not today," he laughed, shaking his hands." Hey, Dean!" he called to his co-pilot in the cockpit, "try that switch again for the turret. The mechanic said he replaced the solenoid that had crapped out."

"Is that turret jinxed?" Steven asked.

"The damn thing is never going to work. I can just see some slant-eye in his Zero coming in from my six o'clock high position, guns blazing, and I can't do a damned thing to him but smile."

"If you get off with surprise, you'll be gone before they know what hit them," Danny said.

"That's what Colonel Doolittle says, but I dunno. We're talking about Tokyo, not some godforsaken outpost. But whatever it takes, we gotta succeed. The country is depending on us," Lawson said, looking up to the dorsal turret to see his engineer-gunner Sergeant David Thatcher, spinning around freely. "Ha! It works. I guess you Navy guys can do something else besides play poker."

"Are you worried about getting off the ship?"

"You know, Steve, I'm more concerned with that then anything," Lawson said, an expression of angst coursing his face. "Look how angry those waves look. How do you guys do it day in and day out?"

"First of all, we train at it day in and day out. Second, we don't do it flying bombers designed to use a mile of runway. Third, we learn to swim real, real good. How do you think I survived this?" he said, waggling his arm in its sling, and pointing to Morello's wrist.

"You're the guys that went down in that new Navy plane, aren't you? Hell, let me tell you, we Army guys all thought you were goners, but the Navy kept telling us they would find you. We even hate to fly over water. It really is against our better instincts."

The three of them shared a laugh. Steven began to feel humbled about the situation he found himself in. "The country is depending on us." That's what Lawson said. And after the mission, the loss of his leg was to him a small price to pay for the privilege of being able to participate in the raid, and not let "the country" down.

"Just keep your revs high, your nose even with the horizon, and the nose wheel on the white line the crew painted here for you," Steven said, pointing to a white stripe that ran the length of the carrier's flight deck to the bow. "Get your gear up as soon as you've cleared the deck. That'll reduce drag."

"What about if that storm they're talking about kicks up? Won't the ship be rolling and rocking?" Lawson said.

Danny wanted to say, "That's rocking and rolling there, Ted," but didn't. Lawson might take him for some kind of faggot.

"That might actually help you. Your launch will be timed as the bow's rising, so you'll get an extra push upwards. As a matter of a fact, Ted, the Royal Navy has a plane they call the Harrier that uses a ski..."

What the hell was he about to say? Harrier? He saw Lawson looking at him quizzically, and Danny staring at him in disbelief.

"Anyway, Ted, the *Hornet* doesn't roll much due to her design, so don't worry about catching a wing on a wave."

"Thanks. I'll see you guys at dinner I guess."

"Take care."

"I bet Ted is going to wonder exactly what a Harrier is for a while. When you said "ski," I thought the ball game was over. I could see us in strait jackets," Danny said as they went below.

"I want to tell them so much. I want to tell them that it's all going to be worth it," Steven said.

"I think they already know that, Steve."

In the middle of a hot and heavy game of craps, Steven recognized the faces of the other three men he was looking for. Dean Hallmark and Harold Spatz were laying five dollar bills on the deck with two fighter pilots from VF-8, while Tex Gay of VT-8 shook and blew on the dice and finally threw them, yelling "Seven!" at the top of his lungs. Hallmark and Chamberlain turned away in agony. Steven was going to approach them, but thought better of it. He saw men under tremendous pressure having as good a time as circumstances would allow. He didn't need to satisfy his curiosity as to their personalities or inner thoughts. It was plain to see they were there to do a job, plain and simple. They volunteered for it and had every thought of success. What they really wanted to do at the moment was get their money back from those two Navy guys that were taking them for all they were worth.

In the meantime a deck above, a sergeant had asked Danny for help. He needed advice about a radio tube's worthiness, and was asking Danny if it would be possible to show him how a piece of test equipment already aboard the *Hornet* to service the new radios of the anticipated TBF's worked.

"That guy Waldron up on the bridge says you know the TBF inside and out."

Danny shrugged his shoulders and gave a "what-the-hell" expression and went along. He found the test equipment in one of the little shops that lined the HORNET's hangar deck, and managed to get it to respond as the sergeant wished.

"Here you go, sarge. This one is good as new."

"Thanks, sir. I want everything to work. This is important to us."

"I see that. Where are you from?"

"Kansas. My dad is a farmer out there. I hope he's doing all right. He hasn't been the same since my mom passed on. I want to get this war finished and go back to farmin'. I don't know if I have the courage to continue as a soldier."

"I think you guys are doing just fine."

"Thanks for the kind words, sir. And for the equipment help."

"Glad I could help."

He went back down to the pilots' quarters and ran into Steven coming up the stairs from the other direction.

"I see you met Harold Spatz," Steven said.

"Was that one of the guys you were looking for? I didn't even ask him his name. He was in such a hurry..."

"It's tension. I didn't get a chance to talk to my two guys. I thought it better to leave them as they were."

"Why are they so important to you?"

"Those three will be taken prisoner by the Japanese, along with five others in China. They will be routinely tortured and forced to sign statements that alleged that their mission was to strafe schools and hospitals as well as bomb residential neighborhoods. For a while they were held in Nagasaki, but were returned to Shanghai in June for a mock trial, found guilty, and sentenced to die. On October 15, 1942, they will be paraded out into a small cemetery, tied to crosses as they kneel and blindfolded with a white cloth. A black ink circle will be put on the cloth directly over the center of their foreheads. From twenty feet away, six Japanese riflemen in two ranks will be standing by. On order, the three in the front ranks took aim at the three black marks and fired. Their deaths were mercifully instantaneous. Their wounds will be bandaged, their bodies placed in coffins, then cremated. That's why Hallmark, Shatz, and Chamberlain were so special. Another pilot, Bob Meder, will die of malnutrition and disease a year later. He was Hallmark's co-pilot."

"Dear God in heaven," Danny said. "Do you think they would drop out if they knew?"

"They had the chance. They wouldn't hear of it. If only their planes had a few more legs, it wouldn't have...Danny! I've got an idea! We've got to talk with Doolittle tomorrow morning. I don't think the planes have been armed yet. Remember when you said you wondered if we could change history? Well, we are going to find out."

Early the next morning, Doolittle walked to his B-25s with Mitscher and Waldron in tow. The planes were going through start-ups again, and afterwards would be armed with the bombs they would take along to Tokyo after a brief ceremony on the *Hornet's* deck. Halsey and Doolittle and Mitscher wanted to "give back" a few medals the Japanese had presented to them years ago as recognition of their aerial feats. Walking along with them was a face unfamiliar to Steven, but upon asking another pilot, he found it was Commander Apollo Soucek, the carrier's air officer. All the better, Steven thought. The group approached Ted Lawson's *Ruptured Duck*. Lawson saw Steve and Danny first.

"Hey, you guys! Did you find another chump for poker last night?" he asked.

"No Ted. You were our last hope. 'Attention on deck!' Steve couldn't have timed it better.

"As you were," Mitscher said. "So, Amato, Morello-how are we feeling today? Are you still trying to blame the airplane for your accident?" he said with a chuckle. "Lawson here already knows you're full of shit."

"Just trying to be some help, sir."

"How's the ship, Ted?" Doolittle asked.

"Just fine, sir. All ready to go, except for the bombs."

"Sir, I was thinking...uh, may I?" Steven said, trying to sound as innocent and innovating as possible.

"That's why we sent you to Annapolis. If we wanted you dumb, we would have sent you to West Point. Uh, no offense Jimmy."

"I'm gonna remember that, Captain. What's on your mind, son?"

"Sir, fuel seems to be the primary concern; that is, after you manage to get off the deck, right Ted?"

"Right. One piece of grief at a time."

"Let's say the *Hornet* and her force is detected before we get you within five hundred miles of Japan, your fueled range. Let's further say we have to launch you early to bring our own planes up to defend these precious decks of ours."

"We'd be in a spot, for sure. However, we are prepared to take that risk," Doolittle responded. It wasn't bravado. It was perfect mission planning, with a smattering of guts added.

"I understand each plane will carry two thousand pounds of bombs. Am I correct?" Steven said.

"Yes, you are. Three five-hundred pound fragmentary bombs,and one five-hundred pound incendiary."

"So you'll be dropping a grand total of 32,000 pounds of bombs from sixteen planes over three or four cities, depending on weather, launch points, and whatever."

"Yes. What are you driving at, Lieutenant? I'm not that fond of Plato or Socrates right now. Oh, by the way, Pete, we learned about those guys at West Point."

"Sixteen tons of bombs is not going to do a hell of a lot of damage to the Japanese spread over the area we're talking about. You know that as well as I. Therefore, I have to believe that the material damage is secondary to the mental damage you want to do, and the boost in morale you want the folks back home to get from this. I think that if you dropped a toilet in the Emperor's courtyard, the effect it would have on the Jap military leadership would be just as profound as a bomb dropped on a ball bearing factory. Therefore, why not lessen the load of bombs you plan to carry?"

"He's got a point there, Jimmy," Mitscher said. "It would make the mission a lot more certain of being able to land at your destinations in China, especially if we have to get you off earlier than we anticipate, or your planes suffer battle damage."

"That's right, Colonel. We could also put another gasoline bladder in the bomb bay, or failing that, lengthen the distance the gas you are carrying will have to take you. At the least, it will certainly get you off the deck easier," Soucek added.

Doolittle put his hand to his chin, thinking about this alternative. He had probably thought of this contingency somewhere along the planning stages of this exercise, but had dismissed it by applying the primary axiom of strategic bombing-putting maximum ordnance on the target. His mission profile and therefore all his training was dedicated to taking up a ton of bombs in each plane. But what if they did have to launch earlier? Now, out on the middle of the Pacific Ocean, the lighter load/additional gas option had to be considered.

"What do you think, Ted?" Doolittle asked.

"We planned for maximum damage. I would risk running out of gas if it meant really plastering a target."

"But Ted, there aren't enough of you to really plaster a target, but there are more than enough of you to really put the fear of God into Tojo and his drinking buddies, not to say what it will do to their populace. They'll be looking up in the sky before they take a leak when they get up in the morning for months," Danny added.

"But what about the paper city Tokyo is supposed to be?" Dean Chamberlain joined the conversation.

"A few tons of bombs aren't going to cause a major fire, Dean," Steven said. *If only you knew how badly you would need that gas, Dean,* Steven thought.

"What if a number of us get knocked down before our drops? That will drastically reduce the tonnage of bombs we'd be delivering. We should cause some damage if we've gone through all this, don't you think?" Chamberlain was more adamant than anyone else.

"What if your surprise factor is 100 percent and none of you are shot down? You're going to have a hell of a time getting to the airfields in

China as it is, and that's with the hope that General Stillwell still owns them. Commander Soucek said they're changing hands by the hour. What if you run into bad weather and get lost? Add to that the extra miles if we have to launch you earlier than planned. Every hour we sail west is about twenty four miles you don't have to fly. If one bomb is dropped, you've made your point, and accomplished your mission."

Steven was pressing, and he saw Doolittle become a bit uncomfortable, but Steven knew something Doolittle didn't know-all this happened to Doolittle's crews.

Another of Doolittle's pilots, Lieutenant Everett Holstrom, spoke up. "I don't see any reason to change the profile, sir. I think we should go as planned. We can fly 2,000 miles with a 100-mile gas reserve. Why throw a bomb away to fly a little farther? Hell, why throw a bomb away to add five hundred pounds of gas? I'm out to kill Japs, not save gas."

"Okay. Let's load up the bombs. We'll go as we planned. Thanks anyway, Lieutenant Amato, but I think we had better go the way we trained," Doolittle said.

"I understand, sir. Good luck!" Amato said.

"Hey, Morello. Why don't you tie that kraut watch to one of the bombs? We all tied our old Japanese medals and such to others. Go ahead, son. Make a contribution to the Jap's scrap metal supply we're sending them," Waldron said.

Danny really had no choice. He whispered to Steve as he brushed passed him on the way to a bomb trolley loaded with incendiary bombs for Lawson's *Ruptured Duck*. "When we get back, if we get back, you owe me a watch, you bastard!"

At 3:15 a.m. on April 18, the *Hornet's* electrical general alarm sounded incessantly, and Danny rustled in his bunk as he felt the ship heel to starboard in a tight turn. Sailors ran to their battle stations, pilots to the hangar deck, and Colonel Doolittle's band to the ready room they borrowed. Waldron came down to Torpedo 8's ready room. He looked on a map posted over the blackboard and frowned.

Ray Moore walked up to him and asked, "What's up, skipper?"

"The *Enterprise* reports two surface contacts ten miles ahead. We're turning north to avoid them. It looks like we've run into a Japanese picket line. I don't think we're going to be able to continue westward. Doolittle was to take off at two this afternoon, with the rest of his group following a few hours later. The raid was supposed to occur at night, with Doolittle lighting up Tokyo with incendiary bombs for the rest of the group to home in on. Now, I dunno."

"I sure as hell wished they carried one less bomb and more gas, because now, it's a real stretch," Moore said. "I think Steve Amato was right."

"Well, we can't do shit about it now," Waldron answered, a scowl painted on his face.

"What's all the noise about?" Steven said, entering the ready room. Every ready room on the carrier had an odor that wasn't prevalent on the carriers of Steven's navy-stale cigarette smoke. As he felt the ship heel hard to starboard, he narrowed his eyes and said to Waldron, "I guess we've been noticed."

"The Japanese must have a picket line established out here," he said pointing to the map. "We're almost 700 miles from Tokyo, as I figure it. No one ever said anything about a picket line. The Captain said the subs that reconned this route reported no patrol vessels. Shit!"

"It's Murphy's Law," Steven said, and when Waldron turned his head, he realized an explanation was probably now due.

"Who the hell is Murphy?" Waldron asked.

Way to go, Amato- you shithead! "It's a one of those new sayings that are going around. Basically, Murphy's Law states that if something can go wrong, it will go wrong."

"Fucking Murphy must have been an optimist! Look at what the hell is happening here!" Waldron replied.

"Anybody who makes China now has a real talent for saving gas," Ray Moore added.

Task Force 16 pressed westward. Like Steven had said, every hour meant another twenty-four miles the Mitchells didn't have to fly. The crew ate breakfast at general quarters. Where there was a picket boat, a submarine and enemy air couldn't be far behind.

Pete Mitscher saw an SBD make a low pass over *Enterprise*. Its pilot dropped a bean bag on her deck. It was the way patrol aircraft relayed reconnaissance information under radio silence conditions during the war. Mitscher didn't need a crystal ball to know what it said.

"Get Colonel Doolittle up here on the double," Mitscher directed his aide. Halsey sent him a message that the SBD pilot who had dropped the bean bag on had spotted a string of patrol boats about twenty miles directly in front of the task force. He also said he was sure he was spotted as well. Then another signal from *Enterprise* was transmitted by signal light. It was the one Mitscher expected since 3:15 a.m., but had hoped against hope that he would receive it a few hours and miles later.

LAUNCH AIRCRAFT

If the Japanese had any doubts about the messages they received from their spies, they were all laid to rest when they spotted that American

SBD. A message went out to their coastal bomber units and to the carriers *Akagi, Soryu, and Hiryu*, returning from a victorious sweep of the South China Sea:

ENGAGE AND SINK THE AMERICAN CARRIERS

The Japanese were expecting an engagement the day afterward, when their striking forces would be primed. Their own picket boats spoiled their surprise.

"Colonel, it appears we've been found out. We are turning into the wind. It's time to go," Mitscher said.

"Thanks, Pete."

Doolittle went down to the ready room to get his men. He stuck his head into the ready room, where Steve, Danny and a good number of Air Group 8 pilots were giving last minute do's and don't's, and he simply said, "Okay fellas. Let's go."

Hands were shaken and a few bear hugs were exchanged, as well as apologies for any overly excessive gambling winnings. Lawson hugged Steve Amato, and said something Danny couldn't quite hear in the din. Then Doolittle's men went to their waiting B-25s.

At 8:20 a.m., with 168 more miles to fly than intended, the wings of Doolittle's B-25 caught enough of the fifty knot wind blowing down *Hornet's* deck to fly, just as the bow of the ship came up off a wave trough the storm had kicked up, giving the plane an added boost. Each plane's takeoff after that was helped by the concentrated force of will generated by a thousand pounding hearts and two thousand watchful eyes of the men in Task Force 16. As each one caught the wind, an inspiring cheer rang out from the ships. As one plane hung on the edge of a stall, its tail barely clearing the crests of the waves reaching up to it, it seemed the shouts and minds and hearts actually lifted the plane to safety.

"What did Lawson say to you before he left?" Danny asked. "I saw you were both all teary eyed about it. If you don't want to tell me, that's fine, but I..."

The Ruptured Duck's was making its run into eternity. The wheels left the deck. Atta boy Ted! Steve thought. Nice run! Now get those goddam wheels...thatta boy, Ted. Way to be!

"He said thanks for the suggestion about the bombs and gas, but he really didn't expect to make it to China anyway, and as long as he was going to die, the extra bomb meant the chance of taking that many more Japs with him."

"They are some kinda guys," Danny said, finding his own chin quivering.

"He gave me this letter to mail to his wife in the event he doesn't make it back."

"They didn't listen to you about the gas and lightening their bomb load, so I guess nothing changes. Lawson does make it back, barely, and four guys die. It's history. Why don't you throw it away?"

"Not quite yet," Steven responded, seeing the last of the B-25s turn westward on a direct course for downtown Tokyo. Suddenly, he stomped his feet and burst out, "Damn it! It would have been great to have those planes enshrined in museums around the country. Now their wrecks will be put on display in Tokyo to assure the Japanese people revenge had been exacted. All of them will garbage by the end of the day, all for a lousy 8,000 pounds of bombs one lousy Phantom could easily carry today. If only they knew what was coming in the form of the B-29 in a few years, perhaps this wouldn't have happened and there would be four more guys at their famous reunions years and years later."

"Hey, Steve. Remember your perspective. This is then, not now."

The return trip to Pearl Harbor was uneventful. Steve and Danny established "*The Flying Ronzoni*s Ground School" for VT-8's pilots to acquaint them with the new TBF, and they had great fun doing it. Waldron, a taskmaster to be sure, appreciated their hard work and their sense of duty, and made no bones about letting everyone know. When VT-8 wasn't flying its Devastators, or its pilots weren't doing calisthenics, they were at "Ronzoni Prep".

Steven by chance passed by Waldron's opened cabin door the day before they entered Pearl Harbor, and saw Waldron looking at a picture on his desk. He turned to Steven and said, "Hey Amats. Aren't these the most beautiful little girls you've ever seen?"

Steven looked at the picture and smiled. The old war horse, the blood and guts leader, the tough as nails taskmaster was a bowl of mush when he talked about his little girls.

Steve and Danny were on deck as the *Hornet* rounded Diamond Point and turned up the channel leading to her berthing space next to Ford Island. Cheers went up from the men lining the channel. Although the mission had been a secret, it didn't take the average man long to determine that the HORNET left with Army bombers of the same type the intercepted Japanese messages had identified as having bombed Tokyo. And everybody knew the range of a B-25.

The cheering subsided when the ship passed the hulk of the capsized battleship *Oklahoma*. It died out entirely when it passed the twisted mass of blackened metal that had once been the proud battleship *Arizona*, still flying her battle flag at her stern. The old target battleship *Utah* lay capsized on the other side of Ford Island, where she had berthed by chance on December 5 in the *Enterprise's* spot. Because her topsides were heavily timbered, she somewhat resembled a carrier from the air, and the

Japanese Kate torpedo planes and Val dive bombers plastered her two days later. Pete Mitscher wiped his eyes and blew his nose.

Steven took all this in, himself awestruck at the condition of the ships. All the material he had read, all the pictures he had seen, all the newsreels he had collected, none of it prepared him for the scene of massacre he saw before him, in living color. The backdrop of broken and burned ships against the beautiful Hawaiian skies was totally incongruous, but the odor of burned oil and burned flesh, of molten metal and charred wood, the stench of death, made it all too real. The term of "the Sunday Murders" was used in the fleet to describe the day the world stopped cold.

Ted Lawson's mindset, though not logical, was at the least understandable. Those B-25s ran on hate as much as they did on gasoline. This was not merely a war, that much was evident from what Steven and Danny witnessed here. Death was acceptable now, if it meant the annihilation of the Japanese at every opportunity.

It was a blood feud, pure and simple, but of epic proportions.

Chapter 26

Julie Tate, Susan Amato, and Marcus White arrived on Oahu several hours before Paul and Rena Amato were to arrive. It was Julie's and Susan's first visit to the Hawaiian Islands, while Marcus had taken an "R and R" there while stationed in Vietnam in 1967. Julie and Marcus had sold the Post on the fact that she needed to spend at least two weeks there to complete the story she was working on, and Marcus's help was instrumental to her. Paul and Rena expected the trip to Hawaii to mark their twenty-fifth wedding anniversary, not the point-of-return where Julie said Steve and Danny would probably arrive after their "rescue." Julie's determination and mindset was so overwhelmingly strong that Rena and Paul had almost no choice but to believe in her. The only doubting Thomas remained Lieutenant Commander Riley, who none the less managed to get the Navy to send him, Todd Reuter, and Tommy Ware to Hawaii for "about a month" to determine if all efforts were truly exhausted to recover the bodies" of Amato and Morello. They remained listed as missing. The Navy was using the deep diving submersible *Alvin* to try to locate the lost F-14's forward section to ostensibly recover the pilot's bodies, but more so to salvage the top secret radar and air-to-ground delivery systems and software Vincent Capo had designed.

Julie's and Marcus's first stop after depositing their luggage at the Royal Hawaiian Hotel was the USS *Arizona* memorial. Every visitor to the island of Oahu, Japanese and American alike, made it a point of seeing the remains of the once great battleship. The ship's superstructure had long been cut away to make room for the memorial that stood amidships across the her beam. When she exploded, eyewitnesses saw the ship literally leap from the water with bodies, parts of bodies, and the personal effects of its men joining the shards of metal that were scattered all over the heretofore neat and tidy anchorage.

"Those of us who live in our generation can't really know the anger and fire for vengeance that the sinking of this ship created," Marcus said.

"Before 8:00 a.m. Hawaiian time on December 7, one of every two congressmen were neutralists, quite willing to let England go under to Germany, and let Japan have China. At ten o'clock, every one of them was quite willing to wipe the Japanese race from the face of the earth. It's funny how one ship can make such a difference. The Pearl Harbor raid has played a dominant role in the foreign and defense policy of this country ever since. And every ship that sailed westward toward Japan had to pass this one we're above right now. Can you imagine the terrible resolve their crews must have been filled with? Americans hate to lose. What compounded it was America's dormant racism. That yellow men did this to them was unforgiveable. It made the dropping of the A-bombs on Hiroshima and Nagasaki all the easier."

"You mentioned Yamamoto. He's the one that planned the raid, correct?" Julie Ann said.

"He told the Japanese general staff that he could run wild for six months, maybe a year at best. After that he couldn't guarantee anything, because the industrial might of the United States would make it possible for Japan to survive. After five months of an uninterrupted string of victories, he got cocky, so much so that he never planned on getting ambushed by the American aircraft carriers he sought so desperately to sink as he tried to extend Japan's defensive perimeter, all this due in no small part to Doolittle's raid. Like I said, many view it as the opening shot of the Midway campaign. Yamamoto and his staff were so confident that they thought the Americans would follow his operational plan, just as if it were a script he had written for them."

"Well, if this was 1942, the actual battle for Midway is set to commence in about three days. I hope we're on the right track, Marcus," Julie said, taking his arm.

"Don't worry, Tate. I'm sure the admiral will be found nonetheless for wear," Marcus said reassuringly. "Even if the whole thing is preposterous," he added, for his own sanity.

Julie was getting dressed to meet the Amato's for dinner at about six in the evening. The phone in her room rang and she picked up her phone.

"Julie? This is Commander Riley."

"How are you, Commander. Have you found anything as yet?"

"Yes, we have. We've recovered the nose section of Steven and Danny's F-14."

"And?" Her heart pounded so. She truly feared for the answer she would receive, for it was the last bit of proof she needed for her hypothesis, as supernatural as it sounded, to be correct.

"They must have gotten out. The ejection seats are gone."

"I knew it! They didn't go down with the plane! Commander, they are alive, somewhere."

"Julie. Please don't go getting your hopes up. Just because they escaped doesn't mean they're alive. They've been missing for almost two months now. They ejected in a violent squall. This is a big ocean, and they could have...hold on a minute, Julie. Something else is coming over the wire."

She heard the whine of what had to be a fax machine in the background, and while she could distinguish Riley's voice, she couldn't decipher what he was saying on the other phone in the office used by the search and rescue squadron.

"By sheer luck, the *Alvin* also came up with their helmets, and their ejection seats, about a mile from the wreck."

"That's wonderful! That confirms it!" she squealed.

"If you want excitement, wait till you hear this. The helmets and seats were found within twenty yards of the wreckage of a TBF. The damned plane must have been down there since the war. *Alvin* at first thought it might be the Tomcat because of the sonar signature it reported. I would think they made it out of the plane alive, and shed their helmets to keep the weight in their rafts down," Riley said. "I'm flying back out to the *Alvin's* mother ship tomorrow, Julie. Todd and Tom are still there."

"Keep the faith, Commander."

"I hope so, Julie. Good night."

"Hello, Julie?" Marcus asked as he knocked on the door. "It's time for dinner. Julie?"

She opened the door and Marcus stepped in. "Why the smiles, Tate?"

"Commander Riley just called. They found the F-14 without ejection seats, and Steven's and Danny's helmets about a mile away, next to an old TBF. It seems that..."

"Did Riley get a number off the old TBF?" Marcus asked excitedly.

"He didn't mention any number. Why?"

Marcus ran to the phone and picked up the receiver, asking, "Julie, what's Riley's number?"

She fumbled in her bag, found her black book and handed it to him.

"This is the 85th Air Sea Rescue Squadron. May I help you?"

"Yes, you may. Lieutenant Commander Riley, please?"

A minute later, Riley came on the phone, interrupting Marcus's doodling on the note pad with the Royal Hawaiian's name and logo on it.

"Lieutenant Commander Riley here. May I help you?"

"Commander, its Marcus White on this end."

"Hello, Marcus."

"The TBF you found, Commander. Did *Alvin* photograph it? Do you have the location of it?"

"I would assume it did photograph it. It's procedure to photograph any interesting artifact on the ocean floor. And we would have charted it as well. Why?"

"If I can get a serial number, and I have the location, I can...."

"You can find out when it went down, and who owned it, right?"

"Absolutely."

"Hold on, Marcus. I'll contact *Alvin's* mother ship."

Julie's eyes had widened considerably, and she nervously tapped her teeth with a fingernail and paced the floor. Marcus went back to his doodling.

"Marcus, the information just came through by fax. The serial number was 62-1122. There isn't a squadron number. That's odd, but it's possible it could have eroded away. From the photos, though the plane isn't in too bad a condition considering its demise and the years of salt water corrosion. I would venture to guess that it hit the water at a fairly shallow angle, as it's fairly intact."

"What's the position, Commander Riley?"

Marcus carefully wrote the information on the pad, and then said to Riley, "I'll get a check going right now. I have a friend in the Pentagon that owes me. I'll get back to you, Commander."

Marcus hung up, looked up a number in his little black book, and dialed again, thinking that waking up an admiral at two in the morning eastern daylight time might very well mean an execution by keelhauling, but this couldn't wait.

After three rings a groggy voice said, "Hello?"

"Ah, Admiral Tegan. Did I wake you? I'm so sorry."

"Marcus, is that you?"

"Yes, admiral it is. I'm so pleased you recognized my voice. Do you recall that favor I did for you last year? You know, the story of the *Iowa* class battleships?"

"Yes, I do Marcus. That story you wrote about the need to bring those battleships out of mothballs and refitting them with cruise missiles helped us a great deal with the Congress." The voice indicated a fully awakened individual now controlled it.

"Well Admiral Tegan, I'm calling in my chit, so to speak."

"As long as it doesn't involve a state secret. Shoot."

About twelve hours later, at six in the morning, a groggy Marcus White picked up his phone.

"Hello?" he said sleepily.

"Gotcha! Ha!"

"Admiral?"

"Vice Admiral Robert A. Tegan, at your service, sir. I got your information on the TBF."

"I'm all ears," Marcus said, reaching for a pad.

"That bird went down on April 9, 1942. It was one of the first TBFs to come off of Grumman's assembly line, and was assigned to the *Enterprise*'s torpedo squadron for carrier qualification and operational suitability trials. It has been listed as missing all these years. Now, we've found it."

"What about the crew?" Marcus asked.

"Missing as well. They were a Navy test team." There was a slight hesitation in Tegan's voice, and then surprise. "Hey, if I got my facts straight, the *Big E* should have been on the way to Tokyo with the *Hornet* and Colonel Doolittle."

"You have them straight, Admiral."

"What's the scoop? Why are you so interested in a forty-year old wreck for?"

"The Navy lost an F-14 in the same area a few months ago. I thought it odd that..."

"What do you know about that F-14 loss, Marcus? Or should I ask how you found out about it?" Tegan's voice had changed from high pitched jolly to deep toned concern.

"It's a long story, Admiral Tegan. I'll tell it to you in a few weeks."

"I'll be dying to hear it, Marcus. Good bye."

"Good bye. And thanks!"

Marcus shook his head in disbelief. There was too much coincidence here. He dialed Julie Ann Tate's room to tell her the good, yet odd, news.

Chapter 27

The *Hornet* returned to sea with the *Enterprise*, but left Danny Morello and Steven Amato ashore to await Swede Larsen, Al Earnest, and the contingent of TBFs that were winging their way to Waldron. Gene Lindsey of Torpedo Six reminded Waldron that Amato and Morello belonged to him, and Waldron reminded Lindsey that if it hadn't been for *Hornet's* task group, neither Amato nor Morello would be alive, so "back off!" he had said, quite good naturedly.

As Steven had expected, word was filtering back through the rumor mill that *Lexington* and *Yorktown* had gotten into a scrape with the Japanese fleet in the Coral Sea, off Tulagi in the Solomon Islands. Steven had difficulty remaining "in the dark" as to the outcome of it all. When it was heard that the Japanese carrier *Shoho* had been sunk, Pearl Harbor was delirious with the joy of blood lust. When it was heard *Lexington* had been sunk, the mood turned somber. The *Lady Lex* had been converted from a battlecruiser hull as was her sister *Saratoga* to become the Navy's first fleet carriers in 1928. She was huge at 36,000 tons, her block-like island giving her the look of indestructibility. Practically every aviator with the rank of lieutenant or above on any other carrier had served on one of those grand sisters at one point or other in their careers. *Lexington* was known to be a happy ship, loved by her crew and respected for her efficiency. Now she rested on the bottom of the Coral Sea, and the officers and enlisted men who served or had served as part of her crew or air group were shocked to tears.

Steven and Danny saw the faces turn more sour when word also filtered in that *Yorktown* had been mauled as well, and was limping back for repairs.

After futilely sailing at full speed to engage in the Coral Sea battle, the *Enterprise* and *Hornet* returned to arrive at Pearl Harbor on May 26. They fueled and provisioned at a feverish pitch. The crews did not go ashore, working under sunlight and floodlight. The air groups did not leave Ford Island or Kaneohe Naval Air Station. The pace of preparation was near hysterical. Senior officers crawled all over the two carriers and their task groups. In a ceremony on the *Big E's* flight deck, Danny and Steve overhead Admiral Chester Nimitz, the Commander in Chief of the Pacific fleet, tell Roger Mehle of VF-6 as he pinned the Distinguished Flying Cross to his chest, "Congratulations, Roger. I think you'll have a chance to do it again in a few days."

AS TIME GOES BY

Danny and Steven were sought out by a VT-6 pilot who had left his name with several people in their barracks on Ford Island. Finally, they came upon Lieutenant (jg) Charles P. Whitney, whom they found reading the pilot's manual for the TBF on Steven's bunk.

Steven couldn't believe it. Whitney was young and dashing. He sported a thin blond mustache on a narrow face, that did not look all that different from the one Steven had come to know. His blue eyes were even more penetrating in his youth.

"The guys said you were the TBF experts. I heard we're in for a full scale sea battle, and we were sailing with TBFs. Is that correct?" he asked.

"I don't think they'll get here in time, Mr. Whitney."

"Are you sure? Gene Lindsey says that they'd be here by the time...."

"Mr. Whitney, there is no time. The plan is that we're going to ambush the Japanese Fleet off Midway, and we sail tomorrow."

"Why don't you call me Charlie, like everyone else? Why the formality? And how do you know the battle plan already? Lindsey is hearing it now for the first time at a briefing by Nimitz's staff on the *Enterprise*."

Steven wanted to blurt out 'force of habit,' but caught himself just in time. Just yesterday, Waldron was watching Danny pitching baseballs, and when he complimented Danny on his unbelievable fastball and curve, Steven said, "Oh, yeah. The California Angels were really interested in signing him." When he saw Waldron's contorted and confused face, he said, "Oh, they're a minor league farm team for the Yankees."

"Charlie, I guess I'm just a little clairvoyant. Sorry."

"No problem. I'm really disappointed about those TBFs though. I would hate to attack the Japanese fleet with those Devastators. There so damned slow and vulnerable. We're being told by *Yorktown's* air group that it was pure luck that their torpedo guys even got a few hits on the *Shoho*. The damned things misfired, broke, or ran amok. They say if the Japanese gunners or fighters had been any better, they would have been decimated. But how do you know about the Midway..."

"Keep the faith Charlie. Maybe we'll luck out again. Who knows?"

"I've got to do some damage to those fucking Japs. I don't care if I have to crash my damned plane into one of them, like Bombing Five's Johnny Powers from the *Yorktown* just did to SHOKAKU. I heard he's getting the Medal of Honor. I can't think of a better way to go than to take a bunch of them yellow bastards with me, after what they've done to us."

"You'll get your chance, I'm sure," Steven said, trying to sound honest as well as reassuring.

"Hey, Amats!", Danny yelled from his window, "The *Yorktown* is coming in, and she looks like she took a real pounding. She's trailing oil, and her hull and bridge are smoked up. Come and take a look."

Steven ran to the window and saw the great ship had a slight list to starboard. "She took a bomb hit that twisted her insides forward, and several near misses that shook her to her bilges, caved in her starboard side, and peppered her with shrapnel. Look at the holes in her starboard side! It took a miracle to transform her to battleworthiness in the next forty eight hours."

"How do you how hard she was hit? And how can she sail in that condition in only forty eight hours? Her air group came in a few hours ago, and it was decimated! She won't have enough planes or pilots to sortie."

"They'll use parts of *Saratoga's* air group. She left them here when she went stateside to get repaired from that torpedo she took."

"I hear *Saratoga's* on her way back here as we speak," Whitney said.

"She'll be too late."

"And how do you know that?" Whitney exclaimed. "And they'll never repair the *Yorktown* in time. Never! And this Midway deal. How did..."

"Want to lay a few dollars on that, Charlie?" Steven said, again cutting him off at the pass. Danny and I might as well have some fun, he thought, as he saw Danny look on, smiling like the cat that ate the canary. He wasn't going to change anything. Doolittle's mission saw to that...so far. Besides, Whitney was so damned sure of himself, he needed to get taken down a peg.

"And by the way, you better make sure that Devastator of yours is in tip top condition, or you might not get a crack at a Jap carrier."

"I've been to Marcus, Wake, and to Kwajalein, and I've never missed a mission yet. I'll be there when the curtain goes up, Amato. Count on it."

"How about that fancy tie clasp against fifty bucks?" he said. The tie clasp had the insignia of VT-6 in enamel inlaid in gold, over the silhouette of the *Enterprise*, also in gold.

"Fifty bucks? This is real gold! Make it a hundred, pal!"

"You're on, Charlie," he said, shaking Whitney's outstretched hand. "I just hope both of us are around to collect, no matter who the winner is."

"How about another fifty I put a hole in a Jap carrier in this...Midway deal?"

"Why don't we just let it go at that, and not tempt fate?" Steven said.

"I guess you're right. How about I buy you and Morello here a drink?"

"You're on again. Let's go."

They exited into a frenzy of activity. Supply trucks were making their way down to the carriers filled with all kinds of food stuffs, rags, ammunition of all calibers, aircraft spare parts, uniforms, lubricants, cigarettes, paper, mimeograph ink, and the thousands of other items needed to keep the two floating behemoths at sea in harm's way for two weeks. In addition, barges and lighters full of fuel oil pulled alongside each of the carriers and began to pump the "Navy Special" and aviation gasoline deep into the carriers' bowels. Brand new F4F-4s, a faster version of the Wildcat fighter with folding wings, filled the taxiways and hangars of Kaneohe and Ford Island, waiting the word to fly out to their new homes. The folding wings meant the carriers could carry more of them to increase fighter escort for attack planes as well as their self-defensive combat air patrols, or CAPs. To Waldron's and Lindsey's dismay, no TBFs appeared.

Waldron caught glimpse of a truck that had twin thirty caliber mounts that the Dauntless dive bombers carried for their rear seat gunners. He grabbed Danny as he was just passing by, and they followed it to a weapons depot. "You still got that cast on, I see?"

"Yes sir. The doc said it still isn't healed."

"Great! Come with me, Morello. At last, you might be able to do me some good."

"What do you want with those guns?" Danny asked.

"Our Devastators have only one thirty caliber in the rear seat. Those are twin mounts. If I can get them for our planes, I would have doubled our firepower, and from what I'm hearing, we're sure as hell gonna need it, Morello. Let me do the talking. Just back me up if I need it."

"May I help you, sir?" the ensign by the depot's gate asked.

"Yes, you may," Waldron said. "I'm Lieutenant Commander Wade McCluskey, CO of VB-6 on the *Enterprise*. I see you've got my guns. Why don't you just follow me to..."

"Let me check my requisitions, sir," the ensign said in a very official voice. After searching through a clipboard of lists, he said, "I'm sorry sir, but I don't see a requisition for these weapons. From what I have here, they're spares for storage, and not designated for..."

"That's impossible!" Waldron yelped, as he watched the ensign jump back a step. "These goddam guns are for my Dauntlesses. I've been waiting for them since before our last sortie, and I'll be goddammed if...why am I talking to you? Who's your boss, ensign?"

"Well, sir, I'm kind of in charge here. Lieutenant Commander Woods is in sick bay..."

"And he left you 'kind of in charge?' He's in deep trouble now," he said turning away, but just as quickly turning back. "Okay, ensign. Listen up. I haven't got the time to squeal on you up the chain of command. I'm going to let you in on a little secret. We're about to head off into the biggest battle since Trafalgar. You've heard of Trafalgar, right?"

"Yes sir!" the young man said proudly. "At the Naval Academy. We learned that..."

"Very good! I need those replacement guns for my planes. If I don't get them some nip Zero pilot has a better than even chance of splashing one of my boys. Or me! I've got two little girls and a wife that think I'm the greatest thing since chocolate ice cream, and I want to go back to them right after I sink a Jap carrier. So are you gonna help me, or do I tell Admiral Nimitz's nephew there in my jeep, that an ensign is going to make the crucial difference between victory and defeat because he wouldn't give me my guns, the guns I properly requisitioned months ago, and never received because of some shithead of a paper pusher? Jack Nimitz is in my squadron, and as you can see by that cast on his wrist, he's already taken his share of pain from the Japs while you're here safe and sound. Well, what's your answer? I haven't got all day!" Waldron said, lowering his head, and putting his hands on his hips.

"I'm sorry, Commander McCluskey, but I'm not authorized to..."

"Fine! Just fine! Jack!" he called to Danny, who looked up forlornly, "He's not budging!" he said, as he walked with purpose towards the jeep. "He's flushed with power, that paper pusher is. I know you hate to do it, but I guess you'll have to speak to your uncle Chet about..."

"Commander McCluskey!" came the nervous yell. "I'll have the guns shipped to the *Enterprise* now, sir!"

"That's wonderful, Ensign...Ensign..."

"Creamer, sir. Ensign George C. Creamer. Annapolis, Class of '41. At your service, sir. And shoot down one of those nip bastards for me, sir. I really want to get into this war, but I haven't been..."

"Thanks, Creamer. How about those guys follow my jeep over to the *Big E*?"

"Fine. Hey, Maxwell!" he yelled to a driver. "Get your detail and follow Commander McCluskey to the *Enterprise* on the double!"

"You're a patriot, Creamer. And I'm going to ask young Jack there to personally speak to Admiral Nimitz about you and your wish to be assigned to a combat vessel. What kind of ship are you looking for?"

"Battlewagons, sir!" Creamer responded, his chest bursting with pride. "I graduated first in my class in gunnery, sir!"

"Isn't that something? Your parents must be so proud! Well, I understand we're building some magnificent battlewagons these days, Creamer, and Jack and I will make sure you're on the first one by here- if we get back. Me and the Admiral... well, we're very close," Waldron said, trying to act humble. "I don't like to let that out, but in your case, I feel...tell you what, Creamer. Let me buy you a Coke!"

Waldron was having a difficult time choking back the laugh buried deep in his belly. Danny Morello was so hysterical he had to keep his head buried under the dash of the jeep.

He deposited a nickel for each of the Cokes into a vintage machine that would be worth thousands in the Land of Now, Danny mused. Then after opening both bottles, he handed one to Ensign Creamer and toasted, "To the *Arizona*! May the Japanese language be spoken only in hell to atone for her death!"

"To the *Arizona*!" Creamer toasted, clinking his bottle with Waldron's.

Danny was laughing so hard he fell out of the jeep, leaving his wallet on the seat.

Waldron led the truck directly to the *Hornet* dropping Danny off where he picked him up outside the Officer's Club. It was almost dusk and as he suspected, the crew Creamer sent couldn't distinguish the two sister ships. He got the guns unloaded, put onto several pallets and hauled aboard the *Hornet*. Then he noticed a wallet in the jeep's passenger seat and, figuring it was Morello's, put it in his pocket to give it to him later on. Then he went over to the *Yorktown* to talk to Lem Massey, the CO of Torpedo 7, about the Coral Sea engagement.

When Danny went back to the Officer's Club, he found Steven about half in the bag, trying to out-bullshit Whitney, who had to hold on to the bar for balance.

"Yeah," Steven slurred. "They call it panty hose. And it's a real pain in the ass! You can't get the damned things off!"

"For chrissake," Whitney replied. "What the else are they gonna think of next? I like garter belts, ya know? They're kinda sexy, if you know what I mean, Amats!" Whitney said with a wink.

"I know what you mean. The only garter belts I've seen lately are in Playboy magazine. What women!"

"Playboy? What's Playboy? Is it like Esquire? I've never met a woman like those Vargas girls in Esquire. Gawd, they're are beautiful!"

"You never heard of Playboy? Well, this little skinny guy named Hefner started it. He used to work for Esquire, but it didn't show enough skin for him. Those Playboy broads show it all! Everything!"

"Everything? You mean they show the whole tit?" Whitney said, his eyes as opened as wide as he could get them.

"The whole tit, plus...if you know what I mean, Charlie my man!"

"You're kidding me!" Whitney replied, downing another shot of rye. Steven just stared at him and winked. "You're full of shit!" Whitney responded. "I mean, I've seen films like that. You know the kind of films I'm talking about. The ones with no sound, and the guys wear masks."

"Hell, I've seen them in full color!" Steven said, belting down another Jack Daniels. "Back where I come from, that is."

"Full color? Like *Gone With The Wind*?"

Whitney tried to stand up straight, but almost fell. Danny just caught him in time. This was the first time he had ever seen Steven Amato two sheets to the wind. And Whitney wasn't nearly as proper as the old man was in the Land of Now.

"Full living color, Charlie my man. Hell, in some areas of the country, you can even see them on television!"

"Wait a minute. I haven't been gone that long, Amats! I saw that television gadget in the '39 World's Fair, and they weren't even close to putting it on the market."

"There's this one, Charlie, that's called *Deep Throat*, and this woman takes the guy's whole..."

"That will be enough, Steven. Let's finish the drinks and get some sleep, shall we?" Danny interrupted.

"Dan my man! You have returned! I hope MacArthur has the same luck! Ha!"

"Ha!" Whitney responded. "Hey, Amats. What's this 'my man' you always say when you say a name. Charlie my man, Dan my man. What's that?"

"Ah. I had a buddy," Steven said, staring into his empty shot glass. "A great buddy, who said that all the time. His name was Thatcher. Louis Thatcher," Steve said, suddenly melancholy and morose. "What a guy this guy Thatcher was. A helluva man. A helluva pilot."

"Did something happen to him? I mean, you're talking like he's ...he's, you know..."

"Murdered. He was murdered by some fucking Libyans. And he was just as brave about it as Johnny Powers of *Yorktown*, I tell ya, except Thatch didn't have a chance to fight back."

"Let's go, Steve. I think it's time we put you to beddy bye."

"Murdered by Libyans? You can't trust those Arab bastards! I bet they cut his throat with one of those long, curved knives!"

Steven thought a moment, and came back to where he was, and who he was talking to. Glenn Miller's *Moonlight Serenade* was playing on the juke box, and he became somewhat more alert.

"Thatch loved that song. He told me to play it over and over again on my sax and on the piano in the officer's mess on the ship and Pensacola. He didn't like much of this stuff, but he liked this tune. He really liked the black..., er,...negro artists, like..."

"Like Duke Ellington and Count Basie, and Cab Calloway?" Whitney said.

Steven laughed drunkenly. "No. Like the Four Tops and the Temptations, and Kool and the Gang."

"I've never heard of them," Whitney said.

"You will, Charlie my man. You will." He turned to Danny and said, "I think you'd better get me out of here, Dan my man. I'm forgetting where I am."

As Danny helped him out, Whitney said, "You had better keep your money handy, Amato," Whitney said, collapsing into a chair.

"And don't forget to take that tie clasp with you!" he yelled back.

"Chrissake, Steve! Panty hose, Playboy, Kool and the Gang. What the hell did you..." Danny said, but froze. The target of his tirade was already curled up in a fetal position, and fast asleep.

It was glaringly obvious that the men at Pearl were willing to give it all up to kill a Japanese sailor or aviator. The stories of the Coral Sea battle only intensified the bloodlust, be they truth or new legend. The hate that filled the air was disturbing, even for a warrior like himself, Danny thought. It was definitely not bravado. If Pearl Harbor was considered their quintessential home, these guys were the homeowners who watched their homes torched, their wives raped and their goods stolen on a beautiful Sunday morning. Vengeance was the word of the day. They meant business, from enlisted man to admiral. And it was contagious, which disturbed him even more. He began to think that he might certainly welcome a crack at a carrier. He would never get this chance in the Land of Now. He also knew Steven Amato would be happy to lead the way.

Doolittle's group showed the Japanese to be far from invulnerable, and *Yorktown* and the late *Lexington* at Coral Sea showed them to bleed when punctured. Odds for survival attacking the mightiest fleet in the world weren't the factor to measure success today. Today, success would be measured by how many Sons of the Rising Sun were killed outright by horrific explosions in ships and planes alike, how many drowned, and how many Japanese ships were sunk. Losses of friends were not to be taken into account, because if the Japanese won this battle, or won it without taking severe casualties, the war was lost. Hawaii would be next, unless the Americans sued for peace. And everyone, from Nimitz to the enlisted man whose back was breaking as he provisioned his ship, to the Pearl Harbor Navy Yard worker who labored tirelessly to get the *Yorktown* seaworthy, knew it.

He cursed himself when he discovered his wallet was gone. He checked his footlocker as he did every night to insure the bag with F-14 manual and the mission tapes were still there. It was. He could explain the contents of a lost wallet. How the hell could he explain an F-14?

On the morning of May 27th, Swede Larsen and Al Earnest asked for landing instructions as they appeared over Ford Island, each in a brand new Grumman TBF. They were followed by five more of the planes, all designated for VT-8. The planes all landed nicely, but when they were to be hauled to a revetment by tractors, the feverish pitch of operations disoriented one of the drivers. He backed up a little too fast and too far, and jammed the tow rod he was attempting to attach to the TBF's tail wheel into the bomb bay door. The impact knocked the plane's egressing pilot off the wing. He fell to the tarmac and suffered an awful looking compound fracture in his left arm.

John Waldron and Gene Lindsey felt their hearts hit the souls of their feet at the sight. Yet they took no vengeance on the tractor driver, a seventeen-year-old enlisted man who they had seen working for thirty-six hours straight to manage the aerial armada that regularly landed, were fueled and serviced, then departed for Midway. The poor kid hadn't eaten but one meal in that time as well, and he looked as if he'd throw himself into a spinning propeller to atone for his sin, if he could.

"This one is definitely grounded," the base's maintenance chief Captain Fred Richards, declared. A tall, likeable redheaded Virginian, he was a member of Nimitz's staff, and had just come back from one of many briefings he had attended over the last twenty-four hours. "There's no way we can fix these doors. We haven't got the parts or the time."

"What about the other TBFs?" Waldron asked.

"They can go, but I don't know what the hell you can use them for, because the shipment of 24 inch torpedoes they're fitted to carry haven't come in yet, and they're not equipped with bomb cradles. The Army put whatever 24 inch torpedoes we had on the island in the B-26s over at Hickam Field, because nobody expected these TBFs to be here so soon. We think a bunch of them are coming in PBYs from the states, but not today."

They all looked skyward as a four plane echelon of B-17 heavy bombers made its way northwestward to Midway.

"As you can see, fellahs," Richards said pointing to the huge bombers overhead, "we're pulling out all the stops."

"Now what the hell are we gonna do?" Waldron said, running his hands through his hair.

"How about this?" Captain Richards said. "These TBFs can go off to Midway, and we'll send the torpedoes to the airfield there as soon as they arrive. You can't take 'em on your carriers, because there is no way we can get those torpedoes to you at sea. But at least they may show up in time for the battle. It's your call, John."

"Are we leaving soon?" Lindsey asked.

"Don't let this get around, but those carriers are to sortie in a few hours. The crews are aboard, and you're going to get the call to go as soon as the task groups are formed up."

"What about the *Yorktown*?" Waldron asked.

"She sorties May 30, ready or not. We need that deck. The whole Jap Navy is in on this. This is the battle they've been lookin' for to finish us off, but we're gonna head them bastards off at the pass, and bushwhack 'em. It figures that only a Texan like Nimitz would come up with a strategy like that."

"How do you know all this, Captain?" Lindsey asked.

"Let's say you can take it to the bank," he responded with a smile.

Steven knew the reason, as his vision was of course twenty-twenty. The Japanese code had been broken. Nimitz's intelligence team could even identify a Japanese carrier by the way its Morse operator pounded his sending key.

"So what's it gonna be? I gotta know now so I can get these aircraft on the maintenance and fueling schedule so they can leave. Believe me, there isn't a moment to waste. We're running a hot schedule and we're taking a big chance with this operation. We've got no choice. It's now or never, gentlemen."

"How about we fly the dented TBF, Commander Waldron?" Steven suggested. "Danny and I still can't fly combat, but we can sure fly liaison missions between ships, transfer personnel and equipment, you know, the dog work, without causing a loss in strength of the aircraft that are going to take it to the Japanese."

"You're grounded," Lindsey said. "The doc said you can't fly combat."

"We won't be flying combat, unless of course a Zero attacks us, We just might happen to fly a patrol, or a number of other missions we might be able to carry out with a plane unable to carry a torpedo or bomb, sir," Steven replied.

He wasn't going to let those ships sail without him, not after he had come this far. This was Midway, the battle that shaped his being before he knew it was happening, and was no doubt a large part of why he found himself in The Land of Then. It was arguably the most famous and desperate battle the United States Navy ever fought. He knew it inside and out, and a quirk of fate or quark of time, or both, had enabled him to see it live.

And now, to watch these two men he had come to admire and respect long before he had met them "personally," fly off to their deaths on June 4, 1942? Perhaps there was the outside chance, just maybe that he could...

"What do you think, Captain?" He threw it in Richards' lap.

"It'll fly just fine. If it can't sustain this kind of damage and stay airborne and operational, we are in deep trouble, for sure," Richards answered, passing around a pack of Lucky Strike Green. Again he and Danny declined.

"Okay. But I want your word that you won't take your orders liberally and we find you over the *Akagi* making strafing runs. And you went to Annapolis, so you know the code. Deal?" Lindsey said, eyeing him.

He turned to Waldron, who said. "He's your CO Amats, and I kind of like you, even if you are I-talian. I don't want you throwing your life away."

Throwing my life away; what are you two going to do in a week?

"Deal," he said with reluctance, but to Danny's great relief. Amato never broke his word.

Men arrived in speeding jeeps, then sprinted to the various squadron ready rooms handing out sheets of paper, and yelling with wild-eyed abandon. Waldron grabbed a VT-6 lieutenant as he ran by.

"What's cooking?" he asked.

"Yeah, Whitney, what's the scoop?" Lindsey added.

"They're on the way! Midway's it! I've got orders for all pilots to man their planes. Take-off is at 1500 hours. Here!" he said, thrusting the operational orders at Waldron and Lindsey, and then moving on. Then the he stopped to look around and saw Amato standing there.

"If you really want to know what the hell's going on, ask him. He can probably tell you how this turns out! Panty hose, for chrissake! I almost believed you, Amato!" Then he ran off.

"What the hell is he talking about?" Lindsey asked.

"Who the hell knows?" Morello responded. Steven just laughed.

But he was still going to try to turn this around. Waldron and Lindsey were just too good to die.

At their berths, the carriers' stacks began to emit black smoke. The ships were making steam. *Enterprise*'s beloved Captain George Murray was seen joking on the flag bridge with an enlisted man, while *Hornet's* Pete Mitscher shared a smoke with his bosun's mate. The cruisers and destroyers escorting and protecting the carriers sailed first, then the oilers and their destroyer escorts came next. The ships left to a rousing chorus of cheers and waving hats of white and khaki as they made their way down the channel to the open sea.

At 1110 *Enterprise*, carrying Admiral Raymond Spruance, the task force commander, sailed down the channel followed by *Hornet* at 1134. *Yorktown* saluted by blowing her foghorn continuously. Her sisters responded in kind. The harbor was near delirious.

Opposing them would be four carriers, nine battleships, ten cruisers, thirty-eight destroyers, and sixteen submarines, plus a host of auxiliary vessels. To say the Japanese just outnumbered their American counterparts was the cruelest of understatements. They were outnumbered, and outgunned.

Steven stole a glance at Waldron and Lindsey, both of whom had tears in their eyes.

"You know, Gene, we're two lucky sons-of-bitches," Waldron said.

"It's not luck, John," Lindsey replied. "It's a blessing. Let's get our boys together. It's payback time!"

It was May 28, 1942.

Danny Morello looked over to Steven and said, "Not that it matters, but you haven't landed a TBF on a carrier before, have you?"

"It's called on-the-job training, Danny. I'll be fine-I think."

On May 30, *Yorktown* sailed with her task group, which included two cruisers and four destroyers. The Navy Yard personnel went crazy with joy to see "their ship" sail off to glory.

Chapter 28

The restaurant Julie Ann Tate had chosen was on a hill that overlooked Pearl Harbor. In fact, the hill had served as a lookout point for the "diplomats" from the Japanese embassy to monitor the comings and goings of the American fleet in the fall of 1941. Julie sat next to the Amato's at dinner. Susan sat across from her next to Marcus White. Their somber faces were the antithesis of the expressions of every other tourist in the Hawaiian Islands. Julie was the only one who wore a perpetual smile, and tried to keep the group's morale up.

While Marcus White felt compelled to smile at her, she knew that deep in his heart were grave reservations about their purpose here. Marcus was a man of great intelligence and his reasoning powers were second to none. He believed more in her strength of character and her powers of deduction than in her wild thesis based on what he could only believe was unconditional love, circumstantial evidence and uncanny coincidence, or perhaps some kind of psychological trauma each of the "eyewitnesses" may have unknowingly shared. Nonetheless, he felt compelled to play along and support her, partly because he had always respected her intelligence and her spirit, but more so because he developed a deep admiration for her power to love and to hope. Steve Amato was indeed a lucky man, he thought. However, with each passing day, he realized that the little hope of finding the two aviators alive diminished in geometrical progression, if in fact there was any chance at all of them surviving the storm they were thrown into when *Jawn* and the *The Flying Ronzonis* were whacked by the Sparrow missile.

There was one confirmed casualty of the shoot-down incident, however. John Lynch, who's F/A-18 loosed the missile on its own, had tried to drown himself again. This time he was more successful, having been pulled from the pool in the backyard of his parent's home on the brink of death, while on convalescent leave. He was being kept alive by a snakes' nest of tubes connected to all parts of his body, with daily EEGs showing only the most minimal of brain activity that kept his body from serving solely as a cache of organs for donation.

Julie refused to have Susan Amato give up Danny's ghost. She went over the evidence with her again, and immediately after Julie finished her presentation, Susan was uplifted. Then, her own powers of reason took hold, and reason dictated Danny and her brother were dead.

Rena Amato remained stoic. She had to believe her son was alive. She just had to. She was a mother. She gained a new appreciation and respect for those who lost a son in Vietnam under the guise of "missing in action." And for all these years, they still believed that someday, their sons or husbands or sweethearts or brothers would walk out of the jungle and into their arms again. She long ago decided to continue to believe in Julie until they found her son's body. After she buried him, she would then believe he would never come back.

Commander Riley stopped in to have coffee with them, having been invited by Julie to this "business dinner" earlier in the day. He was accompanied by "Roto" Reuter and "Silver" Ware. Each of the officers tried to remain upbeat and showed outward respect for her theory, but she knew she was being patronized.

"Commander Riley, has the *Alvin* found any more of the F-14?" she asked quite nonchalantly.

Riley was convinced she was clairvoyant. "Yes, Julie," he said, after the briefest hesitation. "We've recovered the whole bird now. I was going to tell you that..."

"Did thee inflight recorder confirm the plane's crew ejected successfully?" She scooped up a mouthful of poi.

"Yes. But we knew they had because the seats were not in the nose section we found, and the cockpit showed scorching from the seats' rocket motors."

"What's the date today, Roto?" she asked.

"June 3, Julie. Why?"

"Marcus, what happened on June 3, 1942?" she asked. "Boy, this stuff is amazingly good!" she said, eating the poi non-stop.

Rena Amato felt compelled to smile upon her. She was right all along about her. Julie and her son would have...will produce beautiful grandchildren, she thought.

"The American fleet had gathered at Point Luck, a location on the map north and east of Midway, for the ambush of the Japanese fleet to engage the Battle for Midway. The *Hornet, Enterprise,* and *Yorktown* had chosen the site to be close to Midway, yet within range of the Japanese Fleet, based on the data provided by the broken Japanese code. *Yorktown,* the poor dear, was the last to arrive because the bomb damage she suffered during the battle of the Coral Sea was hastily repaired. She left Pearl Harbor from the Navy Yard, right over there," he pointed with a fork, "two days after her sisters had departed. She couldn't make speed because of her damaged hull, but she joined the parade, so to speak. Her deck and air group were critical."

"So the shooting starts tomorrow, right Marcus?"

"So to speak, Julie."

"The TBF made its battle debut at Midway, correct Marcus?"

"That's right. Six planes flew from Midway. They were attached to Torpedo 8 of *HORNET*. They couldn't fly from the carrier because Midway was where their torpedoes had been sent."

"What's your point?" he said, knowingly she had led him on again.

"Well, Marcus, we know there was already a TBF out here, before Midway. Your buddy Admiral Tegan said one was lost off the old *Enterprise* in April of 1942, with its crew. That appears to be the one that *Alvin* found, right?"

"What does that have to do..."

"On a hunch, I also called Admiral Tegan this morning and asked him to find out if any other TBFs might have been available for the battle, other than the six that *Hornet's* Torpedo 8 contingent flew from Midway. And you know what he said?"

"No. What did he say, Tate?" Marcus said, knowing she had another gotcha in her bag of tricks, just for him. He didn't like being outdone, even if it was her doing it to him.

"Pass the water, will you Marcus? Gad, this stuff is hot!"

"Goddammit Julie! What did Tegan tell you?"

"He said that seven TBFs made the trip to Midway. Seven," she reiterated, wiping her hands and sticking up seven fingers. "One was damaged when it was being hauled from one end of the strip on Ford Island over there." She pointed to Ford Island in the middle of the harbor. It couldn't carry any weapons, and it couldn't be fixed, he told me. But two young guys said they could use the plane sort of as a "go fer" between the three carriers, and took it."

Paul Amato leaned forward, suddenly alive again.

"How the hell did he know that? There aren't records..."

"I'll tell you why he knew it, Commander Riley. After they found the original TBF, his curiosity peaked a bit. He called an old friend, an Admiral Richards, who was the maintenance officer at Ford Island during the Midway campaign, and he told him about the *Alvin's* discovery. It was then that Richards recalled the damaged TBF that was damaged by the ground handlers during the frenzy to get the fleet ready for the battle. Tegan was surprised at how the heat of battle dims facts and memories. Then Richards said that he knew where the seventh plane is today. It was hauled off Midway after the war by a Charles Whitney, who..."

"He's been flying Whitney's plane all along!" Susan blurted out. "He has two of the ghosts from that battle?"

Rena Amato felt faint. Ware and Reuter looked at each other dumbly. Marcus just buried his head in his hands. Paul Amato's face broke open a smile. Julie Ann kept at the poi.

"Why the hell didn't Mr. Whitney tell us?" Susan asked.

"Because Whitney didn't believe it himself, even after I went to him and told him about the Oceana incident to save my own sanity. That is, until now. And when I tried to call him this morning as well, it turns out the old dear is in the hospital. Mrs. Whitney told me that he was so excited by the prospect of confirming what he always thought about Steven and Danny as true, and that he hadn't lost his mind or dreamed it up, his heart went in arrhythmia. He may need a pacemaker."

She stopped eating for a second, dabbed her pretty mouth with her napkin, pulled the hem of her skirt down over her crossed legs, and stared back.

"Well what the hell is the matter with y'all? I told y'all this over and over again. Everything we learn just confirms the impossible. Deal with it. Accept it. Rena, Paul, your boy will be here tomorrow to celebrate your anniversary. Our boys will be back."

"I'm putting Danny's parents on the next plane out here," Susan said, as she broke into a sprint for the pay phone.

"They won't be here," Paul Amato said with tears in his eyes. It was the first time he had shown any emotion at all since *The Flying Ronzoni's* spun in with *Jawn*. No one knew what to make of his comment until he continued. "Do you think those boys are going to give up the chance to take a plane into a classic air-sea battle, especially the one my son has studied all his life? We'll find him on Midway. Or, close to it. Commander," he said to Riley, putting his napkin on the table and leaning forward, "do you think you can put some air-sea rescue crews near the island of Midway?"

"What choice do I have?"

"Marcus, I think we had better look at that battle map of yours again, and find out the routes the planes took back from their close encounter with the Japanese fleet. And you, Miss Julie, you call me dad."

Chapter 29

Lindsey and Waldron had squared it with Wade McCluskey, Stanhope Ring, and Oscar Pedersen, the CAGS of *Enterprise, Hornet,* and *Yorktown* respectively, to allow the "go fer" role for the damaged TBF, and it's not-quite-ready-for-combat crew. In fact, Danny still had his wrist in a cast, and Steven's shoulder was still so sore he still couldn't lift his right arm above his head. The plan would save a serviceable combat plane and combat-ready crew for combat, while providing another line of communication for the fleet.

In one of the most prophetic command decisions of the war, Admiral Raymond Spruance was Nimitz's choice to replace Admiral William Halsey for Task Force commander, because Halsey was stricken with dermatitis. The Midway atoll actually consists of two islands surrounded by a coral reef. Sand Island held fueling stations and a seaplane base. Eastern Island contained the airfield. When Danny and Steven flew out to Midway on June 1 with the six other TBFs of the VT-8 detachment, there were so many airplanes of all types, from B-17 bombers to obsolescent Marine Vindicator dive bombers and Brewster Buffalo fighters, that it was a wonder that Eastern Island stayed afloat.

The atoll bristled with guns of all calibers, and Marines, who anticipated a Japanese invasion and a fight to the last man if the American fleet failed. VT-8's detachment tried to remain collected and professional, even though they had barely any hours at all in their factory fresh TBFs, and weren't quite sure as to the tactics they should employ. Nonetheless, Langdon, Fieberling, A.K. Earnest, Ozzie Gaynier, John Williams, and Swede Larsen were confident in securing a victory; after all, they were trained by John Waldron. In fact, they were planning on landing their TBFs back on the *Hornet* at the conclusion of their mission to blow out the bottom of a Japanese carrier with their new 24 inch torpedoes. There couldn't be rearmed for another mission as the only torpedoes available were the ones that were tucked in their bellies at Midway. Steven and three pilots tried their damndest to open the holed and misaligned bomb bay doors on the crippled plane, but to no avail.

When Spruance was informed that the go-fer TBF was on Midway awaiting orders, he requested that it land on *Enterprise* to collect several charts and transmission codes for the recently promoted Rear Admiral Mitscher on *Hornet* the next morning. The evening before his departure, Steven and "AK" strolled along the runway, and Earnest found a two dollar bill. It was unusual occurrence, because there were never many two dollar bills minted.

"I guess this is a good luck sign."

"I guess it is. Keep it tucked safe inside your flight suit. And show it to your crew, especially that Manning kid in the ball turret." Steven suggested.

"That kid is nervous as hell. He gives me the creeps."

He looked at Earnest and smiled. Earnest would be the lucky one, he thought. The others would be lifeless tomorrow, entombed in a watery grave, their spanking new aircraft turned to twisted shards of metal. And Manning had good reason to be worried. Tomorrow a Japanese Zero's 7.7 millimeter machine guns would fire two rounds into his chest. Only Ferrier, the TBF's ventral gunner, and Earnest would be the only survivors of VT-8's Midway-based detachment.

"AK, let me offer some advice. I'm leaving tomorrow morning for the *Big E*. I'm to report directly to Spruance, so I guess this is really it. Let me make a suggestion. Try to take off tomorrow with those B-26s over there."

"Army guys? Why? I mean, those guys never launched a torpedo before, Steve. They..."

"I know you never did either. And no one else did except for Swede Larsen, and that was only once on a practice range."

"How do you know that?" Earnest asked suspiciously.

Steven thought quickly. "Remember? I worked in the development of the TBF. I know what you guys have done. I also know you didn't have all that much experience in the Devastator. There's strength in numbers and coordination, AK."

"Frankly, I don't think the fucking Japs are that good. I think we're..."

He had had enough of the bravado, the theories that self-sacrifice would win over superior numbers, and still after all their conquests, underestimating the Japanese military. "You're gonna get creamed! All of you!" he shouted. "For Christ's sake, listen to me!" He found himself grabbing Earnest by his shoulders and shaking him as he screamed. "Didn't you see Pearl Harbor? Didn't you see *Yorktown* when she came into port? Do you think she got that banged up in a hailstorm? But you didn't see *Lexington*, did you? And you won't see Wake Island, or the Philippines either for three more years! And after the fourth of June you'll never see Yorktown again. And off this ugly island in the Solomons called Guadalcanal, the *Hornet*..."

"What the hell are you talking about?" Earnest said angrily as he pushed Steven away. "Are you nuts? That head wound of yours must make you delirious from time to time. If Waldron heard you, he'd..."

"Goddammit, man! He's not going to make it either!"

"Why, you son of a bitch! The man treats you like his own son, and you damn him to death! I ought to..."

Earnest swung wildly at Steven, who used judo move to throw him off balance and flip him to the soft sand adjacent to the runway. Earnest glared at him wildly.

"Just stay down there, AK. It's over. I'm sorry, really sorry. Just fly off with the army guys in your torpedo attack."

Earnest tried to get up and charge him, but Steven kicked him off balance.

"AK, please. You're gonna make it. The other guys won't. "

"How do you know that? How do..?"

"Never mind how I know. I just know."

"As soon as they tell me where I can find a Jap carrier, I'm gonna take off with this detachment, or by myself if I have to, and cream that scow full of slant eyes, even if it means diving through their fucking flight deck! That's what we get paid for, Amato!"

That's what we get paid for. That's exactly what Commander Riley said after Thatcher had died. But this was different. These guys would kill themselves by fighting back. They weren't stooges. They ran on hatred.

"You get paid to kill the enemy. Not to kill yourself, or your flight through stupidity, or a lack of good tactics. They're good, AK, the Japs are real good. You know that. We'll need a ton of luck to pull this off. We're outnumbered and outgunned. They're bringing four carriers to the party. We've only got three."

"*Saratoga* is coming in from San Diego with her task group. That'll even..."

"*Sara* will not make the party, AK. She won't be here in time."

AK was silently but angrily staring at Amato. He didn't need to use words to convey his feelings. Danny came running across the runway yelling to them, and this slightly subdued Earnest. He got up slowly, dusted himself off, and said quite calmly, "How do you know all this, man? How?"

"If I told you, you would really think I'm crazy."

"I do. But those Army guys have different ideas. I'm not sure they understand the purpose here, or why we have to think the way we do," Earnest said, taking out a pack of Chesterfields. "Cigarette?"

"No. And you should stop smoking too. What purpose, other than to sink Jap ships?"

Earnest smiled as he put his hands in his pockets, and greeted Danny.
"Hi, Dan."

"What's going on? Practicing for the Japanese."

"Just a misunderstanding. We're all a little on edge." He turned to Steve, and said, "We're throwaways. We have to be. Don't you see that? How can Nimitz guard this island and the fleet at the same time, especially since we're outgunned and outshipped, like you said? I'll tell you how. Through ambush and attrition tactics to keep the Japs on the defensive, but letting them think they're on the offensive. This way, it'll take twice as much strength to accomplish their goals than they have. We hope to keep them off balance so our carriers can be protected, and maybe get a few lucky shots in and knock a couple of their carriers off so they have to call off the invasion, or if they do manage to take us, make them vulnerable to attacks from Hawaii, not the other way around."

"Yeah, but if you attacked together, you might..."

"Steve, be realistic. Look at the planes here. Those Vindicator dive bombers are worse death traps than the Devastator. Those Brewster Buffalos are as useless against a Zero as tits are on a snake. They're all relics, but if they attack in dribs and drabs, the Japanese fleet still has to deal with them. A Vindicator can still do a lot of damage to a carrier if it drops its bomb on a deck full of gassed and armed aircraft. And has a B-17 ever hit a ship maneuvering at flank speed at sea? But nonetheless, the B-17s have to be dealt with. The TBF is a sweetheart to fly and a major improvement over the Devastator, but do you think six of them have any chance in hell of attacking a first class fleet without fighter escort? That leads to my next question. Do you see enough fighters here to escort all these obsolete old planes and four-engine bombers, and defend the base? I know the score, Steve. I know what's expected. I don't need anyone to tell me. And tactics aren't going to amount to a hill of shit. I'm here to die. I'm trying to make myself happy about it."

"But to suggest that you sacrifice yourself knowingly seems a bit out of character. For God's sake, AK, why not try to pull this off differently? Why are you pinning your success or failure on...luck?"

"It's crazy, I know. But we have to take advantage of the fact that the Japanese admiral has to neutralize this island, invade it, hold it, and then deal with the American fleet he knows will have to come with its precious carriers to push him off of it, because Hawaii is a goner if we don't. And we haven't the strength to fight him off on the beaches, or at sea. We gotta nip at his flanks, wait for an opening and hit him hard. It's like a lightweight fighting a heavyweight. The light guy can't go toe to toe with the heavy guy, but can tucker him out, confuse and confound him, and maybe hope then for an opening to land a knockout blow. Now then, with all this in mind, do you really think six TBFs mean all that much in terms of how they attack?"

"You've got to maximize your forces, AK. Concentrate on a salient, attack in strength. You learned that at the Academy, didn't you?" Steven said, frustrated by the logic of AK's argument.

"That's exactly what we're doing, but we're doing it by tactical attrition. Our strength is that we know the Jap plan exactly, from what I've been told. Nimitz supposedly even knows when that cocksucker Yamamoto takes a shit. And the only way to take advantage of our inferiority is to keep the Japs off balance, so they don't know what the hell to do, keep them from launching or recovering because they have to deal with us gnats. Make them think our forces are superior with all these varied attacks, and then whack them in strength with the air groups from our carriers in the midst of their dither.

It made perfect sense. Was it planned that way? Probably-the planners assumed optimum tactical conditions based on pre-war exercises and assumptions, which, in turn, assumed that Midway's defenders and attackers would take "acceptable" casualties. But what did that mean in this particular instance considering the importance of the outcome? Did the losses at Pearl Harbor or Coral Sea redefine the parameters of attritional strategy and tactics?

"Be careful, AK. Don't take a stupid risk. And remember, the Zero is the best fighter in the game. Don't take it lightly."

"Sleep tight, Steve," he said, fateful smile gripping his face. "You're a rare kind of guy, that's for sure. Don't go blabbing your premonitions to too many people. You'd be bad for moral. And tell the guys in the ready room on the *Hornet* I'll be bunking with them in a few days."

No, you won't AK, because even if you had made it to the *Hornet*, they won't be there to greet you.

"Yeah. You bet. Good night, AK."

Steven looked after him as Earnest walked away, and shook his head sadly. He looked at his watch, and noted that it was now officially June 2, 1942. Two days left.

"Hey, Amats. What did you expect? Don't be so down."

"I thought I could warn him off, have him take some initiative. They know what they have to do. I guess it wasn't meant to be."

Steven caught the sight of the *Enterprise's* landing signal officer (LSO) on the stern of the carrier, standing on a small platform on the port side of the flight deck. There was no "meatball" to keep in the center of a mirror, or TV to monitor his landing for him to study later, or to be graded on it. He followed the paddles in the LSO's hands and obeyed them.

"How we doing there, Amats?" Danny asked.

"We're doing just fine. Let me concentrate. I don't want to embarrass myself!" he shouted back over the intercom.

Yes, please, dear God, please don't let him embarrass himself, and get us both killed and lost in time forever.

Steven was within fifty yards of the *Big E's* deck when the LSO brought his paddles across his chest, which indicated permission to land. Steve flared the TBF, pulled back on the throttle, and felt the wheels touch the deck and the tail hook snag a wire. He retracted the hook on order from the deck officer, and taxied forward as prescribed. He had landed the TBF on the carrier as if he had done it all his life.

"I've got to go see Gene Lindsey as soon as we're done with Spruance. And then I'm going to find Charlie Whitney, and rub his nose in my ass," Steven said.

"Lindsey's probably up to his eyeballs in work right now. Why bother him, Steve? Let the poor guy..."

"If things have happened as they should have, Gene Lindsey is not up to anything, right now. As for Whitney, he has something of mine I want."

Wade McCluskey, the *Big E's* CAG, greeted the two flyers with a warm handshake following the obligatory salute. He took them to Admiral Raymond Spruance on the flag bridge, reviewing his operational orders and checking the readiness of his task force.

"Sir," McCluskey began, "These are Lieutenants Amato and Morello. They're your gofers, sir."

"Hello, gentleman!" Spruance said warmly. His bright blue eyes twinkled. His face was kind and scholarly, much more like a college professor's than an admiral charged quite unexpectedly to fight the most pivotal battle of his country's navy.

"I see your wounds are slow to heal. However, that was one fine landing, son. That TBF is quite an airplane."

"Yes sir, it is," Steven responded proudly.

"I hear it packs quite a punch. Do you envision using the same tactics as with the Devastator?"

"No sir, not quite the same. The TBF and its torpedo is designed for a faster run-in to the target and a pull-out farther from the enemy ships. The ball turret increases its ability to in defend itself, yet it still will need fighter escort to be survivable."

"I wonder why they don't design a heavy duty fighter to do this work. It seems that the TBF would make a fine bomber, but this torpedo role still seems a bit suicidal. I don't know why the need for aerial torpedoes anyway. It would seem more logical to bomb ships than to have planes fly across an entire escorting task group, taking fire all the way in and out, at dangerously low altitudes that favor enemy gunners. A dive bomber comes straight down and pulls straight up."

That said a lot about his confidence in the torpedo squadrons.

The thinker, the questioner, the logician emerged in his speech patterns. Spruance was known to be brilliant and gutsy. Nimitz had the ultimate confidence in his abilities. Why else would he make a man who had previously commanded only cruiser divisions the commander of a carrier task force?

"We're supposed to attack in concert with the dive bombers, sir. That way, enemy ships are trapped in vertical and horizontal envelopments. The old Devastator isn't up to the task. It's just too slow."

Spruance stroked his chin and squinted as he thought through Amato's words. He exhaled, saying, "Anyway, here are the charts, codes and timetables I want you to take to Admiral Mitscher on *Hornet*. Tell him that Admiral Fletcher on the *Yorktown* and I had a chance to meet before we sortied, and he thinks I've come up with a few good solutions. Ask him if he has any questions. Better yet, I'd appreciate it if he had a few ideas, so convey that, won't you?"

"Yes sir. I sure will."

"Very well. I guess I'll be seeing you again before all this is over. Happy landings," Spruance said, as he went immediately back to his papers and maps.

"Commander McCluskey, where can I find Lieutenant Commander Lindsey?" Steven asked, knowing very well where he might be.

"In sick bay. Gene is pretty banged up from a crash."

"Commander Waldron will want to know if he has any ideas as to last-minute changes in tactics, sir."

"Come with me," McCluskey said.

Amato and Morello found Gene Lindsey lying in sick bay with obvious pain. His forehead bandage covered a six inch gash. He had broken several ribs and punctured a lung. His chest was bruised black and blue.

"Commander?"

"Ah, Amato," he groaned. "I see you made it out here," he said, managing a very faint smile. "I blew... a landing. I don't know what happened to cause the...plane to...stall. Stack gas, bad airspeed indicator...I don't know. I hit...deck very hard, twisted up the arresting wires for sure...went over the port side. The *Monaghan's* crew rescued me...just...before the plane...went under. Screwed up the ...landing for the whole air group. Shit! I can't....breathe too good. I'm pissing...blood. Doc tells me I...hurt a kidney. I stopped coughing up...blood, though."

Steven and Danny were aghast at Lindsey's condition. The man should have been in a fully equipped hospital, at the least. His tortured speech made their own lungs ache for air.

"Sir, Commander Waldron will probably ask about you. Is there anything you'd want me to convey to him?"

Lindsey's eyes opened wide and his speech became firmer, although the extra expenditure of air was obviously excruciating.

"Tell him...I'll see him on...the fourth, over the Jap ...fleet!" he said with conviction. "That...will be the...day. The fourth. Tell him...not to go for...a mop up role. Tell him...that we,...attack with the... entire air group. No reserve...shit! We...trained too hard for...oh, God!" he grunted, as his whole face contorted in anguish.

"Yes sir. I will. Rest easy, sir."

"Take care...of...TBF! We'll need it soon!" Lindsey said.

"Aye aye, sir," Steven said, saluting, then turning to leave.

"I guess he's one of the guys who survives, huh?" Danny said.

"No. He is actually helped into the cockpit of a TBD, and he flies the mission, leading his boys into the Jap fleet. He doesn't come back. Only five planes from VT-6 do. He doesn't even get to pickle his goddam torpedo," Steven said in disgust. "But there is something he said that made sense. Someone, somewhere had taken the Devastator's total lack of competence into account, and was willing to change the battle plan to let them "mop up." If that was the case, the torpedo squadrons would have lived, maybe to attack the other surface ships. The antiaircraft fire from the ships wasn't the problem. It was the concentrated force of the CAP over the Japanese carriers that was. And the Devastators started their runs from nine miles out. A Zero pilot had all kinds of time to wreak havoc on them as they blundered along at only a hundred knots. That mop up role is a great idea!"

"But what would happen to the dive bombers? The Zeros would fly straight to them, maybe causing a lot of them to miss the carriers. And they sunk the carriers."

"Danny, the dive bombers had fighter escorts, remember? They would have engaged the Zeros, and the Dauntlesses would have gotten by anyhow. We got to sell Waldron and Massey on this."

"I think you'll have the same luck with them as you did with Earnest."

They found Charlie Whitney on the hangar deck, lovingly working over his Devastator, his hands in the middle of his engine, right next to a mechanic's.

"Trouble, Charlie?" Steven said.

"Oh, Amato!" he said with obvious, wry delight. "No major trouble. She's running a little rough so we're playing with carburetor a little. Did you drop by with the hundred you owe me? I've got big plans for the money when we get back to Pearl, mah man!"

"Very cute, Charlie. Come here, my man. I want to show you something."

He walked Charlie Whitney over to the *Enterprise's* port side, Danny in tow. He held a set of binoculars.

"Charlie, what ship is that over there?" Steven asked.

"That's *Hornet*. I don't need binoculars for that, Amato! Now where's the hundred?"

"Not so fast, Charlie my man. Let's stroll to the starboard, shall we?"

Danny saw Whitney's face losing its color, half in rage and half in embarrassment. He knew what was coming.

"Now Charles, I think you know *Enterprise* has two sisters, right? Answer me, Charlie mah man."

"Yes, goddammit. I know that."

"Then if this is *Enterprise*, and the ship to port is *Hornet*, would you agree that it would be a safe assumption to say that ship right over there...here, Charlie mah man, use these," he said, giving Whitney the binoculars. "Wouldn't that ship there be the, uh, what is its name...oh, yes, *Yorktown*? The one in the same *Yorktown* that you unequivocally stated would never, ever make this mission?"

Whitney said nothing. He reached in his pocket, took out the tie clasp and handed it to Steven. Then he glared and walked back to his Devastator.

"Now, Charlie. I wouldn't screw around so much with that engine, son. Let somebody who knows what they're doing take care of it. You wouldn't want to be left behind now, would you?"

Whitney still ignored them, as they left happily with a memento from their visit to the Land of Then.

As they went back to the flight deck with their charts and messages, Steven suddenly felt Julie pop into his mind. He had never experienced her presence before, but he felt she was there, if only he could determine where to look. He shook it off. He missed her so, that was for sure, and he couldn't wait to see her again, if that was to be the case. He looked at Ray Moore's Hamilton as it ticked the seconds off.

"Where do you stop, he asked the watch silently. When is it over? When do I go back home? What else is it that I must do?"

Then his mother's and father's image entered his mind. And he felt incredibly sad. This airpanes onna ships stuff had certainly gotten out of hand.

The deck was bustling with patrol planes taking off and landing. TBDs and SBDs went out on long searches to sniff out the Japanese fleet just in case some bit of intelligence was incorrect. Steven taxied the TBF to the port side of the *Enterprise's* wooden flight deck immediately after a Dauntless launched, heading westward to the sun closing on the horizon.

As he always did before a launch, he asked Danny, "All set back there, Danny?"

"All set, Steven," came the usual reply. He revved his engine, saluted the catapult officer, and put his head back to the headrest, awaiting the one hundred-fifty mile an hour acceleration he was so used to.

And nothing happened.

"Uh, Steve. I think things are a little different here in the Land of Then," Danny said.

He looked to the launching officer, and instead found a man with his hands on his hips staring at him with a what-the-hell expression on his face. Then the man shrugged his shoulders and folded his arms to express either, "what the hell are you doing?" or "what the hell are you waiting for?"

The man gave the launch sign again. Steven released his brakes, and felt the TBF leap forward and then raise itself off the deck. He banked to the left, and made for the *Hornet's* task group, about a mile or so away. He couldn't wait to see John Waldron again and explain his idea of attacking after the Japanese carriers were destroyed by the dive bombers, even though Gene Lindsey abhorred the idea.

He didn't know that Waldron was eagerly awaiting his arrival. He had several questions about the unbelievable photographs and documents that had caught his eye in Danny Morello's wallet.

The photos, their amazing content aside, were in color. The documents were the stimulus for a hundred questions in their own right. Waldron had seen none of this before.

Chapter 30

Steven and Danny found the *Hornet's* flight deck to be alive with action. Planes were launching and landing at two-minute intervals. He taxied forward to the amidships elevator, where the plane was struck below to the hangar deck for a quick maintenance check. Before Danny left the plane, he took his waterproof pouch containing the F-14's manual and the tapes with him. He knew the carrier and its air group would be engaged tomorrow, and that anything could happen with that TBF. Although there was no record of any TBF taking off from *Hornet* after the Japanese fleet, he wanted to insure that the reason was not simply the omission of a footnote to history.

With Danny in tow, Steven went directly to Torpedo 8's ready room, and found John Waldron reviewing some dispatches and poring over several maps with navigational instruments. Ray Moore stood firm by the phone to the bridge. The squadron, while not at battle stations, was sleeping in flight gear just in case the intelligence data, which up to now had been foolproof, had gone awry. It was getting darker by the second, and the chances for any sort of engagement were at best very slim. Waldron, however, true to his reputation, was not about to let down his guard. If this was *Nimitz* in the present day, the ready room would have been full of pilots getting ready for the evening CAP, or an attack or recon mission. A modern day carrier never slept. *Hornet* did, from nightfall to dawn.

"Sir, I've got a message from Lieutenant Commander Lindsey," Steven said.

Waldron had a million questions about that wallet's strange contents, but he was too engrossed in the fact that tomorrow, or the day after at the latest, he would take his squadron into combat for the first time in what was shaping up to be one of the biggest battles in history.

"Well, Amats, Morello. Are you enjoying the grand tour of the fleet?"

"Yes sir. Sir, Commander Lindsey is pretty badly hurt. He..."

"Then it is true. That was his plane that went over the side."

"Yes sir. I don't think he should fly, but he's insistent. He asked me to convey to you his very firm feelings about the idea of not using the torpedo squadrons on the initial attack, but to employ them in a mopping up operation instead."

Waldron's face turned beet red, as his eyes and nostrils widened and his teeth were bared. Danny expected to see steam fly out of his ears before his head detached and headed for the ceiling.

"What the fuck, over?!" he screamed. "Who said anything about using us as a mop up group? I'm not mopping up for anyone, unless it's the blood of the son-of-a-bitch I'm gonna gut for suggesting this! Where'd you hear this, Amato?"

Ray Moore moved forward, face tense, hands on his hips, backing up Waldron. Tex Gay came in out of the hall at the boom of Waldron's voice.

This was the reaction Steven was expecting. So far, he had determined that someone "upstairs" had decided that the torpedo squadrons, still disappointingly equipped with the Devastators, were in fact suicide squadrons if they were allowed to attack the Japanese Fleet. Now, as to how they actually went from rear guard to vanguard was Steven's interest, and he was hoping the chain of events that was no doubt about to commence would explain it.

Waldron took a deep breath, but still scowled at Amato. Then his features softened, and he dropped his defensive stance.

"Sorry, Amats. Now that I think about it, I've got a good idea as to where this originated. Amats, Morello, please come with me. Ray, stay by the phone."

"What about me, skipper?" Gay asked.

"You tell Moore when the phone rings so he can answer it," he said with a laugh.

As they passed by the hangar deck, Waldron stopped for a moment and watched as the twin thirty caliber mounts he and "Jack Nimitz" had "requisitioned" from Pearl Harbor were being mounted to his Devastators. He said nothing, but he did smile and wink at Danny Morello, who nodded his head and returned the smile.

The three of them proceeded to the bridge, where Admiral Mitscher was watching the last few planes of the CAP come aboard from his elevated stool.

"Sir? May I have a word with you?"

He turned and said, "Hello, John. And *The Flying Ronzonis* too! What can I do for you?"

"Sir, has there been any talk about relegating the torpedo squadrons to a mop up role?"

The smile left Mitsher's face. He hadn't wanted a confrontation, but now, here it was. He should have known better. He knew Lindsey and Massey as well as he knew Waldron, and he knew perfectly well what the degree of their reaction was going to be. His would have been the same, if not more...impassioned. Yes, that would be a good way to put it, he thought. Impassioned was a much more positive word that outright insubordinate.

"Cigarette, John?" Mitscher asked, taking out a pack of Camels.

"It's true then, isn't it, sir?" Waldron said.

"It's been discussed, John," Mitscher replied, letting out a long cloud of smoke. He could see Waldron smoking too, but Waldron was without a cigarette.

"Whose idea was it, sir, if I may ask?"

"It was Admiral Fletcher's."

"I knew it! I just knew it!", Waldron exploded. "He doesn't have any guts, and he's assuming we don't..."

Mitscher suddenly slapped the cigarette down to the steel deck and jumped off his stool. His face seethed in anger. "Now you hold on there, Mister Waldron! You hold it right there! You are talking about an admiral and fellow officer in the United States Navy, and I will not tolerate that kind of talk, from you or from anyone else, at least not in my presence! Am I clear?"

Since the war began, Fletcher had gotten a reputation around the fleet for avoiding a fight, and then mismanaging the ones he finally got into. It all stemmed from his reluctance to come to the rescue of Wake Island when he had the chance to actually ward off and destroy the Japanese invasion fleet with *Lexington* and *Saratoga*. At Coral Sea, rumors were circulating that several opportunities that should have been seized weren't, and as a result the battle might well have been a tactical as well as a strategic victory. But then again, the fact that Fletcher was the only admiral to this point who had come face to face with major elements of the Japanese fleet, including their carriers, and was the only one who had lost a carrier, seemed secondary to the accusations. And Fletcher had seen firsthand what the major elements of the Japanese fleet could do, to ships and torpedo planes. His *Yorktown* was the barely living testament to that.

Waldron's face quickly changed from anger to supplication. One thing he didn't want to do was to anger Mitscher, his superior, and more, his friend.

"I'm sorry, sir. We've been training so hard for this, and it appears that now when the moment is at hand, we're being cast aside."

"That's utter nonsense, John. You know why VT-3 is flying from *Yorktown*? Because VT-5 was mauled at Coral Sea, and *Yorktown* needed *Saratoga's* planes to field a squadron. We all expected to have more of Amato's TBFs, but they didn't materialize. Sending you in would be heartlessly sending brave men who are willing to die in the line of duty off to their deaths. And remember, Fletcher was at Coral Sea. Whether he fought the battle well or not will be up to historians to decide. What he did was engage *Yorktown's* torpedo guys and watch them get torn apart. That they got even a few hits is sheer luck, and even that is up to conjecture. That Devastator just isn't up to the task, and we were thinking of finding it a mission in which it can excel, rather than be destroyed with its crew. That's the reasoning. I'm sure there's going to be plenty of room on the hangar deck and flight deck after the battle to remind us how powerful our foe was. We don't need to help that along."

Waldron persisted on the offensive. "The tactics that they used weren't in the best interests of the aircraft, sir. Even Lem Massey knows that. If the bombers would have attacked in unison with the torpedo planes, they could have split the enemy fire."

"John, the problem is the Devastator, pure and simple. It's too slow and vulnerable to work well in fast changing tactical situations. It can't climb very fast and its long slow approach to the target makes coordination with screaming dive bombers almost impossible. And that torpedo is unreliable, if not slow. You would have to practically go it alone to be in range when the dive bombers are ready to attack. We can't change the entire tactical plan just because the torpedo planes can't keep pace with the air group. We saw what happened with that at Coral Sea. For heaven's sake, the Wildcat's stalling speed is just a little lower than the Devastator's top speed. We can't even provide you with good fighter escort."

"So what do I tell my boys, Admiral? That they're second rate? That all that training I've pushed them through is all for nothing? That their commander is nothing more than a blowhard of a martinet?"

"Take it easy, Commander," Mitscher cautioned. "If we thought your men were second rate, we wouldn't be having this conversation right now, would we? As for their commander, I never thought he was a blowhard. If he were, he wouldn't be on my ship."

Waldron dropped his eyes. He looked like he wanted to cry. Mitscher's eyes showed he felt his pain. When proud men are forced to perform anything less than their sworn duty, it is a moment of shame, of disgrace. Steven Amato knew full well of what Waldron was feeling just then.

"Sir, I respectfully request that you and the task force commander review this change of tactics, as I totally disagree with their concept and their outcomes."

"Okay, John. I'll ask. But I don't think this is in your best interests or the best interests of the torpedo squadrons at large. We're going to need incredible luck to pull this off, John. If you go as you want, there won't be enough luck in the world to see you clear."

"I'm not counting on luck, sir. I'm counting on my men's training and courage."

"Very well," Mitscher said, lighting another cigarette and turning away.

Steven knew the torpedo squadrons would be slaughtered for the same reasons that Mitscher just gave him, and others Mitscher couldn't know right now. Steven knew that the torpedo squadrons were unfortunate enough to be launched first, thinking their slow speed would make it easier for the fighters and dive bombers to catch up and overtake them at approximately the point of attack; nonetheless the Devastators would be out-distanced by the fighter escorts, who were charged with protecting both the highflying dive bombers and the torpedo planes. In fact, the fighters elected to stay high because they couldn't climb up to protect the dive bombers as quickly as they could dive to protect torpedo planes skimming the surface-and would lose sight of them. The torpedo planes were unfortunate enough to happen on the Japanese fleet before any of the other attacking planes, including the rest of the entire air group off *Hornet*, which never found the Japanese that day. *Enterprises* and *Yorktown's* air group destroyed the four Japanese carriers.

But the question remained-was there a change of tactics that enhanced the torpedo planes' role of unwitting or purposeful decoys? He knew now for certain that their effectiveness was in doubt. Admirals Mitscher, Spruance and Fletcher had grave doubts, for sure, based on recent history at Coral Sea, and practical observation of the obsolete Devastator aircraft.

"What are you going to do, sir?" Steven asked.

"I don't know what else to do. It seems that I'm up against a wall. Maybe Stan Ring can help me out with this." He said it almost reluctantly.

Waldron found Ring in the officer's mess nursing a cup of coffee, concern all over his face. Ring was a worrier, to be sure. That his air group would have a pivotal part to play in this battle put the burden of the world on his shoulders.

"Stan, do you have a minute?" Waldron asked.

"Yeah, sure, John. What's up?"

"Have you heard that there is an effort for the torpedo squadrons to be placed in a mop up role?"

"What do you mean?" he asked. His face showed quizzical confusion.

He hadn't heard about it. That much was obvious. "Well, Stan, the thinking is the Devastator can't pull its weight in a full scale battle. From what I can determine it seems we're more of an impediment than an asset, and I..."

"How do we split the attack, then? The enemy fighters and AA will crush us. How do we corner their ships? Who's idea was this anyway?"

Ring was agitated. The officer who wanted clockwork precision and detailed planning was obviously trying to figure out how all this was going to work. His plans were much too detailed to have eclecticism play a role. Rightly or wrongly, though, it was Ring's way. He was a dedicated and studious officer, and he didn't rise to command an entire air group if had been wrong a lot more than he was right.

"I don't think that this is the best interest of this air group, John. I shall speak to the admiral myself regarding it. I don't think this is the time to adopt new tactics. I think we go the way we were trained. I would think that McCluskey and Pedersen see this the same way."

"Thanks, Stan. Goodnight."

It was then that Steven was chilled to the bone. It took Ring and his tunnel vision to do it.

They walked back to Torpedo 8's ready room, Waldron with an ear to ear smile. "I've got Mitscher thinking, and I've got Ring convinced. This idea is dead."

"I think you ought to give the tactics Fletcher suggested some additional and original thought," Steven blurted out, and was almost immediately sorry that he had.

Waldron stopped dead in his tracks, and his shoulders hunched as he whirled around to face this...this infidel. "What the hell am I hearing from you?" he said, as his face contorted with anger again. "Have you no idea what you're saying about brave men?"

"Commander, if I may. I think you're getting the wrong message here. I think they're telling you one of two things are going to happen. They've given you, Lindsey, and Massey a choice by the way it was suggested to you."

"Out with it, Amato. I don't like philosophy any more that Jimmy Doolittle did."

"Simply put, sir, they said either you take off after the dive bombers and fighters and finish off the flaming carriers and their less dangerous escorts, or you go in on your own, see what luck you have against the Zeros, and if you don't have luck, all they lose are forty-five pilots, forty-five gunners and a shitload of planes that should be used for target practice anyway. They're saying that Coral Sea proved that the Dauntless is the weapon, the ship killer of choice, at least until the TBF gets here in numbers, because the Devastator is a flying turkey. It's too slow and its ancient torpedoes are no good against a fast carrier. Oh, maybe it could have screwed up a battleship built in the twenties, but not a thirty-five knot carrier. And if this battle is shaping up like they say, ninety pilots and crew and forty five old planes don't stack up much against a ship the carries over two thousand men and a hundred airplanes. *Shokaku* was almost killed at Coral Sea by dive bombers, not torpedo planes."

"*Lexington* was killed by torpedo planes, wasn't it?" Waldron said with a glare.

"That's true, sir. But the Japanese Kates carry an 1800 pound torpedo that's faster and hits harder than your thousand pounders do. The one the TBF carries is similar. But you don't have any TBFs. And don't forget that the Kate is highly maneuverable and has a similar speed to the Val. They can attack in concert. And their crews have trained for years. Half our guys haven't even dropped a real torpedo."

Waldron stared at him, the muscles in his jaw pulsating as he ground his teeth together.

Then Steven remembered this was his boyhood hero, the man he had studied at Annapolis, who had a fierce determination to get the job done he had trained so long and hard to do, and a sense of duty that made Annapolis what it was.

"Sir, I only say this because I care. That's all. When you get the new TBFs in numbers, all your tactics can change. The plane is a superstar. But as for now, I think that the Japs can be dealt a major hammer blow with little loss of life on our part, if you coordinate your attacks and let the dive bombers go in, have the fighters engage the enemy CAPS, and then blow the bottoms out of the wounded and leave your squadrons practically untouched. It's worth a try, sir."

Waldron's face softened a bit, but it was obvious that this isn't how he planned to fight his first battle. He wanted to engage as he had been trained to do, executing the prevalent theory that the torpedo plane was the major element to be used to destroy enemy ships. Dive bombers were to attack land bases. Their secondary role was to blow up ships, to assist the torpedo planes. The reality of it all was crushing, to be sure.

"What do I tell my men? Do I tell them that they now have a secondary role, that they're not up to the task?"

"Sir, I have a feeling that before this war is over, what we once held sacred will be the butt of jokes, like the invulnerability of the battleship. Tell them that they'll be so many TBFs back at Pearl that everything they've learned will have to be evaluated for effectiveness."

Waldron looked long and hard at him, then glanced at Danny Morello, who tried to remain unusually quiet throughout all of this. He didn't need to double team John Waldron. He doubted if it would do any good anyway. Nothing else they tried to do since coming to the Land of Then had amounted to anything.

"I don't think so, Amato. I think I'm here to fulfill a role in history and so are my boys. We're not here to do anything less than what we were trained to do. If the admirals think otherwise, well that's just too bad. I'm going to fight this."

Steven looked back and grinned. "Somehow, I knew you'd say that. May I offer this, sir? How about you prearrange a signal for the fighters to come to support you should you need it? Something simple, like, 'come on down!' May I also suggest that you ask Commander Ring to come to an agreement before you take off as to what course you should follow? In a battle of maneuver like this, people will get lost and screwed up."

"I'll talk to Ring," he said, "for what it's worth."

As he headed to the ready room, he turned for a second and said, "Oh, Morello. Here," he said, tossing the wallet his way. "I've been so busy I've forgotten all about this. I found this in the jeep back at Pearl. Where the hell did you get those pictures? I didn't mean to pry, but I was looking for some identification. The pictures are in color. And is there a VF-41 somewhere? You have a calling card that fell out of the wallet with VF-41 on it."

"Think fast, Danny!" Steven muttered.

"Oh, those. I had them taken at the World's Fair in '39. They cost me a bundle, but I thought it was worth it. They say they're working on cheap cameras that can use color film. I gotta see that."

"You look like a character in *Gone With The Wind*," Waldron said. "This other picture, though, Morello. Why is Amato holding up my picture with the negro fellah? He's all dressed up in what looks like flight gear, and..."

"That was taken at Grumman aircraft, sir. We are wearing a special experimental flight suit that helps us with blackouts from high speed pullouts. That negro fellow is the Grumman employee of the month. He's a porter, but he's well liked. Grumman is a progressive company in keeping morale up, sir. We dressed him up in that fancy flight suit and took him up in a SNJ trainer Grumman keeps on hand to flight test equipment. We took your picture off the wall at Grumman and photographed ourselves with it, because VT-8 was supposed to get the first delivery of the TBFs. It was in the company newspaper. I liked the picture, so I asked for a copy of it myself."

"They have color too?"

"Oh, yes sir. In fact, the Grumman engineers are working on a reconnaissance camera for the TBF that shoots photos in color film. I think it will come to be quite handy."

"Yeah, probably," Waldron said, somewhat suspiciously. Then he yawned. "Oh, well, I've got to turn in. I don't think I'll be getting much sleep until this battle is over. Goodnight."

"Employee of the month?" Steven said, as soon as Waldron rounded the corner. "I'm glad he forgot to ask about VF-41! Shit!"

"What would you say? I hope I wake up tomorrow laughing," Danny said.

"Why is that?"

"Because then I'll know this was only a piss poor nightmare!"

Chapter 31

The American task forces tensely waited at their ambush stations north and east of Midway on June 3, eagerly anticipating news on the whereabouts of the Japanese fleet. Giant PBY Catalinas searched westward from Midway looking for the feathery white wakes on the ocean surface that would mean contact with the enemy. Each squadron lovingly worked over their aircraft, checking and rechecking every switch, dial, gauge, and meter to be sure the manufacturer's specifications were well within their limits. Everyone, from Admiral to steward, keenly felt that tomorrow would be the day of reckoning. Not one torpedoman gave a thought to the tactics suggested by Fletcher. However, Stanhope Ring was giving a good deal of thought to insuring that his bombers got through to their targets. As a matter of fact, he requested a meeting with Spruance on board *Enterprise*, with Pedersen and McCluskey, "to insure the Admiral knew of our tactics, and to inform him of our anticipated battle plan." Of course, Spruance, anxious to be the student and learn everything he could of carrier operations, including making optimum use of the next twenty-four hours, welcomed the opportunity to meet them.

"Commander Ring. Let's start with you. I understand that you have serious reservations regarding Admiral Fletcher's ideas about the deployment of the torpedo squadrons," Spruance said.

"Yes sir. That is correct. Using the torpedo squadrons in that fashion would nullify the practice of diverting the enemy's fire from his CAP and the AA batteries on his ships by attacking from several different directions using several different tactics."

"If I may, sir," McCluskey said, "the torpedo squadrons attack on the ships flanks and box her up, so the dive bombers have a steady target to dive upon, rather than a ship that only has to avoid the threat from above."

"Admiral Fletcher's concern, equally shared with Admiral Mitscher, is that the Devastators will not get close enough to launch their torpedoes with any effectiveness, because it's so slow and its torpedo is as slow as it is unreliable. They state that Coral Sea was a good example of their failure to do any real damage to the enemy fleet. They envision a mop up operation, you know, putting the Japanese carriers out for good, and perhaps attacking battleships. It seems the Japs are lousy antiaircraft gunners, but their Zero pilots are a vicious bunch of sharks. Wouldn't sending the Dauntlesses over the Jap fleet with fighter escort prove to be too much for the Japanese, especially if we concentrate on their four carriers?"

"Sir, the Devastators were able to attack at Coral Sea because of the coordination with the dive bombers. That they were ineffective was probably due more to jitters affecting the pilots than to the planes' or weapons' shortcomings," Pedersen offered.

"That seems to be correct, sir," Ring commented. "Besides, our torpedo men are a brave and nefarious lot. If they think they have been relegated to a Second Hand Rose position, they might turn around right after takeoff and torpedo our three carriers!"

The room erupted with laughter.

"At the least, I know John Waldron would," Ring gushed.

"He would have to fight Massey and Lindsey for the opportunity!" McCluskey added.

Spruance smiled lightly. "I've just seen Gene Lindsey. He's so terribly battered, but he is more determined than ever to lead his squadron into battle. Personally, I don't think there is a way to stop him. Do you Mac?"

"I'm not getting in his way, sir."

"All right, gentlemen. Considering Admirals Fletcher and Mitscher made this issue as only one of suggestion, and considering I believe in the dictum of fighting the way you train, I will go along with your recommendations. However, I think it is vitally important that you come up with a prearranged signal of sorts to lend fighter support where it's needed, either on the surface with the torpedo planes, or up with the dive bombers. We're up against their best carriers and air groups. Coral Sea's Japanese combatants *Shokaku* and *Zuikaku* were the newest ships with the greenest air groups. They'll miss the battle. We play their varsity tomorrow."

"Sir, this will shape up to be a battle of wits, and attrition. I think..."

Spruance cut Pedersen off. "Let me tell you my orders from Admiral Nimitz. I'm under the dictum of calculated risk. That is, I may endanger my forces only if the chance to inflict greater damage on the enemy than I would sustain is clearly on my side. I want you to take this same dictum back to your ready rooms. The Japs have us outgunned in every category. We cannot call this a battle of attrition, for if we do, and use that solely as our tactic, we will come away losers. We have to defeat them soundly. We will cause diversion with aerial attacks from Midway, and ambush them when they least expect it with our carrier air groups. Merely stopping the Midway invasion will be only a tactical victory. We have to cripple their ability to project strategic strength. That means, gentlemen, we must insure that their carriers rest on the bottom of the Pacific before we make steam for Pearl Harbor. And gentlemen, everything, and I mean everything, including our three carriers, is expendable, if it means we can put all their carriers plus a few battleships out of action for good under that dictum of calculated risk. Am I clear?"

"Yes sir," Ring said, ever the dilettante, shaking his head to invoke the same response from the other CAGs. "Thank you for your time, sir."

"What does this all mean?" McCluskey asked, walking Ring back to his Dauntless.

"I think it's simple. If the torpedo guys want to kill themselves while making it all the more likelier that we can shitcan the Japs with these here dive bombers," Ring said, patting his Dauntless's side, "we let them."

"I sure wish we had a few more of those TBFs," Pedersen said, as he watched Steven making an approach to *Enterprise*. At least then they'd have a chance."

"It wouldn't matter," Ring said. "The torpedo game is old hat. The Japanese Navy loves the torpedo attack. We haven't developed the tactics or the aircraft for it, until the TBF. We haven't enough fighters to escort both groups of planes. Someone will have to divert fire while still maintaining the possibility for a hit. That's the torpedo plane's job from now on. I'd be surprised if those planes ever get close enough to get a hit on a carrier. I say leave them to handle battleships and cruisers and tankers and other fleet auxiliaries, but they're too pig headed a lot to accept the secondary role, even if it means putting the coup de grace on a carrier. And those torpedo planes, even the TBF with its ball turret and its free ventral gun, won't be able to stand up to a determined Zero fighter attack because the TBF still has to make a long attack approach, totally vulnerable all the way. Mac, I've got a ton of work to get done. See you over the Jap fleet. Good luck," Ring said.

"Right, Stan. Good luck!"

Ring started the engine of his "double nuts" Dauntless, taxied forward, and a minute later was over the bow of *Enterprise* winging his way back to *Hornet*.

Steven trapped the TBF on the *Enterprise*, and after watching Ring's takeoff, he scooted up to the flag bridge to deliver dispatches and a part for the *Big E's* radar motor drive. Spruance was walking down to the flight deck as Steven bounded up the stairs and almost knocked him over.

"I'm sorry, sir! Are you all right?"

"Yes, Lieutenant, I'm fine," Spruance said with a chuckle. "I haven't been taken down like that since I played in the Army-Navy game. I see you have the dispatches."

"Yes, I do, sir. And the part for the radar motor."

"Very good. Please take this back to Mitscher," he said, motioning Steven to take the pad and pencil from his pocket. "It's better to use a messenger for stuff like this, because I really don't trust the Talk Between Ships communications gear. I feel the Japanese are eavesdropping on me right now!" he said with a laugh. "Tell him that we will stick to the original plan of a coordinated aerial attack on the Japanese fleet. Do you have that?" he asked. Steven, quite involuntarily, put his head up from his writing, just enough to show his eyes. "What's wrong, son?"

Spruance saw the disdain on his face, and it was obviously so deeply inscribed in his features that he had felt obligated to ask.

"It's nothing, sir."

"You don't agree, do you?"

Now what the hell was he going to say? An admiral was giving him a voice, and Spruance's face said he wanted an answer, not because of his rank, but because of his interest in learning.

"Sir, if the torpedo pilots had that TBF, there would be a chance they would make it. Instead they have those old, slow Devastators with their miniscule torpedo. If things go wrong with coordination, if we have unintended consequences to beautifully detailed plans and tactics, the torpedo men will have a rough go of it."

"I think we have to fight the way we train, son."

"Yes sir, and train the way we fight, too. Unfortunately the way we trained is not the way we have to fight. Our tactics and equipment were outdated before the war."

"This battle is very important, Amato. You have to know I have to keep our men confident in their equipment and tactics and training. A change now wouldn't support that."

"Yes sir. I had to pull Commander Waldron's head from the ceiling last evening when he first heard about it. But don't worry, sir. We're gonna nuke 'em!"

"We're going to what?"

"Oh, nothing sir. Just a new expression. Is there anything else?"

"No, Lieutenant. Happy landings."

"Thanks, sir." he said with a salute. Nuke 'em. I'm glad Morello didn't hear that one.

He went back to the TBF and took a long look at the *Big E* before climbing into the cockpit. As he stood on the TBF's wing he remembered that the ship would be the most decorated ship in history. Her tall block-like stack belched at thin cloud of black smoke, and her wake was straight and true. Her men raced along her wooden deck. The smell of gasoline was always present, like kerosene was on the carriers he served on. She was the pure embodiment of everything the Navy and the United States was about in this particular cell of time. Her men had a fierce determination, no less than the *Hornet's* crew to be sure, but *Enterprise* had its own style. And unlike *Hornet* and *Yorktown*, the latter having only a day more to live, the *Enterprise* would survive the war. That her own country cast her aside like an unloved old whore that everyone had had, forgetting how she loved and was loved, was nothing short of disgrace. For now, though, *Enterprise* was young, not only because she was only three years of age, but because she was full of life, full of spirit and determination, just like the country from whose steel, wood, copper, bronze and a hundred assorted raw materials she was created. As he lifted off her deck, he looked back at her high bow wave as she pressed through the blue Pacific. It seemed to say, "Bring spears, enemy. I will not be defeated."

He landed back aboard *Hornet* and reported to Admiral Mitscher, who only shrugged his shoulders upon reading Spruance's note, and said, "Case closed."

Steven went to VT-8's ready room, drew a cup of coffee, and sat down. Gus Widhelm of Scouting 8 came in and asked if he had seen John Waldron.

"No sir. I haven't, but I've just come aboard."

"I tell you that guy is nuts. He had a way out, but..."

"Are you talking about the change in the torpedo mission, sir?"

"Yes I am. He had a chance to survive, but now, I don't think he's going to make it. I dunno. I'm having premonitions. I've never had them before."

"You know him better than me."

"Well, if you see him, tell him I'm looking for him."

He felt time growing ever shorter. It seemed the old Hamilton was ticking faster the closer to June 4 it came. Steven wandered throughout the great ship, sensing a tenseness building in her crew, and even in her steel body. She surged forward defiantly, her men working tirelessly on her systems and on her aircraft. No one frowned, no one complained. Everyone had a smile of anticipation, a grim determination to engage the hated Japanese.

On the hangar deck, in a little machine shop off to the port side, Raymond Moore fashioned a piece of metal carefully.

"What are you up to, Ray?" Steven asked.

"I'm making a model for someone back home. It keeps my mind occupied."

The silvery plane was a perfect replica of the Devastator.

"Are you getting a bit tense?"

He turned off the metal lathe and took off his goggles. "Steve, I'm scared to death."

Steven frowned. It was so very true.

"Maybe we'll all get lucky, Ray. Who knows? Perhaps they'll be a last minute change in tactics. Maybe we'll really catch them with their pants down."

"Don't kid yourself, Steve. We might catch them in a bind, but not with their pants down. That's the Japanese Imperial Fleet out there. We're going to pay for everything we get."

"There's some talk of changing the battle plan. Spruance was thinking about the torpedo planes coming in after the bombers have a shot at..."

"Bullshit!"

The tone and defiance Moore showed was totally out of character for him. The easy going Moore had turned into a Bengal tiger.

"Waldron said that faggot Fletcher thought up this clean-up role. Screw him! We trained for this shot at the Japs and I'll be goddamed if I play second string. Either we go in with the bombers or we go in by ourselves!"

"Take it easy, Ray. I'm just saying that maybe someone will coordinate this battle a bit more. It seems that we have a better shot at success and survival if all the air groups go up together and attack together. That's all."

Moore softened a bit. "You mean an overall CAG?"

"Well, yeah. That would be a good way to do it. This way we won't get chopped up piecemeal. And intelligence will be better as well. Less people will get lost."

"Who will be the overall CAG? Ring? I don't think he's got enough respect. McCluskey-there's the guy. Pedersen may be a bit too gun shy after Coral Sea. Is there any talk of that? You've been flitting around the fleet."

"No, Ray, there hasn't. I think things have happened too fast, but you never know. Spruance is a thinker."

"No matter what, Steve, I'm going to do this right. I don't care what it costs."

"What do you mean you're going to do this right? I don't see that you've made so many mistakes."

"I let people down, Steve. I always have. Funny, I never thought about it much, but now that we're on the verge of eternity here, I guess I've reevaluated myself and discovered that I'm a real bastard."

Steven was astounded. Here was the cocky Clark Gable look-alike, the rich kid with the fancy uniform, thinking he had really fucked up a lifetime. Did he somehow know that it was all about to come to a terrible end?

"What do you mean, Ray?"

Moore looked at him and grinned, then shook his head. "You think I've had it made too, right? Well you are right, and I've done nothing about it, except take advantage of everyone who ever treated me with a shred of respect and love. My dad wanted the best for me. He sent me to a fancy private school in Richmond. He spent every night talking with me about me, and the plans he had for me and the more he tried, and the more he loved me, the more I broke his heart. I was accepted to Princeton. My dad wanted me to be an architect, because I drew so well and have a mind for math. You know what? I refused to go, because it would have made my old man happy. Instead, to show I was a man, I joined the Navy. My mom was shattered, but she never let a day go by without writing to me. My dad never gave up on me, either. He'd fly to the Great Lakes on weekends just to see how I was doing."

"Every guy is a rebel at heart, Ray. Look how you turned out. That's what really counts."

"I needed a kick in the ass, Amats. The Navy wanted to send me to Annapolis. They said I was too smart to be an enlisted man. I refused. What's worse, I told my father I refused. He never lost faith in me, though. My mother cried like a baby when I told her I refused to go, but she still wrote me every day. It took an admiral to tell me I was going to Annapolis. You know how he convinced me to take the appointment? He brought me down to the boiler room of a Great Lakes ore tender and told me that if I refused that appointment, he promised to keep me down there shoveling coal for the next four years. Imagine that?"

"The man had an obvious eye for talent."

"That, and the fact that he got his picture plastered all over the Navy with this boy who 'would join the brigade of Midshipmen.' My dad was so proud when I graduated. That's when he bought me my Ford. He brought my fiancé with him to the ceremony. She pinned on my gold bar. She loved me to pieces, Amats. She was sweet, kind, beautiful and lived for me. And I treated her like dirt, too. If you only knew what I... shit, nevermind."

"Waldron thinks highly of you."

"Waldron is like my dad. No matter how much trouble I cause him, he always takes it in stride. Oh, he screams like a son-of-a bitch, that's for sure. But he always lets you try again. I owe the man, and my dad, everything. When he met my mom and dad at Oceana just before Pearl Harbor, he went on about how I was the best pilot in the squadron, and what a true pleasure it was to have me on his wing. The night before, he pulled me drunk out of a brothel just before the SPs arrived. Some gem, I am, I tell you. That's why I can't let him down. I've got to do something right, for him, for my dad."

"Ray, you're being too hard on yourself. This is no way to go into battle. You've got to have a positive ...."

"Amats. Look what I did to you. I asked you if you had sex with the reporter. If you were a bastard, you would have popped me for insulting your fiancé. I'm like that all the time! If I survive, I'll be a different guy, for sure. If I don't, it's only because I deserved it. One thing, though-I'm gonna get a hit on a Jap carrier. I'm gonna do it with that torpedo underneath that plane over there, or with that plane itself. I told my rear seat gunner Pettry that this is the way it is, and if he doesn't want to come along, I'd understand. I'm not letting anyone down again."

"It's chow time. Want to go get something to eat?" Steven said.

"Yeah. I'm starved."

The day had passed quickly. The talk in the officers' mess was that word had filtered down that long range recon planes from Midway had sighted elements of the Japanese invasion fleet. The carriers couldn't be too far behind. Tomorrow would most definitely be the day.

Danny Morello was silent throughout dinner. He looked around at the men at his table and was overcome with a profound sadness that had him damping his eyes. He got up and went to the piano, the only piece of wood remaining on the ship at the request of the officers, and began playing *Yesterday*, the ballad by the Beatles.

Ray Moore and Waldron were attentive as he sung the lyrics. Tex Gay gave him a standing ovation when he finished.

"Who wrote that song? I've haven't heard it," Gus Widhelm asked.

"It's by one of the greatest composers of our time, sir."

"Who? Guy Lombardo? Cole Porter?"

Danny laughed. It was true-good music was timeless.

"Rogers and Hammerstein."

Night was falling quickly. The ships buttoned up and blacked out. On their way to the bridge to check in with Mitscher once more for instructions regarding the morning launch, Steven spotted Moore on the wing of the TBF, a paintbrush in his hands. He nudged Danny, and pointed to the seriously involved Moore, who must have felt their presence.

"Oh, shit! This was going to be a surprise! Ah, well. I'm almost done anyway. What do you think?"

On the side of the TBF were two obviously Italian looking men, with peaked caps and mustaches, their legs astride an out-of-proportion TBF. Each held a sausage in one hand, and a torpedo in the other. Under the plane was a bowl of spaghetti with Japanese flags intertwined to serve as the meatballs, the bowl lettered with *THE FLYING RONZONIS*.

"You're hot stuff, Moore."

"Ain't that the truth? It's my way of saying thank you, for... well, you know."

"I didn't think bastards said thank you."

"I'm not a bastard. And I'm going to prove that tomorrow, and when I get home."

You won't get home to prove it, Ray, but you'll prove it tomorrow for sure.

Danny just smiled and said, "Can we buy you a nightcap, Mr. Moore?"

"Certainly, Mr. Morello."

Mitscher had no business for them, at least not for the dawn launch. They met Ray Moore in the VT-8 ready room. He was reading a mimeographed sheet he handed to them, then poured them a cup of coffee as they read it. It was from Waldron:

Just a word to let you know I feel we are all ready. We have had a very short time to train and we have worked under the most severe difficulties. But we have truly done the best humanly possible. I actually believe that under these conditions we are the best in the world. My greatest hope is that we encounter a favorable tactical situation, but if don't and worse comes to worst, I want each of us to do his utmost to destroy our enemies. If there is only one plane left to make a final run in, I want that man to go in and get a hit. May God be with us all. Good luck, happy landings, and give 'em hell!

"Death to the Emperor!" Moore said, only half seriously.

"Death to the Emperor!" they responded, toasting with their coffee cups.

Steve suddenly left the ready room for the head, saying he had a cramp. Once inside the locked door, his eyes released a sea of tears and his chest heaved with uncontrollable sobs.

Danny was a bit more subtle. He said he had to check something in the TBF. He went straight to the flight deck, ran to the bow, and tried to stare the Pacific Ocean down. Then quite unexpectedly, and without any planned thought, he found himself praying for the boys of Torpedo 8 as they doggedly prepared for battle, and a peaceful Eternity that would be theirs tomorrow, save one.

Chapter 32

The air crews on all the carriers, including the Japanese, were up and about early this fourth of June, if in fact they slept at all. The American crews were told there would be a climactic sea battle today. The Japanese didn't anticipate facing America's carriers today. Their intelligence wasn't nearly as good as it was before Pearl Harbor. However, the Americans knew generally where and when. The Japanese thought they were to decide where and when, and there lay the seeds for their defeat.

In the early morning hours of June 4, 1942, Admiral Isoroku Yamamoto looked proudly from the flag bridge toward the bow over the massive eighteen inch guns of his flagship the battleship *Yamato*. She was the biggest warship with the biggest guns in the world. As much as he tried to cleanse them, his thoughts were nevertheless conceited and pompous, no doubt due to the string of victories he had experienced since December 7. His plans called for Midway to be his within hours. Then, he would rearm and service his aircraft to blast the American carriers to the Pacific's depths when they sailed, as they must, in a feeble attempt to retake the atoll from him and protect Hawaii. He thought *Yorktown* had sunk with *Lexington* at Coral Sea, and he knew *Saratoga* to be under repair in San Diego. No force on earth's seas could stand up to his Kido Butai, let alone two American carriers. Then, with the American carriers and their task forces destroyed, land based air could be brought to Midway, and the neutralization of Hawaii would begin in a week. For the American Navy, it would be over before it would begin.

Yamato's bow crashed through the ponderous Pacific swells as he would crash through the puny American effort in the way of his next prize, he thought. It was an easy, relatively uncostly war thus far. The coming Hawaii campaign might be costly, but in the next few days the Sons of the Rising Sun would own the Pacific west of California. America's choices would then be to capitulate immediately, giving Japan free rein in the Far East and China, or she would fight and suffer a terrible defeat in Hawaii, and capitulate those islands as well. Secretly, he looked forward to inspecting the wrecks at Pearl Harbor in a few more months.

Yamamoto reflected on how unexpectedly easy this had all been. He certainly had overestimated his enemy's capacity to wage war. He had accomplished all his goals in the six months he had given himself before America's industrial capacity took hold to beat Japan back to her home islands. Perhaps his years in America, in Washington and at Harvard, had led him to overestimate the American's will. Despite the reports to the contrary from the relatively green carriers *Zuikaku* and *Shokaku*, he did not think the Americans had the spirit, nor the weapons to beat him. *Akagi, Kaga, Hiruy,* and *Soryu* had veteran air groups who had flown together for years. Indeed, the ships operated well as a team. They were blooded, their pilots flying together since the China incident. *Enterprise* had never seen a fleet battle, and *Hornet* had only delivered Doolittle's planes to Tokyo. Their air groups were relatively untried. Why not think pompously, he told himself. Why not indeed?

But Yamamoto had not as yet encountered the men whose collective hate for him, his ships, and his race, because of the treachery of the sneak attack the Americans referred to as The Sunday Murders that he had orchestrated. He would have been terrified if it could be personified. Never in the history of warfare were men ever keener on exacting blood than they were of Yamamoto's blood, and the blood of his sailors and airmen. He would learn today that the Americans, as kind and easy going as he knew them to be, could be the worst killers on the face of the earth, far worse than even he imagined. Like the Japanese, they would give no quarter in battle, unselfishly willing to sacrifice themselves to take their enemy's lives. This was not only because of a proud military tradition as was the case of the Japanese. The attitude of execration was heightened due to the antipathy and aversion the Americans felt for their enemies, because of the absolute treacherous and recreant way they began and prosecuted this war.

Yamamoto had characterized the Pearl Harbor attack as only the most basic of tactical victories. It had given Japan a little breathing room to carry out conquest, but also worked negatively to "wake a sleeping tiger, and fill it with a terrible resolve." The last six months had made him euphoric; it was only the remotest possibility that by the close of the day today, he would contemplate suicide for the dishonor he would soon suffer.

Aboard *Hornet*, VT-8 had gathered in its ready room after an early 3:00 a.m. breakfast, anxiously awaiting word of the Japanese fleet's disposition and position. Men smoked, drank coffee, kidded each other, or were strangely silent. Ray Moore's face was one of determination. Tex Gay just smiled at everyone. The others, Gray, Ellison, Kenyon, Teats, Miles all of them were silently eager to get on with it. Down the hall at VS-8's ready room, Gus Widhelm could be heard singing to a Frank Sinatra song. Messengers from the other squadrons ran back and forth between ready rooms sharing as much information as they could muster. On the flight deck their rear seat gunners, Amelio Maffei, Otway Creasy, Ron Fisher, Bill Sawhill, George Field, Hollis Martin, Bob Huntington all of them, worked over their new twin mount thirties that Waldron had gotten for them at Pearl, cleaning and oiling the mechanisms, and loading the belts of thirty caliber ammunition into their breeches.

Every time somebody appeared at the door, the pilots rose and turned, their faces full of anticipation. The air could have been cut with a knife. When a signal flag went up on the carrier's bridge, the gunners sat down in the cockpits and fastened their seat belts, thinking that this time was "it."

On *Enterprise*, Gene Lindsey painfully made his way to the officer's mess, and sat down to a breakfast of powdered eggs. He moved slowly and grimaced as he ate. His executive officer Pablo Riley said, "Skipper, you're still hurting. Let me take the squadron in today."

With a forkful just at his mouth, he turned to Riley and said, "This is the day we've trained so long for, Pablo. I'll take the squadron in."

No one questioned his decision.

Jim Gray, the commander of VF-6, sat down next to Lindsey. Lindsey said, "Remember Jim, if I need you, I'll yell 'come on down.' I know you can come down to protect us easier than you can climb up to the dive bombers. Just keep your ears open."

Gray looked at him for a moment, and the edges of his lips turned downward when he saw how Lindsey was hurting. "Gene", he said, "why don't you come in after the bombers, you know, like we suggested. I have to follow them down in the attack, and I'll be down at sea level in an instant where you'll be anyway. That way, you can whack the Japs when they're hurt and confused, and I can protect you. If the Jap carriers don't get hit by the bombs, I can still clear the Zeros away for your torpedo run. What do you say?"

Lindsey put down his fork, turned to Gray, and with absolute resolution his face, said, "I say that we'll see you at the Jap fleet the same time as everyone else. I appreciate your concern, Jim, but that's not what we're here for. If we go in alone, the bombers will be swarmed over with AA and Zeros. You can't protect us all. There just isn't enough of you. We can't change tactics now anyway. That'll only screw things up some more."

At 0430, *Yorktown* launched ten of her SBD Dauntlesses to cover the northern arc of the tactical battle circle, just in case the Japanese changed course overnight. Then, the rag tag squadrons of Air Groups Three and Five tried to work out some signals of coordination, in an attempt to insure they all met at the same time over the target area. It took an hour and a half for all the call signs and codes signs to be assigned. Still, there was confusion.

It was 0600.

AS TIME GOES BY

Danny Morello had packed whatever few belongings he had, including the tapes and the F-14 manual. Steven and he had a feeling today would be the day that, perhaps, they somehow might effect a return to the Land of Now. What else was he to do here? They both prayed that their experiences here would be short-lived, that Steven had gotten the chance to answer some lifelong questions as well as a few recent questions that had clouded his thinking since Thatcher spun into the Mediterranean. They both were sticking to each other like glue. But then again, Steven mused, was that different from any other time?

Waldron walked down the passageway to his ready room, and smiled at the two young men.

"Today's the day, Amats! Today, we put a Jap carrier in the mud."

"Yes sir!" Steven replied.

Waldron took out a cigarette, but left his lighter in his quarters, and he fumbled in his pockets for matches.

"Here, Commander. I've got it," he said, fumbling for some matches.

He accidentally unzipped the wrong zipper, thinking it was his flight suit. The zipper he fumbled with belonged to the bag that carried his tapes and his manuals, which promptly fell to the floor.

Waldron spotted the manual and bent down too quickly for Steven or Danny to retrieve it first. He quickly leafed through it and his mouth opened wider and wider as he did. When he came upon the photograph that Julie had taken of Danny, Steven, and Vincent Capo posing in front of the new F-14, with *The Flying Ronzonis*" and the letters *JAWN* painted on its nose, he just stared at them. They, in return, said nothing. What could they say?

"Who the hell are you guys?" Waldron asked. "And what the hell is an F-14 Tomcat with a FLIR pod? When did Grumman get into the rocket ship business? And what the hell is my Academy nickname doing on it? And what are these here things?" he yelled, holding up a computer disk. "Are you bastards from Mars?" he said, cocking his head, then reaching for the thirty-eight on his shoulder.

"No, sir. We're not from Mars, but as far as you're concerned, we might as well be. I think we have to talk, Commander Waldron," Danny said.

Waldron remained incredulous as Steven and Danny told the story of their crash and rescue in a scant few minutes. They said nothing of Fords, or of Hamilton watches. What good would that do? The story's roots were unbelievable enough without the explaining the limbs. Nevertheless, Waldron kept his hand close to the thirty-eight.

"How could you have gotten here?" he asked.

"I think I willed us here, sir, plain and simple. This battle has intrigued me since I was a child barely able to read. You were a hero of mine.

Things in our Navy aren't so cut and dry. A great friend of ours was killed by hostile forces without us firing a shot, or having him fire a shot in his own defense. I lost faith. I guess I had to meet you to know about devotion to duty and..."

Suddenly, he realized he was going to tell Waldron what he didn't need to know, at least not at this very minute. He didn't have to.

"Okay, Amato, Morello, or Buck Rogers and Commando Cody...you do know who they are, don't you?"

"We saw the movies, sir. They're still popular from where we come from," Danny said.

"What hostile forces shot your buddy down? Japs?"

"Libyans. But that's not important. The world has changed dramatically. I could take a week to inform you about it, but..."

"Libyans? You mean Arabs? Camel jockeys shot your friend down? They can hardly read! What's the name of your ship?"

"The *Nimitz*," Danny said.

"Named after your uncle, I presume?" he said with a laugh.

"Yes."

"So I can assume that Chester Nimitz is dead in the nineteen eighties, right? They don't name ships after live people."

"Right, sir. He would have been almost a hundred."

"Do the Libyans have planes like this here Tomcat?" Waldron said, admiring the plane.

"Something like it, but not nearly as good. They're Russian MiGs, or Sukhois. There ain't nothin' like a Tomcat," Steven said with a smile.

"Russia? Are you telling me that after all the Lend-Lease stuff we sent them, they turned against us?"

"You don't know the half of it. So did the Chinese. Names like Korea and Vietnam become synonymous with the term cold war. I can go on and on, sir, but..."

Then Waldron's face turned eerily serious. "Wait a goddam minute! You know how this turns out then, don't you? I guess we win, or you wouldn't be here! Too much depends on this battle for you to have...that's why you were so hard on trying to get me to change our torpedo tactics!"

Steven only looked at him, with his eyebrows starting to upturn above his nose. Danny just turned away.

"That bad, huh?" Waldron said. "Shit, I expected it to be bad, but..."

"Sir," Steven began. "get Commander Ring to follow your lead. Beg him if you have to. I can fly to *Enterprise and Yorktown* and Gene Lindsey and Lem Massey to do the same. It's not too late."

Waldron was pensive for a moment, then he picked up his head, his eyes bright. "Well, if you think...wait a minute! I'm getting as nuts as you two guys! What will I tell them? Oh, by the way, Gene, I met these two guys from the future, and they told me that all of you should follow me to the Japs. Yeah, they might believe that! Shit! I don't believe that!"

"Commander! We've got contact!" Ray Moore motioned them to come to the ready room right away.

"Follow me, gentlemen," Waldron said, turning away towards Moore, still shaking his head.

As pilots jotted down the information about radio frequencies, headings, and courses to the Japanese fleet, Sam Mitchell, the CO of VF-8 walked into the ready room. "John? May I see you a minute, please?"

"Sure, Sam. You wait here," he said to Steven and Danny, who nonetheless followed a few steps behind. Maybe Mitchell had something, they thought. When he started to talk to Waldron, it was evident his concerns were the same as others being expressed on the other two American carriers right now.

"John, I've been thinking about this awhile. I talked to Jim Gray yesterday, and Jimmy Thatch aboard *Yorktown*. We're all in agreement that you follow in the dive bombers, and we clear the path in and escort you when the bombers have made their drops and head for home. I don't think the Japs can waste their CAPs on retreating planes and letting fully armed ones get by. What do you say?"

"I say that by our doctrine and tactics, this is to be a coordinated attack. That means we all go at the same time," Waldron said, as implacable as a rock.

"John, we have to change our tactics to accommodate the torpedo attack, especially with those old Devastators. Even if you had TBFs we would have to do something differently. John, those Zeros will swarm all over you on the way in. Nine miles gives those cross-eyed Japs a better than even chance to splash you. I can clear it with Ring, John. What do you say?"

"I say no."

Stanhope Ring caught sight of Mitchell talking with Waldron, and walked to them, his eyes and ears taking in as much of their conversation as possible.

"What's up?" he asked.

"I was asking John about changing the torpedo tactics a little bit to accommodate the vulnerability of the Devastator, Stan. I think..."

"It's too late to think. We got a contact report, and we're off to the Japanese Fleet. Four carriers spotted. We go in a few minutes. No changes in the game plan, understood?" Ring said, flashing his eyes at both of his squadron commanders. "Here are your position reports. Distribute these to your men. We're turning into the wind now."

"Understood," Waldron said. He turned back to the ready room and copied down the position reports on his charts.

"John, I think you ought to reconsider," Mitchell persisted. "Those boys haven't got a chance in hell. We've got to do more to protect them."

"The tactics we have trained with are the best protection. Get up to your fighters, Sam. It's showtime."

Waldron studied his charts, plotting the position of the Japanese fleet.

"Midway reports many planes heading their way," a messenger cried as he ran into the ready room.

"We need a bearing!" Waldron yelled.

"They're coming directly from the 280 degrees northwest."

"Where's the wind coming from?"

"Meteorology reports the wind coming from the southwest."

"That means that they turned in to the wind to launch, then back again to recover their aircraft, then back again to launch, if they care about keeping the distance to Midway constant for their departing and landing planes, and searching for us...which means they won't be here..." he said as he drew a line and an X on the map. "Considering the wind, their speed and the time their aircraft attack Midway and fly back home, land and launch again, they should be..."

"Midway is being bombed!" another messenger yelled.

Waldron did some figuring, used a compass to draw an intersecting line, looked at his watch, and then drew another line with a straight edge.

"Here! The bastards will be right here!" he said, making an X on the map, and showing it to his squadron.

"That's not where Commander Ring just said," Ray Moore said.

"Fuck Commander Ring! We're going here!" he said, pointing to the X on the map with a pencil.

Waldron turned to his squadron and said, "All right! Listen up! We'll be off in a minute or so. I don't want any torpedo drops so far out that you won't have a chance to get a hit. That's what happened at Coral Sea. They dropped too far out, and now everybody wants us to play mop-up because they think we're unreliable and obsolete. To hell with them! VT-8 will show 'em how it's done! Get in close! Remember, that fleet out there is the embodiment of everything evil on this earth. You saw what they did to Pearl. Remember the guys on Wake and the Philippines as well. They're brutal bastards, worse than the devil himself. I wouldn't be surprised to find out the devil is a Jap. However, let's make the devil happy, and return a bunch of his little devils to him!"

"Pilots! Man your planes!"

"Let's go, boys!"

The ready room erupted in a shout of joy, just like a locker room before a big game.

"Commander Waldron! Please talk to Ring! He knows..."

"He knows shit, Amats. You want to talk to Ring? Well here!" he said, taking off his Annapolis class ring, and thrusting it at him. "Talk to this ring. I'll be back in few hours to get it. If I don't make it back, keep it as a remembrance of what a hard headed jackass I am."

Waldron smiled at him as he put on his leather helmet. Then he grabbed both Amato and Morello and hugged them both. "Good luck wherever you guys are from. It sounds like an absolute hell hole. But you two guys will prevail. The good guys always do. And thanks for naming that Tomcat after me. It means a lot. I won't be forgotten, so I guess I'll do some good."

Waldron turned to follow his squadron out the door.

Steven found tears coming down his cheeks. He ran after Waldron and yelled, "Waldron! It's going to be all right, you know! All of it!"

Waldron turned slowly and smiled at him, hands on his hips. "Don't you think I know that, Amats? Do you think I could do this if I didn't believe that? God, just look at you guys and that Tomcat. Happy landings, kiddo!"

And he was gone.

Ray Moore handed Steven a leather flight gear bag as he ran out, saying, "Amats, the registration to the Ford is in here. I won't be needing it. What am I going to do with Ford and a Lincoln?" he laughed. "There's also something else in there that needs getting done. I can't explain now, but it's important. Can you handle it for me, please, in case we...,or I don't..."

Ray Moore almost glowed. His smile was bright, and his eyes gleamed. His face bore the blush of life.

"Sure, Ray. Whatever it is, I'll do it. And here, take this. It'll help you navigate."

"No Steve," he said, holding his hand as he tried to undo the watch from his other wrist. "The watch is yours. I won't be needing it today, especially since big Sioux chief Waldron is leading the war party. But you will. Good luck!"

"Goddammit, Moore. Shake it up, will you? Why the hell is it we always have to wait for you, your highness? "

"I gotta go before Waldron has kittens."

And he was gone.

Danny and Steven scrambled on deck to watch the takeoff. The planes seemed to claw their way into the air, as *Hornet* sailed into the wind with a bone in her teeth. First the Devastators, then the Dauntlesses, and finally the Wildcats flew off, all heading east north east to carry out the biggest ambush in history. It was 0700.

The last Wildcat was aloft when Mitscher ordered them to the bridge. They saw the Admiral with moist eyes, as he turned to them to speak.

"I've seen it a hundred times, but it never fails to get to me. Now, my air group from my ship is going into battle for the first time. I pray for them."

Mitscher lit a cigarette and turned to get a stack of papers from the counter near his perch. "Take this to Admiral Spruance aboard the *Enterprise*. You boys are doing a magnificent job with this. I certainly hope you realize what a help you've been."

"Yes sir," they said, realizing they hadn't even worked enough to pay for the gas to start the TBF's engine. But that was Mitscher- all for one, one for all.

He had to try, at least. "Sir, could you request that Commander Ring make contact with VT-8? Commander Waldron's course to the Jap fleet takes into account their launching and recovery of their Midway strike group. I don't think Commander Ring took that into account. He headed straight for the position given by the PBY that spotted the Japanese fleet."

"Ring commands the air group. I'm sure he will find Waldron's squadron and they will head to the target together."

"Sir, I don't know. It seems..."

"Like I said, Amato, Ring commands the air group. I can't manage his battle from here."

"Yes sir. I'll get this over to the *Big E* now, sir."

Mitscher stared at the specks that were quickly vanishing to the east, as he lit another cigarette.

"I don't believe this! No one is going at this as if they had air groups. If we did this, we'd get our balls in a sling for sure! I can't understand it! It's a fucking free-for-all. Look! There goes the air group from *Enterprise*. They're going off on the wrong heading! Sweet Jesus!" Danny was near apoplectic.

"We are observers, not revolutionaries. It's all meant to be as it was," Steven said resignedly. "Ray Moore just told me that when he told me to keep his watch."

The TBF ran down *Hornet's* flight deck, along the same white line that Doolittle has used to get his bombers aloft. He headed for the *Enterprise* a few miles away. Steven circled her once before landing. The *Big E's* strike was aloft and winging its way to the Japanese Fleet. All of them, except one Devastator, who's pilot tried in vain to start it.

"What happened, Whitney?" Steven said, rushing to the distraught airman.

"The son-of-a-bitch won't start! It won't start! We went over her with a fine tooth comb again last night, but it won't turn over! Goddammit! I hate you, you bastard!" he screamed at the airplane, as if it were an obstinate mule, not that a mule would have moved anyway, and threw his clipboard at it.

"Calm down, Charlie. They'll be another strike. Maybe you were meant by fate to do something else. Today will be...Charlie! Where are you going? You can't do that!"

Whitney jumped into a Dauntless dive bomber that had just been refueled after returning from a search mission, before it's pilot had any idea he was there. He gunned the engine, and taxied it to the bow, only to be told by the launch officer that jumped on his wing that if he didn't get out of the airplane right quick, he would shoot him. They took Whitney below, dragging his feet in total despair.

"Well, that's that, isn't it?" Danny said to Steven.

It was 0925.

They went to the flag bridge to deliver their messages to Spruance. The radios came alive with the first contacts with the Japanese fleet. Waldron's voice was loud and clear.

"I told you I'd find 'em. Radio the position report to the rest of the air groups. Okay, let's go! Spread it out. We're gonna have to watch the gas if we have any hope of getting back to the ship!"

"Sir, shouldn't we wait for Commander Ring and the rest of the air group?"

"Let Ring find the Japs himself. If we wait, we'll run outta gas! We were ordered to attack and attack we will! Let's go in. Watch the ...Zeros! Zeros at twelve o'clock!"

"Zeros at the six! Anybody got 'em?"

"Hey, Tex! Watch that bastard coming in at the seven! Oh, shit! Shit! I'm hit! I can't control it! I'm goin' in..."

"Billy! You're on fire! You're wing....Billy! Get outta there!"

"I got one! Burn, you bastard!"

"Nice shooting, Amelio!"

"Watch the three, two bandits at three o'clock! Christ, are we the only ones out here? Where the fuck is Ring? I...uhh..."

"Head for that carrier directly ahead! Somebody will get a hit! Head right for her bow!"

"She's turning away! Dammit, we can't go round again!"

"Skid it! Use your rudder and skid it!"

"This goddam plane can't..."

"Skipper! This is Tex! You've got one on your tail."

"Dobbs! You got him? Dobbs!"

"Skipper, Dobbs isn't moving! Skid it, sir. Skid it..."

"I'm trying to. She's sluggish, Tex. Oh, Jesus!"

At that moment, Steven knew that Tex Gay's Devastator was the only one of fifteen left flying, and he was bearing straight down on the *Akagi*. A machine gun slug ricocheted in his canopy and imbedded itself in his arm. He squeezed it out, and for some reason, put it in his mouth. He got so close to *Akagi* after releasing his torpedo that he flew only meters from her bridge, so close that he could make out the Japanese staff as he whizzed by. He flew down the carrier's flight deck sending her deck crew scrambling, firing his wing guns as he went. He would have crashed on her deck, but the plane's controls were not responding well to input. His gunner, Robert Huntington, had fallen victim to a Zero's slugs. Just when Gay thought he just might pull off an escape, as sloppily as the Devastator was handling, a Zero made another run that tore off his wing. The Devastator pancaked onto the ocean. He quickly tore open the canopy that had been slammed shut by the impact, took the seat cushion from the rapidly sinking plane to use for flotation. He didn't dare open the raft in the middle of the Japanese fleet that was twisting and swerving to avoid the incoming torpedo planes from *Yorktown* and *Enterprise*. He noted that Huntington sat lifeless in the back seat, one hand still clinging to the new twin thirties that Waldron had gotten for them to double their firepower as the Devastator slipped beneath the waves.

All in all, forty-four torpedo planes attacked from the three American carriers. The men of each torpedo squadron had drank together, whored together, flew together, even were best men at each other's weddings together. Today, they died together. There were no hits, and only seven pilots and six enlisted men survived. Of the six TBFs that attacked with Earnest from Midway, only Earnest made it back, one of his crewmen dead. None of the B-26 bombers made it back. The B-17s fared slightly better-only one was killed. All of Midway's fighters were decimated in the air attack, save a few.

And neither Jimmy Thatch, Jim Gray, nor Sam Mitchell ever heard, "Come on down."

The Japanese fighter pilots had had a field day. But now, they were low on the water, out of fuel, and out of ammunition. Their Midway strike was returning, which meant the four Japanese carriers had to delay launching their strikes against the American carriers, just recently discovered by a scout plane from the cruiser *Tone* that was delayed in launching due to a faulty catapult. The strike's Kate torpedo bombers had already been rearmed with torpedoes to engage the American carriers; they initially had bombs for a second strike at Midway. So in their feverish preparation to strike the American fleet, the Japanese carriers lay fully vulnerable, with armed and gassed planes on deck, thousand pound bombs indiscriminately tossed asunder, gasoline lines crisscrossing their decks, few fighters in the air, and downwind and scattered as they tried to avoid the continuous, if not accurate, strikes from Midway and the torpedo planes from the three American carriers. Mistakes were piling upon fatal mistakes. Disaster was holding all the cards.

It was 1015.

Steven looked at Spruance's face as he heard the debacle conclude.

"Where's the rest of Air Group 8?" he said aloud.

"Probably on the way back to *Hornet* or Midway, jettisoning their bombs in the ocean," Steven said bitterly.

"How do you know that?" Spruance asked.

"Just a hunch, based on the heading that Ring said he was using when I was on the *Hornet* this morning, and the position report Waldron gave just before he died."

"It seems those reservations of yours were realistic, Amato," Spruance said, his chin buried in his chest.

"I think we all should go to church this Sunday, and give thanks for God's blessing today, and for the boys of Torpedo 3, 6, and 8."

"Maybe we can divert Air Group 8 to..."

"How about I fly to Midway to determine if we can? Some of the planes will land there. Maybe I can give them a position report."

The *Big E's* speakers came alive again.

"This is McCluskey! There they are! Best, take your group to the one to the north. We'll take this one." He gave a position report, and then yelled, "Okay, let's do it!"

"Where the hell are the Zeros?"

"Count your blessings."

A minute later, the air was full of war whoops and shouts and whistles. McCluskey's voice came through loud and clear.

"We got them! We nailed two! That must be *Yorktown's* or *Hornet's* group to the west on another. We got three of the bastards burning! Three! *Arizona*, I remember you!"

It was 1020.

In five minutes, the Japanese went from the expected victors to the utterly vanquished, their carriers' decks masses of molten metal, gushing gasoline fires, and exploding ordnance and broiling bodies. Hell had been reinvented.

Spruance walked over to them, almost on air. Suddenly the plight of the torpedo squadrons had been cast aside.

"Take this over to Fletcher on the *Yorktown*. I need his opinion about the next phase," Spruance said.

Spruance saw the disbelief on Steven's face. "I know what you're thinking, Amato, but consider this. Those torpedo boys may have missed with their torpedoes, but they hit with those bombs. It wouldn't have worked without them."

"I guess so, sir. I'll be back as soon as I can."

They left the *Big E's* deck for *Yorktown* operating a few miles eastward.

"Holy shit!" Steven yelled.

"What's the matter?" Danny said anxiously.

"It's almost noon!"

"So you want to stop for lunch? What?"

"Oh, shit, I'm right! Look to the west!"

"Japanese! Where are they heading?"

"For *Yorktown*. She takes three bombs now. We can't land. We'll never get off, and I don't mean that we won't be able to take off."

"You're goddam right we can't! Let's get the hell outta here!"

"We can't go back to the *Enterprise*. The Japanese might follow us, and with our luck, history might finally change."

"Hey, look! That bastard is making a gunnery run on us!" Danny screamed.

"Start working that turret, Danny boy! Hang on!"

Steven dove the Avenger (he figured that this was a good time to start calling the plane by its nickname) straight to the sea. The Zero followed close behind. Danny uncorked the fifty caliber machine gun in the turret, and drove the Zero away...momentarily.

The Japanese pilot rolled the deadly little fighter and came back around, guns going full bore. The twenty millimeter cannons in the wings flashed, and the 7.7 millimeter nose guns spat tracers that caused holes to appear in the wings and fuselage.

"Steve! Keep it going! Slip to the right!"

"Roger that!" Steven replied with his heart in his throat, as he heard the fifty caliber in the ball turret come alive.

The Zero looped underneath and over them, and came back head on. Steven fired the fifty caliber nose gun at the Zero as soon as he came into range. After a few seconds, the Zero suddenly pulled up and over again, quite surprised at the greeting he had gotten. When he did this, however, he exposed the belly of his plane to Danny's withering fire. The Zero began to smoke and pulled off, having had enough of the battle.

The TBF was hit badly. It was losing fuel from its holed wing tanks, and its engine was smoking as the oil pressure dropped. The smell of hydraulic fluid permeated the cabin, and Steven noted the wheels were beginning to drop from their wells. There was no way he could land on a carrier without fouling up its precious deck. He decided to make for Midway, as the chase, lasting not five minutes, had dragged them in that direction anyway.

He tried to radio *Enterprise* as to his intentions, but he found the radio had been shattered by a twenty millimeter slug.

They flew on for fifteen more minutes, the engine beginning to miss. The oil pressure gauge was flat, and the plane began to have control problems. The flaps would only come down half way. Below them, a little island about a mile to the west of Midway appeared.

"Danny, I'm going to try to put down on the beach below us. We can't make Midway. We're too banged up."

"Roger that. I'll buckle myself in real good."

"Here we go."

The Avenger glided over the coral reef and Steven did his best to keep it above stalling speed, even though engine was about to give up the ghost. Just as they crossed the beach, it did. The plane was only about fifty feet above the sandy beach. He pulled the stick back and the plane stalled perfectly, its tail hitting first, then the belly. The Avenger nosed over heavily, and the propeller stopped windmilling and bent at weird angles. After a run of about one hundred yards, the plane stopped abruptly, throwing Steven's head against his gunsight, and Danny's head into the side of the turret. Both of them passed out.

Danny thought he was the first to have awakened. He groggily made his way out of the TBF, and then on to the wing to see how Steven was. He found him awake, with a rag on a nasty cut on his forehead, staring out over the Pacific.

"Where are we?" Danny asked.

"I think this is Kure. It's a little island just to the west of Midway. We'll be okay. We'll begin signaling as soon as we break out the survival kit."

"Let's build a fire," Danny suggested.

"I'd rather not. There are Japanese subs out there. I don't want them to know we're here, at least not until tomorrow. We'll use a searchlight and mirror then, flashing it directly at Midway. We'll also spread out the parachutes on the beach."

They sat down, opened a few C-rations, and ate. The afternoon brought heavy squalls that flushed the smell of hydraulic fluid and gasoline from the Avenger. They slept under the Avenger's wing, using the rubber boat as a mattress. Tomorrow they would begin signaling Midway for rescue.

It was 1900.

The sun was setting quickly in the west. Both were uncontrollably drowsy, and just as the sun went down and the first stars began to shine through the darkening sky, they fell asleep. They heard the drone of aircraft engines as planes too badly damaged for a carrier landing or too low on gas to find a carrier at night, landed on Midway, permanently secure in the possession of the United States.

It was 2100 hours.

They would have been intrigued to know that Ray Moore's Hamilton Chronograph had stopped ticking at midnight, as they slept with the gentle, warm tropical breezes whistling through the palms above them that belied the carnage that marked the day.

Chapter 33

The USS *Vincennes* had her "ears" opened wide. Her powerful listening devices and computerized communications gear were set for full sensitivity to determine the origin of a very weak radio signal emanating somewhere near Midway. The helicopter on her stern was awaiting word on a bearing to follow, its blades spinning just below take off speed. The sea was flat as glass making *Vincennes* bow wave that much more impressive as she sliced through the blue about fifteen miles south of the Midway atoll.

Vincennes is an Aegis-class cruiser, fitted with the most powerful shipborne radar and sonar man could devise. Her communications gear was computer driven, as was all her weapons systems. She could "listen" silently for traces of an enemy submarine, surface ship, or aircraft with the most sensitive passive search systems in the world, or could blast out pulses of electromagnetic radiation to find a seagull diving for fish miles away. Her weapons systems were formidable, to say the least. She was a hornet's nest of surface-to-air and surface-to-surface missiles, and high volume-of-fire cannon. Her anti-submarine capabilities were limitless. *Vincennes* was designed to protect a carrier battle group, as well as herself, from all hostile threats. Now, however, her captain, James L. Spino, had all her appropriate systems concentrated on a barely audible signal coming to her from the north. As there was still a missing crew report stubbornly being kept active by a Commander Paul Riley, the crew's squadron commander, *Vincennes* was compelled to investigate any signal that might tell the fate of Riley's F-14 crew, missing almost eight weeks after a horrendous accident. While Captain Spino entertained no thoughts that an aircraft crew might be alive out here that long, he radioed Midway of his findings, and prepared a search and rescue operation.

Back on Oahu, Commander Riley patiently waited by the communications shack on Ford Island. Riley looked absolutely horrible. He had lost weight and had deep circles under his eyes from the lack of sleep. Rena Amato's face had aged considerably over the past eight weeks. Marcus White stopped smiling at Julie Ann Tate when she accused him of patronizing her, and as a result, she would have no choice but to cut out his heart and stomp on it if he did it again.

Quite to the contrary, Julie Ann Tate never looked more upbeat, or more beautiful. She had gotten Susan to put on new makeup and get a new cut for "Danny Boy" who was due home today. She herself had bought a new Hawaiian style dress that totally accentuated her figure, and the dark blush she developed under the bright Hawaiian sun made her blue eyes even more brilliant, and her blond hair even more striking. Riley just shook his head when he looked at her, thinking she was still hoping against hope. Lieutenants Ware and Reuter tried not to look-if Amato and Morello were still alive, there would be hell to pay and blood to let.

"Sir? I'm getting in a report from *Vincennes*. They've picked up an extremely weak but audible distress signal in their patrol area. They've sent their chopper to investigate. They will report in about five minutes."

"Did she send a position report?" Riley said, as he stood up, as did Julie, Susan, Rena, Paul and Marcus, all of them holding their breath awaiting the answer.

"Yes sir. It's from an island called Kure," the enlisted man responded.

"Where the hell is that?" Riley said.

"Right here, Commander," the enlisted man responded. "It's about a mile from Midway."

"Hah! Hah Hah! I knew it! I just fucking knew it! The boys are back in town!" Julie yelled. Rena Amato started to cry in her husband's arms. Susan sat unsteadily. Marcus White smiled like he knew all along it was just a matter of time. Riley just stood there.

They all paced, or drank coffee a mess attendant had brought to them as they waited for the helicopter's report.

*****

Steven Amato awoke first, as the helicopter's blades thumped out its approach. Danny, who was always the more sound sleeper rolled over, annoyed that the sound had mildly disturbed the most peaceful slumber he had had in weeks. Steven elbowed him.

"Danny, wake up! We're back!"

Danny opened his eyes wide as the helicopter eased up the beach to the parachutes they had laid out to attract the attention of aircraft approaching Midway.

Several things caught their attention, the first of which was their garb. They were dressed in the same flight suits they had worn the day they were "rescued" the first time. However, the leather helmets and goggles they had worn were still near them in the sand.

Their hair was far from regulation length. While not long by the day's standards, it was far too long for Naval Aviators. In addition, the growth of beard on their faces was more in line with that worn by a submariner than a pilot. And they were deeply tanned.

Only a slight scratch remained of the cut Steven received when the Avenger came to a sudden halt. Neither of them had any other abrasions or cuts. Even Danny's arm felt absolutely fine.

Most notably, the TBF Avenger was gone. Not at trace of it remained, not even the ditch it had dug itself into as it careened down the beach.

But that was totally understandable. They knew exactly where it could be located.

Chapter 34

"Where have you been, son?" his mother tearfully asked, running to him as he sat in the hospital bed, looking very healthy and tanned. Steven and Danny were there for twenty-four hours' worth of observation by Navy doctors, just to be sure. With haircuts and shaves, they never looked better.

"Where I've always been. Flyin an airpanes onna ships!" Steven said with a laugh.

Rena Amato just couldn't hold him enough. Paul Amato just beamed. Susan would not let go of Danny, even when his own mother and father flew out to greet him, his mother fainting at the sight of "the men who returned from the dead."

As for Julie Ann Tate, she just wanted to hold him close, and she did so whenever Rena Amato let him go-and all night long, when everyone was asleep in their own rooms.

Commander Riley and a team of other officers interviewed them about their miraculous survival. The story they told to the team was completely different than the story they told to Riley when they were alone.

"You know what your fiancés say, right?"

"Yes, we do," Danny said.

"And you know what I think, right? Officially, that is?"

"Yes sir, Commander Riley, we sure do," Steven answered.

"And now tell me a fairy tale."

"A fairy tale it is, sir," Steven said.

Riley gasped, gaped, and gawked at their experiences. The relics they brought back from the Land of Then left him thunderstruck.

"The interrogation team thinks you found this stuff on Kure- the leather helmets, goggles, the metal airplane model, is that right?"

"Yes. It's possible, you know. Midway was kind of a hot place during the war."

"So it was."

"I didn't show them these, though," Steven said, reaching into his pocket and displaying the contents to Riley.

Riley took the objects, examined them and smiled from the bottom of his heart.

"I wouldn't have shown them either," he said. "Dear God. What men!"

"Yes sir. They were the best."

"By the way, Amato, that woman of yours is the best. She kept the faith in all of us, even when I flat out told her that there was no way you'd ever be seen again. She kept your parents alive. She knew your every move. She even knew the day and hour you would be recovered. How did she...?"

"She did her homework. And she believed. I'm not sure what this project is she cooked up for me over the last six weeks, but I've got a good idea."

"What could that be?" Danny asked.

"Ray Moore, revisited."

"By the way, Morello, the doctor told me your arm was recently broken. Did you know that?"

"Yes sir. It was expertly set by a doctor on the *Gwin*."

*****

Steven and Julie sat with Danny and Susan at the little cafe table in the Royal Hawaiian's outdoor forum. They both laughed at the drinks they ordered with the gauche umbrellas stuck in a chunk of pineapple clipped to the rim of the tall glass.

"I decided to do a little search based upon Ray's age, his dad's age, and those who knew them, including the little housekeeper that found Richard Moore's body when she returned to the house a few years back. She was the only one left in the house. And she started me on the right trail. As it turns out, Raymond Moore didn't have a sister. Ray was an only child." Julie opened a portfolio of photos, clippings, and hand-written letters.

"Then who did the Jaguar belong to? Richard Moore said it belonged to Raymond's sister," Steven said.

"Did Ray Moore tell you, by the way, he had a fiancé?" Julie asked.

"Yes, Julie, he did. He regretted something he had done to her, and didn't want to talk about it. He figured after Midway he'd make everything right again, with her and with his parents."

"The sister Richard Moore referred to was Ray's fiancé, whom was very pregnant with Ray's child when he died at Midway. Ray's daughter was born on August 12, 1942 in a little hospital in Nashville. Mr. Moore was very concerned about avoiding scandal, being from the very proper south of the era, and Raymond not around to make things right."

"What?! That's...that's..."

"That, dear Steven, is the truth. After the war, Richard Moore sent her to live in Europe, Switzerland, to be exact, where the Moore's had banking interests and a very upscale country residence. She traveled back and forth to the United States twice a year so the Moore's could see Ray's little girl. She was blonde and so beautiful, just like her mom, and Ray's mom. They supported Ray's daughter and her mother in a very comfortable lifestyle, probably too comfortable, because Ray's daughter became a spoiled little hellion for her poor mother, who never married, to handle by herself. She ran away from a finishing school with a young aristocrat from the south of France, just before she was to enter Barnard College in New York City."

"Richard Moore must have had a canary," Danny said.

"An ostrich is more like it," Julie quipped. He was heartbroken. He fell into a deep depression and began to regret not having Ray's daughter and her mother live with them, where he might have kept a firmer hand on the young lady. There was a rumor circulating that Richard Moore was about to have the young Frenchman, uh, taken care of, shall we say politely?"

"What stopped him?" Susan asked.

"When he caught up with them, Richard Moore's granddaughter had a very swollen belly."

"All those Moore's must be oversexed!" Susan said.

"That's speculative, dear boy. I'm a reporter. I don't speculate," Julie said, stroking his hand with the nail of her forefinger. She leaned over to kiss him on the cheek. He couldn't help it, but he found himself looking down the low cut sarong dress that gave hint to her ample bosom.

Then it dawned on him, almost in a flash, just as he was about to make a snide remark about reporters and speculation.

"She was pregnant with Derek!"

"How'd you know that?" She threw herself backwards so fast she lost her breath. He had literally taken the wind right out of her sails.

"It just struck me while I was looking at... well, it figures. Richard Moore treated Derek with the utmost care. He never really commanded him to do anything while I was there. He sort of asked, and always smiled at him. Now I see why. It was the last bit of Raymond he would have. What happened to Ray's wife?"

"She passed on two years ago, still living in Switzerland."

"And Ray's daughter?"

"She's living in Richard Moore's residence. She just came back to the United States to live. Derek never really knew who he was until his mother, who was sworn to secrecy under a penalty of disinheritance, would tell him so. Richard Moore didn't want to create yet another spoiled child who would tear his way through the world."

"Like his grandpa Ray?" Steven said.

"Exactly. She took delivery of several documents that arrived by mail to the Swiss office of Richard Moore's bank, with strict instructions that they were not to be delivered and opened until..."

"June 4, right?"

"Right. Marcus was wrong about you, Steve."

AS TIME GOES BY

"How's that?"

"Sailors are not all wet," she said, punching him on his shoulder.

He winced, to her delight. He didn't tell her a doctor on the *Gwin* had fixed him up too. However, the shoulder was still sore. Crash landing the TBF Avenger didn't help.

And when he thought of the TBF, he remembered he had a few stops to make when he got home.

*****

He entered the familiar hangar with some trepidation. What if it wasn't there? What if neither of them was there? As soon as he opened the door, he was relieved that the Devastator, the Avenger, and the Dauntless were there to greet them, all in the same pristine condition he had last seen them in at what seemed like a long, long, time ago. He walked to the Avenger and patted its sides. Then he climbed into the cockpit and powered up the electrical system, and pulled the switch for the bomb bay door.

"It's opening," Danny said.

"I figured it would," he said with a laugh.

Mr. Whitney walked to them with a spring in his step. The old gent never looked better.

"Nice to see you again, Steve, Danny. I heard you had quite an adventure."

"Charlie my man, it was the best," Steven said.

"Then you know," Whitney said. "You know what I tried to..."

"Save it, Mr. Whitney. And I've got something for you," Steven said, reaching into his pocket and displaying its contents.

"A bet's a bet."

"Take it. I'll probably lose it anyway," he said, thrusting the gold tie clasp with the VT-6 insignia into Whitney's hand.

"Thanks! And I've got something for you," Whitney said, "but I'll need a hand with it. Come over here."

They walked to a small shop in the hangar. Whitney took out a crate about three feet by three feet. It weighted at least fifty pounds. He carefully took off the cloth that covered it. As it dropped to the ground, Steven and Danny smiled broadly.

"I took it off the Avenger when we repaired it. I thought that it would come in handy someday," Whitney said with humility.

The aluminum metal panels, were obviously removed with care from the TBF Avenger and attached with equal care to an oak wood backing, then framed and encased in glass. Ray Moore's artistic rendition of *The Flying Ronzonis* looked like it was done yesterday.

*****

John Lynch wrote Steve and Danny a heartfelt apology for something he had no control over. Their visit to his hospital bed brought the young man into recovery with remarkable quickness. He was walking and eating quite well, he said, and had regained enough fine motor control to write the letter. It looked like Midway's last casualty would be fine in no time. As to whether he flew again depended on his own will.

*****

Steven delivered the toy airplane Ray Moore had fashioned to its rightful owner, just as the note he had given Steven requested. How he had known that the initials of the owner would be "DM" is still a matter of conjecture. Steven offered him the Ford, but the young man refused. After all, he said, Steven had the bill of sale in his hands.

He was flattered to have received two wedding invitations in the mail about three weeks later. As a matter of fact, he was so taken aback by this genuine expression of love that he offered his house in Switzerland to the honeymooners, telling them the skiing would addict them forever, and the chocolate and cheese would make them fat.

*****

On their wedding night, Julie wanted to give Steven back his Annapolis class ring. After all, she said, the wedding ring and the engagement ring would more than suffice.

He said they should keep it somewhere and give it to their first child to have as a keepsake. Anyway, he reasoned, he was partial to wearing the Annapolis Class of 1924 ring with the initials JCW engraved inside.

*****

The A-6 Intruders were low and slow having just come off their bombing run on the Iraqi defenses to the west of Baghdad. They were being chased into the Persian gulf by MiG 27s, and the A-6 drivers were screaming for help.

"Pasta One, this is Oscar one. Come on down, Amats! They'll be on us in a second! Amats, you read?"

"Roger that. Commence right turn. Stay on the deck."

"Hurry, Amats! My ECM is about finished with its bag of tricks! Their ground stations got us on visual!"

"Not to worry. Keep burnin' and turnin'"

" Amats, I've got lock on the two closest to the Intruders! Call it!" Danny reported.

"Fire!"

A few seconds later, two MiG-27s became so much high tech garbage as the Phoenix missiles killed them fifty miles away.

"I'm closing!"

"Amats. This is Oscar! They're boxing us!"

"Negative Oscar. They think they're boxing you. Continue right turn. Two, you got me?"

"Right here, CAG." Danny Morello became an F-14 driver. The Navy had allowed present RIOs with correctable eyesight to become pilots. He became one of the best.

"Take the pair to the right. I've got the goalie here."

"Roger CAG."

Danny pulled out and headed due west with his wingman. A minute later, the wingman reported his Sparrows were firing. Twenty seconds later he reported a pair of MiG-27s on their way down to the surface of the Gulf, coming apart as they fell.

"I got two!"

"Very good, Mr. Lynch. Very good indeed."

"Your guy is running off," Danny reported.

"I think not, Mr. Morello. This ruckus was his idea, and I think old *Jawn* here is going to finish it."

With that, he thrust the throttles of the F-14 into after burner. The distance between him and the frantic MiG was narrowing quickly. Then one of the Sidewinders under his wing began to growl louder and louder as the bright tailpipe afterburner of the MiG came into view. Steven squeezed the trigger and the Sidewinder leapt from its launching rails like a falcon after a pigeon. Twelve seconds later, it found its mark. The MiG exploded with a blinding flash.

They were greeted aboard *Nimitz* like a returning Roman generals after a successful campaign. It was then Danny noted that Steve was wearing the Hamilton chronometer for the first time in six years. He almost went crazy.

"Relax," Steven said. "It doesn't work. I wear it for luck, that's all."

He didn't want to alarm Danny. Actually, it worked just fine. It still kept perfect timeless time. He was living his dream, and if he needed to be reminded of that, he looked at the picture of the beautiful blond holding the most gorgeous one year-old little girl. Then he looked at the picture of his nephew dressed up in the Baltimore Orioles uniform. Then he looked at the bronze oak leaf on his collar that identified him as the youngest lieutenant commander in the Navy. It was rumored he'd be a captain by year's end.

He had all the answers he needed.

For now.

AS TIME GOES BY

CPSIA information can be obtained
at www.ICGtesting.com
Printed in the USA
FFOW01n1655230414
4972FF